AUTHOR	**MATTHEWS, TISA**
TITLE	**UNHITCHED**

DUE DATE	BORROWER'S NAME

To my mom, who took me to see Titanic as my first movie in theaters and started my love of love stories.

To the girls who have had the character growth of Brooke
Davis but still miss the way life hit when they were younger.

Mya's Mix

On the Way Down - Ryan Cabrera
(There's Gotta Be) More To Life - Stacie Orrico
Why Can't I? - Liz Phair
So Yesterday - Hilary Duff
Build Me Up Buttercup - The Foundations
Ultimate - Lindsay Lohan
Best Day Of My Life - Jesse McCartney
2002 - davvn, Bowling For Soup
brb ttyl - davvn
What Makes You Beautiful - One Direction
It's Not Over - Daughtry
Here (In Your Arms) - Hellogoodbye
MIRACLE - BOYS LIKE GIRLS
I Think I'm in Love with You- Jessica Simpson
Collide - Howie Day

Author's Note

Wassup peeps?!

I'm so hyped you picked up this book and can't wait to take this trip down memory lane with you. Nostalgia ties us to a simpler era, and I, for one, am way too stressed all the damn time to not vacation there once in a while.

Mya and Kace might not have a strong grasp on relationships, but they do share a love for the 2000s. While touching on all too real depth that comes with turning thirty for many people, their story is jam packed full of memories to whisk millennials back to better days.

This book is for the person who has struggled with the dilemma of whether or not to settle for less because you feel like you're running out of time and frustrated that adulting isn't as black and white as the quiz you took in *Seventeen* with your feet kicked up as you lie on your zebra comforter.

It's for the millennial who loves the ridiculousness of a 2000s rom-com–those who think TV shows and movies just don't hit like they used to.

It's for anyone who misses the days where you'd meet your friend at the mall or chat on AIM until your mom made you go to bed.

For the ones who wish we could go back to playing neighborhood Ghost in the Graveyard (safely) when the street lights came on in place of mindless midnight scrolling.

It's for the millennials who miss the hours it took to make a perfect mixed CD, the ultimate love letter to someone, moreso because we were willing to risk a LimeWire virus on the family computer.

Most importantly, it's for anyone who wants to grow up without completely growing up.

If this is *you*, I hope you enjoy the blasts from the past. I hope a reference sends a jolt of joy through you at a memory you'd forgotten, and you relive moments the way you did when you picked up your disposable camera pictures after forgetting what you photographed. I hope you dust off your N64 or DVD collection and have an epic date night. I hope you message me to share a story that will always be a core memory for you. And if you're still able, I hope you call your mom and thank her for giving you a childhood full of all the little things that we had no idea we'd miss so much.

Happy reading,

Tisa

P.S. Kace is pronounced like Case or Jace with a K. <3

Chapter One

"This is why you didn't want to see me tonight?" I scream, waving a hand like a madman as my feet carry me toward the unsuspecting blonde and her date. Clenching my fingers into fists at my sides, I halt in front of their table, staring her down and waiting for an explanation she won't be able to give me.

Gritting my teeth, I inhale through my nose. I don't know my next step–I didn't think that far ahead. It was supposed to be simple: pick a random couple and ruin their date to prove to myself that it's not *me*–that all relationships are fragile when they encounter an obstacle.

It's the reason I'm standing in a fancy-ass restaurant on this godforsaken Valentine's Day–to convince myself that I'm not a complete moron for being blind to the flames that engulfed my relationship.

There's no rhyme or reason for why I chose *her*. It's just another random part of my plan. *The plan.* What a joke. My life apparently no longer consists of plans, commitments *or security*. My favorite quality ripped from me without my consent. It's fucked up, is what it is. The new "qualities" that have taken over my subconscious? Cynicism and skepticism. Even worse.

The couple is halfway through a pasta course with nearly empty glasses of wine on the white tablecloth–they probably need alcohol to enjoy each other's company. The woman just stares back, her mouth open in shock, undoubtedly seeing the rage lasers shooting from my eyes. It's not like my acting needs to be faked–it doesn't. Just like it doesn't matter that one woman in particular fucked me up. I'm doing everyone a fucking favor by making them see love inevitably leads to broken trust and lies.

Her wide eyes dart to who I assume is her boyfriend sitting across from her. Although, I doubt they'll last. I plan to stick around just long enough to leave a relationship crumbling in my wake, hopeful that the world will gain a couple more miserable humans like myself tonight. *Misery loves company, right?* I've tried everything else to hurt less and nothing has worked, so I'm attempting to fight fire with fire.

Or maybe I'm a masochist. I'm not sure, but I'll stoke the fire either way. "What the fuck, babe?" I fold my arms at my chest. "Are you going to just stare, or is there a lie on the tip of your tongue? Spit it out."

Her gaze shifts back to me. The heat of other people's stares bore into me from all sides, sending tingles of dis-comfort across my skin. Casual conversation at nearby tables turns into whispers. I'm vaguely aware of the man sitting across from this woman asking her who I am, but the rest of the dimly lit restaurant only seems to darken more as she studies my face. What the hell is she looking at with those stupid green eyes that hardly hold an ounce of anger?

I swivel to face the guy. His knuckles are white as he grips his fork. His brows are pinched as he glares at his girlfriend. His shoulders... are slumped? *Fuck.* He looks defeated. He probably thinks she's actually cheating on him. No shit. That's the picture I painted–a painting that's ugly no matter how you frame it.

This was a terrible plan, and I don't feel better in the slightest. My skewed reasoning clouded my mind, but the devastation on this dude's face makes it clear as fucking day that I'm too old to be acting like this. I scoff, angry with the situation for making me act out of character. Or maybe angry with myself for letting it affect me this way. I get stressed or upset as much as the next guy, but I can usually goosfraba myself off the ledge. Apparently that was a power I only possessed *before* everything went to shit.

"Excuse me, sir." My head whips toward a man in a suit with hard eyes, clearly the manager. "I'm going to have to ask you to leave, or I'll call the cops."

"Chill the fuck out," I snap, rage overwriting the script my logic had planned as I tug my fingers through my hair. "I'm leaving." Dropping the act, I spin on my heel and storm toward the door without any clue of who I'm angry with anymore.

Behind me, I hear the woman pleading. "Please put your phone away. I know him. Don't call the cops." *What the fuck?* I sure as shit do not know her, so why the hell is she coming to my defense? *I need to get out of here.* With a shake of my head, I don't waste another second, passing the hostess stand and pushing the cold metal bar that leads me to an even colder outside.

Shoving my hands into the pockets of my bomber jacket, I stumble onto the sidewalk because my feet can't fucking keep up with my racing thoughts. Sucking in a breath, I pause just outside the door to adjust to the bite of the cool night air. Moving to Washington state was one of the best decisions I made in my life, but I refuse to admit that at this moment.

Scanning the downtown street, puddle water sprays over the cement in front of me as a car whirs past, far over the speed limit. *Idiots.* A group of couples wait at the crosswalk a dozen steps ahead of me, arms linked and leaning into each other. I roll my eyes, wishing even more that I had stayed home with my semi-comfortable couch and a bowl of cereal.

As I step toward the crosswalk, the suction of the door opening behind me causes me to turn around. Before I have time to process, the woman whose date I just crashed launches herself at me, throwing her arms around my neck and nearly knocking me over with the force. I steady myself by gripping her waist, my fingers sinking into the texture of her sweater. *What the–*

She squeezes her arms tight around me like we're long-lost lovers or some shit, nuzzling her face into my chest. She smells edible–like fucking marshmallows or something. *Why is she so close that I can smell her?* I brace my hands on her hips, pressing hard enough to encourage her to let go.

Thankfully, she takes the hint, releasing me and allowing oxygen back into my lungs. "Thank you so much," she whispers, the willpower of her tears holding strong and refusing to fall down her face. Her beautiful face. Damn, this girl is gorgeous. The lighting from under the restaurant awning makes her skin glow, the few freckles sprinkled across her nose barely noticeable. Her long blonde hair is in waves past her shoulders. And her green eyes. *Fuck.* They're so bright that they starkly contrast the tan sweater falling off her shoulder. My gaze dips to where it's tucked into a tight black skirt showing off her lean legs–at least what's visible above her knee-high black boots. How is she not freezing?

I shake my head, clearing away the appraisal of the stranger in front of me and shove my hands back into my pockets. *Wait. Thank you?* "Excuse me?"

She twists her fingers into the sweater at her waist, breaking her stare to focus on her nervous fidgeting. "I don't know how to thank you."

"I just ruined your night." I deadpan, unsure why I'm even entertaining her. I'd rather step on Legos than deal with this shit, but there's a gleam in her eyes that keeps me from walking away.

"No." She shakes her head. "You saved it." Confusion must outweigh the *I don't give a fuck* in my features because she continues. "I've wanted to break up with him for a few weeks now. It's just..." Her pause allows me the satisfaction of exploring her eyes again. "It's hard, you know? We've only been together for three months, and I feel like I should give it more of a chance to feel right. But it's like... Do you sacrifice the time you've put in so you can start over? Or settle and not throw away a chunk of your life *again*?"

My eyes widen, fidgeting with my apartment key inside my pocket. Why is this girl confessing her life to me? Can't she see I don't want to be here? She should take this somewhere else. Like a diary. "Am I being Punk'd?"

The corners of her mouth quirk up in a smile. "I *wish* Ashton Kutcher were here, but I highly doubt he is." "Great." I run a hand through my hair. "Well, I'm glad I could help you figure shit out." *At least one of us feels better about this encounter.* Turning away from her, I take a few steps toward the only thing I want in my immediate future–Cinnamon Toast Crunch.

"Wait," she calls after me, and I pivot back toward her like an idiot.

"What?" I mean to snap, but my voice betrays me, coming out calm and patient. Sad maybe. Of course I'm sad. This girl thinks three months is a long time to throw away? Try eight *years*. Almost a fourth of my life out the window like a fly being swatted away, never to be seen again.

Emotions finally catch up to her, a tear carving a path down each of her cheeks, illuminating her freckles even more. "I'm sorry. I don't know what happened in there–considering I've never seen you before–but I needed you to show up more than you could ever understand. I hope that brings a little peace to whatever your heart is feeling right now." Her voice soothes me like a pretty girl curled into your side on a cold night, and fuck if my stupid manipulated brain isn't malfunctioning at her soft and genuine words.

"My heart doesn't feel a damn thing," I manage to respond with what I wish were the truth. I'm convinced it's bad luck that's been building up because I never forwarded those chain emails a decade ago.

"Okay." She sighs and swipes away the tears. "Well, have a good night." I give a curt nod, determined to finally get back to my couch when she continues. "I'm Mya, by the way."

Of course she would have a beautiful name. "Kace," I tell her, even though it doesn't matter. "See ya." I walk away, questioning my choice of words because I'm positive I will never see this woman again.

The crosswalk sign lights up as I reach it. Thank fuck. I was strongly considering jaywalking, which goes against every fiber of my being, considering I've worked in some form of security since I was twenty. People are unpredictable and insane. Mya just proved that. *I* just proved that.

Crossing the street, I turn right, only walking about a hundred feet before I'm standing in front of my apartment building. I let myself in, swiping my key card at the elevator and taking it to the seventh floor. It's surprisingly dead in here for a Thursday evening. Usually there's an excess of people coming home late from work or heading to the gym before turning in for the night. Everyone is too busy celebrating the pointless Hallmark holiday.

I stare at the back of the stainless steel doors. The metal reflection doesn't reveal the intricacies of how shitty I look and feel right now. Glancing at the mirror to my right, I get confirmation.

My hair looks deceivingly good, considering I've been running my fingers through it all night. By some miracle, it appears like I purposely styled it to have that messy look I've heard women find attractive. My facial hair could probably be trimmed a little cleaner, but I've managed to shower every day this week, and that's all that should be expected of me currently.

A plain white T-shirt is crisp under my brown bomber jacket, paired with dark jeans and Chelsea boots. It's what

I would have worn if I were on a date tonight, but I haven't been on one of those in a long fucking time.

I tear my eyes from myself as the elevator rises another floor. I usually appreciate this mirror because it's an added level of security, to be able to see any passengers. But right now, it's a reminder that despite my clothes, it's evident that I haven't slept well in weeks, and my brain is far from functioning at optimal levels. It's probably not a good thing, considering my job requires me to be on top of my game.

The elevator opens, revealing an empty hallway and my front door directly across from me. Slipping the keys from my pocket, I unlock the door and head straight to my kitchen. I can't help but scoff at the irony of my favorite beer from Brothers Cascadia Brewing waiting for me in the fridge. Or maybe it's intentionally clever. Even if you have a shit day, you can drink a Best Day Ever IPA and claim you had... well, a Best Day Ever.

Gripping the fridge handle, a chuckle escapes me at the thought, but it's immediately wiped away when I spot the remains of tonight's trigger on the marble counter. *How did I forget that was there?*

Ruby and I broke up two months ago, and while I've been doing terribly since she dumped me out of the blue, today I found a bag of tagless lingerie in the back of our closet. *My closet.* I had never seen them before. It's not like I wasn't aware our relationship was probably in need of a refresh, but how in the hell was I supposed to know it was bad enough that she was buying new underwear to wear for someone else? I guess it could have been for me, but considering I hadn't seen my girlfriend in anything sexy–hadn't seen her in *nothing*–for a long ass time, I highly doubt it was for my eyes.

Despite the intention or reason, they landed in my lap nonetheless this morning. And from that moment until now, all I saw was a red deeper than the color of the fabric. *And the emerald green of those eyes.*

Fuck. I swipe the bag of infidelity off the counter and toss it in the trash under the sink. Pulling a can of beer from the fridge, I crack the top and take a sip before reaching back for the milk. I set both drinks on the counter as I grab a box of Cinnamon Toast Crunch from the row of boxes lined up under the white cabinets and make myself the world's biggest bowl of cereal.

Happy fucking Valentine's Day to me.

Chapter Two

Kace

Adjusting my laptop bag on my shoulder, I cut across the gym parking lot. It's only three blocks to the restaurant I use as an office for a working lunch to avoid feeling cooped up. I'm smart enough to know if I didn't keep up the habit after Ruby left, I might never leave my apartment again. And after the disaster four nights ago, I need to stick to a healthy routine more than ever.

I pick up my speed, hoping my brisk walk will counter the icy air. I almost make it to the other side of the lot before I notice a pink Jeep. Even with the glare from the midday sun glinting through the clouds, how could I miss it? It's a pink Jeep. Who the hell even knew that combination existed?

A frazzled blonde stumbles out of Barbie's dream car, the strap of her bag falling off her shoulder as she tries to tie up her hair. I stop in my tracks a few parking spaces down be-cause it's hard to look away from a train wreck. Once her hair is secure, she reaches into the backseat of the car, leaning so far inside that the entire top half of her body disappears. I can't help but stare at the way her black leggings cling to her perky ass. *What am I even doing?* I shake my head in an attempt to divert my gaze because I'm well aware I'm being a total creep.

Failing miserably, I watch as she grounds herself, shoving a few more things into her bag. When she turns to close the car door, I'm hit with déjà vu. *Huh.* She looks vaguely familiar. My eyes widen in recognition as a whispered curse slips out.

The girl from the restaurant.

The victim of the date I disturbed. *Apparently* it was disrupted in a good way, but that's hard to believe. The whole ordeal felt like an out-of-body experience that I regretted immediately when I woke up the next day. Valentine's Day aside, I'm not usually a total jackass. For some reason, Mya–I think her name was–didn't seem to think I was. But if she wanted to break up with the guy, why didn't she just do it? Why wait so long? It's the question that's been running through my mind on repeat since Ruby did the same shit to me.

Only Ruby finally bit the bullet and brought me to my knees all on her own.

That memory is burned into my mind, on repeat like an overplayed song on the radio. She didn't come home until after midnight one night–rare for her even though she was the work-late-in-the-office type. She hadn't responded to a single text, but for some reason when she walked into our room, I felt anger over worry and relief for the first time.

"Where have you been?" I asked her, sitting up in bed from where I had been staring at the ceiling.

She kicked her heels off and tossed them to the side. "None of your business," she snapped but then sighed, and a wave of dread washed over me. She sat on the edge of the mattress, and the weight of it felt so much heavier than it should have. Taking out her earrings, she didn't even spare me a glance as she said, "This isn't working for me anymore, Kace. I'm sorry. I've been seeing someone else, and I'm tired of hiding it."

I sat there, a tornado of shock and anger brewing inside me. I told her to fuck off, to get out of the apartment, and she grabbed her suitcase from the closet–already packed, I numbly realized. She left without a fight–without a conversation, or so much as a "nice knowing you, thanks for the company during eight years of my life." The self-hatred didn't kick in until the next day when I realized I should have seen this coming.

I shake my head, clearing the memory, and huff my contempt for the girl I spent the majority of a decade loving–not well enough apparently, but regardless.

Mya locks her car with a beep on her fob and walks toward the gym. Once she's through the glass doors, and before my brain registers what the fuck I'm doing, my feet take me to her car. Despite knowing I should leave it alone, this girl intrigues me more than a passing curiosity. Glancing back at the gym entrance again to make sure she's not within sight, I cup my hands around my eyes and peer through the window.

God, I'm a creep.

But... More importantly, why does her backseat look like it's a bed? There's a pillow on one end, and blankets lying across the leather like she sleeps there. Does she live in her car? There's no way. She's a grown-ass adult. I spent all of three minutes with the woman but she has to be around my age. I'm thirty-one, and I can't imagine she's older than that. Either way, it would be insane for her to live in a car.

My heart feels like it's smashing from side to side against either lung, making it hard to breathe. *Did I do this?* My self-pity rampage caused her breakup, and as a result, she's homeless?

Running my hands through my hair, I step away from the car and take a breath, exhaling a cloud of condensation. I'm overreacting. Everything isn't about me, and I'm sure there is a logical explanation for this.

I shove the thoughts into a compartment in the back of my brain and continue on my way. I had to pick up the pieces of my life when my relationship ended. I'm sure this girl is more than capable of doing the same, and where she sleeps in the meantime is none of my business.

Although, living in a car isn't safe, and I fucking hate that. Vancouver is primarily green on the crime map, but the yellow gets a little spotty here in downtown. It's nothing like Portland, but still.

Still.

No. Not my problem. I have enough of those to deal with at work, which is where I need my focus. I turn down the next street, and the brick exterior of the corner restaurant comes into view. The dependability of my favorite taco and torta joint always being there is just what I need.

Reaching for the handle, I hold the door open for a couple of businesswomen to step through, then follow them in, thankful I no longer have the desire to bite the head off of any woman I encounter. Too bad that wasn't before I became partially responsible for a girl now sleeping in her fucking Jeep. I shake the thought away again.

To the left is a small seating area with mismatched round and square wooden tables, all the chairs looking like they've come from a variety of grandmother's homes. I find a seat on a metal stool at the end of the L-shaped bar against the wall.

By the time my laptop is out of the bag and open on the concrete bartop, the bartender, Rocco, is in front of me, holding up an empty glass. "Hey, Kace. The usual?"

Tattoos scatter his arms–his are random and chaotic in design and color compared to my grayscale foggy forest. I push up the sleeves of my black and white flannel, revealing the bottom half of the design. My forearms flex in the process, reminding me how sore I am from this morning's arm workout.

I nod, but he's already rolling the rim of the glass in black salt. A few moments later, the mezcal cocktail is on a coaster next to my computer. "Thank you." I cross my ankle over my knee, settling my fingers on the keyboard and glancing at the open kitchen in the back of the restaurant.

He hooks a thumb over his shoulder. "The kitchen wants to try out a new dish. You in?"

"Always." I give him a nod. Now that Ruby is out of my life, I'd say I see Rocco more than anyone. It's sad as fuck considering all he really knows about me is my favorite drink on the menu, that I'm always down for whatever dish they want to serve, and that I don't like to be bothered while I work.

He walks away, leaving me to fire up my VPN and bring up my chat window on Discord. I moved here from Virginia when Ruby got a job as director of finance for Columbia Sportswear. I hadn't found my dream job yet, so there wasn't a good enough reason to say no. I could hate her for it, the way I'm pulled to hate everything else in my life that's a result of loving her, but the truth is, the Pacific Northwest is home. I grew up in Charleston, West Virginia, and I didn't dislike it, but I love living in Vancouver. The mountains. The trees. Look in any direction and drive three hours or less and you can snowboard. There are too many small-town breweries to even know them all. And that's not even considering the food.

"They must have known you were going to say yes," Rocco chuckles, setting a tin plate with a fat torta in the space next to me.

The. Food.

Fuck, I love the food. The tortas here are out of this world. And while I've never had this specific one, I've yet to be let down.

"Thanks, Rocco." My eyes lock on the golden toasted bread as I reach for it. He leaves me to my meal as I take the first bite. I groan internally as the flavor explodes in my mouth. Soft bread, crisp on the outside. Marinated pork. Avocado that they did not skimp on even though they never charge me extra. I chew and look at the meal in my hands, examining the flavor profile. I think it's an orange-habanero salsa. Red onions and cilantro. Never enough cilantro, but I'll let it slide.

What the hell is this crema sauce? I would commit a crime for this sauce. That says a lot coming from a guy whose dream job would be snatched away if he did so. I take another bite, savoring the second even more.

Needing to get some work done, I set down my food, wipe my hands on a napkin and focus my attention on my laptop. Lunch hour is the time I use to check in with my cybersecurity "friends" who work for other companies. All of us are white hat hackers, assigned to intentionally break into sites and programs to find holes so they can be patched and sealed. We give insight to companies that have been hacked by either us or someone else so they can learn from their mistakes and work more efficiently. In today's world, identifying threats is a job that constantly changes, and while I'm more of a *keep to myself* kind of guy, the only way to stay on top of it is through collaboration.

"Kace?"

My attention snaps to the voice at the other end of the bar. *Mya.*

The guilt comes back, burning in my chest. *Not my girl. Not my problem.*

I minimize my chat screen, having a feeling she'll be standing in front of me within seconds. Not that I have any evidence to back my theory, but she seems like the nosy type.

Sure enough, she's once again too close for comfort. Her straight, wet hair smells sweet like candy. Or maybe it's the Blow Pop she pulls to her lips, sucking the green sugar into her mouth. In a split-second pep talk, I convince myself that it's not sexy at all. Whether the scent is coming from her hair or the candy her lips are wrapped around, it clashes hard with the Mexican food aroma and ruins my routine.

I drag my eyes away from her lips as she pops the sucker from her mouth and scan the rest of her body. She's wearing the same black leggings she had on earlier with a light purple cropped hoodie revealing a sliver of midriff. And fuck, is that a belly ring? I stare long enough to confirm it's a small, dangling pink heart. I didn't think I was a fan, but the uptick in my pulse would suggest otherwise.

I rest my hand on my ankle, still crossed over my knee, and clear my throat, buying time to figure out how to get rid of her again. I already feel bad enough for wreaking havoc on her life completely unprovoked, and seeing her in front of me isn't helping.

"Oh." She smiles nervously, and I hate the way her green eyes dim. "Did I get your name wrong? I'm sorry. You are the same guy, right? From Valentine's Day?" She sticks the Blow Pop back in her mouth as she waits for my answer.

I should get back to my sandwich, but I find myself drawn to this interaction. "Yeah. Same guy."

She pulls the sucker away again. "Good." Her smile shifts into a real, full-fledged one. I swear her eyes brighten on the spot, and it makes my stomach flip. Or maybe I'm just hungry. "Do you come here a lot?"

"Uh. Yeah." I pause. "You?" I hear myself say and groan inwardly. *At the very least, maybe this conversation will ease my guilt.*

She shakes her head. "First time. Nothing like a first time, you know? There's so much excitement because you have all these ideas in your head based on other people, but then you get to experience it for yourself and make up your own mind. It's my favorite." *Damn, this girl can talk.* "I hate missing out. My ex hated Mexican food, but now that I'm not with him, I couldn't go another day without trying this place." She seems genuinely happy, and it's confusing as hell.

"Are you living in your car?" I blurt, immediately flooded with a wave of regret and embarrassment for how I acquired that information.

Her face scrunches in confusion but quickly morphs into shame. She looks up at the shelf lined with plants above the door, then to the row of tequila behind the bar next to us.

My heart sinks. *Fuck.* I usually love being right, but in this case... "Mya."

Her eyes snap back to me, a hint of a smile making an appearance. "You remember my name?"

"Don't change the subject."

She takes a breath. "Yeah. It's temporary. It's fine. I survived Y2K and the Jonas Brothers breaking up. I can do anything."

"Did that asshole kick you out of your home?" I scowl.

Her eyes flicker with amusement, and I shove the unintentional possessiveness down.

"It is *his* house." She shrugs. "But I don't mind. It's an adventure."

"You can't live in a car. It's not safe."

She twirls the sucker stick between her thumb and pointer finger. "Safe is a relative term."

I stare blankly at her. This girl is insane. Yet, she still made sure I didn't get arrested the other night. My rage could have cost me my job–the only good thing I have going for me. I tug on the back of my neck. "I can't let you be homeless."

She laughs, her smile widening as her free hand lands on my bicep. "It's not your job to let me be anything." Her grip is firm enough that I know she can feel the muscle I've worked hard to build, and for some ungodly reason, I like her touching me. I glance at where our bodies connect, and she jumps back like she just noticed we were touching. "Sorry. I don't have a personal bubble." She pulls her hands to her chest with a nervous smile.

"I've noticed."

"Well, anyway. I'm fine. Promise," she says with false bravado.

"Your ex wouldn't let you stay with him until you found someplace else?"

She hums. "Maybe. Probably. But there's no sense in hanging around in a life not meant for me."

I arch a brow. "But there *is* sense in living in your car?"

She shrugs. "It seemed like a perfectly fine temporary solution until you started crapping on it."

"You really don't have anywhere else to go?" Please for the love of tacos, let *someone* be available to help her.

"Not really. My sister, Ella... I could stay with her. But you see, she and her husband, Mack, just had a baby. Well, he's more of a toddler now. I love him dearly, but I've already seen *Frozen* 872 times, and I might die if I have to sit through it again. Plus, they live in Eugene, and that's too far away from my life."

The rambling continues, and she has no sense of security *at all*. The personal information she's spitting out for free could give someone what they need to easily figure out a password faster than they could hack it. It's terrifying.

"You don't have any friends who have room for you?" She's friendly as fuck. Surely she has a hundred friends.

Her eyes drift to the ceiling like she's mentally flicking through a list of people she knows before focusing back on me and shaking her head. "I don't think so."

My grip on my ankle tightens. "A coworker with a couch?"

She chuckles. "I think most people have a couch. But I don't have a coworker."

She doesn't have a coworker she could stay with? Or she doesn't have a coworker in the first place? The temptation to know wins. "Do you have a job?"

"Yes..."

"But no coworkers?"

She nods. "Correct." A smile lights her face, and for some fucked up reason, it's my tipping point.

I close my eyes, pleading with myself not to utter the words on the tip of my tongue. Despite my poor decisions on Valentine's Day, at my core, I'm more inclined to help than hurt, and this girl is in need–thanks to me. Inhaling a deep breath to contain the immediate regret I know I'll have the second the words leave my mouth, I let them tumble from my lips anyway. "You can stay with me."

A disbelieving laugh leaves her perfectly pink lips, sugary from her sucker, and I'm struck again with how beautiful she is. She must be using the gym for the showers because I've hardly been here long enough for her to finish a workout. Her face is bare from makeup, making the tiny freckles sprinkled across her nose more prominent. The daylight–and my less-ened hostility–is giving me the ability to take in every detail.

"I think I misheard you." Her voice snaps my attention to her lips again.

"I only have a couch to offer." I rub the back of my neck, my eyes dropping to my sandwich. "But it's better than the backseat of your car."

"I told you everyone has a couch!" Shifting gears, she chews on her lip. "There's no way I could impose though."

"I feel obligated. I'm the reason you're choosing to live in a moving piece of metal over a stable home."

"People live in motorhomes and sprinter vans all the time." She grins, pleased with her comeback.

Jesus Christ, this idea is feeling worse by the second. "That's not the same thing, and you know it. Please indulge me." At this point, I'm committed. "Stay at my place until you find your own."

"You're coming off a little bit like a psycho, especially with the way you stormed into the restaurant the other night. What was that about anyway?" I *think* she's teasing, but my stomach twists at the thought of her being put off by me.

"That was... It was nothing." I run my fingers through my hair in an attempt to quell my anxiety. "That wasn't me. I mean, it was. But I've never done anything like that before."

"It's okay." She places a hand on my shoulder, and my stare follows the movement. "Even Troy Bolton made mistakes and acted out of character, and he's still loveable. So I haven't lost complete faith in you yet."

What the fuck is she talking about? The V between my brows deepens.

"Never mind." She shakes her head in amusement, her touch falling away from me. "But still, how do I know you won't chop me into pieces and throw me over the edge of your boat in a garbage bag?"

I can't help the snort that escapes. "Well, for starters, I don't have a boat. I'm more of a mechanic." I hold her stare to see if she catches my reference.

It's only a moment before a spark flickers in her eyes with recognition. "No one is Authur Bishop–or Jason Statham in general–but if you're anything close to him or Dexter Morgan, I suppose it doesn't matter if I stay or go." She shrugs, and I can't tell if the nonchalance is comfort or a defense mechanism. "If you want me dead, there's no avoiding it."

The thought of seeing her dead ticks my anxiety up a notch. Do I look like a killer? *Note to self: Google Ted Bundy.* "I think I'll stick to killing dates instead of women," I retort, convincing myself I'm funny and don't regret my actions the other night.

"You are good at that." She smirks.

Guilt consumes me, and it's my own damn fault. "I'm sorry," I mutter before a sigh slips out. "Will you accept my offer or not?"

"If only to save you from the hassle of having to track me along my wayward path..." *Reckless abandon seems more accurate.* Both of her hands land on my shoulder this time. "Yes, Kace, I would love to live with you."

I glance at her right hand, making sure the sticky sucker pinched between her fingers isn't too close to my hair. "Temporarily."

"Yes." She nods, her hands forming a prayer under her chin. It's fucking adorable.

"Just until you get back on your feet," I reiterate. I don't even know what job she has or if it's reliable. Looks like I'm about to make a second mistake where this woman is concerned, and the unknown timeframe for our new living arrangement has me wanting to crawl into the fallout shelter with Brendan Fraser and not come out until I know it's over.

Chapter Three

Mya

"Wait," Kace says, pulling the key from his door and spinning on his heels. When he's turned toward me, our faces are mere inches apart. He startles at my closeness and tries to back up. Instead, he stumbles a bit before regaining stability by bracing his hand on the doorframe. It only allows me to focus on his features better.

The man is *fine*. The definition of handsome. His brown hair is perfectly mussed in a way that's unclear if he styled it or a woman ran her fingers through it. Although, I'm assuming it's intentional with the way he's spoken about relationships in the little time I've known him. His skin is more tanned than mine, which makes no sense since I spend as much time outside as possible. Plus, no one in Washington should be tan right now with the dreary, sunless winter we're having–must be the genes he was blessed with. I shrug internally, brushing over that fact without jealousy. We all have different gifts, and if I don't want others to feel jealous of mine, I refuse to turn green over theirs. And it just so happens that some of Kace's gifts are benefiting me through an impeccable view.

Seriously. His scruff is perfection. It's neat but also rugged? Can those two things exist at the same time? I haven't seen him smile yet, but I already know it'll be the cherry on top. I wonder if he has dimples. God, I hope he has dimples. *What am I doing?* The last thing I should do is encourage my attraction to the guy giving me a place to sleep.

His deep brown eyes stare back at me, his brows scrunching together. Oh yes, he needed to say something. "Hit me with it!"

"What's your name?" He digs his phone from the pocket of his black jeans, swiping up on the screen. Does he want my phone number?

"Ummm. Mya?"

He makes a sound that I *think* is a chuckle, but there's no smile to confirm it. This guy's light is duller than a glow-in-the-dark ceiling star. "Your full name."

Not wanting to meet his gaze, I stare at where his black and white flannel is rolled above his forearms, revealing his other sleeves underneath. His tattoos are H. O. T. Hot. They're moody, black and gray trees with fog wisping in between them. I readjust the strap of my backpack on my shoulder. "Ask me something else." I lock my gaze on the ink covering his muscular forearms.

His body goes rigid, and he freezes with his fingers over the keys of his phone. "Are you not who you say you are?"

"Oh. What?" I laugh. "Sorry. Nope, I'm me." I reach out, resting my hand on his forearm. He remains tense. "I just hate my real name." Finally, his arm relaxes, like it could have released its own breath.

He considers me for a moment, glancing from where we're touching to my face. "Well, I'm going to need to know. So I can run a quick background check."

My hand flies to my chest in faux offense. The man is letting me stay in his home. He can have anything he wants from me. "Kace. The lack of faith you have in me. Do you see this face?" I beam at him. "This is the face of a girl you can trust."

"I don't trust anyone." His vibe is a flatline, stealing any joy within sight. *Dang.* He's going to be a hard nut to crack.

"I'm kidding. Just promise you won't laugh at my old lady name."

He stares at me, unreadable as a scratched CD.

"On second thought, maybe I do want you to laugh at it, so I know it's possible."

"Do you want to get moved in sometime tonight, or...?" This man has the grumpiest exterior, but something tells me he's a teddy bear on the inside, and I'm making it my new job to find that version of him. Everyone deserves to be more sunshine-y. Especially someone willing to take in a stranger.

"Eleanor Mya Holloway."

He taps away on his screen, unphased by the reveal of the name I've hated since I was a kid. "What's your name?" I pry.

He doesn't look up from his phone. "Kace Levitt."

"Ooooh. Like Joseph Gordon?"

He spares me a glance as he scrolls through the webpage he's on. "No idea who that is. Birthday?"

"What!" I screech. He looks up like he's offended by the sound, but I'm the one who is truly appalled. "He's only one of the greatest actors OF. ALL. TIME." I punctuate each word with a poke on his biceps. He's unflinching as he follows the movement. Damn, this man is a stone wall. Literally and figuratively.

"Uh huh. Birthday?" he repeats.

"February 15th, 1995." His eyes snap to mine, his brows furrowing, maybe like he's realizing it was three days ago–the day after we met, the day after my breakup. I ignore the thought and continue before he has time to chime in. "You've never seen *10 Things I Hate About You*? *500 Days of Summer*? Oh!" I snap my fingers. "You seem brainy. Surely you've seen *Inception*."

His eyes meet my hopeful gaze. "I have seen that."

I clap my hands. "You're not a total loss, then. But don't worry. Now that we're going to be roommates, there's plenty of time to get you acquainted with the classics."

He raises a brow. "Don't mistake this for anything more than being roommates. And only until you figure out your next step."

"I know, I know." I bounce on my toes, leaning over his phone to see what he's doing. "You've made it very clear you're a miserable man who prefers to be alone."

He glances up, our faces inches from each other. Damn, he smells good. Like walking outside on a crisp fall morning. Our eyes lock, and I hold my breath, not wanting to breathe hot air on him. "Here." He reaches his phone toward me. "Put your social security number in."

I hesitate, but follow his gaze to his phone and pull it from his hand. Punching in the nine numbers, I watch them immediately turn to black dots before returning his device.

"Thanks." He taps a few more things on the screen. I lean further into him and watch him press *Submit* on the form. "You really have no personal bubble, do you?"

I shake my head but step back, catching the judgment in his voice. "Sorry."

"It's fine," he says mindlessly.

Seconds tick by, and it feels like we're frozen in time–him staring at the phone screen and me watching him. He's hard to look away from if I'm being honest. I'm not *looking* to date. Even though my last relationship was only three months, it was still serious. We still did all the things–living together, sex, grocery shopping, watching "our" shows, taking turns making dinner. It was civil. Low pressure. Low sparks. Low chemistry. Low excitement. I'm the kind of girl who wants excitement. It's how I prevent myself from feeling my age. Despite all of that, I didn't lose my ability to notice an attractive man. And Kace is the tippy top tier of them. Well, if you take his grumpy personality out of the equation. For my sake, and I think his too, there will be no dating. No vibes. No sparks or interest. Definitely no sex. This is just Eeyore taking in Tigger.

Finally, he scrolls through what I'm assuming are the results from my background check.

"Am I a total psycho?" I grin at him, my fingers looped into the straps of my backpack containing all my makeup, skin care and hair stuff. Two suitcases and a duffel bag sit in the hallway next to us. I'll bring the rest of my things inside depending on what space and storage look like. I don't want to invade his space so much that he finds a way to kick me out sooner than I'm ready to be on my own. The truth is, I say I'm fine. And I am. Relatively. But these past three nights alone were more challenging than I expected after having someone in a bed next to me for three months. Even before that, I hadn't been on my own in a while, and while I fully believe in my ability to survive that way, I'm thankful Kace is giving me this opportunity.

"Not according to this check, but it's still to be determined." He doesn't crack a smile, but I *swear* his brown eyes twinkle a bit.

I feign relief with a sigh. "Oh good. Those lawyer fees were worth it."

His mouth falls open. "Excuse me?"

I chuckle. "Kidding! I'm kidding." I wave my hand toward his locked front door. "Show me the way to the kingdom."

He hesitates, but when he finally puts the key in the lock, this time he completes the turn of the knob, opening the door and holding it in place for me to walk through. "Wait!" I scream, and he turns toward me, startled.

"What?" he asks with wide eyes and furrowed brows.

"Shouldn't I do a background check on you? I mean, just because you say you're not a killer doesn't mean you're a good guy."

I *think* I catch a hint of a smile before he neutralizes his face. He pulls out his phone again, taps on the screen, types a few things and scrolls the web page before handing it over to me.

I scan the form. *Kace Levitt.* "Wait. What is your middle name?"

He shrugs. "Don't have one."

"Why does that feel shady? Like how can I trust someone with no middle name?"

He says nothing, raising one brow like he doesn't believe my concern.

"When I have a kid, I'm making his middle name Danger. How cool would that be? He could say, 'Danger is my middle name.'" I giggle at the thought.

"Already sounds like you, and he doesn't even exist," Kace mutters, and it makes me grin.

"Alright. Moving on." I glance back at the screen. "Birthday. *July 31st.*" I slap his arm. "Kace! That's my mom's birthday AND Harry Potter's birthday. You're so lucky."

"Lucky. That's me." His voice is laced with sarcasm.

I feel like he's funny, but I can't be sure yet. Black dots hide his social security number, and I scroll past it to hit submit.

The way the loading circle ticks round and round has my heart racing with fear that it'll reveal something terrible, but a new page appears a minute later revealing no felonies or misdemeanors–not even debt. "Good job!" I tell him, expecting to see surprise on his face for absolutely no reason. Instead, he looks at me with an expression that clearly says *duh.* "You may now pass go and collect $200!"

He shakes his head in disbelief and holds the door all the way open.

Once one of my suitcases is parked inside, I turn around to retrieve the others. Kace is behind me, wheeling the other rolly in one hand and my duffel slung over his shoulder. "Thank you."

"No problem." He closes the door behind us, locking it and latching the chain. Man, this guy really is a security freak. Better safe than... not, I guess. "Alright." He motions to the right of the entryway. "Bathroom is there." He continues walking, past the kitchen on the left. "I'm sure you'll find your way around the kitchen quickly. Help yourself to whatever."

I cut him off. "Oh. No. That's okay. I can get my own groceries."

He glances over his shoulder. "Just let me know if you finish anything off so I can make sure to pick it up at the store. I hate expecting something to be here when it's not."

I stare back. Why does it feel like he's talking about more than the cereal I see on the counter? God, I love cereal. Giddy at the thought of eating some for dinner–even though I ate tacos an hour ago–I skip-hop my way after Kace toward the living room that's just past the kitchen. There's a worn brown couch on the right wall, and he picks up the solid black blanket that was haphazardly strewn across the back of it. I glance around the rest of the room, but it seems the blanket was the only thing "out of place." His space is moody, the tan walls the only reprieve between the black area rug and TV and the dark brown TV stand and coffee table. "This is where you'll be sleeping." He points to the couch like it's not obvious that it will be my makeshift bed.

"Thank you so much, Kace," I say, resting my hand on his bicep. "I really appreciate this."

"It's not a problem." He shoves his hands into the front pockets of his dark jeans, my hand falling away from where we connect. "Well, I'll let you get settled." He hooks his thumb over his shoulder toward the door next to the end of the couch. "My room is in there. Since the bathroom is in the main space, don't be startled if you hear me in the middle of the night."

"Okay." I give him a thumbs up but immediately regret it and pull my hand back. "And I don't sleep naked. So don't worry about seeing something you shouldn't. Just do your thing."

He scrubs his hand down his face. "Okay. Well." He motions toward his room again.

I tilt my head. "Are you going to bed? It's only–" I spin in a circle until my eyes land on the black metal clock on the wall between the living room and kitchen. The outer circle is Roman numerals, and the inner circle has a mountain range behind the shadow of a snowboarder. "–2:07." For such a small, uncluttered space, I feel like I'm learning plenty about Kace already. Thank god, because I doubt he'd teach me himself.

The time sinks in, and I glance around the room for light as Kace says, "Oh. I didn't realize. Today has been weird."

"Or maybe it's the fact that you have blackout shades over these beautiful full-length windows." I invite myself to tug on the bottom of one, watching it slowly spring up, revealing the most gorgeous view. "KACE!" I yell, glancing back over my shoulder to see him leaning against his bedroom door, arms folded and feet crossed at the ankles, watching me. "HAVE YOU SEEN THIS VIEW?! Are you freaking kidding me right now?"

I run across the room, fingers circling his forearm and giving a yank until he stumbles forward, and I drag him over to admire the view.

Standing in front of the glass, it occurs to me that it feels weird he let me touch him, but I thank the day for this little joy and point out all my favorite things. "Look! You can see the Columbia River."

He deadpans. "I'm aware." It's blatantly obvious. His apartment sits high enough to see the entire front two streets of the Vancouver waterfront and the I-5 bridge that takes you to Portland.

"You know what this makes me think of?"

"I have no idea," he muses in a way that makes me think he's entertaining me instead of making fun of me, so I continue.

"Have you seen the movie, *'A Walk to Remember?'*"

"No." He leans against the glass, and in my periphery, I can see his eyes trained on me instead of the incredible view. "Oh.

Well, it's way better than *The Notebook*, but that's beside the point. There's this scene where he takes her to have one foot on either side of a state line, so she can be in two places at once. Isn't that sweet? It's the little things, you know?"

"I don't think you should stand in the middle of the bridge."

I chuckle. "No, I'm not *that* crazy."

He quirks a brow. "Still to be determined."

"I just randomly thought of it for some reason. It's cool we can hop on over to Oregon whenever we want. I know people who have never left their hometown, let alone their home state."

"Doesn't your sister live in Oregon?" he asks.

My mouth falls open, and I spin on my heels to face him. I know I haven't told him my life story, but he keeps recalling details. It's impressive. "You remember that?"

"You told me like an hour ago."

"Still," I say, looking down at my white Keds, suddenly shy. He's acting like it's not a big deal, but it is. It's not that the past men in my life didn't know little things about me–they did. But for some reason, with Kace, it feels different. He's not trying to date me or sleep with me, so the motive to act interested isn't a factor. Maybe it's just that he likes being aware of what's in his life. Despite my lack of self-awareness–which, ironically, I'm aware exists, thank you very much–I can tell he's always on alert. Like he's waiting for a bomb to go off at any moment.

Sometimes I think it's a result of living through 9/11. That feels so specific, but I think it was the start of millennials feeling like their entire world could crash down at any given moment. I've noticed people my age tend to view life in three different ways: Some live in fear that something terrible will happen and keep their guard up–I think Kace falls into this category–at least from what I can tell. Some become immune and indifferent toward trauma, escaping with denial or coping with a substance that helps them dissociate–my sister took that route for a while. And some, like me, use it as an excuse to make the most of every situation and choose to live in the present moment. While this may seem like a blessing, always seeing the bright side can be a curse too. For example, when I'm stuck in a relationship that my heart is no longer in, I focus on all the positive parts of it and convince myself it's worth it to stay, even when deep down I know it's not.

"I still have work I need to get done." Kace's voice pulls my attention to his very serious, yet very beautiful face.

"Oh. What's your job?" I ask, tugging on the strings of my cropped hoodie.

He pauses, hand resting on his bedroom door knob.

"Cybersecurity," he answers curtly.

"Are you in charge of making everyone change their password every three months so it forces them to expand their childhood pet's name to have nine extra letters and symbols that make it impossible to remember?" I grin, and he smirks. A SMIRK. That's practically a smile coming from this guy–even though the dimples I imagine are still in question. I'll count it as a win.

"You could just make a new password with a less hackable word."

I drop my hands to my hips. "How is anyone supposed to guess that the queen of my ant farm was named Flik?"

"Anyone who has seen *A Bug's Life.*"

"You've seen that movie?!" He's definitely not as hopeless as I initially believed.

Again, he stares back.

I shrug a shoulder. "They would also have to know I had an ant farm in the first place, you know? Who would guess that?"

"No offense, but I've never met anyone as free with information about their life as you. Everything I've learned about you has been against my will. It's terrifying."

"You get used to it." I grin. "I like being open."

"Unless you need to communicate with your boyfriend about wanting to break up?" He arches a brow.

I shut down, one vein pinching closed at a time. Quickly though–all the energy draining from my body like it's on a mission to abandon me at all costs. "Maybe I'm open in every other area of my life to make up for that one area I'm not so good at when it comes to being vulnerable." I whisper the words I've never spoken aloud before. I'm both relieved and embarrassed at the realization.

Kace hums a sound of acknowledgment, then without another word, disappears behind the wooden door. Part of me wishes my remark had led to a heart-to-heart because I feel the need to process its effect on my life, but it's probably best he didn't make me elaborate. He's so contradictory, and I hardly know which way is up with him. He ruined my Valentine's date, but he saved me from a boring relationship. He's fine on the outside, but a total grump inside. That's not the kind of man I need a relationship with.

Wanting to let him get his work done, I get settled for the night. I pull yellow plaid pajama shorts from my suitcase along with a pink sports bra–there should be *some* color in this place, after all. Rezipping my bag, I tuck them under my arm and pad off to the bathroom.

After I've changed and tucked my clothes away in my bag, I go to scope out the kitchen. I open every single cupboard and drawer for no reason–the way my sister and I used to do whenever Mom and Dad would take us on vacation. It was an unspoken first task–searching through every nook and cranny–one I've carried on to every new place I go. Second was always building a fort out of couch cushions in the living room. I consider building one now to give me a secluded space, but I have a feeling it wouldn't go over well. As I pull a box of Cap'n Crunch from the counter, I imagine the reaction Kace would have if he ventured out of his room for dinner and found me hiding under a tent made of pillows and sheets. Giggling at the image in my head, I pour the yellow, sugary goodness into a square matte black bowl. *Who uses square bowls?*

Making my way back to the couch, I sink into the leather. It's not the most comfortable couch, but it sure as heck beats the backseat of my Jeep. I need to come up with a way to thank Kace for this. Starting by making sure not to bother him, I set my cereal on the coffee table and dig my portable DVD player and DVD case from my duffel bag. They're both covered in Happy Bunny and holographic angel and devil stickers, designs faded and cracked from wear and tear. I got this thing for my tenth birthday. It's a miracle that it still works perfectly after twenty years. I swear everything from the 90s and early 2000s were made to last while things today are made to break.

Unfolding the screen, I sort through my choices–all my favorites. *How to Lose a Guy in 10 Days. Sweet Home Alabama. Just Married. Uptown Girls*–RIP Brittany Murphy. Of course *The Lizzie McGuire Movie.* God, I love Hilary Duff. She's the queen. I flip through four other Hilary movies and finally land on *A Cinderella Story. Shocker.* I chuckle to myself as I slip the worn disk from its sleeve, knowing exactly which scenes will glitch from wear and tear scratches. Plugging my headphones into the jack, I rest the player on the arm of the couch and lean forward to pick up my cereal.

The first bite hits my taste buds with perfect texture–part mushy from where the bottom half was soaking in milk and part crunchy. I love the way it tears up the roof of my mouth as I sink back into the leather couch and the opening credits start, instantly capturing me as if I haven't seen this movie hundreds of times.

An hour and a half later, I reach for my phone, knowing I need to bite the bullet and call my sister. She's been blowing up my phone for days. Like my parents, she knows Matt and

I broke up. I told them I was staying with a friend so they wouldn't worry about me living in my car, but I refused phone calls because I wasn't in a place to hear the things they say every time. It's so much easier to not fall apart and to stay in a positive mindset when I'm not being reminded how far behind in life I am.

Ella answers on the second ring. "Hey! Finally! Hold on." The rustling in the background makes me picture her getting my nephew settled with a toy before she sneaks away to the kitchen for a quiet conversation. "How are you?"

"I'm good. Finally got a good night's sleep." I keep my voice low to assure Kace isn't bothered.

"Did you and Matt get back together?"

"No..." My brows scrunch even though she can't see me. "Why would we do that?" Matt really is a good guy, but he didn't see the world in the same way I did. I don't think that's necessarily a bad thing. Differences *can* be good–helpful even in keeping excitement in a relationship–but I think it has to be the right things you have conflicting views on. You still have to be able to support the other person. While he allegedly "supported" my dream, it turned out he didn't have much faith in me at all. I wish my sister understood that sacrifice wouldn't be worth any positives.

"I don't know, Mya. I was hoping maybe you got tired of drifting through life." As long as we're not talking about settling down, my sister is one of the sweetest people I know, second only to her husband. But it's like she used up all her patience getting her own life together that she doesn't think there's any time left for me to do the same.

"Come on, El," I whine. This is why I haven't called her since the breakup. I know it comes from a place of love, but it's too tough for the situation. My family hardly even knew Matt–*my* ticking clock is just driving them insane. I lie back on the couch, flinging my feet over the back. "That's not fair. Why would you want me to be with someone who isn't right for me?"

She sighs on the other end of the line. "I just want you to be happy."

I close my eyes, taking a deep breath. I know she wants what's best for me. She wants me to find what she has because it's what I'm looking for too–someone perfect for me and my dreams. It's part of why I stayed with Matt longer than I wanted to. I thought maybe if I had more patience like Ella, waiting for things to work out with her and Mack, it could be the same for me.

"So you're sleeping on someone's couch again or what?" Even though her words are soft, the jab stings because I've never moved to someone's couch before this. In between boyfriends, I've moved back in with my parents' friends. I had a space there–a bed. But when I started dating Matt, I insisted that this time would be different and that they should rent out the basement apartment to make extra money. I thought that without an escape plan, I'd be more committed.

"It's temporary. I promise." I want to tell her about Kace, but it feels like if I speak it aloud, I'll jinx it. Even though we've only had two interactions, I'm confident the man I first met isn't the person he is. There's a steadiness about him that feels so complimentary to the chaos in my head.

But until I know more about the extent of this situation, the last thing I need is my sister confusing my thoughts more. She has this theory about how when you have a space that's truly yours, it's so much easier to take control of the other areas in your life, and that's not the route I want to take right now.

"Do you need some help to get into an apartment? I can cosign for you."

I'm more than capable of getting an apartment. I have good credit. I can afford it. Maybe not one as nice as Kace's, but I could. The thought of being locked into a lease when I don't know the next step in my life just sounds miserable. It's infuriating that because I don't have security in their eyes, despite the hype my friends and family give me about my work, they don't think my crafting business is sustainable. I know what I'm doing. *Mostly anyway.*

My nephew yells for Ella, saving me. She says something about this conversation not being over and makes me promise to call her soon. Attempting to keep her judgments from infiltrating the bubble I've created for myself, I click another DVD into place.

I'm well into my next movie, invested in Adam Sandler trying to woo Drew Barrymore with a walrus–I love those two acting together–when Kace finally makes an appearance. He glances my way, not even long enough to see what I'm doing, and gives me an awkward wave before heading to the kitchen. Not a minute later, without a second glance, he's back in his room for the rest of the night.

Chapter Four

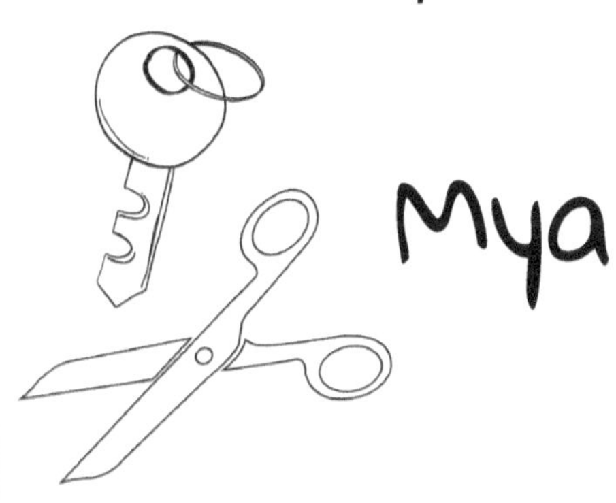

Mya

Before my eyes open, I unstick my face from the leather beneath it. Running my fingers over the sleep marks, I take in my surroundings–Kace's apartment. The room is nearly pitch black with the shades, but slivers of light seep in at the edges.

I sit, adjusting the sheet underneath me. My blankets shifted so much in the night that they're hanging off the edge of the couch and jammed into the cushion cracks. Scanning the room, I see no sign of life. I tilt my head to look behind me but don't detect light or sound coming from behind Kace's door.

I reach for my phone on the coffee table, immediately smiling at the new yellow and pink daisy case I bought for my birthday. Considering all celebrating was canceled when my relationship ended the day before I turned 30, I thought I deserved *something* special. Mom and Dad offered to drive up from Eugene, but I told them it wasn't necessary. That it was fine. I am *fine*. Today is a new day. I'm going to work on this week's business project and go grocery shopping so I'm not tempted to eat Kace's food. I'm choosing to focus on what I can control.

10:37. It's late, but I still have plenty of time to get through my to-do list and then some. Standing from the couch, I adjust my shorts and sports bra. It's not like I'm excessively well-endowed on either end, but I can't be pulling a Janet Jackson on my first full day as a roommate.

I can make out the kitchen from the living room, even in the dark, but carefully make my way to it and flip on the light switch by the fridge. I continue on, peeking my head in the bathroom to make sure Kace isn't there. The light's off, but with the new brightness from the kitchen, I can see the mirror is fogged up like he just finished showering. Maybe he is still in the apartment.

Pressing my ear against his bedroom door, I listen for Kace–or at the very least, Borrowers in the walls. *Nothing.* I knock lightly. *Nothing.* I rap my knuckles a little harder on the wood. *Nothing.* I turn the knob slowly, hoping if I'm interrupting him, he'll have time to stop me. When no objection comes, I push open the door wide enough to step through.

I wish I were surprised by the room in front of me. I hadn't necessarily pictured it, but if I had, this is what it would be. His bed is pushed against the back wall, a rustic wooden bed frame with a dark comforter. His bed is made neatly, with a few throw pillows even. His office desk is definitely *not* from Ikea. It has a rustic vibe too but looks sturdy enough to withstand an earthquake. Three sleek monitors are arranged in a semicircle, turned off as they sit in front of a computer chair that surely supports his back in a way all thirty-something-year-olds need.

Not wanting to snoop, mainly because I don't think I'd find anything I need to know, I get a move on my work day. I grab my jacket off the hook in the entryway, but the moment I'm outside the apartment door, it hits me that I don't have a key. *Crap.* Scanning the hallway, there's no one in sight. I decide to take the chance, just this once, and leave it unlocked while I run to my car. Since my ex had furniture before I moved in, there wasn't much to take with me besides my clothes and my crafting boxes.

Pushing open the front door to the complex, I'm struck with the steady beat of the rain on the pavement. I tug my hood over my head, and run down the sidewalk to my car, raindrops pelting my bare legs as I go.

I quickly pull out the cardboard box labeled "guillotine" and balance it in my grip as I close the trunk. This paper cutter is one of the best purchases I've ever made, but it feels more like a medieval torture device and *my Lanta* it's heavy–even more so when I have to carry it through the downpour.

By the time I make it back to the apartment–thankful someone held the door to the building open for me because apparently you need a key for that too–I'm wet with a combination of rain and sweat.

Maneuvering the knob with a flimsy grasp from under the wet box balancing in my arms, I push my way into the apartment, taking in the space again. There is no room for activities, but I'll make it work. I'm not sure what time Kace will be back, but I'm going to bet on having a few hours to myself. He had his laptop set up at Little Conejo yesterday when I ran into him, and the way he casually sat there makes me think it's a regular thing. I take off my jacket and quickly dry my legs with a towel, then push the coffee table toward the TV and away from the couch. Unfolding the top of the box, I pull out the folder of papers and my paper cutter.

I walk to the floor-to-ceiling windows, tugging on all four black-out shades until they spring up and flood the room with natural light. It's overcast today, but the river is clear, and I love seeing it from this view.

I settle on the floor with my back against the couch and open Spotify, tapping on the top option on my recently played: *Metamorphosis.* "So Yesterday" begins, the intro quiet. I increase the volume by the time the first verse starts and place it on the couch behind me. It's the soundtrack to my life right now, and while maybe I should be crying as the chorus hits, instead, I'm tempted to grab a hairbrush and sing into it like a microphone because I feel floaty in the best way.

Today is going to be great.

Sliding paper from the hot pink folder, I thank one-week-ago Mya for printing these bookmarks. The one thing I did leave behind was my printer because technically, it was a mutual purchase. The look on my ex's face when Kace ruined our date haunts me so much that guilt forced me to leave the thing behind.

This week's project is nostalgic bookmarks. Think: stories you scored at the scholastic book fair and fell in love with. The books that might suck if you read them today, but if you had a Bookstagram back then, you'd make it your entire personality for at least a week. I have ten sheets of paper with five bookmarks printed on each. I'm only making these fifty for two reasons. Reason number one is that if I craft for more than a couple of days on one project, I tend to get bored and abandon it altogether. Reason number two is supply and demand. Simple keys to a successful business.

I flip through the sheets, checking the quality of the titles and background images on each bookmark. I've already lined the back with holographic sticker paper and sealed the prints with holographic lament. These babies will be as timeless as these stories have been for me.

Island of the Blue Dolphins
Among the Hidden
Sisterhood of the Traveling Pants
Daughters of the Moon
The Boxcar Children
Magic Treehouse
Hatchet
Bridge to Terabithia
The Secret Garden
A Little Princess

I know there are so many others I could have chosen, but my business isn't typically for all the mainstream favorites.

You can get *Twilight* nostalgia from anywhere. It's way more fun to bond over secret gems of the world with strangers. The way it makes someone's day to be reminded of a love their brain kept locked away in a childhood compartment is one of my favorite glimmers.

Lining up the edge of *The Secret Garden* print with the blade on my cutter, I lean forward to make sure it'll slice perfectly. The smooth grind of the knife against the metal base is almost as satisfying as the way it perfectly cuts through the cardstock.

I hold the shortened piece of paper in front of me. Perfect. Realigning it back into the cutter, I lean close again, making sure it'll slice my pretty print into a straight bookmark.

Slice.

Fuck.

The smooth chop of my hair happened in slow motion yet too fast to stop.

I sit back, staring at my perfectly cut bookmark covered by a huge chunk of my blonde hair.

Glancing from the freshly cut strands, my eyes cross as I try to look down at where my evenly cut hair is looking not so uniform. I run my fingers through it, thankful I only cut the front chunk to just barely above my shoulder. I mean, it's *a lot* because the rest of my hair is long enough to reach my mid-back, but at least I won't need a pixie cut. That would be too drastic. Not to mention, I don't think I could manage that on my own. This, though, I can fix.

Calmly grabbing my nice fabric scissors from my craft box, and leaving my phone blasting "Workin' It Out," I walk to the bathroom. Flipping on the light, I shut the door behind me and glance in the mirror, my heart rate skyrocketing at the blatant difference in length. Panic courses through me. *Is this going to be what breaks me?* The thing that finally tips me over the edge into accepting I'm not where I want to be in life?

Nope. It's fine. I inhale as deep as possible, my chest expanding as I fill my lungs completely with air. Everything is fine. I've always wanted to try short hair, but I've been too scared. I guess this is the universe's way of getting me over my fears. It's been taking over my life a lot lately.

My pink straightener on the white marble counter contrasts the way it looked on the carpet in my bedroom at Matt's, and it sends my thoughts back to Valentine's Day as I comb through my hair and get ready to make the first snip. Everything happened so quickly, I could hardly process it. If anything though, I was more focused on the way Matt's eyes shifted between Kace and me, filled with questions. Something in my gut told me he wasn't wondering if it was true or not–if I had a boyfriend on the side. I'm sure it only helped his case when I defended Kace to the manager as he was dialing 911. As soon as he stormed off, Matt asked, "Did you plan that?"

I stared back at him blankly.

"Answer me, Mya. Was this some mastermind plan to get me to break up with you because you were too chicken shit to do it yourself?"

What a brilliant idea that would have been, I thought to myself. It's not like I wasn't creative enough to come up with the idea on my own. My first few breakups in high school were "staged." The first boyfriend I ever had was sweet. He was everything I could have wanted, but he was a year younger than I was, and we weren't on the same page sexually. I didn't want to hurt his feelings or make him feel bad for not being ready to have sex when I was, so I decided to break up with him. I logged onto AIM–because my mom wouldn't let me have a cell phone until I turned eighteen like Ella, and I was two months short of that milestone. I *pretended* to instant message my friend that I felt bad and didn't know how to break up with my boyfriend without hurting him. I *intentionally* sent the message to him, and it initiated his breakup with me. *That* was a chicken shit way out. This would have been too, *if* I had planned it. I wish every inevitable breakup fell into my lap that easily. If only it were as simple as folding my arms with a nod and a wink like Jeannie.

Matt had taken my silence from across the table at the dimly lit restaurant as confirmation. "Seriously, Mya? This whole time I thought maybe you were just busy trying to make your little crafts into a career. But you were avoiding our relationship, weren't you?"

That was the nail in the coffin for knowing this breakup was the right choice. Despite my inability to take steps toward it before, it was enough for me to push away from the table and leave without arguing to save a relationship I didn't want to bring back from the ledge.

I sigh, shoving away the final thought of Matt shaking his head before telling me to leave and returning to the pasta he had twirled around his fork.

Refocusing on my reflection in the bathroom mirror, I watch as the chunk of hair mirroring the missing one falls to the floor. I've never cut my hair before, but Ella and I used to cut each other's growing up. I gave my sister the adorable shoulder-length hair she's been rocking for years, so surely I can manage.

Fifteen minutes later, I've snipped away at least eight inches of my hair, leaving the remaining blonde strands sitting right at my shoulder. I tousle my fingers through it, shaking away any loose hairs, and twist my head from side to side to get a better look at my work. I went for the choppy look to give myself some extra leeway, and it looks pretty dang good if you ask me. I spin away from the mirror, looking over my shoulder to make sure the back is more or less even when the bathroom door flies open.

It misses hitting me by a fraction of an inch, slamming against the rubber jam on the wall behind it. With my heart racing, I freeze at the image in front of me. Kace stands there with a look of panic in his gorgeous brown eyes, his hair more ruffled than usual like he was just tugging on it. His chest visibly deflates with an exhale. "Are you okay?"

"I think the better question is, 'Are *you* okay?'" I giggle.

"Jesus, Mya. I thought something was seriously wrong."

I tilt my head. "Why did you think that?"

"I don't know. Maybe because I come home from a meeting and the practical stranger I let live with me is nowhere to be found, and yet, her abandoned phone is blasting music next to a pile of her hair. It looks like the start of a gone missing, then murdered story out there."

"Love Just Is" plays from my phone in the living room, although the sound is faint from here. I can't help but think how *I can't make sense of this guy.*

"Mya," he says like he's trying to get a reaction from me.

"Yes. Hi." I clear my head with a shake, a few newly cut wisps of hair falling to the floor. "I'm sorry. I didn't mean to scare you. I just had a slight accident while I was working, and I got distracted trying to fix it."

His eyes scan my body from head to toe like he's taking in my appearance for the first time. My arms fold over my mid-section, all of a sudden acutely aware that I'm still in my pajamas shorts and a sports bra. His gaze finally stops on my face. "You cut your hair." His tone is so matter-of-fact that his opinion on it is unclear.

I nod. "Does it look awful?"

His eyes scan my head, but then I watch them briefly dip toward the rest of my body. "No." He clears his throat. "It looks good."

"Okay good." I square my shoulders. "Thank you."

"No problem." He taps the doorframe with his fist twice. "Sorry for barging in. I'll leave you to it."

"It's okay. I'll go clean up the crime scene."

A smirk flickers across his face. "Do your thing. I've got to get back to work." With that, he gives a slight nod and exits the bathroom.

I call out after him, "Thank you for being concerned about me being taken, Liam Neeson," and wonder if he heard me.

While I'm in the bathroom, I shower and blow dry my hair to ensure it's acceptable. Tapping my finger against the plate of my straightener to test the temp, I pick out chunks of my hair and twist them in loose waves. The spunky vibe that results is a dream come true and makes me wish I had kept my crimper.

This isn't awful mid-life crisis hair. It definitely isn't the over-gelled scrunched ramen hair from middle school. This is comeback hair, and I'm obsessed. Happy as a bird with a french fry, I peek my head out from behind the door to make sure Kace isn't in the main area. With no sign of him, I make my way to my suitcase in nothing more than a towel and drop it as I dig through my bag when I realize my roommate left again.

I pull out my camo print short overalls that scrunch at the waist–not caring that it's only fifty degrees outside–and a black tee to go under them. It's not as colorful as I usually dress, but I feel edgy with my new hair.

Finding my place back on the ground, I switch the music to Ashlee Simpson's *Autobiography* album and pick up my bookmarks again. I finish cutting them, still leaning into my cutter to get a precise cut, not worried since I'm not sure it could do much more damage to my hair.

Bobbing my head to "Pieces of Me" as I make a neat little stack of my fifty bookmarks, I pick up the top *Daughters of the Moon* one and grin at the black and neon green print, glowing under the holographic laminate. I finish it with a tiny hole punch and an eyelet before tying on a black tassel to match.

I hold my bookmark in front of me, turning it in the natural light streaming through the window. It's perfect.

Happy with my work, I start a pile of completed ones to my right and pick up the next bookmark to finish. An hour later I'm done with all of them plus taking pictures of them on Kace's coffee table. His place might be simple and plain, but I can't deny it's also aesthetic and perfect for product marketing pictures–especially with the light from an entire wall of windows.

I glance at the metal snowboard clock on the wall. *3:52. Dang.* This day is flying by. I mentally toggle through the rest of my to-do list.

List bookmarks.

Grocery shop.

Ask Kace for a key.

All doable in the remainder of the day. But first, food. I haven't eaten.

I pour myself a bowl of cereal–Rice Krispies with a cut up banana on top. It's not like I've seen Kace eat anything besides his sandwich yesterday, but I have a feeling we have similar tastes in food. If only he had marshmallows so I could make us some Rice Krispie treats.

I finish my late lunch, savoring every snap, crackle and pop in my mouth, before putting my dishes in the dishwasher and cleaning up the chaos I left in the living room. After making sure everything looks good enough to prevent Kace from panicking again, I do my makeup. I usually stick with a basic look, letting my green eyes do all the heavy lifting.

Today, however, I'm going for edgy energy–at least until my undeniable bubbliness overwhelms it. I twist the black eyeliner up and apply a *thin* line–more wannabe edgy, less Avril Lavigne.

Satisfied with my look, I finish my mental grocery list. Assuming Kace went to the taco place, I'm going to stop by there first to find out when he will be home. Then I can plan my shopping accordingly or see if he has time to get a key made for me. I lock the door on my way out, not wanting to leave it open for so long, and press the down elevator button once I'm in the hallway.

The steel doors open with a whoosh, and a man stands on the other side of them, nearly falling over from the box piled high with liquor bottles in his hands.

"Do you need help?" I ask, and he peers around the side of the handle of Smirnoff as he steps off the elevator.

"No, I'm good. Thanks though." He readjusts the box in his arms.

I smile at him, and right before he continues on his way, he turns his head back toward me. "Are you new here? I thought I knew everyone on this floor."

"Kind of, yeah." I motion back down the hall. "I'm Kace's new roommate."

The man glances toward the ceiling like he's trying to put a face to the name. "Oh." I can practically see the lightbulb turn on with how his furrowed brows shift to wide eyes and a nod. "The moody guy who always keeps to himself?"

I chuckle. "That's the one."

"Well, I've already interacted with you more than I have with him in the three years we've both lived here, so here's to hoping your neighborly-ness is contagious. This floor is a lot of fun for adults in their quarter-life crisis. Don't let him make you believe otherwise."

I like this guy already. When I was with Matt, we lived in a townhome next to an elderly couple who kept to themselves. I would love to make some friends. "Don't worry, I won't let him bring me down." I grin.

"We're having a party tonight. Starts at six. I know that's early, but we like to be done by midnight instead of 4 a.m. Come meet everyone."

"Oh my gosh," I muse. "Remember the days when we could stay up half the night, then fall asleep on someone's floor using a jacket as a blanket, with a stereo blasting?"

He laughs. "Now my wife and I can't even sleep without a sound machine, an essential oil diffuser, and a blackout shade."

"Thirties hit differently, that's for sure. Sounds like fun, though. I'll let you go so that vodka doesn't take you out too early."

He grins. "We're apartment 708. Stop by anytime after six."

I thank him and say goodbye, then wait for the elevator door again while he walks away.

Thankful the rain has let up, I make the fifteen-minute walk to Little Conejo bundled in my puffer jacket. I see why Kace loves it here. The tacos I had yesterday were out of this world, and the cactus and aloe plant decor screams cute roadside cafe in Arizona desert vibes. Peering through the window, Kace isn't in the same seat he was yesterday. I step inside and scan the restaurant. I don't see him anywhere. I make eye contact with the bartender. "Is Kace here?"

The woman looks up from behind the bar. "No, hun. He hasn't been in today."

"Oh, alright. Thank you."

She nods in acknowledgment, and I turn on my heel, walking outside just to freeze on the sidewalk. *Crap.* I didn't think this through. I don't have a key. I don't have his phone number. I have no idea what time he'll get home. I guess my only option is to go back to the apartment and wait for him to let me in.

The party.

I pull my phone out of my jacket pocket to check the time. There's still another half an hour until it starts, so I head toward the grocery store to pick up a few pantry items.

Snagging only what I can carry in a newly purchased reusable bag, I end up with rice cakes and peanut butter, Cocoa Puffs, Trix and Frosted Flakes. I also grab a few apples and bananas. I try to eat decently healthy outside of my guilty pleasure. If I knew I could get into the apartment I'd also grab plenty of veggies and chicken to stir fry. But cereal is my weakness. Well, that and Blow Pops. I also get a box of almond milk because it won't go bad in my car for a few hours, and that way I can at least stop using Kace's milk. I can hardly taste the difference, and since that time I researched the reason behind the "Got Milk?" ads, I'm convinced there's no benefit to choosing the "real" stuff. Though, I do wonder what Mary-Kate and Ashley are up to these days–more so than any other milk mustache celebrity.

After walking the few blocks back to the apartment and leaving my groceries in my Jeep, I double-check to make sure Kace isn't home yet.

Still nowhere to be found.

I wish I knew more about him so I'd have an idea where to look, but I don't even know where to start. And Vancouver is way too big for me to go looking for a needle in a haystack. I'm not sure if he cares where I am, but on the off chance he comes home and wonders, I should leave him a note.

Back at my car, I find a notebook and rip out a blank page. Pulling my rainbow tiger Lisa Frank pen holder from my glove compartment, I pluck out the orange and green gel pens. I feel like if Kace liked color, he would like those. I tell him I'll be at the apartment party up the hall and leave my phone number. I take an extra minute to fold the note up into a little triangle football and make my way back upstairs to wedge the paper between the bottom of the door and the floor before taking off to hopefully make a few new friends.

Chapter Five

Reaching the door to my apartment, sweat trickles along my hairline. After coming home from an on-site meeting to the state of both Mya and my apartment, I needed to work out the immediate anxiety that consumed me, so I went for a run. I go to put the key in the lock, hoping the chaos behind the door has dissipated a bit but freeze when I notice a paper wedged beneath it.

I pull the folded triangle of notebook paper from its place, thinking it unintentionally landed there until I see my name written across the front. Each letter has ten lines to it, like the letter was written repeatedly over top the previous time. The "K" and the "C" are in green, the "A" and the "E" in orange. It might say my name, but this literally has Mya written all over it. Resuming entering my apartment, I unlock the door and push it open, sure to latch it behind me.

"Mya, I'm home," I yell loudly to announce myself, feeling like Ricky Ricardo. It came out like it was natural–the way my dad used to call my mom Lucy when he got home from work even though that's not her name. I can't recall announcing myself that way with Ruby, but I sure as shit don't need Mya peeping out from a corner in her tiny pajamas and sports bra. She's undeniably hot, and if I were in any sort of place to be looking for a woman, I wouldn't be looking at anyone but her. But I haven't dated anyone besides Ruby in nearly a decade, and I had a bachelor phase that lasted long enough before that. I have no desire to fuck around now that I'm in my thirties. Even if I did, I wouldn't fuck around with a roommate. These are all obsolete thoughts anyway because I can't imagine trusting a single person long enough to sleep with them.

Not to mention the chaos.

Mya is chaos in human form, and I have zero fucking clue what to do with that. She's like the suicide soda you created as a kid, putting a splash of every single one from the machine into your cup, and *somehow* it tastes good.

Remembering the note, I set my gym and laptop bag on the kitchen counter and stare down at the table football in my hand. I haven't seen paper folded like this since elementary school.

I pull the tab neatly tucked inside and unfold the note one triangle at a time. Running my hands over the creases to flatten it against my counter, I immediately confirm it's from Mya.

Kace,
Whoops! I locked myself out of the apartment. Do you think I could get a key? If not, I totally understand! We could just align our schedules better. Is that weird? I don't need to know where you are at all times. That's weird. Anyway, in case you need to know where I am, I'm killing time at the apartment up the hall. The guy invited me to a party. 708. Here's my number.
Mya

There's a string of hearts next to her name as well as her phone number inside a cloud. I'm only distracted by the doodles for a second before panic sets in again. Does she *somehow* know the neighbor? Sure as shit doesn't sound like it considering she didn't mention his name. I fold the paper in fourths, running my thumb and forefinger over the creases repeatedly as my teeth grind together.

I'm not responsible for her.

I'm not responsible for her.

She's a grown-ass adult who can make her own decisions.

As I step into the shower, I repeat the phrases, but as the hot water cascades down my back, they're replaced with new ones.

What if something bad happens to her?

Or someone spikes her drink?

What if she leaves with a guy and can't get home because I didn't make her a key today?

No. I shampoo the sweat from my hair, tugging on the strands and demanding myself to let it go.

I'm not responsible for her.

I'm not responsible for her.

She's a grown-ass adult who can make her own decisions.

Fuck.

I quickly finish my shower, toss on jeans and a gray T-shirt and grab my bomber jacket off the hook on my way out the door. Pocketing my keys, I veer toward the noise.

The door is open when I reach it, and I take it as an invitation to enter. I don't know many of my neighbors. I haven't had the need. I plan ahead so I don't ever need an egg or a cup of sugar, and what other reason could I have for introducing myself?

I step inside the apartment, leaning against the front wall to take in the scene. Not a single person notices my arrival, and that, in itself, is concerning from a safety standpoint. I let it slide because Usher's "Yeah" is blasting from an unseen speaker so loudly that I'm surprised anyone can hear the person next to them.

Scanning the room, I see the group of people sitting on the floor around the coffee table and playing Cards Against

Humanity. There's another group out on the balcony with Solo cups in their hands, taking turns with a life-size version of Jenga. And then my eyes find Mya.

Her smile is so bright that there's hardly a need for the lights in the kitchen. She's leaning against the counter chatting to some woman mirroring her position on the kitchen island across from her, her new hair bouncing as she talks animatedly. God, her hair is hot. Just long enough to grip from behind.

No. Absolutely fucking not.

God, it's been so long since I've had sex. I can't remember the *last* time Ruby and I slept together. That's how far gone our relationship was. I know I need to take some responsibility for our demise. She may have cut the rope, but I can recognize that it was likely easier because we'd both been fraying it, one twine at a time with each step we took away from each other. I need to figure out how to let go of my hostility.

Confirming Mya is relatively safe, I move to leave. I'll text her so she can call when she's ready to be let in tonight. I freeze when she hands her phone over to the woman she's talking to and swaps it for a shot of clear liquor. Jesus fuck. I wonder how drunk she is, and the widening grin on her face tells me I'm about to find out.

The woman pulls her own phone out and taps a few times until the song changes. Within the first few notes, I know what's playing. The woman holds Mya's phone up and presses the record button as the intro lyrics to "Build Me Up Buttercup" start. Mya reaches behind her for the Smirnoff bottle, holding it to her lips and singing the first verse into the cap like it's a microphone.

At the end of the first verse, she sets the bottle on the kitchen island behind her friend and twirls in a circle, her arms up in the air like she doesn't have a care in the damn world. This woman got dumped a day before her birthday–which upon confirmation made me feel even more like shit than I already did–and became homeless. Yet, she's so damn happy you'd think she just got married and moved into a mansion. *It's not natural.*

In the flash of a moment, she presses her palms onto the counter behind her and pushes herself up. Her feet kick in front of her, and the woman recording zooms in on them before zooming back out and following Mya as she slides across the counter. She hops off when she reaches the end. Is she making a music video?

I shake my head, chuckling to myself. This fucking girl. What is her deal?

Glancing next to me, I take a seat on the arm of the couch, set on watching the show. I'm already here. I might as well. A man crosses in front of my path with a bottle of vodka and a stack of plastic shot glasses. I *think* it's the guy who lives here. When I nod, he says "hey" and to help myself to a drink, then follows the voice of a woman calling him from the other side of the room.

I shift my gaze back to Mya as she flings open the sliding door to the patio like there's no resistance. All the party goers outside give her their attention, lifting their Solo cups into the air under the glow of the patio light–one of them handing over their drink. She takes a sip before handing it back, and my chest stutters. I would feel that way if *anyone* did that though.

She squeezes her way back through the crack in the door, and someone else closes it behind her. Glancing toward the ceiling as if the music is coming from there, it's like she all of a sudden remembers the song. She picks up singing at the chorus about needing someone more than anyone, and I can't imagine Mya ever *needing* anybody.

She twirls around a few more times like she's fucking Julie Andrews in *The Sound of Music*. After a few too many spins, she holds her hands out like they'll steady her and grins at the phone her new friend has pointed at her face.

And then her eyes wander to the side, and they land on me.

For whatever fucking reason–recognition, I'm sure–her smile widens.

"Kace! You're here!" she screams like she's been waiting her whole damn life for me to show up. I'd be lying if I said my heart didn't palpitate at the way my name sounds coming out of her mouth, but it's the shock of it. This girl is a stranger, and yet, she acts like we're childhood friends.

The next thing I know, she's hurtling toward me, and the moment after, she's flung herself on me like we're *anything but strangers*.

I guess I got my answer.

Really fucking drunk.

Her thighs slide against mine, hers bare with how short her romper outfit thing is. I'm at too much of an angle for her to sit stable on my leg, so she immediately starts to slide off. Her arms loop around my neck at the same moment one of my hands falls to the small of her back and the other grips her thigh. Damn, her skin is soft, and her vanilla candy perfume is strong enough to barely overpower the vodka.

Unbothered by my touch, she smiles at me, inches from my face. I want to pull away. I should pull away. I'll blame *not* pulling away on shock. This girl seriously has no personal bubble. She met me a few days ago for Christ's sake.

"Hi," she greets me.

I chuckle. "Hey."

"Oh. My. God." She pulls one hand from my neck to slap it against my chest. "You *are* capable of a smile. I'm so happy."

I bite back a grin and level a stare.

"Nooooooo," she whines in the absence of my expression. "Are you drunk?"

"I'm a little buzzy." She pinches her fingers together in front of my face to show me how *little* drunk she is.

I'm tempted to lecture her about all the danger she put herself in tonight, but besides the fact that she probably wouldn't remember it, I'm sure she wouldn't care. "You look like you're having fun," I say instead.

She twists her fingers through the strands of hair at my neck, and it feels fucking good. "Do you know what fun is, my little rain cloud?"

"Rain cloud?" I clarify, although I'm using the majority of my brain power to refrain from brushing my thumb across where I hold her bare thigh.

"Umm, yeah. I know I don't know you super well, but you seem a little gray. You know what I mean?"

"You've known me for two days." I deadpan, refusing to humor her.

She shrugs like that isn't a factor at all. "Technically a week."

"Alright, buttercup." Her grin widens, and I will myself not to let it affect me.

"Did you see my music video in the making?!" She doesn't give me a chance to respond before she continues. "It won't be as iconic as the one Ella and I made to 'Upside Down' by A*Teens during summer camp as kids, but I have high hopes for it."

As if she's been flung onto the next train of thought, she turns toward the people sitting at the coffee table behind her.

"It was awful," one girl says to another. "Every time I tried to ask him a question, he would deflect with a semi-connected trivia fact."

"Like what?" the girl next to her asks, appalled.

"I asked him what his favorite food was, and he asked if I knew that the fear of peanut butter getting stuck to the roof of your mouth is called arachibutyrophobia."

The group of girls burst into a fit of giggles, then one adds, 'That's nothing compared to the guy who touched my stomach and told me that's where his baby would be. *On a first date.*"

"People are insane," another girl claims. She's not wrong.

"I see you got my note," Mya says, pulling my attention back to her as she links her hands behind my neck again. She leans back so far I'm worried she'll fall over and crack her head on the coffee table if I don't hold her tighter, so my grip adjusts accordingly.

"I did." I hold my stare on her glossed-over green eyes, faded in the darkness of the party.

She doesn't respond. She just stares back at me, her face a little pale.

"Are you okay?"

She stares another second, then nods her head. Then she shakes it.

"Mya?"

"Uh huh?" she slurs, her eyes staring past me and her arms loosen around my neck.

I think that last shot took her over her limit. "Are you ready to go home?" Did I say home? I know it's mine, but fuck if it didn't sound like I meant it was ours. *Note to self: watch your fucking language, so there's no misunderstanding between us about what this arrangement is.*

She gives me a smile that's a combination of sleepy and totally wasted even though it's only 8 p.m. "Okay."

I begin to stand, and she stands with me. Her friend, who I didn't realize was still there, holds Mya's phone out for me. I pocket it, and when she says goodbye, Mya perks up. "Bye!" she shouts, pulling away from me to throw her arms around her new friend.

When she releases her and turns back to me, her face pales again and her eyes drop. "Oh my god," she mutters under her breath.

"What?" My brows furrow.

I step behind her, guiding her toward the door, and she looks back toward me–horrified. "I touched you like a girl-friend would."

My tongue swipes across my lip, my brows still pinched.

"That was so inappropriate. I'm sorry, Kace." She seems distraught.

"It's fine," I assure her, although I think my voice comes out more prickly than I intended.

"No, it's not. It won't happen again. Please forgive me. Don't kick me out. I love your couch. It's so much better than my car." Her words slur, and her sentences run together.

"I'm not going to kick you out."

A sigh of relief leaves her. "Thank you."

I respond with a nod and point down the hallway toward my apartment, hoping we'll make it there sooner rather than later.

Once we're through the door and it's locked behind us, Mya stumbles toward the couch. She nearly falls over, but I reach out in time to grab her elbow and steady her.

She glances at where we're connected before her gaze slowly focuses on me. "Oh!" she exclaims, a memory coming to the surface. "I got us cereal! But it's in the car. I'll go get it." She tries to walk past me, but I stop her.

"We'll get it tomorrow."

"But I thought you like cereal?" she pouts.

I chuckle. "I do."

"What's your favorite?" She stumbles into the kitchen and leans against the counter next to the fridge.

"Did you eat dinner?"

"Nope," she says, popping the "P" as she shakes her head. "Let's have cereal. Make me your favorite."

I study her face, her insistence on learning something about me while she's drunk is impressive. "Alright."

She hoists herself up onto the counter, and I fill a glass of water for her. She takes a sip before abandoning it on the marble beside her in favor of watching me. I reach for the Cinnamon Toast Crunch from the counter next to her ass. She follows the movement as I open the box and make two bowls. Handing one to her, I prop my shoulder against the refrigerator and cross my ankles.

We eat for the next few minutes in silence, except for the crunch of the cinnamon sugar squares. Having Mya in my space is so odd compared to sharing it with Ruby, who was always put together with her perfectly pressed pantsuits and brown hair pulled back tightly–always caring what everyone thought. Despite the unfamiliarity, somehow all of this feels somewhat normal–*better*.

She hops off the counter and places her bowl in the sink, but as she backs away, she loses balance, gripping the edge for balance. "I think I need to lie down," she whispers, and I'm thankful she's not the kind of drunk who wants to keep drinking more.

"Alright." I put my bowl in the sink next to hers and walk past. Opening the door to my room, I swipe my pillow off my bed because I'm too damn old to sleep without the right type. I return to the living room with Mya right where I left her, tracking my movement.

"What are you doing?" Her eyes still follow me as I walk toward the couch.

"No fucking clue," I mutter to myself, truly baffled by my behavior. It's not that I'm *not* a gentleman. I know how to open a damn door for a woman or make sure she comes before I do. But for *my* woman. And Mya is far from *mine*. I don't want her to be either, but something about making her sleep on the couch while her world is likely spinning feels wrong.

She steps closer to me. "What?"

"Nothing. Here." I hand her pillow over.

"I thought you weren't kicking me out?" she says, her voice small. In the glow of the light from my bedroom behind her I have a decent view of the way the curls in her short hair have fallen, and the thought that I wish I could mess them up myself slips into my mind uninvited.

I shake my head. "Just kicking you off the couch. You can sleep in my bed tonight."

She glances toward my room. "Are you sure?"

I nod. "Yup." I take a seat on the couch, making my point. Mya is already going to feel like shit from her hangover. It'll help if she doesn't wake up with a sore back on top of it. Reaching for the remote, I try to distance myself. "Get some sleep. Try not to throw up in my bed."

Glancing at her over my shoulder, I can't decide if she looks afraid of my fake threat, or thankful for my gesture. Either way, she whispers a "thank you," and with her pillow clinging to her chest disappears into my room.

Chapter Six

Mya

A screech worse than dial-up internet jolts me awake. *God, make it stop.* Yanking my pillow from under me, I crush it over my head to drown out the sound. The smooth sheets under my cheek cause me to raise my head from the mattress. What the–

The room is almost completely dark from the blackout shades, but I know where I am, even if I've only caught a glimpse of this space once before. I'm in Kace's room. How did I get here? I sit up, rubbing my temples and glance down at my body while I put the pieces together. My clothes are still on.

The party.

Shots. A lot of them.

My new friend and me planning a music video for my favorite song of all time.

Kace showing up.

Kace.

Oh my god. I sat on his lap. I touched his hair.

It all floods back in pieces between each pound of my head.

His hand on my thigh.

Him making us cereal.

Then giving me his bed.

I groan, mortified. How am I supposed to face him? My second night as his roommate and he already had to play babysitter. He probably regrets his decision so much that he's out there planning how to get rid of me.

Despite not having the mental capacity for it right now, I decide to get it over with–even if only because in the dim lighting of the room, I can tell my phone is not in here, and I have no idea what time it is.

When I slide my feet onto the floor, I stumble over my shoes. Well, at least I had the sense to take them off before I climbed into Kace's bed. Thank god for that.

I attempt to open the door in stealth mode, but the damn thing betrays me, squeaking enough that as soon as I peek my head out, Kace's gaze snaps to me.

He freezes, then rakes his eyes over my body.

I glance down at myself to once again make sure I'm wearing clothes. Sure enough, I've got on the same thing I was wearing at the party. Maybe he's just surprised I'm still alive after how drunk I was last night.

"Morning," I whisper, breaking the silence. I slide onto the stool at the breakfast bar, actually thankful for the blackout shades in the living room and that only one of the lights in the kitchen is lighting the space. My head rests on my palm as I lean over the counter with another groan.

"Morning." Nothing in Kace's voice gives away his emotions. I hold his stare for a moment before glancing at the culprit of the deafening noise from a few minutes ago. He reaches for the blender, takes the top off and sets it in the sink before pulling two glasses from the cupboard.

"I should have had a V8," I mutter to myself as I let my palms slip so they dig into my eyes.

He chuckles. "How about a smoothie?"

"Yes please." I pause, glancing at him and trying to gauge the state of my internal organs. "Maybe." I think he smirks, but I don't have time to tell if it's a figment of my hungover imagination before he turns around to pour the berry-pink cocktail.

He places the glass in front of me, then turns to the stove where he picks up a spatula and loads three pancakes onto a plate. Were those cooking when I sat down? I shake the confusion from my head when the clinking of the plate against the marble sends a shooting pain through my head. I groan. I look up in time to catch Kace's expression–or lack thereof. He stares at me, and I can't tell if he's annoyed, frustrated or wishes he could laugh at me for my stupidity. I'm a grown-ass adult. I should know by now how many drinks put me at my limit. But he also made me pancakes and let me sleep in his bed. I feel weird and foggy like I'm living someone else's life that I know nothing about. I wonder if this is how Rob Schneider felt waking up trapped in Rachel McAdams's body.

Not wanting to dissect his thoughts while my brain feels like mush, I focus all my attention on getting carbs into my stomach to soak up whatever alcohol is left. I take a hesitant first bite, wanting to make sure that once I swallow, my breakfast will stay where it's meant to. When the fluffy goodness hits my taste buds, I can't stop. It's so fluffy and sweet and somehow perfect even though there's no syrup or butter. I wonder what his secret is.

I don't take time to ask, partly because the sound of my voice might be too much for my hangover before these pancakes hopefully work some magic. Before starting my next one, I spare a glance at Kace, to see if he's eating too.

He's staring at me. A tingle runs across my skin at how unnerving it is.

"Was the pancake good?" He gives me a pointed look.

I nod. "Yes."

"Did you chew it?"

I grin. "Mostly."

He just stares, and for the first time this morning, I have the brain power to take him in. He's wearing jeans that hang perfectly on his hips, his chest unfortunately covered by a gray T-shirt that at least highlights his muscle tone. I vaguely recall it being the outfit he showed up to the party in, which makes sense since I was kind of holding his room hostage. I glance over the edge of the counter to his bare feet, and it's even sexier to me. I think I need some water. And more pancakes. Something to clear away any thoughts that don't belong. Until then, I blame the hangover for being this attracted to my strictly platonic roommate. And that his hair looks *that* good. Dark, sexy and just long enough to run my fingers through. It takes everything in my power to stop staring and stab at my pancake again.

"I've got to work," he tells me, and I risk another glance up. He takes a moment to stare before grabbing his plate of pancakes and disappearing into his room without waiting for me to say a single word.

I finish the rest of my breakfast, thankful it all stays down. Finding my phone on the coffee table, I unlock it and check the post I made yesterday with all my bookmarks on my business account: All That and a Bag of Crafts.

I'm so thankful I have space to work at Kace's. I've worked outside of a house before, but I was a little concerned about keeping my business running successfully from my car. It would be a lot of work to dig through all my art boxes and stay organized from my trunk. Crafting may be a flexible hobby, but it usually requires space to spread out the chaos. Dragging everything to the library is something I've done before, and I don't particularly want to revert to that option again. I would have done it though. I've created and sold a different project consistently once a week for years, and I'd hate to break that streak.

Taking a quick glance through the comments, it looks like almost all of them have been claimed, so I hop in the shower to wash off the previous night and focus on my plan to get orders processed and mailed out today and tomorrow.

I opt for my oversized "Perkis Power" shirt–because nothing beats Ben Stiller acting like a total psychopath–and a pair of spandex shorts. If I get all of my work done, I should have time to work out later. Pulling my hair half up with a flower clip–thankful it's still long enough to do so–I put on my One Direction playlist and get to work sending invoices and addressing envelopes for my bookmarks. I wish all my deliveries could be local so I could thank everyone in person for loving my creations and helping me live my best serial entrepreneur life–but if I'm thankful for one thing in this decade, it's social media and a speedy postal service helping my dreams become reality.

Surprisingly, I'm done working by noon. It leaves me plenty of time to scroll social media; I love that my algorithm has been perfectly curated to help me come up with new craft ideas. A notification pings my phone that another payment has come through. I calculate how many days until the end of the month. Still over a week.

I pause, my finger frozen on the screen. I'm no longer responsible for paying utilities and groceries like I did when I was with Matt. I hum to myself, mulling over the changes in my life. I have to help Kace out somehow. I know he said this would only be temporary, so maybe he doesn't *expect* rent, but I'm not a freeloader. And while he *might* take cereal as a form of payment, I wouldn't be okay with that.

Standing from where I've made a workstation on the living room floor again, I walk to Kace's door and press my ear against it. I still don't know exactly what he does, but it doesn't sound like he's on a call or anything, so I knock lightly.

There's a quiet moment, and a few clicks of a computer mouse, then a "come in."

Turning the knob, I peek my head inside his room, surprised the blackout shades are up and letting in a warm natural light. He's sitting at his desk, all three computer screens turned on, but with nothing pulled up. It's just one continuous snowy mountain scene across all three monitors.

He watches me as I step inside his room, his eyes appraising my outfit for a flash of a moment before settling on my face.

"Hey, sorry if I'm bothering you," I say, awkwardly linking my fingers in front of myself.

"You're not." He leans back in his chair and reaches for two Chinese stress balls sitting in a red velvet box. They clink together as he rotates them in his palms, and I'm mesmerized by the motion. "Can I help you with something?"

My gaze snaps to his. "Yes. Well, actually, I was hoping to help you."

He arches a brow.

"I was wondering about rent. I'm guessing it's due soon?"

He stays locked in thought for a moment. "Don't worry about it."

"Kace. No."

"Mya. Yes. It's not a big deal. I said I'd help you out until you got back on your feet."

"I didn't fall over. I'm fine. I made almost three hundred dollars today. I can help."

His brows furrow like he's confused about how I did that, but he doesn't pry. "You can help with groceries," he concedes.

"No," I say firmly.

"No?"

"That's not enough. Please let me help." I release my intertwined fingers to tap on my chin, trying to think of an idea. He stares again. Why does he keep doing that? I wish he would stop. "Oh." A lightbulb goes off in my head. "It's because you don't want me to stay a whole month, huh? It's okay. I understand. I'm *a lot*. Especially after last night." I sigh. "I'm not usually like that. It's just really freaking hard to make friends as an adult." Living with Matt, I spent most of my time with him, and the majority of my friends still live in Eugene, near my sister. I know that not having a local support system is hurting my ability to process my stressors and live my life fully, and it didn't feel like Kace wanted to be friends. So when I locked myself out, the party felt like the perfect opportunity.

"It's not an issue. As long as I can get my work done, it's fine."

Brainstorming a way to convince him, a memory swirls to the front of my mind. "Remember last night when we were eavesdropping on those people at the party?"

He arches an eyebrow again like there's no possible way there's a point to this recollection, or he's surprised I remember it.

"They were bitching about terrible dates they've been on," I prompt.

"I remember."

Sighing, I admit, "The worst part about breakups is recreating routines and realizing you're going to have to start dating from the beginning again."

"Good thing you like experiencing things for the first time." With one foot firmly planted in the carpet, he swivels the chair back and forth, and I'm starting to wonder if he got his hands on the *Limitless* pill or something because this man seems to have a whole storage unit for Mya notes.

"There's always an exception to the rules." I shift my weight to one hip. "People are crazy, and sorting through them can be hard."

"You don't know the whole story," he defends the gossip girls from the party. "What if they did something equally as annoying?"

I mull over the thought. "Even if they did, I think most people put what they believe is their best foot forward at the beginning."

"Maybe that's the problem." He zones in on the circular motion of the stress balls in his palms. "Maybe if we showed the worst sides of ourselves first, we'd save time."

This man is CYN-I-CAL. He's not wrong though. Sometimes when people feel comfortable enough to be themselves, they become entirely new people. "I'm guessing you're not excited to start dating again?"

He eyes me like he knows I'm prying for information. "No," is all he gives.

God, I'd kill for the details of Kace's last relationship. Okay, not kill for. But I'd definitely help the Pretty Little Liars do some shady shit. "I do think it would be easier if everyone showed all their cards from the start, so you'd know if you wanted to keep them or not."

"Yeah," Kace mumbles.

I snap my fingers, an idea forming. "Idea! I'd say it's safe to assume neither of us is interested in dating right now? I mean, I don't know your story. Although, if you'd like to tell me, I'm more than happy to listen."

I pause, giving him a chance to take me up on my offer, but he's still as stone. He even stops rotating the stainless steel balls in his hand. "I really need to get back to work." It's not mean, just serious.

I take that as my assumption being correct. "Wouldn't it be fun if you could go out with someone and be as *you* as you wanted without stressing that you're wasting a real chance?"

"I'm not following." He leans against the back of his chair, settling in for this conversation.

"You go on a date–you know, because they're fun if they aren't being interrupted by grumpy men." I gauge his reaction, catching a smirk. "Don't you miss them?"

"I guess," he admits, and I'm surprised he owned up to that much.

"If there was no pressure for your date to be *the one*, you could enjoy the fun of dating."

His brows pinch. "Still not following."

I need to stop talking in circles and land my plane. Men can't read between the lines for shit. "How about we make a bet?"

"A bet?" he clarifies.

"Yeah. Like a competition. If I win, I get to chip in on rent. If you win... You get a cupboard constantly stocked with Cinnamon Toast Crunch."

He mulls over the idea. "What's the bet?"

I squeeze my fists, resisting a happy dance. "So what if we have a contest of who can plan the most genuine date–"

He cuts me off. "I'm not going on a date with you."

"Ouch." My hands fly to my chest like I'm physically wounded. "Way to kick a girl when she's down," I sass, only a little offended.

"You just assured me you weren't down."

"Right. Well, it will be a fake date, dummy."

"I'm not going on a fake date with you," he reiterates.

"Why are you so grumpy?" I pop my hip, resting my hand on it. "You're Monday in human form."

He smirks, and I count it as a win in my column. "Still, no."

Sheesh. This girl must have done a number on him to make him not even want to go on a fake date. "It's like friends hanging out."

He raises a brow. "Are we friends?"

"We will be once we hang out!" I ignore his questioning stare. "Hear me out." I pause for him to give a sign that he's listening. Holding eye contact without objection is enough permission for me. "We each plan a date we would love to go on if we weren't worried about the other person in a new relationship thinking we're crazy."

"How is that a bet?"

"Hmm." I actually have zero clue what I'm thinking. My idea hasn't gone much further than that yet. I snap my fingers again. "Whoever has the most fun during the other person's date wins."

"How will we do that?"

Yes! I fist pump in my mind. I've totally got him on the hook. Keep the questions coming. "I think we know enough about each other to know if we're choosing something out of character just to make sure the other person would have fun. You and I are practically opposites, but surely one of us will surprise the other with something they didn't realize they'd enjoy."

"How about you just live here and focus on your life instead?"

"My life is fine, thank you. Come on," I beg. "It will be nice to get out of our heads, just mess around, and not worry about being perfect. We'll be forced out of the house so we don't stay inside to wallow over people we are better off without." His eyes snap to mine like that last thought got his attention.

He takes a deep breath before exhaling a dramatic sigh. "Alright. What exactly is the deal?"

"Do you have plans this weekend?"

"No."

"Perfect. We'll each plan a day. We can come up with whatever 'date-ish' activities we want, and at the end of the weekend, whoever's date was the most enjoyable to the other person wins."

"You really expect one of us to have a good time when it's clear you and I like different things?"

"We both love cereal." I beam, teasing him. "But seriously, it will be fun to plan an uninhibited date."

He gives me a pointed look.

I shrug. "If you're scared of losing, just tell me now. I'm betting on winning this. I'm pretty sure you're incapable of planning something fun, so you could save time by giving in."

He hides another smirk. "Anything is fair game?"

"Yup." I consider telling him nothing illegal, but I have a strong feeling that Kace would never go for that anyway. "Find something that you think would be fun but would be nervous 'subjecting' a girlfriend to–for whatever reason. Maybe it's a weird thing you like or a non-traditional date. You're smart enough to plan something." I grin at him. I know he's smart. I mean, I don't *know* know, but look at the man!

If there's anything he oozes along with grumpiness and sex appeal, it's intelligence.

"Alright." He rotates the balls a few more times in his palm before twisting his chair back toward his desk. "I do have to get back to work now."

"Okay, you do you." I tap my finger against my chin. "I'll be planning a date that tricks you into happiness faster than Hallie and Annie got their parents back together." With a smile on my face and more determination than I've had in a while, I practically skip out of his room. Closing the door behind me, I wonder if it's concerning that something I'd be nervous about in any other circumstance is hyping me up more than anything has in a while.

Chapter Seven

Kace

Dave looks as if Mountain Dew were a person. His hair is brown, I think? But it could be *dirty* blond. On the East Coast, you'd call it scraggly, but in the Pacific Northwest it can pass as rugged–either way, it tiptoes the line of mullet, and somehow it pairs perfectly with the soul patch. His green jacket is worn, the patches on it faded to the point that they're unrecognizable. His jorts have unintentional holes, and his sandals with socks complete the look.

He's stopped on the other side of the street, his foot on the ground holding his balance on his bicycle. He's a real-life Forrest Gump, biking here from New York after he got back from the war, and he's got enough stories and a good enough memory that I've never heard the same one twice. He goes on a daily bike ride from the homeless RV camp, and our paths cross at least once a week.

The bike has a milk crate strapped to the back that carries a speaker and a Charlie Brown tree. I know this because oddly enough, Dave is one of the most consistent people in my life. He has been ever since I discovered my favorite taco and torta joint a few weeks into moving here. I took an immediate liking to him the first time he biked past me beatboxing the *Wheel of Fortune* theme song, and it reminded me of my parents. After our timing aligned for the third day in a row, I invited him to share lunch, and apparently, that's how I landed my only friend.

When the crosswalk sign changes, he starts pedaling just fast enough to move forward and not fall over. He doesn't have a care in the world. As he approaches my picnic table outside Little Conejo, his singing voice projects through the air. It's loud and sunny, despite the overcast weather, going on about not worrying and being happy. *I wish it were that easy.*

"Good day, Kace," he greets me, coming to a halt on the sidewalk before me.

"Dave. I ordered an extra sandwich with your name on it. It should be ready in a minute." It wasn't actually for him. It was for Mya, not sure if she had a chance to go grocery shopping today like she planned, but now that he's here, I know Dave needs it more.

"I love you, man," he says with a firm squeeze on my shoulder. "The way Jason Segel loves Paul Rudd."

"Do you think that's a good thing?" I smirk, ignoring the fact that I don't know what I'll do for a groomsman when I need one. Ruby and I talked about getting married, but she got promoted to VP of finance a few years back and became set on a promotion to CFO before planning a wedding.

"Sure is." He gives me a partially toothless grin.

I glance at the approaching bartender, thanking her as I take my bag. I have too much to get done today, so I opted for a to-go lunch instead of working here. Pulling the extra sandwich from the white paper, I hand it over to Dave. He thanks me and grins, showing off a few of his missing teeth again, and tucks it safely into his milk crate. Giving me a salute, he aligns his foot with the pedal, presses forward and picks up the song right where he left off, like he was never interrupted. His singing about how if you frown it brings everyone down fades as he gets further away.

The lyrics bring Mya to the forefront of my mind. I'm baffled by how she's absurdly fine after a breakup with someone she lived with. I can't help but wonder if it's more of a "fake it until you make it" thing or if she's one of those people who can see the upside of everything. I don't know if I should be jealous she's handling it better than I am or concerned about her coping skills.

Deciding it's none of my business, I head home with only one sandwich.

Turning the key in the lock, I push the door open and immediately hear voices coming from the bathroom off the entryway. I lock the door quietly, convincing myself it's because I don't want to interrupt whatever is going on and deny that I'm being a creep. For as open as Mya is, I don't understand her, and it's one of the most unsettling things not to know the details and intentions of those around me. I've been this way since I was a kid, never able to count on my parents being around consistently. At the time, I thought they just didn't understand me. I wanted to take apart my Gameboy and see how it worked. They wanted to watch game shows. Now that I'm an adult, I wonder if because I was such a smart kid, they thought I could raise myself or weren't sure how to relate to me. Either way, the damage is far past done, and now I only talk to them on Christmas and birthdays.

I set my lunch on the kitchen counter, thankful for once that the apartment is small.

"You really don't miss Matt?" a woman's voice echoes on the other side of the bathroom door. Oh. She's talking to someone on speakerphone.

"I'm fine, really. I mostly feel bad that I wasted his time. We should have broken up sooner. He's fine. Great, even," Mya insists, and I wonder again if she's putting on a brave face or means what she says.

"Just not great for you." I can't tell if the woman says it as a statement or a question.

"It was a red flag when we argued over our Valentine's Day plans." Mya sighs, and my stomach and brain flip through a range of emotions about how things could have looked different for us if she wasn't at that restaurant.

"What did you want to do?" The inquiring voice and I are both curious.

"OMSI has a new exhibit where you learn about and play with light. I thought it would be fun," Mya says wistfully. "And they had a special whiskey bar set up that I thought Matt would love."

"You wanted to visit the museum of science for Valentine's Day?"

"They have an 'after-dark' event. It's adults only. I thought it would be cool. There's also a laser show, and I don't know. I wanted to do something besides *just* go to dinner. The only places we ever went for dates were restaurants. I told him there should be more to dating than dinner."

"And he took you to dinner anyway." I can hear the woman's eyes roll in her voice. I want to judge the guy for not giving his girl what she wants, but would I have chosen differently? Despite being tired of going out to dinner with Ruby *too often*, I'd still be down for cliche because it's comfortable and predictable. I don't have to stress about things going awry when it's something I've done a hundred times.

"Yeah. It's fine. I just thought it would be fun and different. You know me, I hate doing the same things twice. There's so much to explore and experience." My heart thumps in my chest, Mya's words both exhilarating and terrifying. I'd kill for that mindset. Part of me does think that way, but a more significant part is too consumed by everything that could go wrong. The security at events. The discomfort in an unfamiliar setting. Being self-aware and a creature of habit isn't great for *living*, but it sure as shit eliminates risks, which is what I'm best at and paid to do.

"Why don't you come home? You can stay with us, and we can go on all the adventures," the woman on the other end of the line suggests. *Home?* I wonder if she's talking to her sister. I think Mya said her family lives in Eugene–two hours from here.

"Yeah, because living with a happy little family won't make me think about how far away I am from having my own." Her voice cracks, and it's the first sign of negative emotion I've had a glimpse of. "No offense, El, but I'm barely holding it together here as it is."

Guilt swarms through me at my eavesdropping, but selfishly I'm thankful as fuck to get this insider view.

"Okay, what about Mom and Dad? They would love for you to stay with them for a while. Until you get your own place."

My own worst nightmare.

Mya chuckles, but it's sad. "You know I love them, but living with your parents as an adult? It would massively feel like going backward in life."

"And living on a stranger's couch isn't?"

I wonder if Mya took that jab like a punch in the gut because there's silence on the other side of the door.

"It could be fun," her sister says, taking the hint and redirecting the convo. "Your bedroom still looks like it did when you graduated high school, Damon Salvatore poster and all." A laugh sounds from the other end of the phone.

"What can I say?" Mya's voice feels lighter. "I'm a sucker for mysterious bad boys who are secretly squishy on the inside."

I internally groan. Hearing a conversation about teenage heartthrobs is my karma for eavesdropping. I move to unwrap my sandwich and sit at the kitchen island but freeze mid-crinkle of the paper.

"Speaking of mysterious, tell me about this stranger you're living with. Are you sure he's safe?"

Mya giggles, and even though I have a feeling it's at my expense, it's a sweet sound. "Trust me, the only place I'd be safer is Emily Gilmore's panic room."

"That locked down, huh? What's he like? Give me the de-tails. Is he hot?"

"He'd be hotter if he smiled more. He's grumpier than Luke Danes."

"You've been binge-watching *Gilmore Girls* again, haven't you?"

"It's the only show I own on DVD! I don't want to mess up Kace's Netflix algorithm. It's already hard enough to contain my chaos with all my crafting."

"He asked for it by letting a woman he knows nothing about move in."

"Yeah. That's wild, isn't it? He feels responsible for my breakup. Technically he was the catalyst, but it was needed. It's not his *fault*." It's nice to hear her say that, but it doesn't make it feel any less true.

"But you moved in anyway?" her sister asks.

"Besides the fact that the ache in my back reminded me daily that I'm too old to sleep in a car, I don't know, Ella. Something pulled me to say yes. I know it's only temporary, but I like being here. As much as I try to tiptoe around Kace, I like his company."

"So his hotness outweighs his grumpiness?" My sandwich has officially been abandoned.

"Yes." Mya giggles. "He's very hot. Think Josh from *Younger* but more ripped. And obviously more moody. But the rest is spot on."

Note to self: Google search "Josh from Younger*" later.*

"Even the tattoos?" Ella questions, and I shake my head in amusement. I feel like I'm a fly on the wall at a sleepover a decade ago–every high school boy's dream or nightmare.

"YES!" Mya squeals. There's no other way to describe the sound she made, and I have to hold back a chuckle.

I'm flattered she finds me attractive, but it's a moot point. Starting to feel guilty now that I've become more than a side note in a conversation, I sneak out the front door, leaving my sandwich behind. This time when I enter, I swing the door open with a little more force and loud feet. I manage to hear Mya whisper, "Gotta go, I'll call you later," before ending the call and immediately turning on the shower.

Chapter Eight

"Good morning!" I chirp at Kace the second he walks out of his room. My grin widens when he looks up, and I can practically see his startled heart from here.

"Jesus, Mya." He digs his middle fingers into his eyes to rub the sleep from them.

"What?" I shrug. "You've been gone for work before I'm awake every day this week. I thought you were a morning person." The past two days have flown by with Kace working most of the day from his home office or the taco place and me working on my next craft of the week. I've been research-ing how to make resin bookends. I want to make a mold from an iPod and cast it in different colors. I'll paint the details and a few songs of each person's choice. My main concern is seeing if it's possible in the limited space I have without destroying Kace's apartment.

"I am a morning person," he grits out.

"Could have fooled me."

He rolls his eyes. "By myself."

"Uh huh. Do you know what I wish?" I grab my flower clip from the coffee table and fasten it in my hair. I'm ready for the day–for our *not date*–wearing jean shorts and my purple cropped hoodie because they are easy to change out of.

"What's that?" he asks, although I get the impression he doesn't care as he makes his way to the kitchen and pops a pod into the coffee maker.

"I wish you could experience your own energy."

"Huh?" He spares me a glance before reaching for a mug from the cupboard.

I join him in the kitchen, hopping onto the counter across from him. "Your energy. You know how when you meet someone for the first time or they walk into a room in general and you can *feel* their energy? It changes the ions in the room or something. I don't know the science of it. That's not my point."

"What *is* your point?" He presses start on the machine and turns to face me with a raised brow. His hair is pushed to the side, and his white T-shirt contrasts his black sweatpants. When I moved in, I was concerned by the lack of art on the wall, but I've realized there is no need for art as long as I have Kace to look at.

"My point is that I wish you could experience your energy. I wish you could watch yourself walk into a room. Maybe you'd adjust your personality a bit."

"Why does it feel like you're insulting me?"

"I mean, I'm not *not* insulting you." I grin, reaching for the cup of coffee he just pulled from the Keurig.

He eyeballs my wiggling fingers in front of him, debating his next move.

I drop my hands to my lap. "I just think you have the potential to be happy, but it's like you wake up every morning determined to be Ray's brother from *Everybody Loves Raymond*. Does your mom not love you either?"

"Not particularly."

I freeze, my eyes widening. "Oh, shit. I'm sorry, Kace. That was insensitive."

"It's fine. I don't have mommy issues." I wonder if he's telling the truth, but I'm distracted as he stretches the black mug full of steamy goodness toward me.

Accepting the gesture, I give him a weak smile.

"Don't look at me like that," he demands in a voice that says he refuses to accept pity as he inserts another pod inside the coffee maker.

"Would you rather me look at you like I'd like to have you for breakfast?" His eyes flick to me as fast as my free hand flies to cover my mouth. *Crap*. When am I going to start thinking before I speak? His mouth tries to form words, but nothing comes out, so I try to recover. "I mean, I didn't mean it like that. I was trying to lighten the mood."

His reply comes in the form of a pointed look.

I throw my hand in the air dramatically. "Fine. You're hot. Sue me."

He smirks but says nothing as he watches the last few drops of salted caramel coffee drip into his mug before taking it. On his way back to his room, he pauses next to where I'm sitting on the edge of the counter. He's close enough that I can feel the heat of his body through his sweatpants against my bare leg. His hand closest to me holds his coffee mug and the other is slipped into the pocket of his sweats as he leans in and holds my gaze. "Today is not a real date, Mya," he says firmly, then continues on his way like he didn't just cause my near death by self-induced suffocation. The way my name sounded on his lips overpowers his point, my heartbeat restarting as I slide off the counter to finish getting ready.

I'm psyched about my plans. They're things that I've always wanted to do with a boyfriend, but I knew they'd never go for it. I know it kind of defeats the purpose that Kace doesn't have much choice in the matter, but I'm choosing to ignore that tidbit of information and have the best day ever.

And tomorrow, I'll be over-the-top hyped for Kace's date. I can have fun almost anywhere, and that gives me a leg up.

I'm not convinced he even knows how to have fun. Although the forever optimist in me is hoping, praying and wishing that Kace has a good time. He doesn't seem like the type who could fake it, so there'd be so much satisfaction that I wouldn't mind if he won. But if worst comes to worst and he hates it so much, he might concede, and I'll get an easy win.

Twenty minutes later, we're walking out the door. Kace's keys jingle as he pulls them from his pocket to lock the apartment. "I'm driving by the way." I pull my own keys from my fanny pack by the dead Tamagotchi I use as a keychain. I wanted to keep him alive, but like everything else, I got bored after a few weeks.

He stiffens, the key frozen in the lock. "No."

"Umm. Yes. I planned the date, so I'm driving. You can drive tomorrow." He eyes me like he's wondering if he has a chance to win this battle, so I put a nail in the coffin. "Either you let me drive or you concede now and let me pay half of the rent." I looked up rent for the apartments we live in out of curiosity, and the amenities, luxury and view make it super freaking expensive. It might actually be a struggle for me to pay half, but I have a lot of crafty ideas in my brain, so I'll do whatever it takes.

"Fine." He finishes locking the door and slips the keys back into his pocket. "But promise me you'll drive safely."

I feign offense. I can't *really* argue considering I have a *hot girls hit curbs* sticker on my bumper. "Do I look like someone who doesn't drive safely?"

"You look like someone who doesn't pay attention at all. You have zero awareness of your surroundings and situations. Possibly play Pac-Man with the lane dividers."

"Well, that's rude." I glare at him as we step inside the elevator. He reaches in front of me to press the button to take us to the lobby, and his nearness sends a tingle through my body. He steps out of my space with nothing more than a shrug.

Exiting the lobby in silence, we're met with the bite of cool air and the chirping of the telephone wire birds. We walk down the sidewalk, wet from the overnight rain and decorated with evenly-spaced potted trees, to where my car is parked alongside the road.

The parking situation is one downside to living in such a prime location. I found out Kace has a garage spot for his car, but it's over a hundred dollars a month, and since I don't know how long I'll be here, it doesn't make sense for me to apply for one yet. I'm not on the lease either which I'm sure would be an issue.

A street up, Kace pauses, groaning at the sight of my Jeep.

"I forgot your car was pink."

"It's *We Peep*, thank you very much."

"Like the marshmallow?"

I grin. "Exactly. Who knew that was an official color? Not me. But now here I am with Peep the Jeep, living our best life."

"You're weird as shit. You know that, right?"

I shrug. "I was the kid who caught grasshoppers at recess and kept them in my desk as pets."

He's frozen in place, staring at me under the awning of a downtown winery.

"You know, in those desks that had tops that opened so you could keep all your notebooks, pencils and erasers inside them."

"I knew what you meant."

"Then stop looking at *me* like *that*," I repeat his phrase from earlier, unlocking my Jeep with the fob.

He looks both ways in the street before holding my door open, leftover rain dripping off the metal.

I slip between him and the car frame and glance back with a smirk as I get in. "I bet you were the kid who stabbed pencil holes into your pink eraser for fun, huh?"

He shakes his head, hiding yet another smile. It's like he's afraid to be happy, and in whatever time we have together–however long it lasts–I'm determined to find out *why*.

I adjust myself on the front seat, buckle up and wait for Kace to join me. Pinching my lips together, I hold back my laugh as he hesitates before opening the door and sliding in next to me. Is he *that* afraid to drive with me? I think he's being ridiculous, but I still vow to be extra cautious as we head to our destinations.

"Where are we going?" He peeks through the front window at the cross-street signs like they'll answer him.

"You'll see." I pull the flower clip from my hair and set it in the center console.

He follows my movement, his brows furrowing.

"I read this article once about how a girl got into a car accident, and the clip impaled her brain. That's not how I plan to go."

The way he's always staring back at me should feel unnerving. Instead, it makes me feel like he's more curious than anything–like he wants to understand what makes me tick. That's probably hopeful thinking though. He's emotionally unavailable. It's just that sometimes I feel like people begrudgingly put up with my quirks, and it's refreshing that they seem to amuse him or at the very least, temporarily distract him from his grumpiness.

"Well, at least you've got a sliver of safety sense," he muses as he buckles his seatbelt.

With my music queued up, I check my mirror and blind spot before pulling onto the road and hitting *play*. "Ultimate" from the *Freaky Friday* soundtrack starts softly in the background. I wait a minute before I turn it up, although I spare a glance toward Kace to check his reaction. If he has an initial feeling toward bubblegum pop, I either missed it or he's hiding it well. He's just sitting there handsome as ever, gripping the "oh shit" handle like I'm incapable of merging onto the freeway. The man needs to relax. He needs a distraction.

"I know this isn't a real date," I blurt, realizing immediately I'm probably making the tension worse.

He hesitates before glancing my way. A moment later, his eyes are back on the road. "Good."

"I know I'm not ready to date." I feel his eyes back on me as I continue driving. "And I don't want to date you," I amend for good measure.

"Glad we cleared that up." His monotone voice cancels out the good vibes of the music coming through my speakers.

"Alrighty then," I mutter to myself, and then there's silence.

Well, silence between me and Kace.

The chorus of "Ultimate" kicks off in the catchy way that only teenage Lindsay Lohan nails. I will never get sick of the instant serotonin boost all my girls bring me: Hilary, Lindsay, Ashlee, Jessica, Britney, Christina, Demi, Miley, Aly & AJ. The OG versions of them, anyway. Before life aged us all and altered the meaning of songs.

I focus my eyes on the road and will myself not to have a car concert–which is nearly impossible. Changing lanes, I move to the fast lane, feeling like Frogger as I get around a semi.

We're only halfway through the song before I realize I'm speeding because the beat has me cruising along. After slowing down to five over the limit, I become aware of Kace again. He's staring at me. I don't have to look at him to notice.

I feel his eyes on me for the entire three minutes that the song plays again. Somehow I can *feel* his grip tighten on the "oh shit" handle.

He makes it to the fourth listen before he finally says something. "Please tell me you're not serious."

"About what?" I feign innocence.

"The song," he grits.

"Do you know this song?" I beam, faking excitement.

"I brush my teeth to this song." He delivers the joke without missing a beat, completely devoid of humor. Realizing Kace might actually be funny deep down sparks so much joy for me. After a pause, he adds, "There is no way you like this song *that* much."

I shrug. "It's one of my favorites," I say, sinking my teeth into my lip to prevent my grin from slipping through. "It's so catchy, don't you think?"

"Do we seriously have to listen to this the whole way there?"

"Yes. I only do this when I'm alone because I think everyone else will judge me."

"Play annoying songs?"

"No, dummy. Put my favorite songs on repeat. Be happy I'm not starting them over whenever I zone out or get interrupted during a lyric I like."

He mumbles something unintelligible with a slight shake of his head.

I flick my gaze toward him long enough to shoot him a wink. "Welcome to the best worst date of your life, Kace."

Fifteen minutes later, we're pulling into the classically crappy parking lot of Goodwill. I move to unbuckle my seatbelt and catch Kace staring at me with an eyebrow raised. "What on earth are we doing here?"

"Hey, don't judge. What if I buy all my clothes here?"

He holds his hands up in defense. "I *love* your clothes, Mya."

I narrow my eyes. "I can't tell if you're being funny or not."

"I'm never being funny."

I shrug. "I'm still holding out hope. Now, let's go!"

I hop from the car and lock it once Kace hesitantly joins me on the curb outside the dirty tan building.

"Are you ready?" I rub my hands together.

"No." He grimaces.

"Okay, so. This is the plan. Here's twenty bucks." I pull the bill from my pocket and hold it out to him, but he just stares at it. "Take it." I reach out and shove the money into the front pocket of his jeans, really wedging it in there before realizing how close I am to *him. Whoops.* Pulling my hand back, I continue. "We're both going in there to pick out an outfit for each other. The only requirement is to pick something you think perfectly fits the other's personality. Although, it'll be more fun if we also pick the most ridiculous version of an outfit."

"You're way too excited about this."

"How could I not be? This is a once-in-a-lifetime opportunity, Kace."

"Or is it my worst nightmare?"

"No way. Part two is your worst nightmare." I bend over in a fit of giggles, knowing what comes next. When I finally regain my composure, I find Kace still stone-faced, his arms folded across his chest.

He sighs. "How did I let you rope me into this?"

"Must be my charming personality." I grin. He raises his brow. "My hard-to-resist face?"

"Yeah. You're lucky you're cute," he mutters before turning on his heel and reaching for the door handle.

My mouth falls open as I walk backward through the door he holds open. *Did he just admit he's attracted to me?* I'm not sure if he's being serious, but on the off chance he's joking, I play it off to be safe. "You think I'm cute?!" I'm tempted to prance around like Rudolph screaming, "I'm cute! I'm cute!" when Clarice notices him, but I won't push my luck.

"Go." He holds his hand in front of us to point inside. "Let's get this over with."

"See ya on the other side!" I stick out my tongue, throwing a peace sign behind me as I skip toward the men's section. I *think* I hear a chuckle in my wake, but even if I didn't, I'm choosing to live in denial about it.

Sorting through the racks, I think about how I view Kace. It's not a secret he's guarded. It's clear from how we met that *someone* hurt him. And in the way he's made it clear we would never date. I genuinely don't think it's my ego believing it has more to do with dating in general than specifically a me thing. He doesn't know me well enough to know he doesn't want to date me. It's more than that. He's overly cautious of everything. Strangers. Drinks. Locked doors. I can't help but wonder if it's who he is at the core or if it's a side effect of being hurt so badly that all he wants is to be in control. There's nothing wrong with the safety-forward part of his personality. It's just... I can't help but believe there's a side of him that doesn't want to be so stressed all the time too. A part of him that wants to have fun but he doesn't feel safe enough to do so.

Maybe that's me being a typical "but I can fix him" girl.

I slide another hanger across the rack, this time with more intention and awareness as I examine the shirt. It's a vintage pattern that reminds me of those white paper cups with the light blue and purple zigzag through the middle... *Jazz cups*? I think that's what they're called. It's fun, but not what I'm looking for.

Next.

The metal hanger screeches across the bar as I push it to the side. This one is a no-go too. I swipe the next shirt out of the way to find a puffy vest mixed in.

Oh. My. God.

Light bulb.

It's tan–that burnt brown shade that only people in the Pacific Northwest can pull off. The top has a Lion King vibes sunset scene printed onto the plastic-y fabric, and all I can see is Adam Brody as Seth Cohen on *The O.C.*

Yanking the vest from the rack, I drape it over my arm while I find the second piece I need in the button-up section. It doesn't take me long to find the perfect shirt–a light blue long-sleeve with faint pink pinstripes. "Perfect." I squeal to myself.

Thankful that Kace can wear the jeans he currently has on with this, I make my way to the register, shocked to find him waiting for me with a bag in his hand. I try to distinguish what he picked, but all I can see is a teal fabric barely poking out of the plastic.

"Ready?" I exclaim as both a statement and a question as we walk out the door, bags in hand.

"No," he says with an annoyed look in his eyes that makes it very believable.

I grin wider. "Channel your inner Carl Allen. Today is more of a *yes* day, don't you think?"

"No," he repeats.

"You could just agree to let me pay part of the rent, and this can all be over with a snap of my fingers." I mimic the movement with my free hand.

"Or I could kick you out."

Panic constricts my voice box. My body is physically frozen, but my mind is running a 5k. *Would he really kick me out? He didn't have to agree to this in the first place. Should I just concede? Should I have planned something that he would actually think is fun? Although I thought maybe, regardless of how crazy today's plan is, he might enjoy himself and relax a little.*

"Jesus fuck, Mya. Take a breath. I'm not going to kick you out."

A rush of air leaves me. "Okay." My next breath brings frustration. "Harsh much?" I still don't really understand why he did this in the first place. Is it just because he felt guilty about me sleeping in my car? It probably would have been easier to find me a Craigslist roommate. I chuckle to myself. Kace. A Craigslist roommate. That's definitely something he would never allow. Not even if we were in the 90s when kids were safe to play in the neighborhood on their own and just come home when the street lights kicked on. "You'd think you'd at least *try* to have fun for the sake of winning."

"Are we doing this or not? I'm assuming you will make me wear something ridiculous in public?"

My grin returns, excitement bubbling inside me as I nod. "Yours is easy. You can change in the front seat. I'll change in the back. No peeking," I direct him as I unlock all my Jeep doors with the fob. We swap bags, and instead of climbing in the passenger seat, Kace sets the bag on it. He pulls the two pieces of clothing out, his face giving nothing away.

Then, right there, in the middle of the Goodwill parking lot, Kace Levitt pulls his plain white tee over his head, leaving him shirtless. And suddenly, I'm left with no good thoughts and very little will to resist. This man is... my mind is literally blank. No adjective or comparison will suffice in describing his chiseled abs alongside the rest of his toned and slightly tanned upper body. It's the first good glance I've gotten of his tattoos–a grayscale foggy forest running the length of the sleeve, a waterfall cascading down the side of his forearm and a mountain peak inked into his shoulder, bleeding into part of his chest. My eyes flick from muscle to muscle as they all work to reach for the shirt on the seat.

Slipping one arm into the sleeve of the button-up, he pauses mid-reach of his hand behind him to find the hole in the other. "No peeking, Mya." He smirks. That freaking smirk. At least he's upfront about not wanting to date anyone, but he's also painfully aware that it couldn't possibly prevent anyone from looking.

I stare a beat longer, clearing the lust from my eyes before sliding into the back seat. He probably thinks it's shitty of me to be drawn to someone else so soon after a breakup, but you can't help who you're attracted to. Even if I was in a serious relationship, it's not like he would all of a sudden become ugly.

My curiosity switching focus, I pull a pile of teal fabric from Kace's bag and break into a smile. No. Freaking. Way. Layers of lace alternating between teal and blue make up the entire strapless Betsey Johnson dress, with a satin bow tied around the waist. A millennial packrat must have recently decided to let go of all her high school dance dresses because that's exactly what this is, and I'm obsessed.

Hardly thinking twice about whether or not Kace can see through the windows, I awkwardly shimmy out of my jean shorts. Sitting on the leather, I slide the dress up my legs, bouncing my butt off the seat to get it over my hips. I undo my bra under my cropped hoodie, pulling the dress above my chest and hoping it'll be tight enough to contain my boobs. They aren't super big, but they're enough to love–C cups on a good day. I'd rather have them smaller anyway, so I'm not tempted to duct tape them down like Christina Ricci in *Now and Then*.

With one arm across my boobs to keep the dress in place, I tug my bra and sweater off with the other. I attempt to reach around for the zipper, twisting my arm in a completely un-natural way. Just like when I give up trying to apply sunscreen to my back on my own, I sigh in defeat.

I poke my head through the gap between the front two seats to find him leaning against the door frame, facing away from me. When he turns my way, I'm given a perfectly clear view of my real-life Seth Cohen, but with more edge and less curl in his hair. I'm convinced his heart is the same though–he seems to mean well but puts on a front around certain peo-ple. I hope he learns that there will be a girl who loves him when he's himself, the way Summer fell for Seth. But for the record, that was not the reasoning for this vulnerable date plan–the outfit is just a happy coincidence for this bet. "Kace?"

"Yeah?" he says the words before his gaze snaps to me, and he slides his phone into the front pocket of his jeans.

"Umm. Can you zip me up?"

"Yeah." He clears his throat. "Sure."

Opening the door to the back seat, he waits as I scoot to the edge and kneel on the leather facing away from him. Holding my dress up with both hands on my boobs, I wait for the tug of the zipper against my skin. His hand braces against my waist at the edge of the zipper before the teeth of the metal lock together slowly. I inhale instinctively, holding my breath for the simultaneous two seconds and eternity that it takes Kace to complete the task. It's not like I'm sucking in. It's his touch that has me searching for my next breath.

I might be fresh out of a breakup, but something about his gentle tentativeness feels more intimate than any sex I've experienced in a while.

He pauses when the zipper reaches the top for a sliver of a moment before letting go. "Alright. You're good."

"Thanks." I turn to him with a smile and hardly give him time to get out of my way before sliding from the seat onto the ground. I run my hands over the front of the lace to flatten it out, although the layers make it naturally poofy. I can't even see myself yet, and I love it. I shut the door, clearing a view in the side mirror to check myself out.

I grin, turning to Kace. "How do I look?"

He takes me in, his eyes raking up and down my body without giving away any emotion until they stop roaming, and a smirk sneaks in. "Like my high school prom date."

I play slap him on the chest. "You got me an outfit that reminds you of your ex?! Please tell me you at least liked her."

"My favorite of all my exes," he teases, and I have zero clue if he's serious.

"For real, though. What made you choose this?"

He shrugs, slipping his hands into the pockets of his jeans, and it takes everything in me not to get distracted by the way his pinstripe button-up clashes with the outdoorsy vest. "It's kind of fun but also makes no fucking sense."

I laugh. "And here I was thinking you don't know me at all. That's exactly what I go for."

He shakes his head, amused. "Don't read into it. It's also bright and crazy and gives me a headache if I stare at it for too long."

"Hey!" I put my hands on my hips, then shrug. "Whatever. I love it. I'm keeping it forever."

"Of course you are," he muses. "It'll be useful for an art project one day, I'm sure."

My grin widens. "Maybe you do know me, Kace Levitt."

"It's hard to miss the killer maze of crafts you've set as a trap in our apartment."

Our apartment. I know he didn't mean it like *that*, but tell that to the butterflies in my stomach that just awakened from their long slumber. I shake my head, wishing it would shoo off the flutters in my gut as well. "Onto the next stop?"

"If we must," Kace says as we get back into my car.

Chapter Nine

Kace

"I can't remember the last time I was at the mall," I admit, leaning forward to peer through the windshield. I knew they still existed, but I didn't realize people still *go* to the mall. I'm pretty sure I haven't been since I was sixteen–the year I refused to accept any back-to-school clothes from my mom unless they were graphic tees from Hot Topic or Spencer's.

As much as I love the tech industry now, it has its flaws. Besides the whole black hacking industry, there's nothing like having to *buy* memes as bunny stickers instead of opening an app on your phone to see them everywhere.

"Well, you can't say that anymore," Mya's peppy voice comes from the driver's seat. How is she so fucking happy all the time? I've never been one to catch sickness from anyone around me, but the way she exists is starting to make me wish she was contagious. "Come on!"

I groan, getting out of the car and following her through the automatic glass doors leading inside. Today has already been a day, and while I'm growing comfortable around Mya at a concerning rate, I'd rather not be in public dressed this ridiculously. Besides the fact that Mya looked like she wanted to rip my clothes off–in a good way–there is nothing attractive about this outfit. But truthfully, her planned activities could have been much wors– "No." How I have any clue what's next is beyond me. But I do, and I refuse. I stare up at the giant white JCPenny letters above the entrance to the department store. "I'm not doing this."

Mya spins on her heels to face me, the skirt of her short dress flaring. I didn't purposely find one that short. I didn't even look that hard. It was like the third thing I saw on the rack. It's not like I wasn't playing along. I got lucky. If any article of clothing screams the bright bundle of chaos that is my new roommate, it's this dress. And for how retro it is, she pulls it off–especially with her new hair half tied up in Princess Leia buns on top of her head.

Her grin widens, and it's annoying that I find her so cute. "Fine. Just forfeit now, and let me pay."

Here's the two things: Without being privy to Mya's entire financial situation–not wanting to ask and not knowing how much crafting pays on a consistent basis–I'm not sure she makes enough to cover half of my rent. I don't want to assume or sound like an arrogant asshole. I'm not rich by any means, but my place is not cheap. When Ruby and I moved into it a year ago, we both had well-paying jobs.

The second issue is that I still feel responsible for her predicament. It's insane to deal with that guilt by taking in a complete stranger, but here we fucking are. I didn't see a better option then, and I don't see one now. It's only short-term anyway, and all of this will be a blip in the matrix of my Groundhog Day life.

Regardless, this date day is absurd. Who even thinks of this? Groaning, I press my hand against her lower back to nudge her forward. "Let's go." I'm not one to half-ass something, even if it's something I don't want to do. And Mya is right. I should at least *try* to have a good time if I want any chance at winning this bet.

She glances over her shoulder with a smile that makes me simultaneously feel more at ease and on high alert. This girl is a walking contradiction. Calming chaos. Is that a thing? I sure as shit wouldn't have bet on it.

We approach the JCPenny Portraits counter, and Mya sweet-talks her way into squeezing us in between appointments. Of course she didn't call ahead. Between this and her out-of-date registration sticker I noticed before our fast and furious drive here, I'm wondering if this girl ever truly plans anything in her life or if she just flies by the seat of her pants.

"Follow me," the photographer says, leading us to a private room. *This is insane.* Ruby made us take professional pictures a few times for Christmas cards, so it's not like I can't make it happen. I'm more than capable of following guidance and mustering all the patience I possess for thirty minutes. "So, what vibe are you going for?" the lady asks Mya.

"Well, you see. Kace and I have known each other since we were in high school. For our graduation, we took silly pictures for our yearbook–something fun to look back on, you know?" The lady nods with an appreciative smile, and Mya continues. "I was hoping to recreate it now that we're older. Keeping the spark and memories alive and all that."

"That's so sweet." The photographer clutches her hand to her heart. "I can't wait. We'll get you the perfect shots. I have a few ideas from when I did this job in the early 2000s if you don't mind me taking the lead?"

"Not at all," Mya replies, linking her arm with mine. "Just don't be disappointed if this one doesn't smile. It might be best if we go for those creepy straight-face looks, so it's one less thing he has to worry about. He's mastered staring at me in a way that gives no emotion. It's actually quite impressive."

This entire story is made up, but the last part... does she think I stare at her? *Have* I been staring at her? It's possible. Besides my working lunch breaks, I don't get out much. And since I was in a committed relationship for nearly a decade, I wasn't actively looking at women. But Mya is hard to avoid.

Yeah, she's beautiful. But she's also captivating in every sense of the word. The way she's unapologetically herself. Her energy–it's charismatic, magnetic and annoyingly enigmatic at the same time, even to someone who would rather be left alone and is content not talking to anyone.

Mya is the sun. She's bright in a way that makes you want to both step closer or hide in the shade. She's tempting in a way that melts your icy heart or burns you. I just don't know which side of the sun I'm standing on, and worse, I'm not sure which side I *want* to be on. All I know right now is that I need to get through the next thirty minutes, and then I'll go from there.

"I can work with that," the lady says, guiding us toward the light blue backdrop. The setup looks like it followed her here from the 2000s. "Okay, how about we start with a traditional prom pose? What a cute nod to the original pictures!" She's downright giddy about this fabricated story. "Oh, I wish I could see them!"

"You would love them," Mya gushes like she's in love with photos that don't exist.

The lady clasps her hands under her chin like this is the dreamiest fucking story she's ever heard in her life. "Alright, you two. Let's get you situated. Mya, you stand right here, honey." She points to a small "x" on the blue backdrop that extends straight from the wall and onto the ground. Mya walks into place, glancing up with a grin and awaiting the next direction. "Okay, Kace. Now, why don't you stand right here." She taps her toe in the space directly behind Mya.

Knowing that if I complain or argue this will only take longer, I oblige the woman, stepping behind Mya and leaving a few inches of space between us.

"Okay, now put your hands around her." She grabs my wrists and places them on Mya's waist. My hands slide over the satin of her bow until they're resting on the layer of lace right beneath them. Fuck, this dress is short on her. It doesn't fall much past where my palms rest, and my natural urge to do *something* else with my hands is strong.

Luckily, in the next moment, the photographer adjusts Mya's hands so they rest on top of mine, holding them in place. Thank fuck for that. Who knows where they'd end up. My entire life feels surreal right now, like I'm hovering outside of my body, watching it be possessed by someone I've never met.

I can't quite figure out how I feel about that. As much as this is *not* my idea of a good time, I don't hate being around Mya. She feels like the friend that drags you to the pool when you're convinced it'll be way too cold, and then you have a blast. I need a friend like that. I can drag myself to lunch every day, but that's not enough to *live*. But on the flip side, there is a level of attraction here. Whether it's because I haven't had sex in months or specifically because it's Mya is still up in the air.

Her hands are warm against mine as she brushes her thumb over my knuckles, and I hate that I like it.

"Perfect." The lady picks up the camera that hangs by a strap around her neck. "Absolutely perfect. Mya, honey, stop smiling. Give me the best straight face you've got."

With my face next to Mya's, my eyes nearly cross trying to catch her expression. I barely see it *attempt* to change, but I'm not sure this woman could keep a straight face if her life depended on it. I mean, she accidentally hacked her hair off and wasn't bothered at all. "It's so hard," she murmurs, glancing back at me slightly.

I lean in to whisper in her ear. "If you don't want to give this your all, you could quit now."

Mya spins in my arms, my hands automatically locked on her waist. Her palms fall to the minimal space between us, landing on the chest of this puffy fucking vest. Her wide eyes meet mine, and I can't help but smirk as her mouth opens and closes again without saying anything. "Don't underestimate me, Levitt," she snaps back. She's trying to be sassy, but her smile gives her away.

"Oh my god," a voice comes from behind Mya, and I glance up to find the photographer swooning. "You two are adorable."

I refocus on Mya, sarcasm dripping from my tone when I mutter, "I think she meant to say, 'terrific actors.'"

"This is almost the perfect shot. The only thing that would make it better is if you kiss," the woman says.

With my eyes on Mya, I watch her flip through thoughts as fast as a kid clicking through images on a View-Master. She turns back to the photographer. "No, it's okay. Kace isn't big on PDA." Turning back to me, she gives me an apologetic smile.

"Oh, come on," the woman presses. "There's no one else around, and these photos are just for the two of you anyway."

Mya looks at me, eyes begging like I'll come up with a better out than she will. I want to tell her no and leave, but Mya is determined to help with rent because she wants to stay at my place. The vision of her packing her bags when this becomes something that doesn't work for her because I won't play along for five fucking minutes keeps me in place. While it seems like Mya has a better relationship with her parents than I do with mine, she was adamant about not moving home. I can't imagine going backward, and while I'm sure Mya would find another solution, our current arrangement works for her. At least for now. "It's fine." I sigh. "It's just a kiss."

"But we're not dating." Her voice is low enough that I'm the only one to hear her.

I hold firmly to her waist. "Have you never kissed someone you weren't dating?" Suddenly, I'm curious to know if Mya had a bachelorette phase the way I had mine.

She nods. "I have, but..."

There's no thought to follow, just her eyes searching mine for sincerity or maybe a sign that an alien has possessed me. "It's fake, Mya. Just like this date–"

And then her lips are on mine.

Shock vibrates through me as her hands slide up my neck and into the ends of my hair. She presses up on her toes to level us out, triggering me to kiss her back. My fingers dig into the lace at her waist, and all the space between us disappears.

Neither of us press for access, but I can already tell this is all wrong. It's weird. Unfamiliar. Foreign. I hate it. She's not Ruby. I don't want her to be. I don't want to be kissing Ruby either, but after not touching anyone else for eight years... eight fucking years... it's too fucking weird. Especially with someone I'm afraid to let into my space more than I already have.

Dropping my grip on her, I hold my hands up in surrender, breaking our kiss and stepping back. I watch Mya's eyes go wide and only take in her shock for a moment before I shake my head. Overwhelmed, I make a break for the exit, needing air.

I vaguely hear Mya apologizing behind me, then she's calling my name. Her voice gets louder with each pass until she's nearly screaming when we reach the car.

"Kace! Stop!"

I spin to face her, my fingers threading through my hair and linking on top of my head. "No, Mya. You stop. Let's just go." I reach for the passenger door handle, yanking on it to no avail.

Instead of walking to the driver's side, she invades my space. "What did I do wrong? I thought you said it was fine if we kissed?" Her brows pull together, and I think it's the first time I've seen her so genuinely concerned. But her worry isn't strong enough to pull answers from me. I'm not mad at her. I'm angry at myself for being fucked up over this. Of course I want to kiss Mya. How could I not? She's beautiful, interesting, and the brightest light in my dark fucking world lately. A real kiss would probably feel like a jolt of electricity waking me from death. But it's weird or too soon or *something*, and I don't know how to fix that.

"I don't want to talk about it, Mya. Just drop it. We're not going to have a fucking heart-to-heart about our past relationships because of one half-ass kiss."

If her heart were outside of her chest, I'd swear it just dropped with all her hope. "Yeah, okay. I'm sorry," she says quietly and defeated.

"Let's just go home, please."

"Of course," she whispers, digging her keys from her fanny pack clutched in her hands. Making her way to the other side of the car, she drives us both home with tension so high I'd rather be listening to her excessively bubbly pop shit on repeat.

Chapter Ten

I half-expect to open my bedroom door to a bright and chipper Mya, but it's still dark when I step into the main space. Glancing toward the couch, I find her curled against the arm, a glow coming from her lap.

As I approach, I realize it's a portable DVD player. I had no idea those things still existed. Mya doesn't acknowledge me until I'm directly beside her. She glances up, slightly startled as she pulls headphones from her ears.

"Oh. Hey." Her upbeat charm is nowhere to be found.

I shove my hands into the pockets of my joggers, thankful I put on a T-shirt because I'm fucking uncomfortable. I hid in my room like chickenshit from the moment we got home yesterday. "Morning."

She hits pause on whatever she's watching. "I'm sorry about yesterday."

"Why?" My brows furrow. If anyone should be apologizing, it's me. "You did warn me you were planning my worst date ever."

Her face falls even further, which I didn't think would be possible. "We don't have to hang out today if you don't want to. I understand."

"I was a jackass, and I shouldn't have taken it out on you." She opens her mouth to speak, and I already know what she'll say, so I cut her off. "But I don't want to talk about it."

"Okay." She closes her DVD player and sets it on the coffee table.

"But–"

She freezes, glancing back at me.

"I know this is bad timing, but something with work came up that I can't miss this afternoon. Can we rain check for next weekend?"

"Yeah. No problem. I love rain." She gives me a weak smile, and I feel like a fucking asshole. I could probably rearrange the date and make everything fit this morning or an evening this week, but I hate being crammed on time. I could also cancel the second half, but we may as well wait. On the plus side, the movie I initially wanted to see will be playing next weekend at an old theater near Portland.

I've only ever gone alone. Though, it would have been nice for Ruby to join me on occasion. The place is retro, a classic theater like none of the others that exist these days. Plus, they have beer on tap and killer pizza. She never understood why we'd drive thirty minutes to see a movie when a brand-new theater is within walking distance. She doesn't understand. Nostalgia ties us to a simpler era, and I, for one, am way too stressed all the damn time to not vacation there once in a while.

"Thanks. Sorry again. I'm going on a run then. Are we good?"

She nods too enthusiastically to possibly mean it. "Yup. I wanted to work out anyway."

"Good."

"Good," she echoes.

We stare for a beat before I cut the tension by turning away. Not bothering to change, I slip into my navy Brooks and swipe my keys and headphones off the counter before I leave.

I've run one marathon, but I wouldn't say I'm a runner. I've got the typical natural talent many men have–the stupidly annoying ability to accomplish athletic endeavors without much training. It helps that I lift weights, but it was absurd that I knocked out 26.2 miles after only three months of training. Mainly I did it because I wanted to prove to myself that I could. That was a few years ago. I'd rather snowboard to keep in shape, but it's not always practical. So I just run one *or six* miles here and there, depending on my stress levels.

By the time the elevator hits the ground level, I've added fourteen songs to the queue, which should be enough to get me through six miles. "Face Down" by The Red Jumpsuit Apparatus blares through my left earbud at full volume. Leaving the right one out to stay somewhat aware of my surroundings, I head down the sidewalk leading to the waterfront.

It's not raining, and it's not cold enough to snow, but there's a fine mist in the air that stings my face. Hoping to warm up quickly, I take off running to the beat of the music. Without looking at my watch, I know the music's perfect tempo already has me on a good pace, and the cool air feels warmer against my skin by the time my playlist switches to "Weightless" by All Time Low. *Damn.* They don't make music as good as they used to.

Right.

Left.

Right.

Left.

Skip down the steps two at a time.

Right.

Left.

I let the steady beat of the song and my feet carry me along the waterfront path, trying to lose myself in the lyrics.

Right.
Left.
Mya.
Fuck.
I want anything *except* her in my head.
Ruby.
Definitely not her.

I pick up speed, pushing myself until I'm nearly breathless, but hold my pace anyway. I hesitate a step, enough to veer around a couple walking in the opposite direction who are too focused on each other to notice me flying toward them.

I slam my feet on the pavement harder than a runner should but not hard enough to erase that kiss from my mind. Half a kiss. A Peck. It was *nothing*. I made way too big of a deal out of it.

I already knew I had no desire to date.

Of course I'm attracted to Mya. I have eyes. She's like Jennifer Aniston–everyone's type. But attraction does not equal *interest*. I don't know nearly enough about her to make that call. Plus, until I figure out how the fuck to resolve my trust issues, I don't *need* to be dating or kissing anyone. I'll just pray that by the time I'm ready, any muscle memory and familiarity for only Ruby will be gone.

I follow the path along the river, under the I-5 bridge and through the tunnel of maple trees. It's a perfect three miles to Marine Park.

Once I hit the park, filled with barbeques and a grassy area that will be covered in volleyball nets come summer, I take a quick drink from the fountain before heading back. I glance at my watch; I'm on a good pace to land a time under forty minutes.

I push myself the entire three miles back, focusing on nothing more than the words to each song.

I don't think about my roommate as Taking Back Sunday's "Cute without the 'E'" plays.

I don't think about the fucking rays of sunshine that constantly emanate from her as Papa Roach screams "Last Resort" through my left earbud.

I don't think about wanting a real taste of her lips on mine as "In the End" by Linkin Park takes me back to the Vancouver Waterfront Park.

Fuck.

Coming to a stop against the railing overlooking the Columbia, I take a breath and stop my watch. A top three time. Slipping my hands under my T-shirt, I bring it to my face, wiping away the sweat and feeling a rush of cool air on my stomach.

My heart pounds in my chest as my lungs work to get me oxygen to recover. I take in a deep breath of fresh, earthy air, and that "just rained" smell is soothing enough to help bring my heart rate down. I opt to lean my hands against the railing to take in the view before going to get water.

"I knew it was fucking you," an angry voice projects from my right.

What the... I scan my surroundings to see who this man is talking to.

"I'm talking to you." He points directly at me, and my eyebrows scrunch. Who the fuck is this dude? "Don't act like you have no clue who I am when you were screwing my girlfriend."

Shit. I should have known my Valentine's Day antics would come back to haunt me, but I thought inviting a stranger to move in with me might have kept karma at bay. I wouldn't be able to place another person I saw that night besides Mya and only because she followed me out to the street. I consider defending myself because I haven't been screwing anyone's girlfriend. I can't even kiss a woman without needing a date with the pavement. Instead, I stare back like I don't have all day.

"Whatever, man. Mya is all yours now." His eyes scan me, and he chuckles.

Suddenly I'm aware of my clenched fist, and I realize maybe the anger building inside me might be a strange possessiveness taking over.

"Chill out. No need to punch me over it. Let me do you a solid–man to man. Watch your back. Mya is a classic serial dater. She's never happy because she gets bored too easily. She checks out by the time three months rolls around."

"Maybe you weren't interesting enough," I defend her for god knows what reason as I run my fingers through my sweaty hair. It's sure as shit going to seem like I've been screwing her now.

He chuckles again. "Whatever helps you sleep at night, man. But tell me. Have you ever seen her stick with one of her silly art projects for more than a week? She can't finish a workout program without hopping to another one. Hell, she can't even get through every season of her favorite TV shows without jumping ship for a few months. You think people are any different for her?"

What the fuck am I supposed to do with this information? The accusations filter through my mind again as I take them in. I can't attest to the second two, but every time she crafts, it's something completely different. Not to mention she was living in her car–literally living life like she could flee at any moment. *Fuck.* Maybe he's right.

It doesn't matter though.

Regardless of what he thinks, I'm not screwing Mya. I'm not dating her. I have no desire to do either. So none of this is a concern. "I guess that's not something you have to worry about anymore, is it?" I level him with a stare, holding my ground to defend my honor or some shit. Whatever.

Without giving him time to reply, I take off running back to my apartment.

Back to Mya.

Chapter Eleven

Mya

I collapse onto the living room floor, feeling like a puddle of sweat, as Shaun T's voice tells me that I did an amazing job through the TV speakers, and Britney's "Toxic" fades into the next song on my phone.

Learning Kace's routine during the past week, I've noticed he works out in the apartment gym every morning. Weightlifting, I'm assuming, based on the way he fills out his clothes and the glimpses I've had of him with his shirt off. And then on days he's extra stressed, he also goes for a run. I'm not sure how I figured that out because the man is always agitated.

I've considered using the gym downstairs, but I'm invading Kace's personal space as it is, and I want him to feel like he has somewhere to go to escape me if he needs to. I got a free week-trial gym membership when Matt and I broke up so I could shower, but it's expired now. It's all good anyway. I prefer working out in my own space–for the sole reason of not needing to wear shoes and blasting my music as loudly as I want.

Today's choice was my 2000s Girl Power playlist and an Insanity workout video. I thought people were being dramatic when they said turning thirty changes your body, but even in the past year, I've noticed how much harder it is to keep up with my health, even doing the same things I've always done. But the high-intensity cardio always makes me feel like I can conquer the rest of the day. Any movement helps really–especially since I do most of my crafts crouched over on the ground because I've never had a designated workspace for it.

Lying on my back, I force myself to do five minutes of stretching, because again, I'm thirty now. With one leg straight, I wrap a resistance loop around my other bare foot for assistance. I tug slowly, pulling my leg toward the side and working on my flexibility the way Luna pretends to be a clock on *The Big Comfy Couch*. How in the hell did she get her leg to her head? There's no way unless you're a Cirque du Soleil acrobat. I switch the other leg once I get stuck around the three on my invisible clock, stretching my inner thigh in a way that burns so good. I would definitely fail the flexibility part of the Presidential Fitness Test if I had to take it now.

A click of the front door whips my head toward the entryway, which I can barely see from my position on the floor. I freeze, suddenly aware of my spandex shorts rolling up my thighs enough to look like underwear and my crotch on full display as my leg stretches to the side.

Kace is frozen too, staring, but I can't read his mind. Is this hot to him? On TV, this would be an innocent position the guy finds sexy, but me? I'm awkward and clumsy and always think I look cute, but then I see a video or picture and it's as traumatizing as looking into the self-checkout camera at Target.

I've been told awkward moments build character, but I'm not sure I believe that. Self-consciousness flies through my veins like Miss Frizzle in her magic school bus, and I sit up. Of course my resistance loop gets tangled on my foot, and I nearly fall over trying to get it off. Meanwhile, Kace still stands there, staring, music so loud in his earbud, I can make out Eminem's "Lose Yourself" over my own "Since U Been Gone." Our differences are blatantly obvious, and I don't know why that bothers me so much.

I pause my playlist because the clashing of personalities, paired with the tension, is overwhelming. "Hey," I manage. "How was your run?"

"Fine," he snaps, shaking his head to clear his trance. A few drops of sweat fling off his hair.

"Ooooooh-kay." I stand, the tone in his voice making me feel like we are not as good as we established this morning. We shouldn't have kissed yesterday. He didn't want to despite saying it was fine, and now everything is weird. "Well, I was going to make some stir fry for lunch and probably leftovers for the week. I know I'm weird, but I could eat the same thing every day as long as I like it. I was thinking chicken, veggies, rice and teriyaki? Do you like that? Of course you don't have to eat it. But I want you to know you can feel free to help yourself." *Oh my Lanta*, Mya, shut up.

Uncomfortable in my sports bra–not because I'm not confident in my body but because I'm convinced a shirt would help contain my vulnerability–I move to the corner behind the couch and dig through my suitcase. I pull out my oversized "Easy Bake Coven" tee and tug it over my head, only sparing myself a moment to love the little witches surrounding one of my favorite 90s toys. The hem falls lower than my spandex, but at least I'm not *as* exposed.

I make my way to the kitchen, passing by Kace, who is frozen in the space between the fridge and the entryway and hasn't answered my question that was hidden somewhere in that ramble. Opening the freezer, I reach in for a bag of veggies.

"Did you work out?" His voice comes from the other side of the appliance, and I close the door.

"Yeah, why?" I hold his gaze, the frozen broccoli cold against my hands.

He pulls the earbud from his ear and the faint music cuts off. "In the gym?"

"Uh. No. Here." I nod toward the living room. "I follow a program on the TV."

He lets out a breath that feels like a sigh of relief, and I'm confused as heck. "So you have a program that you stick to?"

"Yes. Well, kind of. I'm more of a mood exerciser. So I choose a workout from different programs based on the day or what my body needs."

His face falls. "I see."

I open my mouth to speak but close it again. Does he not think home workouts can be effective? *Now* I'm feeling a little insecure about my body. Tugging against the suction of the fridge, I pull out a package of thawed chicken. As I stand, I face Kace. "Any other questions, or?"

"No. I'm going to shower. Then I need to work."

"Aaaaaaall riiighty then," I say with all the enthusiasm I can muster, but it does nothing to lighten the mood. Not a smile. Not even a smirk.

Kace holds his stare for another beat before disappearing into the bathroom. I listen for a moment until I hear a Blink-182 song blend with the sound of the shower. That was weird, right?

Yeah. Weird. I shake the feeling from my head and make lunch. Once I'm finished, I portion the meals into the new prep containers that arrived yesterday and align them neatly in the fridge. I may not be the best planner, but if my meals are easy, it allows me more time to thrive in the chaos of my crafting, and that makes perfect sense in my head.

In the middle of cooking, I only see Kace in the time it takes him to leave the bathroom and slip into his room. His music has stopped, so I assume he must be working. I swear I hear the faint sound of conversation, but I'm not sure if it's a phone call or work meeting, and I don't want to spy.

I move to the couch with my lunch and a notebook, writing a to-do list for my next art project. Usually, I make crafts on my own and put them up for sale, but after posting about a crochet *Land Before Time* dinosaur set I made for my nephew, a woman reached out to me. She asked if I could come to her monthly girl's night and lead the activity. It's not something I've done before, but why not? Part of the reason I switch up the projects I offer through my business every week is because I'm easily bored, but it's also that I love learning new skills and seeing what I'm capable of creating.

I talked her into making chunky knit blankets instead though. Even being semi-competent in crochet, I barely have the patience to make tiny animals. I want everyone to have a good time and be able to complete their project in the allotted time. After researching the average prices for party hosts, I landed on charging one hundred dollars per person. With the yarn I ordered, I'll make about fifty dollars off each of the nine women. It helps that they won't need needles. Not bad for a day's work. That's tomorrow night, so between now and then, I need to pick up the yarn and make a practice one as an example. I got a light pink color for the class, as requested, but found a navy blue color that I think will look good in Kace's living room as his throw blanket.

Despite our little competition to decide whether I chip in with rent, I'm determined to find ways to make his life better at the very least. And whose life *isn't* better without another soft blanket?

No one.

Chapter Twelve

Mya

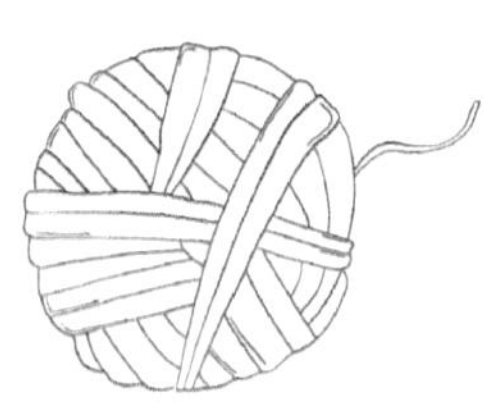

"Thank you so much for doing this last minute." Amber pulls the door open wider, welcoming me into her gorgeous home. It took me nearly thirty minutes to get to Camas–the town next to Vancouver. I rarely come this far east, even though I should. The town is quaint–very Stars Hallow-y. I wouldn't survive without a Target, but the antique store makes for a fun adventure. Despite its lack of amenities, parts of the town are *rich*. The gray stone home I'm walking into looks more like a mansion. It has to be at least a two and a half million dollar place. It's too big for me–although it would be cool to have a crafting room.

"Of course. This is going to be so fun," I say as she leads me through the open concept living room with floor-to-ceiling windows and down a hallway.

"My husband helped me clear out the second living room, so we'll have plenty of floor space for everyone to work." Her brown hair is perfectly pulled away from her face with a soft bow headband, and her smile is wide and inviting as she pushes open a door. We step inside an empty room with only a wine bar in the corner next to a TV mounted on the wall. On the screen, *Mean Girls* is queued up.

By the time Amber helps me bring everything inside and set up, her friends begin to arrive, all of them just as sweet. I wish I had friends like this–ones who make time to see each other even if they're married and have kids. The more my friends start checking off those milestone moments, the more distanced I feel from all of them. *I miss my sister.*

The group circles around me as I start the demonstration, then find their places on the floor to copy me. The movie plays as background noise as they work on their blankets, and I work on another in between helping them when they get stuck.

"How are things going with Johnny?" Amber asks one of her friends–Chloe is her name, I believe.

"Ugh." Chloe sighs, her auburn hair sliding down her back as she tilts her face toward the ceiling dramatically before reorienting herself. "Not any better. He's *so* clingy. It's too much. I mean, I love that he's into me, but not like this. He doesn't understand that I need time to myself, and it has nothing to do with him. I'm suffocating."

"Did you try telling him?" another friend asks, pausing her blanket-making.

"Yeah. But he makes me feel guilty that I don't want to spend all our time together when we're such a new couple."

"Just dump him," Amber says. "There's more fish in the sea."

Chloe rolls her eyes at the cliche. "If only it were that easy. I've tried several times to say that maybe we have different priorities that don't mesh, but he doesn't get it. I've tried not responding. I've tried telling him I'm busy. It always results in him blowing up my phone." She checks said phone. "He's texted me nine times since I've been here. NINE. And he whined all afternoon about how I was 'missing our show.'"

"Maybe you should block him," a blonde who has been quietly crocheting suggests.

"I thought about it," Chloe says. "But I think he would just assume something is wrong with my phone and show up at my house." Her face scrunches. "I don't know. Maybe I'm overreacting. Or crazy. I should be psyched he's so into me."

"Don't gaslight yourself." The blonde freezes her hands holding the chunky yarn. "But if you're really unsure, you could invite one of us to hang out with you two and we can help."

"Good idea," Amber adds. "You know we'll be honest with you about if we think you're just nervous about this level of commitment or if he's really not right for you."

Chloe nods. "And if he's not right for me?"

"We could help make sure your break up sticks," Amber says.

"Having one of you there would probably make it a hell of a lot easier to follow through and not back down when he gives me sad puppy eyes." She chuckles.

"I think it's worth a try," the blonde insists.

"Why is it so hard to break up with people? Even when it's not meant to be?" Chloe asks but is met with silence from her friends as she brushes her thumb repeatedly over the yarn in her lap. I wonder if they all have ideas running through their heads like mine. *Because confrontation is hard. Because it sucks hurting someone. Because what if this is the best there is? What if the other fish in the sea are all sardines?*

"I don't know, but I think this plan is worth a try," Amber says, and the rest of the girls agree.

"It won't hurt. Anyone free on Thursday? We have plans to go to the food truck pod. It would be an easy place for a friend to crash the date."

"Damn. The twins have dance class," Amber says.

"Shoot, I have night classes on Tuesdays and Thursdays," the blonde says.

The other six girls list their excuses for not being able to drop their plans at the last minute.

"I can do it," I offer, and everyone's heads spin in my direction to where I'm finishing the end of my blanket.

"Really?" Chloe asks.

I shrug. "Yeah, why not? I don't know you well enough to tell if he's specifically right for you, but I think I could go off your vibe when you're around him." I'm not sure why I jumped so quickly at the opportunity. A small part of me wants to feel included, and I'm drawn to Chloe's friendship for some reason. Maybe she's just a kindred spirit. I *know* I'm not the only one who struggles with breakups, but lately, it's felt like maybe at this age, I'm the only one who still struggles with having a good grip on life.

"I'll totally buy you dinner. Or wine. Or beer. Or cider. They have such a good selection for everything."

I chuckle. "I'm not worried about it. I know how hard it is to decide if someone is *the one*, and even harder to break up with them if they aren't. I'm happy to help."

"God, you're a lifesaver," Chloe tells me, her hands abandoning her blanket to fold over her heart. "Thank you. Thank you."

"You're welcome." I smile as I tie my yarn off at the end.

"Thank you again for doing this," Chloe whispers as she links arms with me and leans in on our walk to the entrance of Oak Tree Station. After the blanket party, we swapped numbers and made a game plan. I'm here to tag along as an out-of-town friend.

"It's not a big deal. I just hope it works." Based on how she talked about him, I have a feeling she already knows for certain he's not *right*. Sometimes we just need to be validated though, and I understand her pain of wanting a relationship to end but feeling so stuck when it comes down to it. I wish I would have had help. I guess I did if you count Kace.

"Oh, there he is." She points to the typical Pacific Northwest man headed toward us–you know, cargo shorts, T-shirt, flannel, a short beard and a hat from a local brewery. I find the vibe attractive overall, even though they all start to look the same.

"Johnny!" I run toward him at full speed and throw my arms around his neck. I catch him off guard, nearly knocking him over in front of the glass door entrance, but he half-ass hugs me back as he braces himself. When I met Chloe, she gave me a tight hug, like we actually had been friends forever. She's sweet, and welcoming, and while I don't know much about her, I feel confident she should be with someone just as comforting as she is.

"You must be Mya." He has a strained smile and a slight look of horror in his eyes. I know he's a guy forced to hug a stranger, but he emanates *get the fuck away from me* vibes, and I don't like it.

"Sure am! I've heard so much about you. It's shocking there was time to learn anything considering you keep our girl captive, but I've managed."

His eyes widen before he shifts gears. "I haven't heard that much about you," he says like it's an insult.

I shrug. "Buy me a drink, and I'll tell you everything you need to know."

"Yeah." He leans past me to kiss Chloe–not even noticing how uncomfortable she is–then holds the door open for us.

I grab Chloe's hand, pulling her away from Johnny and straight to the bar–just to see how supportive he is about his girlfriend seeing her long-distance friend. I sense him standing next to Chloe a moment later.

"What are you having?" Chloe asks me.

I scan the cider section of the electronic board above the taps. "I can't decide between the mango cider or the blue raspberry! You?"

"That's what I was looking at too!"

"Perfect. Let's get both and share?" I know Chloe already has her own group of friends, but I'm hoping she has room for one more.

"Let's do it!" she says.

"Wait," Johnny cuts in. "I thought *we* were going to share two beers? That's our thing."

Their thing. They've been together for less than a month. He can't claim basic friendship things as *theirs* yet. And even if he can, it doesn't seem like something to throw a fit about.

"I'd rather have cider tonight. Sorry," Chloe tells him, making eye contact with the beertender to get her attention.

"That shit tastes like sitting in a hair salon," he mutters. *Judgy much?*

"Hi. What are you in the mood for?" the woman behind the bar asks with a bright smile.

"One mango and one blue raspberry cider please," Chloe answers. "And whatever he's having." She nods toward Johnny, who begrudgingly orders a porter. It's funny to me that he doesn't even see the benefit of getting to try a beer that Chloe clearly wouldn't like based on the way she mutters "gross" under her breath.

We get our drinks and choose a picnic table on the patio. Even with the awning heaters and our sweatshirts, it's a little chilly, but the fresh air is perfect. "Can you watch our drinks while we go get food first?" Chloe asks her boyfriend.

"Uh. Sure." His brows furrow like he's angry about having to share her. The two of us leave him alone, wandering through the twenty food carts. We land on sharing a smash burger from The Cravory and a pulled pork grilled cheese from Bahn Reade.

Johnny takes his turn, going to get food alone, and then the next thirty minutes are spent eating while Chloe and I catch up on life like we're best friends. I tell her about my breakup with Matt and about Kace—because why not?—and she asks a million questions so she doesn't have to talk about her own relationship. Once I get Chloe all caught up on how Kace and I have barely spoken a word to each other all week, I actually try to include Johnny in the conversation, asking him questions about his life. Each time he barely gives a response, brushing me off like he couldn't care less. I may not always love my significant other's friends, but I at least make an effort to get to know them.

"I have to go to the restroom," I tell them both, and Chloe stands too.

"I'll come with," she says before turning to Johnny. "We'll be right back."

Without waiting for a response, she follows me inside as we weave through the cafeteria style tables to the bathroom.

"What do you think?" she asks the second we've rounded the corner into the three-stall room.

I scan her face, eagerly waiting for my response. "I think you're hoping I tell you he's not the one," I say.

She chews on her lip with wide eyes. "Yeah, I just wanted to know I wasn't crazy."

"I don't think he's necessarily a bad guy. He just doesn't match your energy. I do believe that sometimes opposites attract, but I get the impression he'd try to keep you from some of what makes you *you*. I don't want you to have to settle."

"That's my biggest hold up, you know. I feel like the next guy I pick has to be the right one. I'm torn between making sure he's perfect and just committing and hoping things work out."

"I get it. It's terrifying. I'm the same way, but even if you never found your soulmate, I don't think Johnny is the person you should settle with."

She sighs. "Me either. I have to break up with him now, huh?"

I chuckle. "Yes. I'd offer to do that for you, but it is not a skill I possess."

"It's okay. I should be the one to do it anyway. Do you want to get us another round, and once he leaves we can hang out for a bit?"

"Sounds perfect." She turns to leave, but I reach out and touch her shoulder to get her attention. "You can do this, Chloe. You're amazing, and even if he thinks he sees that, it doesn't matter if he doesn't allow you the freedom to be all that you are."

She pulls me into a hug. "Thanks, Mya. I'm glad you're here with me."

"You're welcome," I say as I hug her back.

Chloe heads back to the table, and after I go pee, I make my way to the bar. I pick out two more ciders for us but wait while she talks to Johnny. It's only about five minutes before he pulls his keys from his pocket, gets up from the picnic table and walks toward the parking lot.

Taking that as my cue, I head back to my new friend. "How did it go?" I set the drinks in between us as I sit across from her.

She smiles, but it comes off a little guilty. "I feel bad, but it's over."

"What did he say?" I take a sip of the honey pear cider.

"When I sat down, he told me I ambushed him by inviting you on our date."

"You know what the Spice Girls say! 'When you get with a girl, you also get with her best friend.' Or something like that." I laugh.

"So true." She grins. "Before I even said anything about breaking up, he argued that he didn't appreciate being third wheel and that if I wanted to just hang out with you, then I should have said so."

"You did tell him that on Monday for the party, and he threw a fit."

"Exactly. I reminded him of that. Then he tried to guilt trip me by saying I shouldn't fault him for wanting to spend so much time with me."

"Oooh. And then what?" I rest my chin on my fist, invested.

She chuckles. "I told him that I have a lot of things that are important to me, and I don't think I can give him the attention he deserves while also making time for everything else I love."

My eyes widen, impressed. She has more balls than I do. I practically avoid confrontation at all costs and just hope everything works out.

"And this time he actually agreed. He said he doesn't want to be with someone who doesn't put him at the same priority level. So I told him I was sorry, but maybe he should be with someone else. Then he left."

"Wow. I honestly can't believe that went so well."

"Me either," she admits, taking a sip of the cider the bartender described to me as "alcoholic grape Kool-Aid." "Thank you again. I think it was mostly helpful having someone here to keep me on track with the break up. It's easier to redirect the plan or make an excuse to delay it when you're alone."

"I totally get that. Maybe we all need a designated break up buddy until we find *the one*."

"Oh my gosh. YES!" Chloe slams her hand on the table. "Wait. Seriously. That's a great idea, Mya. You should do that."

I scrunch my brows. "Do what?"

"Be a designated break up buddy!"

"Umm..." I don't know what to make of that.

"I've seen your Instagram. You work for yourself, right? Always doing different projects?"

"Yeah."

"You could do this on the side. I bet people would pay for the service too. I would have. *I should have.* The rest of our drinks are on me."

I laugh. "It's really okay. I'm having fun tonight." I can already tell she could easily become a Top 8 friend.

"Me too." She smiles. "Seriously, think about it. You're creative enough. I can tell by talking to you and the fact that you helped me get through this."

"I'll think about it."

We spend the rest of the night talking about random things, but my mind keeps pulling toward the idea that maybe I could help people with the very problem I have myself.

Chapter Thirteen

Kace

Closing my bedroom door behind me, I scan my main living space. I've been holed up most of the day working on a big project, so I haven't had the chance to see Mya today. Though, to be fair, I've hardly seen her at all this week. We're like ships passing in the night–or maybe we're avoiding each other. Ever since our half-assed kiss and my run-in with her ex, I don't know how to act around her.

Heading into the kitchen to find something for dinner, I take in the silence and darkness with no sign of Mya anywhere. Even though things are difficult between us at the moment, and we owe each other nothing, I can't help but wonder where she is. Shaking the thought, I reach for the fridge to see what I've got and notice the folded paper on the counter.

Another note.

This one is folded a bit more intricately. It's in a rectangle, but somehow she's managed to fold a diamond into the top. How the hell do I even open this thing? It takes me a minute to undo the folds without ripping the note, then I flip on the kitchen light, leaning against the counter as I read.

Kace,
I realized I still don't have your number. Just wanted to let you
know I'll be out late with a new friend so you're not startled
when I come home. Feel free to have the last of the leftovers.
You should eat something today.
Mya

What is with this girl and her trust in strangers? Yes, I'm aware
that I'm one of those strangers, but it had to be reassuring
that I did a background check.

Walking back to my room, I slide open the drawer of my
desk and shuffle through the pens and sticky notes. I pull
out Mya's first note–folded like a normal person would fold a
piece of paper.

Skipping to the bottom, I punch her number into the contact area of a new text.

> Call me if you need a ride.

It's not that I care where she goes or what she does. I just
don't want her driving drunk.

Microwaving the teriyaki chicken, I plop myself down on
the couch. I haven't spent much time in the living room since
it became Mya's space, but I have been wanting to have a
Back to the Future marathon since they added it to streaming. Setting my plate on the coffee table, I get situated. My
hand brushes against what I assume is Mya's vintage *Lion
King* comforter–it reminds me of the *Goosebumps* one I had
growing up. But instead, it's a soft, navy blanket I've never
seen.

Checking my phone as Marty picks up the phone call from
Doc, I see Mya replied.

Kace? Hiiiiiiiiiiiiiiiiii

She sends another text with an entire row of heart emojis, and while that tracks for her sober personality, I have a feeling she's drunk.

Dif yoi eat dinner?

Definitely drunk.

Did you?

Yess. With Chloe. And Johnny. No more Johnny though.

What in the actual fuck is she talking about? Sometimes I swear she's speaking a different language.

Where are you?

333666 66630877788222550727 7755

That actually *is* a different language. How drunk is she?

What??

No typing bubbles appear this time. I put my phone down, forcing myself to focus on the movie and eat dinner. She's with Chloe. I don't know her, but she's mentioned the name before. I'm sure she's fine.

By the time the credits are rolling on the first movie, I'm kicked back on my couch, the new blanket keeping me warm enough to not need to turn on the heater. I reach for both my phone and the remote.

Nothing from Mya. I consider calling her now that it's nearly nine, but my phone buzzes in my hand first.

My mom? What the– Did someone die? Panic races through me as I sit up straight, my heart pounding as I swipe my thumb across the answer bar.

"Mom? What's wrong?" The fact that it's midnight in West Virginia isn't the issue. My parents are night owls. The concern is that they never call, regardless of the time of day.

"Hi, Kace. Yes, everything is fine." Her voice isn't soothing in the way I suspect other mom's voices are to their kids, but it's nice to hear it after so long. It's been three months.

"Good." My heart rate levels out a bit, but my mind is still swirling. "What's going on?"

"I was just calling to check-in, see how you're doing."

Red flags shoot up in every direction. Does she want something from me? They've never asked for money, but they know I make plenty. Are her and dad getting a divorce? I noticed at Christmas they each called me separately instead of on a joint speaker call like usual. "I'm fine..."

"How's Ruby?" she asks.

I sigh. "I don't know. Ask her new boyfriend."

"What?"

I run my hand through my hair. "We broke up."

"I'm so sorry to hear that, Kace." Her voice sounds genuinely apologetic. "Are you okay?"

Am I okay? Even though I know my mom always cared about me, we never talked about anything personal or emotional. I think when they realized we liked different things, they figured we wouldn't be able to connect about anything else either. It's ironic that my mom is the first person to ask me if I'm okay. She's also the first person I've directly told, but that's not the point.

I'm fine. The only part of my life it affects are things I don't *need*. Mainly sex. Not that we were having much of that. And conversation with someone who isn't behind a computer screen or serving me lunch. Someone I can count on. Although it turns out, I couldn't count on Ruby. "Yeah. Staying busy. How are you?"

The question feels foreign when it comes to her, and guilt racks through me for the first time. I accepted long ago that I wouldn't have a strong relationship with my parents, and because it's not a *bad* relationship, I haven't wasted too much energy on changing it.

"We're good. Your dad and I started seeing a therapist."

Wait, what? "Yeah?" I'm not sure what else to say. Do I ask why they're going to therapy?

"Yeah. It's nothing we can't work through. We just hit a rut, you know? Same thing, different day." I can picture them perfectly, sitting down after work with TV dinners on trays in front of a screen playing back-to-back game shows. It's not like they are zombies though. They're the lively kind of watchers–yelling at the TV, cheering and throwing out answers as if the contestants could hear them. Laughing. My parents laugh a lot. They're like Matilda's parents except not criminals or assholes.

"I know what you mean." I slouch back into the couch and adjust Mya's blanket over my lap.

"Our therapist has helped so much. We know we're getting older, and I think we've been paralyzed by that fact to the point of just going through the motions instead of taking advantage of the time we have."

The idea seems contradictory, yet I understand what she's saying.

"She also had us read this book together. It's called *Maybe You Should Talk to Someone*," my mom continues, and I try to not get distracted by the fact that I don't think I've ever seen my parents read. "One of the takeaways I had was about how sometimes people make endless bucket lists. It can create the mindset that they have endless time. But when you shorten your list to the things that truly matter, you're more focused on the urgency of crossing things off because you're more aware that there is an expiration date for your list."

Nothing my mom has ever told me really stuck. She never pep-talked me when I got bullied in school for being the nerdy kid or when my first girlfriend broke up with me for the senior guy who had a car. On the flip side, she never said anything mean or harmful to my self-esteem. My parents have just always been neutral. They were never against me, but it didn't feel like they were strongly *for* me either. "I like that." It occurs to me that I don't know any of my parents' dreams. Does that make me a bad son? "What's on your list?"

"We'd like to travel more. Come visit you, if you'll let us."

"Yeah. I have a roommate right now, but after she leaves." For some reason, voicing the idea of Mya leaving aloud makes my stomach flip.

"*She?* A new girlfriend?"

"Just a friend, Mom. Hardly even that."

"Oh, alright. Well, keep us posted."

"Yeah. Okay," I agree, still in shock from this entire conversation.

"I'll let you get back to your night. Just know we're thinking about you, honey. And we're going to be better going forward."

It's the first acknowledgment from either of my parents about not being present. I don't know what to say.

"I love you," she adds.

"Love you too, Mom." The words slip out, surprising me, and she replies with a goodbye that holds evidence of a smile before hanging up.

I can't remember the last time I said those words. I'd be willing to bet it was the day Ruby and I broke up because I know we said it every day. When one of us left for work or the store. Before we went to sleep. I did love her, but it was a habit more than anything.

I wonder what might have happened if Ruby and I had tried therapy. Would we have been able to work past our relationship's decline until it rose again? How the hell do you know when a roller coaster is made to keep going round and round instead of letting it crash? *A therapist may know.*

Pushing the thoughts away, I check my phone again to make sure Mya doesn't need me, then play the second movie.

Nearly four hours later, the credits are rolling on the final *Back to the Future*, and Mya still hasn't texted me back. I'm sure she's fine, and there's no need to call her. I don't have a hero complex. I'm concerned about her like I would be about any other roommate, and this is exactly why I don't have many friends. There's too much to worry about.

Still, I pick up my phone, and as my finger hovers over the *call* button, the front door clicks open. My eyes flash up to meet Mya's, hers going wide. "Oh my gosh," she whispers, although I don't know why–I'm clearly awake. "I didn't know you were still up."

I sit up straighter on the couch. "Yup."

She looks comfortable in leggings, tall boots and an over-sized sweater. Her curled hair brushes against her shoulders as she sets her fanny pack on the kitchen counter and makes her way toward me. "I didn't keep you up waiting, did I?"

"No," I deny, even though I strongly considered going to bed after the second movie. I do have to be up early for work.

"Oh!" A smile lights her face. "You're using the blanket."

"Yeah, sorry. I hope that was okay."

"Of course. It's yours. I made it for you." She plops down next to me like this entire situation isn't still weird.

She *made* this? It looks bought. I turn toward her on the other end of the couch. "Wow, Mya. This is impressive." Ruby only ever got me snowboarding clothes from her work. She never put in much thought or the time I'm sure it took Mya to *make* this.

"Thanks." She chews on a nail, and I realize I've never seen her shy before.

"Did you have a good night?" I don't know if I'm asking to make conversation or to be invasive.

She tucks her feet under her. "I really did. I made a friend, I think." She beams like she's proud, but I can't imagine it's hard for her to make friends.

"Oh yeah? Where were you?"

"I told you. The food truck park."

I arch a brow. "When did you tell me?"

"Earlier." She bites into her lip before her face splits into a grin. "Not my fault you don't speak the language."

I hold my stare.

She reaches her hand out and rests it on my blanket-covered thigh. "T9 silly!"

My gaze snaps to where she touches me as I process. T9. I chuckle, forcing my attention to her face. "How the hell was I supposed to guess that?"

She shrugs. "Anyway. We went to that food truck park thing in Camas, and I helped her break up with her boyfriend, and then we drank cider and chit-chatted. I think it was what I needed. I haven't relaxed like that since Matt and I broke up."

The mention of her ex sends a bitterness through me, but I push it aside and scrunch my brows. "Excuse me, what did you do?"

"Uhh. Talked? By the firepit. We had to stay until we were sober and could drive."

"No. Before that." Although, I'm glad she's smart enough to not drink and drive.

"Chloe and I shared a lot of french fries. They have a taco truck there, Ay Caray, and everything on the menu looked amazing. I bet you'd like it." Nothing will ever beat Little Conejo, but she is observant for an unaware person.

I give her a pointed look. "*Before* that."

"Oh, when I helped her break up with her boyfriend?"

"That."

"What about it?" She gives me a quizzical look. "She needed help, so I helped her."

"I didn't realize that was a thing."

"I mean, *you* helped *me* break up with my boyfriend." Her face glows in the dim light of the rolling movie credits.

"Yeah." I scratch the back of my head. "Again, I'm sorry about that."

She waves me off like it's nothing. "I'm thankful for you, Kace. Really."

I shift on the couch. I didn't do anything for her. If anything, it's all derived from being a selfish ass who can't get over his breakup.

"And guess what? Chloe had the best idea. She thought I should start my own business–helping people with breakups. Kind of a fun idea, don't you think?"

"Breakups aren't supposed to be *fun*."

"Oh, I know. I didn't mean it like that. I just mean, I've realized I'm not the only person who struggles with leaving a relationship they're settling for. What if I could help people the way you helped me?"

For fuck's sake, I do not want to be associated with this ridiculous idea. "Or maybe people could grow some balls and break up with people on their own like fucking adults." Mya's eyes widen, and I regret saying the words aloud despite fully believing them. "I didn't mean–Fuck. I'm sorry."

"It's fine." Her face falls, and I feel like even more of a dick. "Maybe it's true." Her gaze rises to meet mine. "But that's not real life, Kace. In an ideal world we know what to say and how to say it without help from anyone. But sometimes love is hard. Relationships are hard. And what if I could help make that a little easier for people?"

I can't help but think about how maybe Ruby would have used Mya's service instead of cheating. Would that have been better or worse? "You already have a business," I counter.

She sits up straighter, her hands folded in her lap. "I think I want to do this."

"If it's about money, I told you that you don't have to pay rent."

"I appreciate that, but you made it clear that this is only until I get back on my feet. I want to contribute while I'm here and save enough to get my own place. The more jobs I pick up, the sooner I can get out of your hair."

Isn't that what I want? Of course it is. I want my space back. I want my routine. So really, it only makes sense to let her work this job to save money. That topic reminds me I still never got to play out my half of our bet. If I win, she won't owe rent and everything will be back to normal before I know it. There's no way I'm avoiding this date again. And this time, I have a new idea.

Chapter Fourteen

Kace

I was set on nothing traditional for my *not date* with Mya. If I can't kiss her without being a bitch about it, I sure as shit can't make it through a real date. And considering how epically bad her date ended for me, I don't feel a ton of pressure when it comes to planning something Mya will enjoy. While I'm a little hesitant about part two–considering it's something I've never done, let alone with a woman–Mya seems easily entertained. I think I have a chance at winning the bet, being justified in refusing rent, and getting Mya on with her life in no time.

Exiting my room, I catch Mya right as she stands from the couch, still in her usual sleepwear–tiny shorts and a sports bra. *Fuck me.* I beg my dick not to jump at the reminder that my roommate is hot, and push the thought of trying a second kiss from my mind. *This is a* not date *with a girl who gets bored too easily to trust with something as fragile as dating.* "What's the plan for today?" she asks.

"Do you actually want me to go over it with you?" I'm fully willing to give her the rundown if she'd like.

"On second thought, no." She grins. "Just tell me what to wear and where to be."

I point toward the barstools at the kitchen counter. "Meet me there in a minute. No need to change yet."

She gives me a quizzical look but bounces toward the kitchen nonetheless.

I retrieve today's first activity from my room. Something Mya said when she suggested the challenge triggered an idea. When I was settled into my relationship with Ruby, every compromise between us seemed like less of a deal as time passed. It's like I got so used to making sacrifices, the impact of it faded as each decision became a habit. One main issue we had was Ruby's constant need to try new foods. There's nothing wrong with that–I'm willing to try almost anything once, but she never understood the comfort I found in consistency. In leftovers. In tried-and-true go-to dishes to take away a stressor of life. But after a long day at the office, she'd have us both meet at a new restaurant in Portland. It was never in Vancouver, and now that I'm thinking about it, I'm sure there was some fucking affair reason for that. It was always without a reservation too.

Every.

Single.

Night.

The world jokes about the majority of women who can't make up their mind when you ask where they want to eat. Well, Ruby is not part of that statistic, and as first-world problem as it sounds, it was a huge stressor in my day.

The thing is, I want to try something new sporadically. I have activities I want to experience and foods I crave, but it always felt like it would turn into a slippery slope. If I told Ruby I wanted to try something, she would find every restaurant in the city that served it so we could taste and compare.

Yes, I crave routine. That doesn't mean I don't want to experience something outside of it. I just don't want it to turn into a whole damn thing.

And that's why I'm sliding a black bag with red flames labeled *The Death Nut Challenge* across the breakfast counter toward Mya. Because it can be a one-time deal–not a whole fucking thing.

Her eyes immediately widen. "I don't know what that is, but it sounds terrifying."

"I did have to accept the terms that it involves risk of personal injury to buy it." I resist a laugh. "But it's just a spicy food challenge."

"We're just going for it, aren't we?"

I grin with a lick of my lips. "Sure are."

"Okay, I'm ready." She grins, and it's mesmerizing enough to keep my stare locked on her face instead of falling to her bare stomach. Okay, well, at least not for more than a second. Maybe she doesn't stick to a program, but her workouts *work*. Her smooth skin is toned, the outer ab lines faint, but there. Her posture is impressive too, for someone I've seen hunched over a project on the floor for hours at a time.

"Are you sure? What's your spice tolerance?"

"I don't like anything hot except for Chad Michael Murray. I might die," she says with a perfectly straight face that she holds for a full second before breaking into another smile.

I smirk. "Alrighty then." I reach for the bag, ripping it open and laying the five individual packets in front of us in order from one to five. I pick up the two pairs of latex gloves and hand one to Mya. "We have to eat one nut from each of the five levels of spice without eating or drinking anything during or for five minutes after."

"Have you done this before?" She wiggles around on the bar stool until she's comfortable, then pulls the black gloves onto her hands.

"No. You?" I reach for the first bag after I put on my gloves and rip it open.

She shakes her head. "Have I ever purposely burned off my taste buds?" She giggles, and it's so fucking cute, I *almost* want to kiss her. Then I remember last weekend, and all the weird ass feelings come rushing back. "But there's no one else I'd rather trauma bond with than you," she says, her voice thick with sarcasm. She sticks out her tongue and scrunches her nose as she reaches her hand out. "Hit me, Blazer."

"The first pack is mild. It probably won't be too bad." I sprinkle one pepper-covered peanut into her palm.

Mya tosses it into her mouth like she's not concerned in the least. I follow suit. I chew, my saliva mixing with the dryness of the nut and the powder coating, as I watch Mya. It actually has a good flavor. I could probably snack on these.

"It's not that bad." She proceeds to chew a few more times. "Okay, maybe it's a little spicy," she amends.

I chuckle, reaching for the second bag between us and ripping it open. Mya holds out her hand again. "The Party Is Starting." I pop the nut into my mouth.

"What party?" She places the nut on her tongue and licks the residue off her glove-covered fingers.

"That's what level two is called." I show her the packet label.

She grins, holding the peanut between her molars. "Nah. Every day is a party with me."

That wouldn't be my word of choice, but the sentiment is not wrong. "This one has a kick." It would probably be okay in trail mix with something sweet.

"Uh huh." She barely gets the words out before she hiccups. "I'm not sure this is going to be my type of party." The smile still present on her face contradicts her words.

"You ready for 'Question Your Commitment?'" I tear open the third bag.

"If you mean the nut, then yes." She plucks the next one from the bag in my hand and takes a deep breath before biting into it. She chews slowly, like she's disgusted, and I hold off from popping my own nut into my mouth. Her eyes are wide when a bead of sweat forms on her brow. "This is not good," she manages, shaking her head.

"Are you 'questioning your commitment?'" I smirk, finally eating my nut. Fucking hell, it's hot. I can tell before I even bite through it. I choke a tiny bit, covering it by clearing my throat.

Mya's palm slams on the counter. She swallows. "Dammit, Kace. You make your first joke ever, and I nearly miss it because you're killing me. Was that your real plan?"

I school my face to keep Mya from realizing how much she affects me. Hell, I'm not even ready to process how much she's been affecting me. I'm not sure why I don't want her knowing that I enjoy her presence. Maybe to avoid the whole kissing shit again. "Do you want to forfeit?"

"No. I'm in this. Next!" She reaches for the fourth bag and rips it open herself. "Boom! Fire It Up!" Tossing the nut into the air, she tilts her head back to catch it in her mouth. "Winner!" she says but immediately starts choking. "Not winner." She coughs while shaking her head. "Not winner," she repeats with strain in her voice.

"Are you okay?" I stand to get her a glass of water.

She continues with her alternating between coughing and choking while shaking her head and waving for me to stop. "I'm good," she manages as her eyes water. "Fuck me, this is hot."

I can't help but smile at her cursing as I stand, leaning against the counter next to her. It's not that I haven't heard her swear, but it's rare, and coming from her pretty lips, it amuses me.

"Are you going to suffer with me or not?" She coughs again, tears sitting in her eyes, and her cheeks flush.

"It's not *that* bad," I insist, putting the level-four nut in my mouth. I chew. Slowly. *Fuck.* I need more saliva to be able to swallow this, but the powder is so fucking dry. Sweat prickles along my hairline.

"Yeah, clearly." Mya rolls her teary, red-streaked eyes as a bead of sweat drips down the side of her face.

I swallow–barely. "Are you okay?" I try to ignore the fact that my tongue is tingling.

"Uh huh." She smashes her face into a fake smile and nods her head too enthusiastically.

"We don't have to do the last one."

"No way. We're doing it. I'm not wimping out! I'm finishing, and I'm going to like it, dammit."

"That's what she said." The words tumble out of my mouth, and I feel seventeen again.

Her gaze snaps to me, her hands flying to her mouth. Right before they touch her skin, she thinks better of it and pulls them away. "Kace no middle name Levitt! Are you actually a *good time?*"

I can't help but wonder in what sense she means those words, but I decide to take them literally. "No." I deadpan.

"Whatever." She brushes me off with a wave of her hand. "One more, right?"

"The Death Nut." I reach for the bag and my mouth waters at the thought–not in a good way. The darkness of this powder is so terrifying my stomach flips. It's worse than when your jaw pings in pain at just the sight of a Warhead sour candy.

"Oh god." Fear flashes across her face.

"Last chance to back out."

She shakes her head. "No. But I don't even want to touch it. I'm pretty sure it'll melt right through my gloves like lava. You do it." She leans forward, opening her mouth and sticking her tongue out like a plate for me to serve.

This fucking girl. Not wanting to touch the nut myself, I rip open the bag, and pinching one nut between the plastic and my fingers, I shake the other one onto her tongue.

Before she even closes her mouth, she stands, leaning against the counter with her palms. "Oh my god. Oh my god," she says between chews and sucked-in breaths.

I chew my own nut, not realizing why she's freaking out. It's not that–*FUCK ME*. I move to run my hands through my hair, wanting to tug until the pain overrides the fire in my mouth, but my common sense makes an appearance just in time. Instead, I grip the edge of the counter. *Fuck.* Tears spring to my eyes. Sweat soaks my hair to the point that I can feel it without touching it, and a bead trickles down my jaw.

"I hate you," Mya curses, and I glance at her long enough to notice she looks like she's going to pass out. For the smallest flicker of time, I hate those words coming from her lips, but then I'm right back to being hyper aware of every sensation my body is feeling.

She rips the gloves off her hands, pulling them inside out as they slide from her fingers, and she drops them on the counter. Reaching toward where my palms are pressed into the granite, Mya pinches the band at the top of my gloves and tugs to remove them for me. I release pressure enough for her to pull them off and into a ball next to hers.

"My entire body is tingly." She laughs, despite the tears now streaming down her face and sweat matting her hair to her head. "Is this normal?"

"According to the reviews." I manage a weak chuckle through the pain in my mouth that is now being shared with my stomach. *Fuck.* I read all these reviews online and thought they were exaggerating. One person claimed the peanuts "stole their soul." Why would I take that seriously?

"We need like water, or milk, or I don't know. What do we do?" She bares her teeth, looking at me like I have every answer.

"Milk." I remember reading a review. "But we're just supposed to swish it around and spit it out."

"Do I even want to know why?" She glances over her shoulder as she makes her way slowly to the fridge, stumbling around the breakfast bar like the heat has intoxicated her brain.

"No." She glances back at me, but I don't elaborate. The milk protein breaks down capsaicin–the chemical in peppers that gives it heat–in your mouth, but in your stomach, it could stimulate the acid and make everything worse.

She trusts me blindly, pulling the milk from the fridge and gulping it straight from the jug. Handing it over to me, she moves to the sink while swishing the liquid in her mouth.

Oh fuck. I love cereal. I love the way milk makes it twice as good. But it does not compare to the way I fucking love this milk right now. The coolness bites through the burn in my mouth. I swish it around, feeling it transition from refrigerator cold to room temperature as it absorbs the heat in my mouth. I already feel a million times better.

Mya spits into the kitchen sink before standing and backing out of the space. I follow her lead, then take a deep breath and stand to face her.

She bursts into laughter so loud, happy and contagious that I can't help but chuckle. "What?"

"You *wanted* to do that?" She manages between laughs, now hunched over in her fit. "You were worried I was a secret psycho, but you've just given me cold hard proof that it's *you*."

"We did complete the challenge. You have to admit it's satisfying." I lean my back against the counter.

She stands, gaining some composure. "Technically not because we didn't wait five minutes." She reaches out and touches my arm. I follow the movement, my gaze locked on where our skin touches. When I refocus on her, she's looking at me. "But we're going to pretend we did, then never do that again."

I'm tempted to redo the challenge without "cheating," but in a situation like this, I can let the rules slide. "One and done. It's not like I'll ever find someone willing to do it with me. At least not without a bribe or a bet."

"True again. God, please tell me that whatever comes next is less rough."

I weigh the answers for a moment, knowing the next part might fuck me up more mentally than this challenge did physically. And with Mya refusing to confront her feelings and just pushing them to the side, it might not go well for her either. "We'll see."

She shakes her head amused, and the fact that she's not concerned about what could be next after that is extremely unsettling. "Can I at least shower first?"

"Yeah. We have to leave in half an hour."

"Got it, Cap'n Crunch." She salutes me and walks merrily toward the bathroom, leaving me standing there like the idiot I feel like when I'm around her.

The feeling is overruled by anxiety thrumming through my body at the thought of what comes next, already regretting my plan and wishing I had another bag of nuts instead.

Chapter Fifteen

"How cute should I look?" I yell at Kace through his bedroom door, still wrapped in a towel. I was so focused on washing off the sweat and spice, I forgot to grab clothes before hopping in the shower.

He cracks the door open, his face a few inches above mine as he looks down at me. He takes in my lack of clothing for only a second before snapping to my eyes. "Just wear something comfortable."

I scan the bits of his outfit I can see through the crack in the door. Corduroy pants and a maroon hoodie with a "VT" logo on the front. I wonder what that stands for. "Okay. Thanks." I turn away, the door closing behind me as I make my way to my suitcases in the corner of the living room on the far side of the couch.

I dig out black leggings with an oversized bright blue crewneck that says "Super Nova Girl" in galaxy block letters. Perfect. I dress quickly and make my way back to the bathroom to put the top half of my hair up into two space buns.

I turn my head from side to side as I look in the mirror. Nailed it. If only my eyes weren't still red from the burn of the nut powder in the air alone. I have to admit, despite the physical pain that challenge caused, part one of Kace's date day was surprisingly fun. Seeing a new side of him–one that apparently does know how to crack jokes–unlocked a new level to my crush. I didn't expect him to come up with something creative, something I've never done. I might not have come up with the idea on my own, but even if I had, no guy I've ever been with would have done it with me. I picture Matt saying something like, *Why would we eat something bad when we could get something that tastes good?* He doesn't understand that sometimes it's about the *experience.* Maybe Kace gets that more than I thought he would.

Leaning closer to the mirror, I swipe on a coat of mascara, then reach for my tweezers to take care of stray eyebrow hair. I swear they grow faster than any other hair. It's like every time I take a shower, I become a Chia Pet.

"Ready?" Kace calls through the door.

I flick off the light, slipping into the entryway. "Let's zoom zoom zoom, Proto Zoa." I flash him a smile as I swipe my pink and white checkered fanny pack off the kitchen counter, and it widens the longer he stands there staring at me like I'm E.T. "Let's go!" I give him a light push on his shoulders until he finally turns toward the door and leads us out.

He glances over his shoulder. "You look like candy."

"Oh! My perfume." I turn back, slipping inside, finding my marshmallow spray on the bathroom counter and spritzing my neck. Kace is waiting for me when I reemerge. "And now I smell like candy." I grin.

"You do know you're an adult, right?" he asks with another one of his blank stares.

"You do know you can be responsible *and* still have fun, right?" I mock him.

He looks at me with an arched brow, like he's still not convinced I know the meaning of responsibility.

"My bills don't get paid based on how I dress. Adults get to choose what they wear or smell like and don't need the approval of anyone."

"I think most employers would disagree."

"Well, it's a good thing I'm my own boss then, isn't it?" I grin. No matter what he says, I'll have a comeback. Am I still uncertain about a lot of things in my life? Yes. Especially my love life. And I question daily if my little crafting business will be sustainable forever. But it works for now, so why would I change it?

"Did your parents stunt your self-expression as a child?" He reaches behind me to lock the door, and we make our way to the elevator.

"No way." I step into the metal box and push the parking level button as soon as Kace is inside. "They're the best. Straight Sonny Koufax. Except instead of letting me wear a strainer on my head and pee on the sides of buildings, they let me wear my hair like Pippy Longstocking every day for a year. And instead of calling me Frankenstein, they called me JJ because I was obsessed with Junie B. Jones."

"You still don't go by your real name."

"Damn. I was hoping you'd forget that."

"I don't forget things, *Eleanor*."

"No. Nope. Absolutely not."

A smirk escapes him along with a twinkle in his eye. "What's so bad about it?"

"It's an old lady's name, first of all. Second, do I look like an Eleanor to you?"

He contemplates it as the elevator jolts to a stop in at the garage level. "So how'd you end up with the name anyway?"

The question strikes me simply because it's the first time Kace is asking me personal questions that aren't for a background check. "Well," I say as he lets me out of the elevator first. I look over my shoulder as I make my way to the parking garage. "My parents are obsessed with the Beatles. My older sister, Stella, got the cool name. I was named after my mom's favorite song."

"That's depressing." He pushes the black metal bar on the tinted door leading to the garage.

I pause as I pass by him, the cool air of the garage hitting my face. "At least they gave me a workable middle name. Can you imagine if it had been Rigby? Oh the horror that would have been."

He looks baffled by the entire situation. "But they named you after a song about a woman who is lonely as fuck."

"I guess. But I don't know, I think it's a reminder to me that knowing you're isolating yourself is half the battle. I can choose to put myself into situations where I don't feel as alone, even when I'm feeling detached, or I'm convinced no one understands me. That's part of why I prefer Mya. It's my active choice to be the person I want to be, rather than the version of me who feels trapped." It's the first time I've spoken that thought aloud, and a wave of shyness overcomes me realizing that Kace was likely not the person to reveal it to. "That sounds stupid, I know," I mutter, walking ahead, even though I have no idea what Kace drives.

A hand touches my arm from behind. "It's not stupid," he says, and then with a light grip, he guides me in the other direction, toward his... truck apparently.

"So where are we going?" He unlocks and opens the passenger side door to his black Toyota Tacoma. "Thanks." I slip past him, hopping onto the seat.

Walking in front of the truck to the driver's side, he slides in next to me, pausing with his key halfway to the ignition. He glances over to meet my waiting stare. "Therapy."

I laugh. "No, really. Where are we going?"

"I told you," he says, the key clicking into place as his glance shifts to the backup camera.

I open my mouth to speak but snap it shut, not knowing how to respond, or how I feel about it. I've never been to therapy.

"Don't tell me I finally figured out the secret to get you to stop talking?" He spares me a glance as he drives out of the dark parking garage and into the daylight.

I quickly recover. "Saving all my talking for therapy."

He accepts my response, keeping his eyes on the road. He didn't put a location into the GPS, so we're either not going far or he's been to this therapy place before.

"So," I start, unsure how to phrase the question I want answered. If we're going to therapy, it's something he *wants* to do–that's the point of this challenge. It also means it's something he feels he'd be judged for or unsupported through. Not wanting him to feel either of those things from me, I shift directions. "How do you want to play this?"

He flicks on his blinker, coming to a complete stop before looking both ways and turning right. "What do you mean?"

"We should pretend we're in a relationship, right? For this to work."

"Yeah. I mean we did last week. So I figured we could manage it today." He spares me another glance that looks... vulnerable, I think. I consider harassing him for a second about how it probably didn't look like we were together after he ran out on me, but I decide against it.

"Absolutely. Let's just wing it. We'll follow the other person's lead and stick to each other's stories."

His grip tightens around the steering wheel. I don't know why he's so tense when this was his idea. "Okay."

"Okay," I echo, unzipping my fanny pack and pulling out a Blow Pop. I unwrap it, sucking the burst of strawberry into my mouth. Ignoring the strained silence between us, I flatten the candy wrapper between my fingers. I fold it the way I used to fold starburst wrappers to make a necklace, focusing all my attention on that rather than the chaos of the "what ifs" running through my mind.

Kace's thumb presses into a button on his steering wheel and a loud drum and guitar intro fills the space between us. I glance at the display. "All I Want," by A Day to Remember.

I never got into the punk rock scene as a teenager, but I recognize the name. He doesn't bother to turn it down as the beginning vocals blare through the speakers at a deafening volume.

The next ten minutes pass without a word between the two of us–not like he could hear me unless I snuck in a word between songs. It flipped to BOYS LIKE GIRLS next, then Fall Out Boy. I surprisingly knew both of the songs. They must have been really popular.

He pulls into the space at the back of a lot in front of office buildings. Yanking the key from the ignition with more force than necessary, the music cuts. The whoosh of cars speeding by replaces the song, but it's not nearly as loud as the tension filling the air.

I set my dwindling Blow Pop carefully on top of my folded wrapper on the dash, then meet him behind the truck. I wait for his lead, since I have no idea which office we are going to. He hesitates as he shoves his keys into his pockets. then glances at me–well, at my hand. Before I have time to piece together his thoughts, he laces his fingers in mine. I let him and don't pull away even when his clammy hands dampen mine. Is he nervous? What is happening right now? I've seen angry Kace. Indifferent Kace. Annoyed Kace. But nervous Kace?

I squeeze his hand lightly, reinforcing the unspoken support between us all of a sudden. If Kace is trusting me with something as vulnerable as therapy, I'm going to take this seriously.

We make our way to the glass door in the middle of the quiet row of suites. Kace takes a breath, wiping emotion from his face as he drops my hand to open the door. I follow him into the waiting room, and Kace takes it in. "This is a bad idea," he mutters, turning to leave.

Right as I'm about to reassure him, one of the two doors in front of us opens. "Kace and Mya?" The woman waiting for us in the doorway looks exactly like the mom in *Freaky Friday*.

To be determined if she's the Jamie Lee Curtis version or the one with Lindsay Lohan trapped in her body.

She takes a few steps backward, and I nudge Kace. "It'll be fine. Promise. You can kick me out if it turns into your worst nightmare." I try to lighten the mood, and he smirks. I know he wouldn't actually kick me out, but if it makes him feel better, I'm happy to entertain him. As we enter her office, the woman holds out her hand. "Hi, I'm Angela. It's so nice to meet you both." She shakes Kace's hand first, then mine.

Kace clears his throat. "Thank you for fitting us in."

"Of course," she says in a sweet and comforting voice that reminds me of my mom. "Please, take a seat."

Kace and I glance around the room, both of us settling our eyes on the couch next to an armchair. Kace sits first, leaving both feet planted firmly on the ground as he shifts around for a few seconds until he's settled enough. I take a seat on the other cushion, but quickly realizing we should probably be closer, I scoot until our thighs are touching.

Angela situates herself in the armchair with a warm smile. "There's something I like to ask my couples before we dive in, if you're open to it." She shifts her glance between the two of us.

"Okay," I say as Kace gives a curt nod.

"Great. How do you prefer to receive support when you're feeling stressed? Kace, why don't you start."

He rubs his palms against his jeans. He seems pretty nervous for a *not date*. He clears his throat. "I like routine. Having things I can count on. Knowing exactly what to expect."

"That's specific and helpful. Thank you, Kace. Mya?"

"Umm. I've never been asked that." I hum, thinking about my breakup with Matt and navigating the past week. "I think I need my feelings to be validated–to know that the person doesn't think I'm stupid or have no clue what I'm doing. It helps if someone brainstorms practical solutions with me instead of criticizing and expecting me to be receptive." I chew my lip. "That's so much different than Kace. Is that bad?"

"Not at all," Angela assures. "Knowing how to support your significant other is one of the keys to success–as long as you're willing to love them in the way *they* need instead of how *you* need."

Nerves race through me at the idea of Kace and I being together. I know it won't happen, but the thought of learning how to understand someone better is exciting. Thinking about someone taking the time to understand me better is all I hope for.

"So," Angela starts. "What brings you two here today?"

I glance at Kace, planning to take his lead, but the more seconds that tick by, the more his face hardens. He seems to be drowning in the anxiety he had outside the office, and I would sell my collector Polly Pockets to know what thoughts are whirling around with that rage building inside him. *Whoa.* I actually care about Kace. Not in a curious way. Not in an "I can fix him" way. Genuine concern washes over me. I clear my throat, not knowing what exactly I should say. Kace's eyes snap to me like he's hoping I'll take over the conversation, and I feel my cheeks heat from the attention. I want him to feel comfortable and supported, and while I don't have experience with therapy, I want him to get whatever he's hoping for from this.

Angela is patient, waiting for me to speak. "Umm..."

I must look frantic because she softly says, "Take your time."

"Getting older is hard." The words tumble from my mouth, and a sideways glance shows me Kace's furrowing brows.

"How old are you?" the therapist asks.

"I just turned thirty."

"That's a milestone year for a lot of people."

"Yeah. It is. But I don't want to talk about that." If we dug into that insecurity, Kace definitely wouldn't have time to get anything he wanted from this.

"What would you like to talk about then?" she asks without prying or judgement.

"Umm..." I try to get a grasp on what I actually want to say. "This morning Kace said something to me about dressing like a child."

I feel him tense beside me. "That's not what I said," he mutters under his breath.

Angela turns her attention to Kace. "What did you say?"

"I said," he snaps, "she looks like candy."

Aaron Carter's version of "I Want Candy" pops in my head. *My Lanta*, Mya, focus. I wave my hand. "This is not the point I'm trying to make. I'm not offended by what he said. I'm struggling with the bridge between things I love from my past and what should remain in my future so I can live the life I want to."

"Could you elaborate on that?" Angela asks.

"I'm a firm believer that growing up in the early 2000s was the best. There's never going to be anything better." I pause, putting together the rest of my thoughts. "Everything has become dull. We discovered new things and expanded our minds playing Where in the World is Carmen Sandiego, and now we have Chat GPT and could never have to actively learn anything. We used to play neighborhood hide and seek until the street lights kicked on, and now the best part of the day is being sucked into our phone at the end of the night, doomscrolling through uninspiring crap. It's just... everything about being a kid screamed *life*."

"Your life isn't that far off," he mutters.

I shoot him a glare. He's so far off base. "I know the point is to grow up and move on from it, but why does being an adult have to be so much worse? Why does it have to be so hard?"

"It doesn't *have* to be hard," Kace tells me like it's simply a choice. If it were a choice, he'd be leading by example.

Glancing from the therapist to him, I glare. "Says the guy who is letting his ex control his fears every day by avoiding his feelings about his last breakup."

"Don't act like you're not stuck in the past when all you do is think about things from twenty years ago," he fights back, and the truth of it stings.

"Well, it would help if you didn't criticize me when I try to go out and make friends–or do anything that screams 'fun' for that matter."

He rolls his eyes. "Sorry for caring about your safety."

"Kace," Angela cuts in. "Try to remember that when Mya is stressed, it's helpful for her to feel heard. Do you feel like you're listening to her before you respond?"

He clenches his jaw. "I'm sorry." His chest deflates with a sigh. "I'm open to hearing your logic."

I take a breath, trying not to be angry at the fact that I'm not sure he means his words. "I'm obsessed with the 2000s because things were easy then. You'd walk through your beaded curtains, plop down on your blow-up armchair, and flip through *Seventeen*. Quizzes told you what you like and how to live your life. You had a manual for being a teenager. There's no guide once you're an adult." *There's no one to tell me when to choose having a baby over having a happy marriage, amongst other things. At what point should I settle for less than a 'soulmate' because there's no chance of having both?*

"You're romanticizing it." Kace runs his fingers through his hair. Taking a breath, he shifts to face me. "I mean... I understand what you're trying to say, and I agree with the fantasy of it. But I think you're blocking out all the days you'd leave a cryptic song lyric as your AIM away message because you felt like your life was falling apart. It's the same thing you do now–block out the bad and pretend it's all good."

I glare at him, not impressed by his half-assed attempt to support me and feeling the urge to scoot to the other side of the couch. I face him instead. "It's not misplaced nostalgia, Kace. As a kid, it's acceptable to be whoever you want and try different things until you figure it all out. Then we become adults, and we're expected to understand everything and get it right on the first try? Not to mention, all the decisions we have to make are so monumental that making mistakes completely changes the trajectory of your life. That's a lot. When did I become qualified for that?"

"You don't figure it out by flitting about without a care in the world," Kace says under his breath. My body freezes, but my mind twists through my thoughts faster than a Conair Quick Braid. Are we here because he thinks I need therapy? Is he playing a role or did he choose this because he thinks I'll never get back on my feet? Is this his way of getting me to leave? *He had to know that comment would hurt.*

If this *is* real, then I'm going all in. "Is that what you really think about me?" Tears spring to my eyes, but I hold them back.

He scans my face. Is he taking in my vulnerability, or is the mask thick enough? "You say you want all these things for your life, but you're so distracted by shiny objects." *Another hit.*

I can feel Angela's eyes on us. I'm surprised she hasn't cut in again, but I don't know how therapy works.

"I'm just trying to do things that make me happy." *Because that feels like the only thing I have control over*, I add to myself.

Kace stares, not adding anything, and Angela's voice breaks through the tension. "Kace, do you mind sharing how you believe adulting should work?"

Something between a sigh and a groan leaves him. "It's not that complicated. You come up with a plan to make sure getting what you want goes smoothly, and then you stick to the plan no matter what."

Oh. This is about his ex. "Kace." I touch his arm, feeling his body heat through his sweatshirt. "I'm not going to leave without warning like Ruby." He's never told me what happened with her, but based on the little I do know, I get the impression she tore herself from him.

He pulls his arm away. "How do you know her name?"

Whoops. It wasn't easy, but Chloe and I went down a social media rabbit hole until we found Kace's ex. It was hard, considering Kace has no social media, but eventually, finding Kace's LinkedIn and searching through his connections took us down the right path. I shrug. "I did what I had to do. You don't tell me anything."

He takes a breath with a slight shake of his head, like he's letting go of my invasion of privacy. "It doesn't matter. You say now that you won't leave. Like she fucking said." I hate that I was right about her leaving him. "But you can't sit still to save your life."

My face scrunches as I pull my fists into my sleeves. He's not talking about me, right? Because there's never been any romantic interest between us–at least not from him. But maybe he means as a friend? Or maybe he's talking *to* Ruby. "No. I'm going to be here as long as you let me stay. I *like* being here." I realize I mean the words as soon as they're out. Are there downfalls or frustrations from living with Kace? Yeah. Space is an issue for sure. Would it be nice if we did things together like friends? Of course. But I like being in his presence, and his space feels comfortable for me.

"Yeah, we'll see if you're singing the same tune in three months."

My brows furrow. "What?" Seriously, is he talking to *me*? "I thought you wanted this to be temporary?"

"No." His eyes widen like he surprised himself with the admission, but then they flick to Angela for a moment. "I mean. Fuck. I don't know why we're here." He runs his hands through his hair, and it really hits me that he's struggling–although with *what* I'm not quite sure. The way his thoughts are whiplash, it's like he can't decide how he feels or what he wants to admit.

He tries to stand and leave, but I reach for his hand. His gaze snaps to where our skin touches. After a moment, he glances back at the door like he's contemplating leaving anyway, but resituates himself on the couch, leaving his hand in mine.

Angela clears her throat, and both of us look toward her. I'm shocked she hasn't caught onto our ruse, or worse, pointed out that we're terrible together. I mean, we aren't together, but aside from that, there's no level of understanding between us or clear form of communication. Yet, for some reason, I don't want to leave. There's something comforting and grounding about the warmth of his hand holding mine.

"How much quality time do you two spend together?" Angela asks neither one of us in particular.

Kace jumps in. "None. She's off playing around with crazy ideas. She doesn't plan anything. She jumps on ideas spur of the moment without a single thought."

He keeps mentioning "having a plan." Is it really that simple for him? Would making a plan create a monumental shift? I tuck that piece of information away for now. "Me helping Chloe was totally planned. And my new business venture is thought through, thank you very much."

He raises one brow.

"Kace, would you like to share your true concerns about Mya's ideas?" the therapist asks.

"Yeah, Kace. Tell her about my plan that's so stupid even though YOU acted on it first."

He tries to pull his hand from mine, but I hold tight. Flashing through a range of emotions from anger to conceding, he says, "I don't think she's being safe."

"I'm a big girl. I can take care of myself. Plus, I have a taser."

He rolls his eyes. "You shouldn't trust everyone the way you do."

"You shouldn't distrust everyone the way *you* do," I snap back. I haven't heard him mention friends, family or even coworkers. Why does he care so much about *me*?

"Okay," Angela says. "Do either of you want to elaborate?"

"No," Kace and I say at the same time. I'm not sure what his reasoning is, but I'm now self-conscious about an idea that sparked so much excitement. I just really think that I could help people during their breakup process.

"That's alright. Is there a way to compromise? Is it something that you could do together? Maybe that way, Kace, you could understand better why Mya is so excited. And Mya, maybe you could give Kace the comfort of knowing you're safe. Is that a possibility?"

Kace is about to object, his hand tensing in mine.

"Actually..." I tap my chin, and his eyes snap to mine. "Do you want to?" My face lights up with hope. I love the idea of having a sidekick on my missions, even if he's a little grumpy. We'd be like Shawn and Gus from *Psych*. He might even provide ideas and necessary points of view I don't consider. I can see Kace's concern about safety, especially if I turn this into an actual business. Plus, I don't know... I think I want to get to know Kace better. He's a kaleidoscope. Every time he's twisted, he shows different colors, and I want to understand all of his patterns. "We talked about getting out more. Not staying at home," I remind him, hoping he remembers how we agreed that the best way to get over our exes was to avoid holing up and being depressed.

He narrows his eyes. "Why do you need a side hustle anyway?"

"I like trying new things." I shrug. "Plus, multiple streams of income. Duh."

"Your current business has plenty of potential with how good you are. Why can't you focus on that?"

The compliment feels more like a slap in the face. "You think my crafts are good?"

He sighs. "Of course I do, Mya. You're extremely talented."

My heart warms, and the feel of his hand in mine shifts from tense to comforting. "Thank you." I take a breath. "It's just... I love crafting, but I love this new idea too. I want to give it a try. Please?"

"I think it's a bad idea," he grumbles.

"Please, Kace," I beg him with puppy dog eyes, going in for a kill shot with my thumb brushing across his.

His jaw flexes as he grinds his teeth. "Mya."

I sigh, my grip on his hand relaxing.

"Kace," Angela says. "Are you open to sleeping on the idea?"

He closes his eyes and takes a deep breath. "Fine. I'll sleep on it."

My heart remains deflated. I can't imagine him changing his mind.

"You set up this appointment today," the therapist adds with her eyes still locked on Kace. "Is there anything else you want to touch on before we're out of time?"

"No." He unlinks our hands to rub his palms against his jeans. "I already got more than I bargained for."

"Alright." We both look at Angela as she clasps her hands together on her lap. "I think we made some progress today. I'd love for you two to come back in a couple of weeks for a follow-up."

Kace stands like he's more than ready to get out of here. "Thank you," I say, as I follow him out the door.

Chapter Sixteen

Kace

I crack my neck, and between the release of tension and it sounding like the snap of a glowstick, it's a pure serotonin boost I desperately need. Fuck, I'm exhausted. What an experience that was. For some idiotic reason, I thought I should try therapy based on the only advice my mom's ever given me. I should have gone alone. Then maybe I wouldn't feel pressured to take part in a crazy Mya scheme.

I toss my keys into the leather bowl on the edge of the kitchen bar. Mya unclicks her fanny pack and hangs it over the back of the barstool. "Sooooo," she says, twisting her hands in front of her. "That was fun." Her gaze shifts slowly to mine.

I open the fridge and pull out a Best Day Ever beer, expecting her to push back a little. Despite that ridiculous appointment being my idea, I want nothing more than to run away mentally. My self-awareness makes me feel like even more of a coward. Will I forever be the guy who runs from the things he can't control instead of facing them head-on or trying to gain perspective? *Fuck.* I don't like the thought of that.

I run my fingers through my hair, keeping my back to Mya so she can't see my distress. Therapy was supposed to meet the rules of our bet and give me a chance to satisfy my curiosity about whether it could have worked for Ruby and me. But I put Mya in that awkward ass position, and she rose to the challenge. I turn to face her. "I owe you an apology." I rub the back of my neck. "I didn't expect things to get so..." I shuffle through a few words before settling on, "real."

"It's fine." She gives a dismissive flick of her wrist as if people hurting her feelings is no big deal.

Suddenly I'm furious with myself, the cold condensation of the beer wetting my fingers under my tight grip. "It's not fine. I'm angry with myself, and I continue to take it out on you."

Expecting hurt to be written on her face, I'm shocked when her features soften. "Thank you," she whispers. "Do you want to talk about it?"

I crack my beer. I'm not trying to reject her again, but talking is the last thing I want to do. "I'd rather not."

"Okay, what would you like to do instead?" There's so much hope in her voice that I think I *actually* want to hang out with her.

Taking a sip, I relax when I realize she's letting me off the hook. "Uhhh."

"I saw that you have a Nintendo 64." Her eyes light up, and I stare at her. "Do you have *Mario Kart*?"

I take another swig of my beer. "I do."

She tugs on the end of a curl. "Do you maybe want to play?"

If I didn't clean my apartment fairly regularly, there'd be cobwebs on my console. It's not that I don't enjoy playing. It's that I either didn't have the time or Ruby wanted to do something else. "Sure."

"Yay!" She bounces up and down before turning on her heel and heading to the living room. "Can I be Yoshi?" she asks over her shoulder.

"Yeah." I like to be him, but with the way her ass looks in those leggings, she can have anything she wants. Not to mention, it's the least I could do after that disaster of a therapy session.

Putting my beer on the coffee table, I set up the N64 in front of the TV and plug in the AV cables.

"There's a drink in the fridge for you if you'd like." I unwind the cords neatly wrapped around the controllers.

"Oh, no thank you. I don't want a beer."

I keep my eyes on what I'm doing. "I figured. I got you some cider."

"You did?" I can hear the surprise in her voice without looking to confirm. It's not a big deal. I saw it and thought she'd like it.

"Yeah," I say, but she's already on her way to the fridge.

She comes back a moment later, cracking the can on the way. Her lips press against it, her eyes lighting at the first sip and sending a rush of satisfaction through me. "Holy crap. This tastes like the red, white and blue popsicles I had as a kid."

I chuckle. "It's called 'Rocket Pop.'"

"This is so good. It reminds me of running through the sprinklers in the summer." I glance at her in time to catch a smile before she takes another sip. "Thank you."

"You're welcome." I hand the transparent green controller to her as she settles on the floor with her back against the couch. I take the black one for myself as I sit on the cushion and select Luigi so she can choose Yoshi. "What track do you want to play?"

She tilts her head back, glancing at me over her hair twisted into buns on top of her head. "Rainbow Road is my favorite." She smiles before fixing her gaze on the TV.

I toggle over to the "Special Cup," and scroll down to select "Rainbow Road."

Mya sits up straighter, her thumb hovering over the "A" button.

A giant "three" flashes on the screen. Her thumb, with chipped pink polish on the nail, presses down on the blue button.

The two flashes, and she presses it again. I'm not sure why I'm surprised she's played this before.

I wonder which of her exes of three months she played with. I press my own "go" as the countdown ends, and we both take off down the rainbow.

"So who won?" She tilts her controller and leans her body to the left like it controls her turning.

"Huh?" I curve down the road, barely ahead of her, using the controller joystick.

"Our dates. Rent." Yoshi flies off the edge of the rainbow road in a gap in the yellow star railing and into the darkness. "Whoops." She rests her controller on her lap as the Lakitu carries her back to the track. I don't answer her, running straight through the mystery box and waiting for the carousel of options to flip through in the corner until it lands on bananas.

I immediately drop the fruit in her path, and it's only a few seconds later that Mya–aka Yoshi–slips, and I catch her spinning in circles in my periphery.

"Hey, rude!" She spares me a glance, sticking her tongue out and refocusing on the screen as Yoshi straightens out. "I was thinking..." I block out the bottom half of the screen, focusing on Luigi. She hits pause, and the game freezes. She turns toward me and sighs. "I hate to admit it, but I had some fun today."

"Because you enjoy frustrating me?" I hit *play* and take off down the rainbow track again. Mya focuses in the nick of time to keep her from flying into the sky again.

"And it was better than you running away after I kissed you."

Fuck. She's still thinking about that kiss? I was hoping she erased it from her memory like I've been trying to do all damn week. I glance at her just long enough on the curve for Luigi to fly over the edge with the finish line in sight.

I don't say anything, because what the fuck do I say to that? I press forward as soon as Luigi is steady on the road. I'm not too far behind because in my silence, Mya got eaten by a Chain Chomp. Recovered, she unlocks a mystery box–a Spiny Shell–and fires it. *Damn.* It finds me quickly, and I spin out.

"Ha!" she yells, tilting her body again, along with the joystick, as the road turns. "Anyway, I don't want to concede, but I think despite us nearly dying from nuts and our obvious irritation at therapy, we'd probably both agree your date was more enjoyable."

What I refuse to admit aloud is that I did have some fun on her date, but the majority of today has been *good*, and I can't remember the last time I thought that. I regain my place on the road and take off. "So I win," I tell her, coincidentally right as I cross the finish line a few cart lengths ahead of her. She cruises over the line as the winner screen flashes and turns toward me. "I hate this."

"Sorry." I shrug. Scrolling through the options, I select "Frappe Snowland." "But a deal is a deal."

"Okay, then can I at least contribute any money I make from my new business?"

Dammit. I groan, sinking my head against the back of the couch. I managed to forget about that. I was hoping she forgot too. "You're *that* set on it?"

She nods, twisting on the floor to face me. "I am."

I go to press *start* but set the controller on the coffee table and grab my beer instead. "And you actually want me to help you?"

"I mean... I think you might have good ideas or push me when I need it. Plus, I think it would be nice for you to understand that..."

"Understand what?" I search her eyes.

"It's just that you seem bothered by the fact that you were the catalyst of my breakup–enough to let me move in. I think it would be cool if you could see that sometimes the things we're taught are bad, could actually be good. You aren't the villain you think you are."

I guess I do feel that way. I scan through my conversation with my mom and our session with the therapist. Reframing my mindset is probably the start of the path to moving past all this shit I've struggled with since Ruby.

"Plus," she adds. "We might make a great team, and this is how we figure it out. Like Nicole Scherzinger suggesting the 1D boys work together." I give her a pointed look, and she waves her hand like she realized she's speaking a foreign language to me. "Never mind. Please?" Her puppy dog eyes send me over the edge to insanity.

"Fine." My hand reaches for hers in concession before my mind can put up a fight.

She stares blankly at it. "Really?"

I nod. "On a trial basis."

"Okay. Okay." She shakes my hand with a burst of excitement. "Yay! This is going to be fun."

"If you say so." I drop her hand, the warmth leaving me immediately.

"Thank you." She grins wider, reaching for her controller.

"Yeah, don't mention it." I pick mine up and settle back into the couch. "Do you even have a plan?"

"I don't need things to be premeditated."

"Uhh." Just like that, I'm bothered by the idea again. "You're not a murderer. You have such a drink-out-of-the-hose mindset."

She scrunches her face. "What does that mean?"

"You do reckless things and don't think twice about it." I take another sip of my beer, then set it on the coffee table.

"You act like that's a bad thing. I never once got sick from drinking from a hose, thank you very much." She beams like she's proud of it. "But anyway, I do have my next job."

I raise my brow, already regretting my decision. How am I going to manage this without any sort of plans? "Already?"

"I'll get some water from the filtered tap, then fill you in." She smirks.

This fucking girl. I can't wait to see what her version of a plan is. "Yeah, alright."

She twists her body, resting her elbow on the couch cushion and her chin in her palm. "Sooooo, we can put the earnings toward rent?"

"Sure," I say, mainly to get back to the game.

She shifts her chin on her fist, apparently just joking about the water. "And let me pay utilities."

"Fine," I concede because I don't want to put up more of a fight. "But that's it."

"Okay, enough talking for today," she says, surprising me as she hits the start button. "Let's just play."

I opt to not press her about her first job in favor of relaxing. We play all sixteen tracks before Mya is ready to call it quits. "Okay, I think I've hit my video game limit." She rests the controller on the coffee table. "Are you hungry?"

I stare at the three empty beer cans at the end of the table. Realizing I've only had alcohol and nuts since breakfast, my stomach growls. "Starving."

She stands. "What do you want? I don't think we have much, and I'm too lazy to cook."

Damn. I meant to go to the store today after therapy, and now she's going to suggest we go out.

"How about this?" She slips her fanny pack from the stool and snaps it around her waist. "I'll walk down to Little Conejo and bring us back dinner."

I stand, more relieved than I should be that she doesn't want to go on an adventure for food, and I'm surprised by my willingness to join her. "I'll come with you."

She shakes her head, grabbing her jacket from a hook in the entryway. "I saw you eyeballing *Call of Duty* when you pulled out *Mario Kart*. Why don't you play while I get food?"

"You sure? It'll be dark soon."

Unzipping her bag, she pulls out a purple rectangle. "Taser. I'll be fine. I promise."

"Alright." I walk to where my wallet sits in the leather bowl on the counter. Opening it, I pull out a couple of twenties.

She shoos me away with a flick of her hand. "I got it."

I don't fight her as she leaves. Instead, I switch to my PlayStation and pop in *Call of Duty*. I have the older version because I don't play often, but it only takes a few minutes to be reminded of how calming it is.

Most of this day has been a stress relief, especially tonight. Going out to dinner with Ruby every night, I'd come home feeling overstimulated. I'd need to relax after, but it was never something we did together–or even in the same vicinity. We'd both either work after-hours on projects, read or watch a movie–but almost always in separate rooms. If I was working at my computer, she'd take her book to the living room, claiming she couldn't focus with the click of the keys. If I sat on the couch and turned on a video game or a hacker-related channel on YouTube, she'd go to our room because "it's more comfortable." The only activity we consistently did together was snowboarding, and that's not exactly a quality-time hobby. Looking back, I'm now starting to piece this all together, and I feel like a fucking moron for not seeing we were drifting apart–hell, maybe we were never even really a match. I didn't realize until it occurred to me how comfortable it is just existing with someone else in my space.

As I toggle through the menu of *MW2*, I wonder if Mya will try to find a separate space after dinner–if she's ready for a break after being around me all day. Not that Mya is comparable to Ruby because we aren't dating, but there's a small part of me that just needs to know it's not me driving women away.

Forty-five minutes later, Mya returns with a bag full of food. I greet her without pausing the game, wanting to get through this mission. She organizes dinner on the coffee table, making sure to not block the space between me and the TV. I glance over quickly, realizing I never told her what I wanted.

To my surprise, my favorite torta sits in front of me. "How did you know what to get me?"

"Would you believe me if I told you that I'm magic? Or a mind-reader?"

I pause my game, raising a brow at her.

"Fine." She chuckles. "Rocco told me."

"Are you on a first-name basis with the bartender now?"

"Oh, we're friends. We bonded over our favorite grump." She grins before biting into her sandwich, and I can't help but smirk as I reach for mine.

I sink my teeth into the soft bread and through the juicy meat, coated in a spicy avocado spread. Fuck, it's good.

We finish eating in silence, both of us hungry from not eating all day. When we're done, I help Mya clear the table before picking up the controller again.

"Hey." I move my gaze toward her voice before hitting *play*. "Would it be okay if I go into your room? I won't mess anything up," she hurries to add, but my stomach has already dropped at the request.

"Yeah." I push *play* on the game to avoid revealing how disappointed I am about her wanting our day to be over. Stop being a moron, Kace. You're roommates, and she has better things to do than watch you play video games.

"Thank you." She skips in front of me, quickly passing across the screen, and digs through a box that's pushed against the window. I will myself to not watch what she's doing, focusing on killing the guy in front of me. As I bob my head around her to not miss my shot, she slips past me again, and I can feel her energy leaving the room. My shoulders sag, and my avatar barely avoids an attack. I scowl and give the screen my full attention.

I do a double take when she comes out only a few minutes later and plops down in the gap between the couch and the floor-to-ceiling windows covered by the blackout shades. She must feel me staring because she glances up. "What?"

"Nothing." I shake my head, thankful that I'm still alive when I get back to the game.

"I wanted to make sure I liked the sparkle of this suncatcher paper," she says, holding up a clear sheet that draws my attention. "It's easier to hold it against your window since the shade isn't down and the sun sets on that side."

"Oh," I say, not knowing how else to respond.

She stares at the TV long enough that it forces my gaze back to my game, and she starts fidgeting off to the side.

The rain dripping from the roof and balcony railings blends with the gunshots of my game and becomes a faint sound-track of the night. At one point, it's interrupted by the sound of a printer, and I glance over long enough to see a thin white device grazing a needle over the black paper feeding into it. Apparently it's cutting.

Mya stays focused, constantly moving in my periphery for the next two hours that I play. I haven't played video games this long in one sitting since I was a teenager, but this form of coexisting is comforting.

"All done," she announces, and I exit out of the game. "Oh. You don't have to stop playing."

"It's alright. I'm done for today. My eyes hurt." I set down the controller and press the heel of my hands to my eyes.

"Mine too. I was going nearly cross-eyed trying to weed these tiny little letters."

What the hell is she talking about? "What did you make?"

"You really want to see?" Hope flashes in her eyes in a way that makes me feel like it's been a while since someone asked to see her art.

I give her my full attention. "Yeah."

She sits next to me on the couch, a stack of decorated clear paper in her lap. She holds the top one up, and I now see the sticker is cut into a circle, but instead of being fully clear it has a crystal rainbow stained glass effect. On top it says,

"Let your glimmers guide you." She holds it up toward the living room ceiling light. "It's kind of hard to see." She tilts it back and forth, trying to catch the light. "But it's a window cling. You stick it on your window and when the light filters through, it streams rainbows into your room. It's pretty."

My eyes meet hers. "It is."

She beams, holding up the next one. This one says, "Without cracks, there would be nowhere for the light to shine through." She tracks my eyes as they read, then sets it on the coffee table and reaches for the next one. "Live so brightly that it doesn't matter if the sun isn't shining." When my eyes shift from the inspirational words to her, she stacks the rest of the pile on top of the ones on the table. "The rest of these are repeats."

"Those are amazing, Mya."

"Yeah?" Her face lights at the validation, but I can tell she's already proud of them. She knows her work is impressive, and I can't deny it's an attractive quality. "I thought it would be a fun project. Between the sunlight sparkles and the quotes, it'll be a little reminder through people's day that magic exists because you decide it does."

I open my mouth to speak, but nothing comes out. How do I even respond to her when I can't figure out how she exists? She seems to be *all good*, despite her chaos. And yet, what Matt said nags at the back of my mind. She must be too good to be true. Why else would her relationships never work out? "Everyone will love them," I say, and it's enough for her smile to make another appearance. It's pretty, happy and a little tired.

"Thank you." She pauses, pulling her fists into the sleeves of her crewneck. "I was thinking about going to bed after I clean up. But you can totally stay up and play longer. I can sleep on the floor."

I chuckle. "No sleeping on the floor. I should get to bed anyway." Standing, I tuck the controller into the drawer of the entertainment center below my TV. "Goodnight."

As I reach my bedroom door, Mya says, "Thank you for such a good night. It's one of the best I've had in a while."

I glance over my shoulder and nod. "Me too," I say before disappearing into my bedroom and closing off every guilty thought about her sleeping on the couch.

Chapter Seventeen

Mya

"I used to ride my bike along the Willamette River growing up in Eugene. It's beautiful and leads to here, but it's nothing like this," I tell Kace as we lean against the railing overlooking the Columbia River.

The I-5 bridge is to the left, taking cars to Portland on the other side of the two-thirds-of-a-mile-wide river. My favorite part of the view is the strip of motorhomes opposite us, surrounded by trees. It's a clear enough day that I can see them, and I'm thankful for the first signs of spring popping up along the waterfront boardwalk–patches of grass trans-forming from brown to green and the silvery-green stems of Russian sage getting ready to bloom the prettiest indigo flowers.

"How did you end up here?" Kace asks. His forearms rest on the silver bar, and his gaze stays locked on the flowing water below. I spare him a glance, but only for a second, so I don't dwell on how cozy he looks today. He's wearing an olive hoodie under a jean jacket with black jeans that makes me wish I could snuggle into his side. And *my Lanta, his hair*. It's perfectly imperfect, like all he did was run his fingers through the strands, and I'm jealous of his hands.

I internally groan. It's safe to say I have a crush on my roommate. I'm trying hard not to, mainly because he ran away after kissing me. The grumpiness I can get over. The hesitation around relationships I can work with. But the man can't even kiss me without being turned off, and that's where I draw the line. "My sister is two years older than me. When I graduated high school, she had already started her photography business, and it had grown enough that she could afford to pay me as her assistant. I did that for a couple of years. Back then she was doing more family sessions–before she broke into the music industry–so I would help her create aesthetically pleasing sets.

"We came up here for a photography conference, and I fell in love. My parents had a friend who was looking to rent out their basement, so I lived there for about five years while I worked on growing my own business." Kace doesn't respond, so I shoot him another glance to make sure he's still with me–even though I can feel his presence about six inches away. "Sorry, that was more than you bargained for."

He looks over, and his dark eyes contrast so starkly with the sunlight peeking through the clouds and reflecting off the water. "You're brave for taking off on your own like that."

"It's not that big of a deal. It's not like I couldn't have gone home if my life fell apart."

"Don't downplay it," he says.

"Well, you did the same, didn't you?" I cross my fingers, hoping that he'll share something.

His shoulders shrug, and I can't help but watch the way his jacket resettles, open over his sweatshirt. "I guess. But I wasn't alone." He pauses. "Ruby was with me, and she had a job before we got here."

"Oh, wow. I didn't know that."

He arches a brow like he doesn't believe me.

"I swear. I didn't stalk her *that* much." I chew my lip.

He smirks, and it eases my nerves. "We met in grad school–Virginia Tech. Got jobs out of college and worked for two years until she was offered a position at Columbia."

"Whoa. That's a big move. Was it hard for you to leave?"

He refocuses on the river, evading my question.

"Mya?" a woman's soft voice comes from behind us, and we both turn to look at the beautiful brunette, more put together than Blair Waldorf on the steps of the Met.

"Hi, yes. That's me." I smile at my client, Olivia. I reach to shake her hand, feeling underdressed in an oversized Rory Gilmore sweater as a dress with brown boots and my hair half pulled back with a ribbon tied in a bow. "And this is my partner, Kace."

"Oooh," Olivia coos. "Partner partner or business partner?"

"Business," Kace answers all too quickly, reaching out his hand for Olivia's. It's like he can't even entertain the idea of anything more than platonic roommates, and I don't know whether I should take offense or remind myself that he's likely on edge from talking about his ex. "Nice to meet you."

"Should we sit?" I plaster on a smile and gesture toward the stone steps behind us. They're wide enough that they are commonly used for lunch breaks since there aren't any picnic tables at the waterfront park.

Kace and I take the second row from the bottom, his feet firmly planted on the step below, while I curl one leg under me. The cold of the stone sends a chill through my bare legs as Olivia sits on the step below, twisting to face us. "Thank you again for meeting with me. This is pretty time-sensitive."

I check our surroundings. Cute trees frame us on one side, giving privacy. With it being so chilly, the only other person out here is on the far side of the stone steps. "Why don't you explain the situation to Kace," I tell Olivia, hoping he doesn't roll his eyes or say anything insensitive.

"Yeah. My parents set me up with this guy. He's exactly the kind of guy they expect me to marry, but I can tell you after one date, there's not a chance in hell I can survive spending more time with him." She takes a breath, vulnerability in her eyes. I hope she's not worried about Kace judging her because she didn't seem nervous going over the details with me. "My boyfriend doesn't have much patience for the situation."

"Do your parents know you have a boyfriend?" Kace clarifies.

She nods. "I've told them so many times. But I turn thirty later this year, and they refuse to believe anyone who hasn't proposed by this age is a serious contender. So they set me up with the son of one of their friends from the golf club. Besides the fact that I'm not interested, the guy is as boring as the sport itself. He even hates *Happy Gilmore* because, according to him, 'It disrespects the sanctity of golf.'"

"Red flag," Kace agrees. "Can't you tell your parents to fuck off?"

She worries her lip and shakes her head. "They're getting older. They had me right before they turned forty, so I know they're just worried about me. They want to make sure I'm taken care of. I can only fault them so much for that. My boyfriend and I have talked about getting married, but we've only been together for a year. I don't want him to feel pressured, so I was hoping you could help me convince this guy that we aren't a good fit so he calls the whole thing off."

"Did you try telling *him* you have a boyfriend?" Kace asks, and I can tell that he thinks everything should be cut and dry, that problems are simple to avoid. He sees the world in black and white, whereas I see it in tie-dye.

I frown, wondering if that's exactly why he didn't see his own break up coming, and I hate that for him. Hate that he got hurt. Hate that he's still not seeing the point of all this. "It's not that straightforward," I cut in for Olivia, sensing how overwhelmed she is by the situation. "Her boyfriend is upset, and this other dude straight-up didn't believe her."

"Imagine Barney, from *How I Met Your Mother*. Completely delusional and couldn't possibly fathom why any girl wouldn't want to be with him unless they just couldn't handle so much of him.'"

"Sounds like a jerk," I say at the same time that Kace says, "Barney is the star of that show."

I turn to glare at him.

"What?" Kace shrugs with so much nonchalance that I want to slap him.

"Stop it," I mutter, knowing Olivia can hear me anyway. I turn back toward her. "Sorry about him. He's Marshall in this situation. Right after Lily abandons their engagement to follow her dreams."

"Oh. I'm sorry," Olivia sympathizes with him. "That's awful."

I can feel Kace's eyes shooting daggers in my direction, but I don't care. I'm here to help my client, and he's making it freaking hard. "That's part of why Kace wants to help out," I fib, trying to get us back on track. "He doesn't want anyone to suffer in a relationship they shouldn't be in." I glance his way expecting to be met with another glare or objection, but it looks more like realization hitting. *Maybe it wasn't a lie.* "We'll get this figured out, I promise." Olivia manages a half-smile. "I have one idea, but it's a little crazy."

Kace chuckles. "Your ideas are always crazy." This time when he speaks it doesn't feel like judgment. It almost seems endearing, and it throws me off for a few seconds. This man is starting to give me whiplash.

Shaking my head to clear my mind, I continue. "I think we should Andie Anderson him."

Olivia's eyes light up. "Oh my gosh. YES. Can we?!"

"Why not?" I shrug with a grin.

"What the hell is 'Andie Anderson-ing' someone, and why is a person a verb?"

Olivia and I laugh, and I clue him in. "It's from the movie *How to Lose a Guy in 10 Days*. Basically you become so annoying that the person can't stand it and breaks up with you."

Kace stares. But this time, I feel like I can read his mind. It's saying, *Wow, how mature,* with full-fledged sarcasm. Instead of confirming my thoughts, he says, "What kind of things?"

I focus on Olivia. "You're hanging out with him tonight, right?"

"Yeah, at a charity auction," she confirms.

"Here's what I'm thinking... Don't do one big thing. Because everyone thinks they can fix one problem."

"Fuck, is that true," Kace mutters under his breath, and for some reason, it makes me smile.

"Start by showing up late. Not fashionably late either. Like after dinner is served so he has to wait to eat." I picture the guy–if he's a gentleman at all–sitting around a fancy round table with no food on the china plate in front of him while everyone else eats.

"And when you get there, complain about what he's wearing," Kace chimes in, and I'm shocked by his helpful idea–and that he is contributing at all.

"He's going to look like Nate Archibald at his worst–so that won't be hard." Olivia laughs.

I marvel at the fact that she and I are on the same *Gossip Girl* wavelength. "Then when the server comes to bring your food, tell them you're not hungry."

"There is nothing more annoying than a girl who won't eat on a dinner date," Kace mutters, more to himself.

I shake my head, wanting to pull out my Blow Pop at the thought of food. "Yeah. Couldn't be me."

"Me either," Olivia agrees. "I'll have to eat before."

"OH! And then while he's eating, pull out a stick of gum," I suggest.

"That's *good*," she adds.

"Chew your gum obnoxiously too." Kace draws our attention to him.

"Yes, think Violet Beauregarde chomping away as she talks." I laugh, picturing her chewing as she turns into a blueberry. I can imagine him giving her a disgusted side-eye.

"Be rude to your server," Kace adds, and Olivia makes a note on her phone.

"Ugh. Yes," she says. "Nothing is more of a red flag than that."

"You should also interrupt him whenever he's talking," I suggest. "So inconsiderate."

"Especially when he's talking about himself," Kace adds. "And don't ask a single thing about him." I'm shocked by that suggestion because it seems contradictory to the times that Kace has appeared annoyed by my questions.

Olivia makes another note. "I think this could work. I'm feeling hopeful just thinking about how annoyed I'd be if I were him."

"I think it will too," I assure her.

"I definitely wouldn't like you at all after that." Kace smirks.

"That doesn't say much," I tease. "You hardly like anyone to begin with."

"Not true." He pauses. "I like you."

My heart palpitates as I study his face. He's so nonchalant that I'm tempted to believe he means the sentiment, and my heart rate clocks in at an all-time high.

"Business partners, my ass," Olivia whispers under her breath.

I slap her playfully. "He didn't mean it like that."

"Uh huh." She grins, focused on me. "Okay, well, I feel great about this. Can I text or call tonight if I need anything?"

"Absolutely. You have my number."

"I really appreciate this, and thank you for meeting me in person. I hate talking on the phone." Olivia stands.

"Unless it's my parents or sister, it's straight to voicemail." I shake my head in amusement. "Can you believe we used to pay for ringtones?"

She laughs. "No. That was insane. We should have just stuck to HitClips."

My smile widens. "Agreed."

"I'll talk to you soon–at least let you know how it goes. Thanks again," Olivia says, and with that, she walks away, leaving Kace and me sitting on the stone steps of the waterfront park as the sun sets to our right.

"That was not at all what I expected," Kace admits, leaning back against the step behind us.

"What did you expect?" I twist my body to face him more, the chill from the evening air making me pull my fists into my sweater sleeves.

"I don't know. Seems like Olivia wouldn't have gotten along with this dude in the first place. Time would have revealed that without an obnoxious game plan."

I pull my arms closer to myself, the chill in the air nipping me more than usual. "She doesn't have that time considering she has a boyfriend."

"Yeah," Kace says.

"I'm so glad my parents don't meddle." It's meant as more of a fleeting thought than part of the conversation, so I'm surprised when Kace tacks on a, "Me too."

"Are your parents in your life?" I hope his earlier comment about showing interest in someone also applies to him.

He hesitates like his answer is top secret information but then sighs. "Supposedly they're turning over a new leaf and are interested in being more involved now. But they've always let me make my own decisions."

I want to pry, but my heart thumps in my chest in discouragement. I want to get to know him, but he doesn't seem interested in me that way, and the closer we get, the harder it'll be to truly accept that. "When do you think we become qualified to make our own decisions?"

He leans forward and rests his forearms on his knees, staring out toward the river. "I'm not sure if it's a *when* so much as preparation. Research. Planning ahead. Being sure about someone before committing."

I hum, unsure if I agree.

He glances at me. "What?"

"It's just… What about trial and error? Don't you think that sometimes learning from experience is necessary? When we're young, we only have skewed frames of reference from our parents and our own lack of experience. And we all know Google is the wrong place to go for advice but rely on it anyway. You know," I digress. "If I was Lou, from *Hot Tub Time Machine*, I would have gone back and done a lot more than change the search engine's name to Lougle. I would have programmed it to prioritize only facts."

Kace chuckles. "You'd have to learn how to program first."

"Hey, I used to be able to code my Myspace backgrounds. I couldn't tell you how, and I definitely couldn't do it today, but still."

"I'm sure you could figure it out again." His eyes scan my body. "Are you cold?"

"I'm okay," I say, willing myself not to shiver. "I'd get you to program, then add in fun designs and a positive affirmation every time someone opens the site."

He smirks, licking his lip, and I give myself a gold star for amusing him. Tugging his jacket off, he tosses it over my bare legs.

"Thank you." I flash him a smile.

"I still think you're overthinking it. It's a step-by-step process."

Consider my curiosity piqued. "What do you mean?"

"You're friends with someone first. So you learn about all those things that would bother you if you were in a relationship with them. *Then* you date them. I bet it would prevent so many breakups."

"We've already been over this though. Before people get comfortable with someone, they have their guard up–they are afraid to be one hundred percent themselves."

He shrugs. "If you go into everything only expecting friendship and you take the time to get to know them, then in theory you'd be yourself."

"But," I argue. "Despite anything else, when you live with people they're different. It's a fact. There are habits and quirks everyone has that aren't evident until you're in their space all the time for all their routines and behind-the-scenes parts of their day."

"So what's your solution? Move in with everyone as soon as you're interested in them to see if they're *the one*?"

That's the second time he's suggested something oddly specific, but it's likely a coincidence. "It's an easy way to find out," I admit shyly. He scoffs. "What?"

"I don't know, Mya." He tenses beside me. "You tell me. You're the one who apparently moves in with people just to see if you should be with them."

I throw my arms up. Okay. Maybe he was specifically talking about me. How the heck did he know that? "It's not like it was a planned test, Kace! I liked them. I *wanted* to live with them."

"How many guys are 'them?'" He glares, and I wonder why he cares so much. Probably because if I had my own place, I wouldn't be in his space.

"Only three," I mutter.

"Ha." He shakes his head, and all of a sudden I feel small. "This isn't something you just decide and hope for the best. Relationships are supposed to be taken seriously."

"I do take them seriously!" I clench my fists inside my sleeves.

"Did you make bets with them too?" His slumped shoulders, furrowed brows and bite in his tone make it unclear whether he's mad, hurt or disgusted by me.

"Kace, no. Stop judging me. You're the one who asked ME to move in, remember?!"

"Knowing you, you probably masterminded that plan somehow."

Screw him, accusing me of the same thing Matt did. Any chill I had immediately disappears with my now boiling blood. I stand, ready to leave, barely catching his jacket before it slips from my lap. "You don't even know me, Kace!" I stand, throwing it at his face as I walk away.

Considering we are going to the same place, he stomps after me, and I catch him grabbing his jacket in my periphery. "Why does it even matter when we aren't in a relationship?!" he calls after me.

I stop so abruptly he crashes into me when I turn around. His hands fly to my elbows on instinct, steadying both of us. We stay frozen, park-goer voices and rustling leaves growing distant as we stare at each other. Hating this fight, I hold eye contact. "You're right. It doesn't matter," I snap. I consider threatening to leave but don't have the energy to be met with the rejection of him not begging me to say.

He takes a deep breath and drops his hold on me. "Let's just go home."

Chapter Eighteen

Kace

Quietly pushing open the door to my apartment, my senses are hit with the smell of bread and butter. "Oh, hey," I greet Mya as the kitchen comes into view. I'm surprised she's awake. "You're up early."

She spins in her fuzzy sock-covered feet to face me, in nothing else but an oversized tee, and for my sake I'm pretending she has shorts on under it. "I couldn't sleep. I thought I'd make you breakfast for after your workout."

She turns back to the stove, and I move behind her, looking over her shoulder. "What are you making?"

"Eggs in a frame," she tells me, cracking an egg into a circular cut out of a buttered slice of toast.

I scrunch my brows. "That's not what that is."

After cracking another egg into a second piece of toast, she faces me again, her brows furrowed. "What is it then?"

"Toad in a hole."

She chuckles. "That doesn't even make sense."

I shrug. "Doesn't matter. That's what it's called."

"Agree to disagree." She grins. "What matters more is if you like it."

"It's bread, butter and eggs. What's not to like?"

"Exactly." Using a spatula, she flips both of the slices of bread to crisp the other side. "I'm hoping to butter you up. Get it?" She laughs at her own joke.

I shake my head, amused. I'm still not feeling great after our disagreement yesterday, but I'm trying really fucking hard not to let my internal rage make an appearance in the real world. It doesn't do anyone any fucking good. "What do you need?"

"I was wondering if you're free after work? There's something I want to take you to do." She slides the two slices of perfectly golden Toad in a Hole onto a plate and hands it to me.

I take it from her and move to the breakfast bar. "Thank you. What do you want to do?"

"You'll feel better if you know, huh?" She uses the lip of a glass to cut out a hole in two new pieces of bread.

Maybe she is paying attention more than I give her credit for. "Yeah." I cut into my breakfast with a fork, the yolk oozing out. *Damn, she cooked this perfectly.*

"I want to go to a smash room. Have you been?"

I finish my bite. "A what?"

She places the toast in the pan and reaches for an egg from the carton beside her. "A smash room. It's basically what it sounds like. A room where you smash things. I read this article about how it can provide a short-term outlet for anger." I pause my chewing to stare at her, not knowing if I should be offended. Her demeanor immediately shifts to insecurity. "I was thinking... I don't know. Maybe it's dumb. I thought it might help you release some tension."

I waffle over the idea. I'm sure this isn't a great long-term solution. It seems it would encourage aggression as a coping mechanism. But as a one-time thing? I could see how it might be beneficial. "Alright." I direct my gaze back to my breakfast and dive in for another bite.

"Yeah?!" I might not be looking at her, but I can sense her excitement.

"Sure. I can probably be done with my work by four today."

She claps her hands, and it's fucking cute. "Perfect. I'll make a reservation."

A reservation? My eyes widen, tempted to be impressed. "Have you ever made a reservation before?" I arch a brow.

"Shut up." She rolls her eyes. "I'm doing this for you." She flips her breakfast in the pan.

"Hey." I wait until she looks up. "Thank you." Surprises have always been such a deterrent for me, but this reservation gives me time to be excited about another method of stress relief besides my workouts, and it's refreshing.

She gives me a half-smile. "You're welcome."

Pulling on the metal handle of the warehouse door, I hold it open for Mya to walk through before me. I hate Portland enough as it is, and we're in one of the more sketchy parts of town. Considering the giant black business sign says "Rage Room" with a glowing blood red light behind it, it feels appropriate.

Once the door closes behind us, we both scan the space and approach the check-in desk. A woman around our age greets us, looking terrifyingly similar to Kim Possible.

"We're here to check in," Mya says, peppy as ever. "It should be under Mya Holloway."

"Yes, perfect. I've got you right here," the woman says. "Have either of you been here before?"

"Nope!" Mya answers for both of us.

"Alright, let's go over the rules then." She reaches behind her to a shelf with stacked bundles of white fabric. "Here are your jumpsuits. You'll have to wear them the entire time you're in there." Mya and I each take one from her. Next, she hands us each a clear plastic face shield. "Please wear these whenever anything is being smashed. We have a camera in the room to make sure you're being safe." She nods toward a screen that's divided into six boxes, each with a view of a different room.

She goes over a few other rules which mostly consist of different versions of, "Be smart, be careful, don't hurt anyone, and be aware of your surroundings."

"Here's the waiver." She hands each of us a single-sided form that looks more like a contract. Mya takes her copy and signs it without reading a single line. I stare blankly at her. *This girl.*

She must feel my gaze because she glances up once she draws a heart connected to the swoop of the "y" in her last name. "What?"

"You're not going to read that?"

"Nope." She shrugs. "She went over the rules with us."

"Why do I get the feeling you don't read any fine print?"

"It's boring and usually confusing. I call my dad if I think it's important and have him translate for me. That's what dads are for." She grins, and I feel a twinge of jealousy over the relationship she seems to have with her parents. I can't remember the last time I asked my parents for help with anything. I took AP math and science classes in high school, and to them it might as well have been a foreign language. When I got accepted to James Madison University in Virginia–which meant leaving home for the first time–I didn't feel like I could ask them for help. I applied to scholarships and grants daily until my eyes would burn from staring at the computer screen. Ever since, I've only relied on myself.

I hold my gaze on her until she nods toward my paper. "You going to sign that or what?"

Glancing at the waiver, I start at the first line, reading the entire thing. She doesn't tease me, but it takes longer than it typically would with her eyes on me the entire time. I scribble my signature and hand it over.

"Thank you," the woman says, slipping both forms onto a neat stack on the corner of the check-in desk. "Last thing. What music would you guys prefer?"

Mya looks at me. "You choose."

I shuffle through my favorite rage music in my mind. "Suicide Silence?"

The woman looks at Mya for confirmation. She gives a pointed nod with a grin. "You heard the man."

She queues up a playlist, and we thank her before following her directions to our room. This warehouse looks like it's been divided into the six rooms by makeshift walls. They look stable enough, but they don't extend all the way to the vaulted ceilings. I can hear muffled music overlapping each other in the connected rooms. I can barely make out a weapon smashing into glass over the sound of an Ed Sheeran breakup song in the space next to ours.

Closing the door behind us, I take in the space. Fluorescent lights hang from the high beams, illuminating the rooms and the piping above us. The room is fairly small–the size of my living room maybe. Along the back wall, there's a trough full of broken glass and technology. A metal pole sticks up from the middle of the floor, with a platform soldered to it that's just big enough to hold a glass bottle–designed to hit it like a baseball off of a T-ball stand.

On the floor to the right of the stand is a TV monitor. It's at least a fifty-five inch screen. To the left is an old school computer tower, and on the wall behind us is one bucket full of glasses and another full of tools–an ax, a baseball bat, a crowbar and a mallet. The walls were originally painted black, but it's chipping away in the places not covered by graffiti. None of it is done by a professional, so it's mostly overlapping images and words that are hard to make out. They must let people bring spray paint in here.

Mya finishes taking in the room around the same time I do. She unfolds the plain white jumpsuit, unzipping it and stepping inside the nylon outfit. I do the same, and reach for my face shield. Anticipation thrums inside my chest.

Mya tugs her own shield in place, the band secured around the back of her head, leaving her blonde waves the only part of her exposed. "I feel like Dexter about to do a blood spatter analysis."

I chuckle. "You're much cuter than Dexter." She beams at the compliment, but right as she's about to respond, the intro to "You Only Live Once" blares over the speakers.

"Ladies first!" I yell over the deathcore and gesture toward the weapons bucket. Mya takes a look and pulls the metal bat from where it's wedged between the mallet and the crowbar. She picks a glass bottle from the bucket next to it and places it on the stand. Glancing over her shoulder, she makes sure I'm out of striking range, then steps up to the tee like she's actually playing baseball.

Without any more leadup, she swings. The bat smashes into the glass, and it all happens too quickly to tell if it shatters on collision with the bat or the wall above the trough. Fragments of glass splinter against the wood and clank against the broken bottles from the previous groups.

Mya glances at me, the biggest smile on her face. I can't help but crack a grin. "Did you see that?!" she screams over the music, like there was any chance I *didn't* see.

"Yeah, you crushed it," I yell back.

She grins wider at the double meaning, and I love how easy she is to please. The smallest words and gestures bring her joy, and while it makes it easy to keep things peaceful between us, it could also be a dangerous line to tread.

"It felt so good. Like an adult version of Kick the Can."

I grin at the throwback.

"Your turn," she adds, stepping to the back corner of the room and motioning to the bucket of weapons.

Chapter Nineteen

What a rush. I eye the computer tower in front of me. I can't wait until we start smashing technology. I'm not one for violence, but when I saw a review online about how someone felt like their negative energy was transferred straight from their body to whatever they were smashing, I wanted to try it myself.

I use the book *The Energy Bus* as my bible, and for the most part, it helps me keep energy vampires at bay. Though I do think this could help the extra frustrations I've felt lately, I think Kace needs this even more. I know he works out daily, but since we met, I feel like his tension and bad vibes have been compounding inside him. If this doesn't work, I am not opposed to getting him a Pez dispenser filled with Xanax.

He glances into the weapons bucket, his eyes scanning the options before he reaches for the crowbar. Turning toward the next bucket, he plucks out a bottle and sets it on the tee.

There was something so thrilling about the way smashing glass to smithereens vibrates through the bat and your body–something so satisfying about hearing and watching it shatter in a way it can never recover from. Normally it would be upsetting to see anything break, especially to the point of not being able to fix it. But, when the point *is* to break it, it soothes my recent anxiety.

I wonder if I'll feel this way when I get more into my business. I felt a similar thrill when Olivia texted me after her event last night, gushing about the success of our plan. This music on the other hand... I'm not sure if it's just a far cry from what I listen to or a cry for help. Either way, it's *angry*.

Chills shoot down my spine as Kace smashes his glass so hard that the crowbar seems to go straight through the target for a moment before it flies toward the wall. Even over the beat of the music, the intensity of his hit sends a vibration through the tee, the floor and *me*.

He flashes his gaze my way to let me know it's my turn, and I swear his eyes are red. God, I hope this helps him not be so uptight all the time. I take my turn, smashing another glass. He does the same. We alternate back and forth, picking up speed as we cycle through our props. The playlist provides a steady intensity that Kace continues to match.

When the bucket is empty, I turn to Kace.

"Ready for the finale?" he asks.

I nod. "Yes, sir."

He stares a beat, his eyes darkening. "Don't call me that."

Staring back, I debate my retort. If I don't put myself out there, I might never get a chance. He's told me we won't ever date and rejected my kiss, *but* he's also made it clear that he thinks I'm cute, so maybe I should make my thoughts clear too. "I would have said, 'Yes, Daddy,' but that seems inappropriate for someone I would sleep with." Kace's eyes widen, and my every muscle tenses with his shock. I roll my lips together, giving me a second to decide on my reaction. I shrug. "I blame the adrenaline for that outburst."

"Uh huh." He smirks. The way the words flow from his lips, I'm convinced he's feeling a little lighter–or at the very least, let that confession slide. He holds his crowbar to me, offering a trade. I hand over the bat, and after he makes sure I'm out of the way, he proves me wrong.

He must be feeling *anything* but lighter as he swings the bat, smashing it straight down on top of the standing TV. It's so sturdy that it hardly dents, and the effect of that is clearly seen in the way Kace curses, shaking out his shoulders. I expect him to take a break, but he takes another swing. This time, instead of striking down, he swings like he'd hit a baseball, directly at the screen. A crater forms at the point of contact like it was struck by an asteroid, and the glass splinters like a spiderweb in every direction.

Watching his frustration loosen feels like an invasion of privacy. He's too in the zone to notice my staring, but in case he does, I give him space. Firmly gripping the crowbar, I swing it at the computer tower. The outer layer of plastic cracks, a few pieces flying in erratic directions. *Oh my Lanta*, this is satisfying.

I take another swing, my elbows jolting when the crowbar gets wedged perfectly in the CD slot. An electric shock pain shoots through me like when I hit my funny bone. Despite my tingly hands, I yank on my weapon, tugging it loose. Shaking out my arms, I wait until the pain subsides and strike again. After a few more hits, the casing of the tower is completely destroyed, revealing the inner workings of the computer. Without its protective skin, the bits and pieces of the brain splinter off at an alarming rate, green and gray metal breaking off in chunks.

Out of breath, and already sore from such a different type of workout, I shake my muscles out and refocus on Kace, where his TV hardly resembles one anymore. He glances up and surveys my space. "You done?" he yells, and it feels louder because it hits right as a song ends.

"Yeah, but we have a few more minutes. You don't have to stop."

He shakes his head. "I'm good."

The next song starts, a harsh voice filling the air, hardly understandable paired with the guitar and drums. I meet him in front of the weapons bucket, dropping the crowbar into the orange plastic.

Kace glances just quickly enough to line up his bat with the bucket, and then brings his gaze to me as he drops it. He steps closer, invading my space. My heart pounds against my chest, and I'm not sure if it's the thrill of the smash room, the vibration of the music, or my proximity to Kace.

I take off my face shield, my hand accidentally brushing against his jumpsuit-covered stomach. My heart rate doubles as he pulls his own shield off, never once taking his eyes off me.

"Thank you," he says. His eyes flash to my lips. It's unmistakable, and my stomach flips.

I inch forward on pure adrenaline and lust, close enough to feel his warm breath on my face. "You're welcome," I whisper. There's no way he heard it over the music, but I can hardly breathe as it is.

The music pulses through my veins, a tingle flickering across my skin as my thoughts take off in a million directions before they focus on one. All I can see is Kat Stratford and Patrick Verona in a paintball war, tumbling over–him brushing paint off her cheek before kissing her. *I want Kace to kiss me like that.*

He stares at me with an intensity that almost feels uncomfortable, pupils surrounded by black speckles mixed into a deep whiskey color that feels like they're casting a permanent mark on my soul.

I lean in, ninety percent, waiting for him to commit to the other ten, like Will Smith says.

But he doesn't touch my face.

And he doesn't kiss me.

Instead, he clears his throat. "Our time is probably up." My shoulders slack with frustration, and I swear he looks guilty. But it doesn't matter. Whether he feels guilty or not, the rejection stings as bad as the first time.

"Yeah." I nod. "It probably is."

Chapter Twenty

Kace

Adjusting my black tie, I take a look in the mirror hanging on the back of my door. This suit isn't anything special–a traditional black suit I've used for business meetings or work events. I've never worn it to a wedding though. I've never even been to a wedding.

Most of Ruby's friends were either already married or focused on their careers. My acquaintances are the forever single nerd type or already settled down.

For a while, I thought the first wedding I attended would be my own, but here I am, going to the wedding of a complete stranger–considering Mya met with the client while I was working. Although it is our job to break up the wedding, so I suppose this doesn't even fucking count.

God, this job is absurd. I've never heard of something so immature in my life–not that I've heard all the details. This entire week has been tense, ever since Mya and I argued on the waterfront. And then there was the rage room. All the tension I released during those twenty minutes came rushing back the second Mya invaded my space, practically begging me to kiss her. And fuck, did I *want* to. But I didn't. Choosing lust over logic would have ended badly.

I thought maybe after telling Mya in therapy that I do better with plans, that she would at least do a bare minimum outline for me. Yes, she made a reservation for the smash room, but I've gotten next to no information on this wedding. It made me contemplate backing out of this whole stupid arrangement, but hell if I'm going to let her go off with strangers, especially with the outburst she'll be participating in today.

I leave my room to check on Mya. If we don't get going soon, we'll be late. I know we'll sneak in the back, but we can't exactly follow through if we show up after the ceremony. I tap my knuckles against the bathroom door. "You almost ready?"

The door clicks open, and Mya steps out, smoothing her hands over the front of her dress. My heart rate skyrockets, and I struggle to keep my breathing steady. Jesus fuck, she's sexy. Her dress is hot pink. Thin straps lead to a lace top that cuts between her breasts that have never been on display like this. The bottom part flares out with a sheer mesh fabric over a layer of silk that lands above her knees.

The urge to thread my fingers through her short, soft curls and push her against the wall has my hands twitching at my side. I shove them in the pockets of my suit instead.

"Do I look okay?" she asks, with a half-nervous smile. She twirls in a circle, the edge of her dress fluttering, and by the time she's facing me, there's a grin on her face.

"Isn't it bad wedding etiquette to look better than the bride?"

Her grin widens. "You don't know what she looks like."

"I don't need to." I stare for an extra beat. I know it's too long, but I can't fucking help myself.

"Thanks." She reaches to straighten my tie, and I let her, even though I know for a fact it's straight. "You look handsome." She rolls her glossy lips together as she drops her hands and walks past me, her arm brushing against mine. I can't tell if it's intentional or not. I follow her movement where she grabs her fanny pack from the counter.

She digs through it, pulling out a card. "Can you put this in your wallet for me?" She holds out her ID, and I hesitate before I take it from her. Pulling my wallet from my back pocket, I slide her ID in, feeling like I checked off step one to being in a relationship.

Is that something I want?

I mean, eventually.

But right now?

Not until I can trust someone.

Would I ever consider that person to be Mya?

Yes. No. Maybe. Fuck. No. We don't even see eye to eye on the details of relationships.

I clear my throat. "Alright. Let's get going," I tell her, holding my hand out for her to lead the way out the door. She takes the cue, and I watch her for a second, her lean legs looking even longer in her strappy black heels.

"Can we go over the plan?" I ask her, hitting the button to call the elevator.

I glance over my shoulder in time to see her shrug. "There's no plan really. How hard can it be? All I have to do is object. And it's not like I can predict how the crowd will respond anyway. I can't plan for a million scenarios, so I'm just going to go with the flow."

Confirmation that there's no way this would ever work out between us. She *could* plan for at least the most realistic scenarios. She *could* set herself up for a higher probability of success. How can she not see that?

I hope that my silence during the entire walk to the parking garage speaks louder than words, but Mya doesn't seem to take the hint as she climbs into my truck. Our therapist's voice pops into my head, reminding me it might be less frustrating if I meet Mya where she's at.

"Hey," I start as I slide onto the driver's seat.

Settling on the leather, she flicks on the seat warmer, then clicks her belt into place. "Yeah?"

I clear my throat. "I can see why it would feel overwhelming to prepare for a dozen possible outcomes."

"You can?" Surprise is evident in her voice.

"Yeah." I start the truck. "Would it help if we brainstormed a couple of the most likely outcomes?"

She hums, her brows furrowing as she stares at the polish on her fingernails. "Okay." She sighs. "I guess I've been avoiding thinking about it because every outcome that happens in the movies is a big deal with a lot of emotion and all the attention on the person objecting."

"Are you nervous about that?" I take a risk, hoping it doesn't come off judgmental. "I've gotten the impression you don't mind having all eyes on you."

She looks over, chewing her lip as I back out of the parking space. "I don't mind it. It's just... this is a pivotal moment in their life. I know that no matter what I do, they still get to choose what comes next for them, but my decision could alter the course of their life. That's a lot of pressure."

I sink against the leather seat as I stop at the red light and take a breath. My gaze flicks to her before it's back on the road, pressing the gas when the signal turns green. "I'm sorry I didn't put that same thought into my crusade on Valentine's Day." Feeling her stare, I glance over long enough to see her wide eyes before merging onto the freeway. "I was being reckless because I was fucked up and hurting."

Her hand lands on my arm attached to the steering wheel, and the touch sends an immediate warmth through me. "It's okay. It all worked out."

"That doesn't make it okay, but regardless, this is different. You've put thought into this plan. And obviously someone else did too, right?"

"Yeah." She pulls her hand back to her lap. "I mean I don't think the decision was made lightly. Falling out of love is a big deal–*a sad deal*. That's what happened to Allison and Eli, you know?" The bride and groom of today's wedding.

I rub my thumbs against the leather steering wheel cover. "So it's a mutual thing? Why didn't they just call off the wedding?"

"To my understanding, they've never talked about it. Allison's mom overheard the back end of a conversation between Eli and his mom. She was going on about how committing to someone forever changes everything. You're all-in, 'til death do you part, and any hesitancy you have while you're dating someone you love goes away."

"That makes no sense."

"You don't think so?" She doesn't seem to be debating me but rather actually asking my opinion.

"I mean, I wouldn't propose to someone if I wasn't one hundred percent sure."

"Is that why you never asked Ruby to marry you?"

I grind my teeth. My hands tighten their grip around the wheel, my knuckles going white. "No."

She takes the hint, but I feel bad for the edge that takes over at the mention of my ex. "I think when they got engaged, they were still in love. At least they still loved each other. I get the impression they do even now."

"What's the problem then?"

"They've been together for a decade–high school sweethearts. They don't know anyone or anything else. Allison's mom said she's been watching her daughter's connection with him fade the longer they go without connecting to anything else outside of each other.

"Her mom has noticed a change in demeanor lately, music choices, whispering phone calls with a few of her friends. She can tell Allison has been questioning the wedding, and said she could hear the uncertainty in Eli's voice when he was talking to his mom. But he also told her Allison deserved the world and that he'll always love her enough to give her that." She sighs, and in my periphery I see her head fall against the headrest. "The mom thinks they're both on the same page, but neither one of them has the courage to leave what they have behind. Plus, the wedding has been paid for and is non-refundable. She's confident that's part of why Allison hasn't called it off, and she doesn't want her daughter's financial concern to be the main factor in her getting married."

"She can't just talk to her daughter?" I ask Mya, despite thinking about how my parents struggle to talk to me about anything. I remember asking them if they thought moving across the country was the right choice and their response was to do whatever makes me happy.

"Apparently, she tried. Ali brushed her off and refused to talk about it. She also didn't clarify any assumptions her mom made."

"So without you, she'd marry someone she doesn't want to be with forever?" I shake my head as I come to a stop at a light. I can't wrap my head around this shit.

"I think so. You really don't see how hard this is, do you? You've never hesitated to break up with someone? You just do it the exact moment you have the first thought?"

I keep my eyes trained on the road. "I wouldn't know."

"What do you mean? You've never broken up with someone?"

"No." I can feel her gaze on me, waiting for more. "My only other serious relationship was in high school. We both just agreed to break up when we went to different colleges."

"Oh."

I know Matt's version of Mya's dating life–or at least the clipped 'attack a stranger who broke up your Valentine's Day dinner and is likely now fucking your ex-girlfriend' footnotes version–so maybe I should give her a chance to share her side of it. "What about you?"

"What about me?"

"How did you break up with your exes?"

She's silent. I glance over to see her face fallen, and she picks at the hem of her dress, making it slide further up her thighs. I debate asking again, but she eventually responds.

"Umm. The first guy... I told him I needed to move back in with my parents' friends to help them out. He said he didn't want to go backward in our relationship so if I left, then we'd break up."

"Did they actually need your help?"

I catch her shaking her head out of my periphery.

"So you lied?"

"I shouldn't be with someone who wouldn't support me trying to help a friend."

"But they didn't need your help."

"That's not the point, Kace."

I raise an eyebrow.

"Anyway. The guy after him... I didn't have room to work at our place. So I would take my projects to the library."

"You don't have room at my place, but you make it work," I counter.

She sighs. "He didn't want me to work there. He wasn't a bad guy–just not for me. I felt bad, and I probably could have made it work, but at what cost? It felt like the blame should be put on me for not compromising on my home/life balance, so I withdrew until he decided there was no point in us being together if we were never 'together.' That way it was my fault we broke up instead of me blaming him for not caring about my work."

That *almost* makes sense. But it's still a million times more complicated than it needed to be.

"Then Matt. Well, you were there for that."

"And if I hadn't been?"

She visibly cringes. "At this point, I'd probably still be with him."

"What does that mean?" I contemplate telling her about my run-in with her ex, but I can't imagine it going over well.

"I don't want to talk about this anymore. I want to focus on our job," she tells me, and with how many times I've redirected her questions, I can't exactly push–despite my curiosity.

Note to self: don't try to extract reasoning from Mya.

She makes no fucking sense to me. Her logic is weak at best, yet there's some level of good intention. I think. Either way, she doesn't handle serious things well. Or at least, not in any responsible or mature manner. "How did you get this job anyway?"

"Allison's mom is friends with Chloe's mom. Chloe gave her my number, thinking I might be able to help."

"How did you get Olivia's job?"

She doesn't respond right away, and I look over in time to catch her rolling her lips.

"How?" I repeat.

"I don't want you to think girls are any more psycho than you already do," she whispers.

"Just tell me."

"She overheard my conversation with Chloe when we were at that food truck park. She found me through the bar's Instagram when I tagged them."

"Not psycho at all." I shoot her a sideways glance before my eyes are back on the road. I have to admit, women can find out a terrifying amount of information from the internet. They probably make better hackers than men.

She shrugs. "Unhitched fell into my lap. I might as well take advantage of it."

My brows furrow. "Unhitched?"

"Yeah. The name was Chloe's idea because I'm Will Smith in *Hitch*–except in reverse."

Huh. That's pretty clever.

"Anyway..." She adjusts the straps of her dress. "Allison's mom thinks if someone else stands up to object at the ceremony, it can create the tension needed to force the break without making anyone from either side angry at one of them."

"Is this really the best plan she could come up with?"

"I think there are pros and cons of every option that helps them move on, and she believes this one is the best."

"And when they ask why you don't want the couple to get married?"

"I thought about pretending to be in love with one of them, but I don't want to make either person look like a cheater." I'm not sure why that gives me some reassurance about her. "I also thought about being their marriage counselor, but that would be a major invasion of privacy."

I shrug. "I mean you're not *actually* their therapist."

"I know, but what if someone questions that authenticity?" She's talking like she did think this through. Fuck, she's confusing.

"True." I flick on my blinker before turning right toward the waterfront wedding venue. "So what did you land on?"

"Concerned friend who finally stopped biting her tongue."

"Do you really think this is going to work?"

"Confidence is half the battle, Levitt. Have a little faith in me." She grins. "But also, have the getaway car ready."

"Nothing good starts with that." I smirk, pulling into a parking spot in the lot designated for wedding guests.

She reaches for the door handle but pauses, looking over at me with worry flooding her eyes. "This is sad, though. Right?"

I stare back, unsure of the right answer. It's fucked that people settle for a life they don't want, but it's also terrifying that things can just not work out after so long.

"I have so many questions," she whispers, pulling her hand back to her lap. "I wish I knew the answers to them before I did this."

I pull the key from the ignition and turn toward her. "Like what?"

"Do you think they'll feel like they wasted a lot of their life being with the wrong person?"

"I couldn't tell you. Depends if they think everything happens for a reason."

Her eyes flicker over my face, like she's debating whether to ask me what she wants to, and I know what her question will be right before the words spill from her lips. "Do you feel like you wasted your life being with the wrong person for too long?"

My grip tightens around my keys, my thoughts spinning around the silence. It's a loaded question, but now that I've had some space from the breakup, I know my answer. "I wouldn't be in Vancouver if it weren't for Ruby. And I love it here."

"Is that what happened with you and Ruby? You fell out of love?"

Taking a breath, I divert my gaze away from her. "Maybe it is. Or maybe we were just broken."

"Or maybe it just happens sometimes," she whispers.

I sigh. "Maybe."

"Kace?"

I run my thumb across the blade of my key. "Yeah?"

She waits for me to look at her, and when I do, she says, "Thank you for being here with me."

"I wouldn't let you come alone."

"I know it's just because it's a job that you felt obligated to be a part of, but–"

"It's because we're friends."

"You consider us friends?" Her eyes widen with hope.

"I do."

She grins. "At least someone is saying those words today."

I laugh because that was fucking funny, and tension that seems to always be present lately dissipates a bit. Mya's face brightens like my reaction is contagious, and for a weighted moment, our eyes lock, our smiles mirrored, and I have the urge to kiss her.

Before I can do something I'd regret, she shakes her head like she's clearing a thought and pulls on the door handle.

Forcing my own thoughts to the back of my mind, I open my door. "Hold up," I say and walk around the front of my truck to open the door for Mya, reaching my hand out for hers.

"Ready to ruin a wedding?" she asks, slipping her palm into mine. I'm tempted to hold on, but as soon as her feet are firmly on the ground, I release her.

"Ready as I'll ever be."

Chapter Twenty-One

Mya

"This isn't going to be anything like that movie *Made of Honor*, is it?" I whisper to Kace as we sit in the back row of white folding chairs, soft instrumentals playing as everyone waits for the bride. This venue is incredible with its floor-to-ceiling windows behind the altar that allow for a perfect view of Mt. Hood on the far side of the Columbia River.

"Never seen it," he whispers back.

"What!" I whisper-yell, taking my eyes off the view to look at him. "It has Derek *and* Owen from *Grey's Anatomy*. So good. Even if I can't stand Owen. He's the worst." I glance back out the windows. By some miracle, the morning rain passed through quickly. The only remnants of it are the dampness of the shrubs and grass dividing the venue from the rocky shore.

"Mya?" He holds his stare until I meet his gaze again.

"Yeah?"

"You're rambling. You don't have to do this."

"Yes. I do. It's my job," I counter, practically shaking in my seat. I don't have stage fright. I'm the furthest thing from shy—as confident as Lizzie McGuire during her rhythmic gymnastics routine, even if I don't love what I'm doing. But this–it's a lot.

"Are you sure?" Kace shifts in his seat toward me.

I nod, holding his gaze, only flinching a little when he reaches up to touch my face. His thumb brushes my cheek. "You can do this, Mya." His words are soft and sweet like he's shifted from being prepared to talk me out of it to full-on supporting the mission.

My eyes flicker back and forth over his. I hold my breath to avoid pulling away from his touch, but I don't lean into it either. This is exactly how I wanted him to touch me the other night. How am I going to survive the *next* job with him? Half of the reason I haven't been focused on the logistics of this job is because the one I managed to get roped into a few days from now will be even more stressful–not because of the job, but because the location comes with more pressure than being a wedding crasher. It's so far out of town, Kace and I will have to not only spend six hours total in a car together, but stay overnight in a hotel. We'll have separate rooms, but still, it'll be more time spent with just the two of us than ever before. That says a lot considering we live together, and I'm terrified not knowing if it'll bring us closer together or send our tension off the charts.

I reluctantly move away from Kace's touch, linking my hands in my lap to calm my nerves and focus on the present task. The wedding processional song begins, and I recognize it immediately. "Somewhere Only We Know," by Keane, plays, and I can't help but focus on the words. Maybe it's the horo-scope effect, but this song seems to fit Allison and Eli. It feels like it tells the story of them wanting to go back to a simpler time–one where they did love each other and there wasn't any more to it.

Regardless of the truth in my interpretation, I sit up straighter, ready to take on this challenge and hoping it works out for the best.

The next few minutes fly by. Allison makes it down the aisle. The officiant welcomes the guests and asks us all to be seated. He then gives a short speech about the sacredness of marriage, which I block out so I can focus on the task at hand.

And then he says the magic words.

"I ask that if anyone here can show just cause of why Allison and Eli should not be lawfully married in the presence of God today, speak now, or forever hold your peace."

I take a breath.

Then I stand.

Immediately, I feel the surrounding eyes jump to me.

And then in slow motion, the rest of the guests turn–I swear it happens one head at a time.

My pulse is so strong in my ears it feels like a sound machine blocking out all the noise around me. I internally snap my fingers like it'll pull me out of hypnosis, and the room comes spiraling back and into complete silence.

There's not a single sound as a hundred sets of eyes stare at me. I can feel Kace's gaze, but mine is focused on the bride and groom. I'm the only one looking at them. I'm so keenly aware of it, and I wonder if they are too.

I clear my throat. "I object." Squaring my shoulders, I speak loud enough for everyone to hear. The words feel so cliche and formal, but what the heck else was I supposed to say?

A collective gasp echoes through the room. Ali seems to ask Eli if he knows me, and he shakes his head. They both stare back at me, but with the way their shoulders relax, this feels right.

Heads swivel back and forth between me and the bride and groom. The whispers start, people leaning in closer to one another to gossip but still shifting their eyes back and forth between the back and front of the room.

I keep my eyes on the altar, ignoring the growing chaos that surrounds me. The officiant leans in, forming a huddle with Allison and Eli. The couple nod their heads after he speaks a few words to them, and then they all glance my way.

"Uh." The officiant's voice is louder than mine, coming through the microphone attached to his lapel. "Sorry for the interruption. Please give us a moment," he addresses the room before focusing on me. "Young lady, please meet us in the back of the room." He points to the freestanding partition where Allison had waited to walk down the aisle.

Taking another breath, I glance at my path. I have to shimmy past Kace, and as I squeeze between his knees and the chairs in front of me, he grabs my hand, giving it a quick squeeze before I continue on my way.

The gazes of a hundred people propel me toward the back of the room, and I disappear behind the black divider to find the officiant waiting with the bride and groom.

"Who are you?" Allison whispers in a tone that doesn't necessarily sound angry–it's more concerned and curious than anything.

The three of them focus on me, waiting.

"Umm. A concerned guest?" I know I need to exert more confidence to be able to drive my point home, but this pressure is nerve-wracking.

Eli stands frozen as the officiant speaks. "Do you have valid reasoning that these two should not be wed?"

I swear on my Princess Diana Beanie Baby that Allison is holding her breath in a "please tell me you've got something" way. I just know.

"Yeah." I take a breath and stand straighter. "They love each other, but they aren't in love."

The officiant looks between them. "Is that true?" They share a look of hesitation, but neither one of them confirms or denies. The man sighs. "Are either of you feeling reservations about spending the rest of your lives together?"

Eli wets his dry lips, and Allison bites the corner of hers. It's silent for a moment. Any gossiping whispers from the other side of the partition might as well be on another planet. Then

Allison nods. "Yes," she whispers, glancing up at Eli, her eyes watering. "Well, I was…" Her voice cracks. She tries to look away, but he catches her chin with his thumb, keeping their gazes connected.

"Tell me what you're thinking," he says gently.

She takes a deep breath, her gaze flickering over his face with worry. "I love you so much, Eli. Lately, I've been thinking that's not enough…"

He hesitates, but then slides his hand to cradle her face. "And now?"

"Now… I can't stand the thought of you being taken from me." A tear escapes, carving a perfect streak down her otherwise flawless wedding makeup. "But that's not fair to you. That I could have those thoughts and not be fully committed to you until I was faced with losing you."

He smiles. "I'd be lying if I said I haven't had cold feet or questioned if we're making the right choice."

Confusion washes over Ali, and I feel it too, unsure where he's going with this. "Really?" she asks.

He nods, pulling her closer to him by her waist. "This is scary as shit. You're the only girl I've ever been with. It's easy to wonder if that's how life is supposed to work, if I can know you're *the one* without being with anyone who isn't."

She breaks eye contact, staring at his tie. "Yeah."

He shifts her gaze back to him with his grip on her face. "But the thought of losing you today… It makes me realize if I don't choose you, I'd spend the rest of my life regretting it."

She reaches between them to press her hands to his chest. "What if someday you change your mind?"

He contemplates his response. "How about this? We put divorce on the table."

Her brows scrunch. "What?"

"Not in an 'escape plan' way, but rather knowing that we're choosing to be together instead of forced to be."

"We're not trapped." She says it somewhere between a question and a statement.

"If we ever feel trapped, we'll tell each other. Do you feel that you are? If we do this? If we get married today?"

"Not anymore. Now that I have an out, I don't want it." She lets out something between a laugh and a sob but doesn't break his stare. "I'm sorry it took a stranger–" she turns to me, "no offense–" I hold my hands up, unoffended and surprised she even remembered I was here. She continues, "to make me realize it." Her face falls. "I didn't want to let you down."

He pulls her into a hug, her chin settling on his shoulder. "I know, baby. It's okay."

Ali pulls back and looks at me. "But seriously, who are you?"

"Umm. I'm Mya." I don't want to betray her mom's confidence, but I'm sure she'll find out eventually. "Someone who loves you asked me to give you the push they thought you needed."

Allison chuckles, her gaze flicking to Eli. "I bet it was your mother."

"No way," he says with an amused grin. "This has your mom written all over it."

She leans into him, and he wraps his arm around her shoulder, pulling her close. "Whoever it was," Allison says, not prying any further. "Thank you."

So many questions I want to ask them battle for space on the tip of my tongue. But they don't owe me answers or life lessons, and this day is chaotic enough for them. "You're welcome," I say, feeling more unsettled than not.

Eli turns to the officiant. "I don't know what protocol is here, but do we just start over and go back in there, or?"

"I'll take care of it," the man assures him with a squeeze to his shoulder. "Why don't you two take a minute, and I'll make sure everyone resets."

As soon as the officiant disappears, Ali addresses me again. "You're welcome to stay."

I shake my head. "Thank you, but I don't want to intrude more than I have. Have fun." I tack on a smile even though I'm really freaking upset inside. Like Cory and Topanga breaking up level upset, but I can't help but wonder if these two need real time apart before finding their way back to each other.

"Well, the offer is open," Eli adds. "Thank you, Mya."

I take the cue, scanning the room for my escape. When I spot a back door, I peek my head around the partition long enough to find Kace in the crowd. His eyes meet mine almost immediately, and when I turn away, despite the chaos lingering in the rest of the room, I can feel him stand to follow me outside.

Taking a deep breath, I push through the door, feeling like I might fall over if I don't have something to steady me soon. Why am I so emotional right now? Cold air bites me as I step outside and press my hand against the wood exterior of the building to ground myself. Taking a shaky breath, I stare at the sliver of river I can see from the backside of the venue, watching the water rush past like what just happened was the smallest rock incapable of diverting its path.

I hadn't heard the click of the door opening again, so when Kace touches my shoulder, it startles me. "Are you okay?"

I shake my head, not able to form words. His hand falls to my lower back, and he gently shifts me until I'm facing away from the venue and leaning against the building like he knows I need the support. Goosebumps erupt across my skin as the cold sinks in, but I hesitate to make my way to the truck. Kace's hands land on my arms, and even though they're warm, the goosebumps hold their ground as he rubs his palms against my skin. "Talk to me," he says, and I'm shocked by the gesture.

I nod, then shake my head. "I don't know."

"What happened?"

"I failed." I sigh, and his hands tense against my arms, transferring his confusion to me. I'm suddenly aware of how close he is, the jacket of his suit brushing against my dress in the space between us.

"Because you didn't tear apart a relationship?" I can't tell if there's judgment in his tone or if I'm imagining it.

"But I was supposed to break them up." Turmoil rattles through me, and my stomach feels sick.

"Mya." His hands slide up my arms, stopping above my collarbone. The warmth of his skin settles against my neck as his thumb rubs across my jaw. This time, my goosebumps dissipate under his touch, and it takes everything in me to not be distracted from the thoughts running through my mind. "This is a good thing."

I shift my gaze across his face, wondering if he could possibly be telling the truth.

"They want to get married, right?" he clarifies.

I nod. "That's what they said. But her mom was so sure…"

"Ali's mom isn't Ali or Eli. Only they can know what they want. If they want to get married and you helped them be sure of that, then you did your job."

"How are people supposed to know?" I whisper.

He mindlessly brushes his thumb across my jaw like he's doing it out of instinct to comfort me more than anything. "Know what?"

"When to give up and when to keep trying?" I look at him like he has the answers I need, but the more time that passes without a response, I know I'm kidding myself. Even if he did have the answers, he wouldn't open up to me. He might consider us friends, but he doesn't see me the way I see him.

His gaze flashes to my lips before they're back on my eyes–although I'm sure I imagined the motion because he drops his hold on my face like he just realized it's too intimate. "There's no rulebook, so I don't know," he says, confirming my assumption either way.

Still, his presence eases the conflict swirling inside me, and I chew on the corner of my lip to keep from trying to kiss him again.

"Was everyone freaking out while I was talking to Ali and Eli?"

"I'm not really sure. I was worrying about you," he admits, shoving his hands in his pockets like it'll keep me from mis-interpreting his confession.

Despite his internal struggle, hearing him say that feels like a win. "Thank you for being here for me–for listening." Searching his eyes, I bite into the side of my cheek as I wait for his reply.

His hands slip from his pockets and link around my fore-arms–the contact against my bare skin strong enough to warm me. He grows serious as his fingers drag down my arms until they link with my hands. "Thank you for being here while I work through my shit. I know I'm not always easy to be around."

My mouth falls open, shocked by the shift, my mind pro-cessing what he's saying and relishing in the comfort I find in his hands holding mine. "You're welcome," I whisper. "I'm here if you want to talk about it or anything else."

"I know." He squeezes my hands. "You ready to go home?"

I nod, and he drops his hold on me before leading us back to the car and taking me home.

Chapter Twenty-Two

Kace

"It's so early." Mya groans, looking up at me from where she's crouched on the other side of the couch, presumably packing her bag.

"Early bird gets the worm," I tell her, closing my bedroom door behind me, duffel bag in hand.

She shoots me a glare. "I don't like worms."

I chuckle, wondering if she's regretting agreeing to an out-of-town job. I recall the other day when she told me the only thing that got her out of bed in the mornings before school was hoping to catch one of her favorite music videos on MTV. "Do you want me to pull up YouTube while you get ready?"

Her smile turns sweet when she looks up this time. "It's not the same, but thank you."

"I'll queue it up just in case. Are you sure you won't want to snowboard?"

"I'm sure." She looks back to her bag, shoving a few things into it on the couch.

"I don't want you to be bored all day." I set my bag on the floor in the entryway and fill my Hydrojug with tap water.

"I won't be. Promise." She holds up a bag even though I can't see what's inside. "I have a book I've been wanting to read, so this is perfect."

"Alright." I was going to offer to bring Ruby's board she left behind when she moved out so Mya didn't have to rent one. But truthfully, a day on black diamond runs sounds more fun than helping Mya up every time she falls on the bunny hill. She showed me a picture of her as a kid with a broken arm standing outside a cabin with her sister. I guess her family went on vacation and Mya tried to learn to ski, but it didn't end well. She looked cute though, her arm in a sling, a pink cast sticking out. Her pigtail braids were under a beanie, and she had on hot pink snow pants.

I appraise her outfit as she stands, resisting a chuckle. This version of Mya seems so similar to the version of herself twenty years ago. *Except now she's sexy,* and seeing her this way makes me wish she *did* want to spend the day on the mountain with me. Her black leggings are tight, contrasting her oversized pink crewneck with the word "Roxy" splashed across the front. Her short, blonde hair peeks out under the white beanie with a puff on top. She bends over to pull on... are those Ugg boots? I thought those went out of style a decade ago. They're gray with bows on the back, and combined with the rest of the outfit, it looks like she stepped out of a winter magazine from the 2000s. If I were a girl, I'd buy everything based on how fucking good she looks. She's a mountain lover's dream.

I shake my head, clearing the thoughts that keep making an appearance without permission. "Ready?"

"Yes!" She holds a duffel bag by the small handles with both hands in front of her. "I'm so excited for our road trip."

"Me too. Let's go." I open the front door for her and flick off the light before following her out. I'm probably more excited than she is. I only went boarding once around Thanksgiving last year, and now that it's spring and the snow season is almost over, I'm so thankful our next job is taking us to my favorite place that I didn't even ask how she managed to get hired this time.

And, let's be honest, this little side business is all Mya anyway. I'm just here for moral support, I guess. And to make sure she doesn't get kidnapped. Seeing her so invested in the wedding job last weekend weakened my defenses a little. I could feel my outermost wall crumbling as we stood outside of the venue after the wedding.

She looked so damn sad, and even though I couldn't quite wrap my head around why she was so disappointed, I felt drawn to comfort her. It hit me that somewhere along the way, Mya became my friend. I enjoy spending time with her. I like learning new things about her. I *want* to be more open with her, but I'm just not there yet.

The past few days since then have been good. I stuck to my usual routine–work out in the morning and then work split between home and Little Conejo. Mya crafted. I caught her working out during the day a couple of times. Tuesday and Wednesday night she hung out with her new friend Chloe. Last night, we went over the plan while we watched *The Hangover*.

I was surprised when she had already come up with a loose timeline and a site pulled up to book two rooms at the mountain resort. She figured it made the most sense to give me time to snowboard first, and her work the job at night, without having to worry about making the two-and-a-half-hour drive back. Of course I didn't want to miss an opportunity to spend a day on the slopes, but I also didn't expect her to plan around it. It took me a solid few seconds of heavy heartbeats before I realized how much that meant to me.

Once Mya gave me the rundown, it was mainly me securing all the details while she went into repeated giggle fits over... well, every single *Hangover* scene. She'd never seen the movie, and it gave me a strong urge to force her to watch all the classics. *Eurotrip. School of Rock.* Anything with Ben Stiller or Adam Sandler. But where the fuck does that land along the friendship and relationship line? She only focused on the planning long enough to insist on paying for both rooms. I tried to fight her, but she said the girl who hired us would reimburse her for one room, and Mya was set on getting a second one for me. The countdown timer to reserve the room was about to expire and with these being the last two rooms available, I finally gave in, deciding arguing more wasn't worth the risk.

It's still dark out, the orange glow of sunrise barely invading the night sky as we pull out of the parking garage. It's calm and quiet. There's no one on the road yet, and it's also apparently early enough that Mya has nothing to say.

I have the BOYS LIKE GIRLS complete playlist playing softly as Mya sips her energy drink through a pink spiral glass straw. The first thirty minutes go by without talking, outside of Mya explaining to me that she had to stockpile this Witches Brew flavor of Alani because they only sell it in the fall. It apparently tastes like those caramel apple suckers you'd get as a kid, and after she forced the straw between my lips, I can't argue her assessment.

Then she went on about how her second favorite flavor is the winter one and how it tastes like if you wad up a Fruit Roll-Up and shove it into your mouth all at once. Oddly enough, I felt I could taste it, but I also called her a psycho for not punching out the shapes like a normal person.

"Am I the only person who drives behind a logging truck and worries they're going to be impaled?" Mya asks out of nowhere.

I chuckle. "I'd say that's morbid, but I think we all have *Final Destination* PTSD." I take in the highway lined on either side with snow-dusted Douglas firs. Fog floats between the trees, and while it would feel ominous if *The Ring* soundtrack was playing, it's what makes the Pacific Northwest so beautiful.

"Thank god I'm not alone. You don't have any siblings, right?" She switches gears as the sun makes enough of an appearance to be considered morning and allows me to see more than a car's length ahead of me.

"No." I keep my eyes on the road, my hand loosely draped over the steering wheel since we're on a straight, empty freeway for over an hour longer.

"How did you keep from getting bored on road trips?"

"We didn't really go on trips. I hadn't been out of West Virginia until college."

She sucks at the end of her drink, the gurgling sound of her trying to get every last drop combined with the clinking of her straw against the can. "That's so sad," she finally says, setting her empty drink in the cupholder between us. "Car games are so much fun. Like I-Spy. Oh! Or the license plate game." She scans the road on all sides of us. "I guess that would be a little hard right now. My memory isn't good enough for that 'I'm going on a picnic game.'"

"I have zero idea what you're talking about." I reach to turn down the music a notch, now that we're talking.

"Okay. Okay. We could play 'Two Truths and a Lie.'" She says the suggestion like I've agreed to play anything with her.

"Nah." I don't know the game, but I can take a solid guess about how to play. "I can't look at you to watch for tells."

"That's not the point! It's mostly just guessing. But okay." She hums, and I see her tapping her chin in my periphery. "I've got it! Let's play 'Would You Rather?'"

I do know that game. I remember playing it when I was younger, coming up with the most ridiculous and disgusting things as a teenager. "Alright," I agree without arguing, knowing it will make time go by more quickly.

"Yay!" She tips her seat back a little, slouching enough to rest her sock-covered feet on the dash. I spare a glance in her direction, taking in her light blue crew socks with snowmen on them. I consider scolding her, telling her to get her feet down, but she looks pretty damn comfortable with her puff beanie still on her head even though I have the heater on. I'm almost too warm in my snow pants and long sleeve thermal.

Ruby and I used to wear sweats and change in the car, but I didn't want to have to worry about the logistics of that with Mya. "Okay. You go first." She clasps her hands together and slips them between her thighs. *I wish my hand was sliding up her thigh.* I glue my eyes back on the still empty highway.

I search my brain for something that will be challenging for Mya based on the little I know about her. "Would you rather eat Cap'n Crunch as your only cereal for the rest of your life or any cereal *except* Cap'n Crunch?"

"How do you know Cap'n Crunch is my favorite?" I can *feel* her grinning next to me.

"Mya." I give her a side eye. "We've been through four boxes since you moved in. Normally a box lasts me all month."

"Oh." She chuckles. "My bad. I really love that stuff. Can I have any version or just the original?"

"Uhh. Any version, I guess."

"Okay Cap'n Crunch then. But don't tell the other cereals. I still love them too. But man, the way Cap'n explodes flavor onto your taste buds before cutting up the roof of your mouth. It's like the cereal form of a Sour Patch Kid, ya know?"

God, she's weird, but I can't deny it's fun to know someone who loves my favorite food as much as I do. "That tracks."

"Okay... If you were reincarnated as your favorite animal, would you rather come back as a wild animal or in a zoo/captivity?"

Humming to myself, I consider the question. "Could I choose which zoo?"

"Sure."

"Alright." I settle back against my seat, my hand falling to the bottom of the steering wheel. "I'd want to come back as an animal at the Wild Animal Sanctuary in Colorado. They rescue animals from illegal or abusive situations and bring them to their 33,000 acre property. They have it designed similarly to their wild habitats, and the viewing is a mile-long elevated walkway, which keeps the animals from feeling fear."

"That sounds so cool. How do you know about that?"

"I watch documentaries sometimes. I saw one a couple of years ago where they talked about taking the tigers from that *Tiger King* show there."

"Why would you rather go there than live in the wild?"

I shrug. "I don't know. Easy life. Wouldn't have to worry about finding food or shelter or humans ruining my home. But I wouldn't have to watch children like Dudley Dursley press their faces to the glass all damn day."

She giggles, and it's so sweet that I flick my music off altogether with a button on my steering wheel. "Your turn."

"Would you rather have to catch a fly like Mr. Miyagi with chopsticks or like Mimi-Siku with a blow dart?"

She chuckles. "That's a good one. Blow dart for sure. Although one time my sister and I had a contest to see who could eat a whole bowl of rice faster with chopsticks one grain at a time, and I totally kicked her butt." I love when she freely shares the most random details of her life with me. "My turn. Would you rather be a character in *Jurassic Park* or *Ghostbusters*?"

"I don't think I believe in ghosts, so I'd say Jurassic Park."

"*Jurassic World* though, right? You could be Chris Pratt's character. You give off that vibe."

I cock a brow. "I seem like the dinosaur-wrangling type?"

She hums, and I spare her a glance in time to see a blush creep across her face. What the fuck is that about? "No." She shakes her head. "Main character energy or something."

It strikes me that she could be saying Chris Pratt is her celebrity crush, but I shove the implication of that thought away. I take a breath, focusing on my chest expanding. Despite there being attraction between us, all we could ever be is a hookup–and that's a terrible idea. I've seen *Friends with Benefits*. I ignore her comment, not wanting to dig deeper. "Would you rather have a pause or a rewind button on your life?"

She hums. "Like *Click*? Or can other people be active in the pause too? Like I can keep doing the same thing I'm doing in that scene of life?"

"Whoever is in the room with you."

"Then I choose that. Pause."

I'm surprised by her choice. "You wouldn't want to go back and change anything?"

"No." She shrugs. "If I changed a mistake or a regret then I would never learn from it, and I'd probably make the same mistake again down the road. But if I could pause in a moment, I could soak it up and savor it."

Her answer is good, but I can't help thinking it doesn't align with the fact that she's repeatedly been in relationships she sucks at getting out of. I decide not to press it and ruin our good morning–to stay in this moment. "Your turn."

"Would you rather give or receive?"

What the hell did she just say? My eyes snap to hers for a brief second before back on the road, and I catch no hint of joking.

"What?" she asks with an innocence that I can't tell is fake or not. "Oh shoot." She laughs. "I meant gifts!"

I quirk a brow. "Sure you did."

"No, really!" she insists, but I'm not sure I believe her.

I keep my eyes on the road. "I prefer neither unless I know the person really well. And then I enjoy both."

"Kace!" She slaps my arm with the back of her hand, but I keep my expression neutral.

Two can play that game. "Would you rather have sex in your childhood bedroom or your parents' bed?"

"Hey! That one is intentionally about sex!" she whines.

"Is there a rule that it can't be?"

"No..." She shifts next to me. A quick glance shows her pulling her feet from the dash to cross one leg over the other, and a little part of me hopes she's uncomfortable in a *good* way. "Well, my parents have a waterbed. So that could be fun? I guess they make it work, right? That feels weird though.

But my room..." She pulls her hands from where they're still pinched between her thighs to cover her face and shake her head.

"Tell me about your room, Mya," I taunt, feeling lighter than I have in a while. Maybe the best I've felt since Ruby and I broke up.

She pulls her hands from her face and glances at me with a grin that lights up her face. "I'll set the scene. You enter my room walking through a pink beaded curtain. You know, the plastic ones that are strings of little hearts? To the left is my double bed, covered in a fluffy pink and black zebra comforter. There's a Damon Salvatore poster hanging directly above my mattress. Sticking out from under my bed is definitely a pair of light-up Heelys. To the right, a pink blow-up chair–the translucent ones, you know where you can see your spit inside when you blow it up?"

I can't help but chuckle at that. I remember my high school girlfriend having one. It squeaked every time she tried to sit on it.

"Next to my chair is a collage of magazine pictures glued to a poster board with all my favorite couples. Chuck and Blair. Rory and Logan. Seth and Summer. Quinn and Clay."

The last couple is the only familiar one to me. *One Tree Hill*. This whole situation is starting to feel a lot like when Ruby forced me to watch that show. I hated every second of it, but at the same time, I wanted to know what happened next. A few seasons in, I'd be secretly mad if she watched without me. I think Mya feels like that. She's the girl it doesn't make sense for me to like, but I'm enamored by her. And that's more terrifying than admitting I like some stupid high school drama show.

"There's a lava lamp on my nightstand. Let's see. What else? OH. I had my sex bracelets hanging from thumbtacks on my wall."

"Sex bracelets?" My brows scrunch. "What the fuck are those?"

"You don't know what sex bracelets are?! They're colored jelly bracelets. But each color is assigned to a different sex act. Basically, if a boy broke your jelly bracelet, it would be like them getting a coupon for the thing associated with the bracelet. I think purple was kissing. Blue was oral... or you know gift giving." She looks over at me and grins. Little shit knew exactly the question she was asking earlier. "Black was sex."

"That's... interesting." I must have missed that whole phase in school.

"The 2000s were wild times."

"You were like ten. You can't tell me you actually participated in the game."

"No way. I didn't want anyone to snap my bracelets. I had pretty ones with sparkles in them!"

I chuckle, but can't help but wonder how innocent Mya is as an adult when it comes to sex.

"OH!" she shrieks, thankfully pulling me from a dangerous path of thoughts. "There would definitely be a Furby chatting from the top shelf of my closet... but not until the moment got heated of course."

"Of course," I muse.

"And we'd have to be able to tolerate the excessive amount of Cucumber Melon scent everywhere. I'm pretty sure it's fused into all of my belongings at home to this day."

"We?" I tease. I think it's a tease anyway. Because I'm sure as shit not picturing fucking Mya on a zebra bed in her childhood room.

She waves me off with her hand. "Anyway. All of that being said, I choose my room. I'm all for living on the wild side... but wild, or exhibitionism or whatever is different than gross. I don't need to have sex on the bed I was likely conceived on, you know?"

The mention of exhibitionism makes my dick strain against my snow pants. Not *a lot*, but enough. *Fuck.* The idea is enticing, which sounds insane considering the kind of guy I am, but while I like safe and secure, my job would also imply that in the right situations, I also like a thrill.

I ignore her response because the last thing I need is to think about fucking Mya for the thrill of it. Luckily, she continues right along with our game. "Would you rather have sex with *Spongebob* or *Rugrats* playing in the background?"

Did she have to stick with the sex questions? I can't help but chuckle though. "Two of the shows with the most annoying character voices." I mull over my answer, not realizing how dry my lips were until I swipe my tongue over them. Sex talk with a girl like Mya makes me feel like a fucking teenager again. "Doesn't matter what's playing." I flash her a glance. "If I'm into the girl enough, I won't see or hear anyone but her."

Chapter Twenty-Three

Kace

Putting pressure on the heel edge of my snowboard brings me to a stop, chattering on the firmly packed snow in the base area. The abrupt end to my ride sends powder flying from under my board and off my helmet and jacket. That last line was insane with a sketchy cliff band that almost ate me alive, but I was able to stomp the landing and ride it out as the powder flew around me.

I may have missed most of the season, but a day like this makes up for it quickly. The only thing that would have been better is if I hadn't let those 'Would You Rather?' questions run on repeat through my mind–if I hadn't had visions of Mya under me, along with her zebra comforter, her blonde curls splayed across her pillowcase as she looked up at me. I've been trying so hard to shove any need I have for her deep down inside, but every time she flirts–especially when she says something sexual and desperately honest–more of my resolve withers away like an Avenger after The Snap.

I couldn't stop a new scenario playing out in my head with each run down the mountain. You'd think an entire day of fantasizing would be enough to expel the ideas from my mind, but apparently not. I lift my goggles from my face before falling back on my ass to unclip my bindings.

I gauge my surroundings, the sun beginning its descent on one side, and the final stragglers from the mountain heading toward the lodge on the other. A liftie walks past me, and I turn back to see that the lift has stopped spinning for the night.

Damn. How late is it? I bite the tip of my glove, tugging to free my hand. The chill of the air prickles my skin, matching the sting on my face. Digging into the Velcro pocket of my snow pants, I pull out my phone and tap the screen. *5:17.* It's not as late as I thought. I still have time to find Mya, check into our rooms, shower and get situated before we need to hunt down this guy.

His girlfriend hired us because she's convinced he's cheating on her. So the plan is for Mya to hang around him and see if he tries to make a pass at her. If he doesn't, Mya will actively flirt to see if he takes the bait, just to make sure. This entire job is idiotic if you ask me. If this girl is so convinced her boyfriend is cheating on her, why would she want to be with him in the first place? Not to mention, if this guy is shitty enough to cheat on his girlfriend, then I don't fucking like the idea of Mya being that close to him.

At least I'll be there to keep an eye on the situation.

Standing, I take my helmet off, the cool air freezing the sweat in my hair. With helmet and gloves in one hand and my board under my other arm, I head toward the lodge. I stop by the rack and secure my board. I'll take it to my truck when we go to grab our overnight bags.

Walking toward the patio of the lodge, I check my phone again. There's nothing from Mya. I took a break for lunch earlier and found her sitting next to the fireplace, drinking hot cocoa and reading what looked like a Christmas book. The title was some play on *The Grinch*, which brought about more questions aside from her being in a holiday mood in March. But I didn't want to interrupt her focus, and I figured we'd get dinner together at the end of the day. It's not like she's required to check in with me.

I pull open the heavy wooden door with its brass handle. Taking a step inside, I feel warmer with each inch the door closes, trapping me in a loud bustling room. For such a small bar, it holds a lot of people. I scan the place. To the left are scattered couches near the fire, full of couples cuddling and friends playing life-size Jenga. Mya isn't there any longer. The rooms weren't ready earlier in the day, but I don't think she'd check in without me. Maybe she moved to one of the booths on the opposite side.

My eyes shift toward the bar straight ahead.

Oh. *Hell no.*

I freeze in the entryway.

Mya touches some douchebag's arm, her hand resting on his bicep as she laughs at something he said. Her smile is bright, and she looks so fucking cozy in her oversized sweatshirt and leggings that make her ass look too fucking good in the glow from the lights behind the bar. She's not wearing her beanie anymore, and her blonde curls bounce as she laughs.

The guy takes a step closer to Mya, tucking a strand of hair behind her ear.

Absolutely fucking not.

She's not yours, man. It doesn't fucking matter what she does or who she does it with.

He's just a regular fucking guy, flipping his hair in a way that was only cool in 2007 when Ryan Sheckler did it. She could do so much better.

Oh. Shit.

I think that guy is *the one*. The guy we were hired to find. A breath of relief leaves me. *She's not actually into him.* But still. Mya was not supposed to do this on her own.

She's not into him, right? I try to inspect her body language from across the dimly lit room. Her arm has moved to rest on the bartop, and her thumb picks at the corner. They're not touching, but his sweatshirt is brushed against hers.

Her eyes remain impressively locked on his, but he's not even paying attention to the ways she's clearly uncomfortable. One of her arms is folded across her stomach with a fistful of sweatshirt fabric. She's twisted slightly away from the bar rather than directly toward him.

A gust of cool air hits my back, and I turn to see a couple walking in the door behind me. I pull my attention back to Mya, but that two seconds costs me. His hand is on her waist, and he's leaning in.

I take a step, but it's a step too late. His lips are on hers.

He sure as shit is a cheater, and that's all the information we need before we get the fuck out.

Thankfully, Mya pulls back before I even reach them, and it's the only thing reassuring me that she wasn't into him. But still. They kissed. Her lips were on his. And not mine.

The intensity with which that thought slams into me nearly knocks me back out the door. I'm swept straight out of delusion because now there's no way I can deny how much I want to touch her–especially after watching someone else do it.

Her head jerks to me, but my eyes are still on him. He's watching her like "what the fuck happened?" and I'm two seconds away from punching this guy.

I flash my gaze to Mya to find her looking at me like a Mogwai who took a bite of food after midnight. I didn't think I was that mad, but her wide eyes say she thinks I'm about to turn into a Gremlin and fuck up anything in my wake. "I suggest you get the fuck away from her."

The guy's eyes snap to me. He takes a step back, putting his hands up in defense. "Sorry, man. I didn't know she had a boyfriend. I would have never made a move."

Yeah, sure he wouldn't have. *Piece of shit.* I narrow my eyes. "You need to leave."

"You can't kick me out of here." He puffs his chest, trying to get in my space. I have at least four inches on him and way more muscle. He's the kind of guy who somehow makes it look like he works out but doesn't actually do shit. I could take him in a heartbeat.

"Where else am I supposed to go?" he snaps.

"Go Ask Jeeves," I snap back, and a giggle escapes Mya until she slaps her hands over her mouth.

He glances at her for a second before focusing back on me. "Fuck you," he spits before turning on his heel and storming off. I don't doubt he'll find a replacement for Mya soon, and I feel bad for his girlfriend. Hopefully this at least gives her the information she needs to leave his sorry ass.

When I turn back to Mya, she's scowling at me. "What?" I ask.

All her amusement from a moment ago is gone. "What the heck was that, Kace?!"

"What do you mean? That prick touched you when you're not his to touch."

"Oh yeah? And who do I belong to?" She flings her arms into the air as if it punctuates her sentence.

Fuck me. That did not come out right. I take a step closer and face her, pressing my palm against the bar. "I meant he has a girlfriend."

"Don't you think I know that?" she snaps. "I was literally hired by her."

"You were supposed to wait for me. We're supposed to do this together," I defend, knowing damn well she doesn't *need* me for any of these jobs.

"So sue me. I came to the bar to ask for a dinner menu because I thought you'd be hungry when you got here. When I looked up, he happened to be here too. I wasn't going to miss an opportunity."

"You could have waited until later."

"No, Kace. I couldn't have. He started talking to me. I had to shoot my shot before he disappeared with someone else."

I know she's not wrong, but I'm still irritated as fuck. "You have to be more careful."

Her brows pinch together with a deeper glare. She's pissed, but she's fucking cute. Her emerald eyes glow in the overhead bar light, the freckles sprinkled across her nose more noticeable since she's hardly wearing makeup. Her fists are curled into the sleeves of her sweater. "Stop telling me what to do." With a huff, she turns and walks away from me.

"Where are you going?" I yell after her, surprised more people aren't paying attention to us.

"Far, far away," she screams over her shoulder, and for once, my brain knows exactly how to fix this.

"Say hi to Lord Farquaad for me," I shoot after her, really fucking pleased with myself.

She freezes, spins on the heels of her Uggs and holds my stare. I stay where I'm at. "Okay. That was funny, but I'm still pissed."

"How can I make it up to you?" I only give her a half grin, not trying to press my luck.

"Let's just get checked in and find some dinner. Maybe we'll both be less angry after we eat."

"As you wish." I motion toward the exit with my hand, not being able to hide a smile this time.

She shakes her head, biting into her lip like it'll hold her grin at twenty percent power. "Just because you figured out the way to my heart, doesn't mean you can get away with things, Westley."

I take a few steps until I'm right behind her. "You got it, Buttercup." I wink, meaning the nickname playfully, but loving the way it reminds me of the night she got drunk at the apartment down the hall.

She rolls her eyes, but I have a feeling she's smiling as I follow her to the check-in desk.

Chapter Twenty-Four

"You don't have to walk me to my room," I say, rolling my eyes at Kace over my shoulder, making sure my irritation is still evident. I realize it's not a huge deal that he went all caveman when someone else kissed me, but trying to understand him is like trying to find your way through Ikea without the maps. I mean, it's not like *he* wants to kiss me–he's made it clear we're *friends*. My daydreams of Kace coming to find me reading by the fireplace and pulling me to his room are trying to convince me otherwise, but the truth of it is, he's had two distinct chances to kiss me that he didn't act on.

I shouldn't have taken our 'Would You Rather?' game in the direction I did. He has made it clear he doesn't want to date me. And yet... he sure did play along with my questions and added some spice of his own.

"It's not a problem," he says from behind me. "It's on the way to mine."

Judging from the sign on the wall, our rooms are next to each other, so I don't continue my fight. It's nice of him to carry my bag, but also, mixed signals much? We walk down the hallway in silence, stopping in front of my room. I pull the keycard from the pocket of my leggings and tap it against the black sensor. It clicks, and Kace reaches for the handle, pushing the door open.

"Thanks," I whisper, walking past him. I take a few steps, ready to explore my room, but freeze.

"Where do you want your–" Kace crashes into me with an oomph, then follows my gaze.

Staring back at us are two pairs of eyes belonging to a very naked couple. He's leaning against the headboard and she's riding him, seated on his lap–thankfully her body is turned away so we can't see any parts we shouldn't.

The moment we all use to take in the situation feels like it lasts forever. The man in front of us breaks the trance when he tugs the sheet sitting below the girl's ass to cover her body.

"Oh my gosh. I'm so sorry," I blurt. "They must have mixed up my room." I cover my eyes way too late, turning toward Kace, who is standing with his eyes wide. I push him with both hands on his chest. *Oh my Lanta*, his chest is so... firm? Ripped? His muscles are evident under his thermal, but touching him has me wanting to slide my fingers down, exploring the ripples of his abs that I'm sure to find. "Let's go," I tell him, and he snaps his attention to leaving, turning and leading me out the door along with our bags.

The lock clicks behind us, and I lean against the hallway wall, laughter bursting from me. "I can't believe that happened," I choke out. Glancing up to see Kace's reaction, I catch a smirk, along with a shake of his head.

"Me either."

"What a mix-up." My laughter fades out. "Well then. I guess we should go talk to the front desk, so they can assign me another room."

Kace cringes. He tugs on the back of his neck. His forest tattoo peeks out from the sleeve of his thermal that rises enough to show a sliver of his abs between his shirt and his snow pants. My eyes don't know where to look. Focus. He has something to say.

"What?"

"We got the last two rooms, remember? Plus, I tried checking us in when I came in for a lunch break. They said they were running behind because they're fully booked."

"Oh."

"Yeah."

"Well, that's okay. I can just stay in your room, right?"

"Uhh." The tugging on his neck continues. Jesus, he looks so stressed by the thought of being in the same room with me. It's not like we aren't already roommates.

"Or not. It's okay. I'll go talk to them. Surely we can figure out something. Or I can sleep in the truck. Nothing I haven't done before." I smile, assuring him it's fine. I don't want him to be uncomfortable or to make things more tense between us. I turn to head back down the hallway.

"No," he says, and I stop in my tracks, turning to face him. "It's fine. We'll make it work."

If he's going to agree, he doesn't have to make it sound like such a hassle. "Are you sure?"

"Yup." He slaps his key card against the sensor on the other side of me, holding up his hand for me to wait before checking to make sure this bed is actually available. He pokes his head back into the hallway. "Good to go."

I follow him inside, stopping in front of the bed with our bags on top of the white comforter. The very small bed. Ironically, the size of my childhood bed–a double. As if I wasn't having enough trouble refraining from revisiting that vision over and over. Kace hovering over me, claiming me in a way that totally makes me forget Ian Somerhalder's face staring at me from the ceiling.

There's a small chair in the corner, and a sliding glass door that leads to a balcony. Other than that, there's hardly even room to walk around the bed. This should be interesting to say the least. Kace grabs his bag and sets it on the chair to dig through it.

"Are you sure this will be okay? I don't want to invade your space."

Without glancing over his shoulder, he says, "It'll be fine, Mya. After a long day, I'm sure I'll be out cold. I won't even notice you."

Ouch. "Okay."

"I'm going to shower." He turns around with a pile of clothes in his hands.

"Alright," I manage, but he's already walking past me to the bathroom.

I unlatch the sliding door and pull it open, stepping onto the balcony. The sun is almost set, but I can make out the mountain, lift and trees. The stars are starting to pierce through the darkness as it drowns out the day, and I love it. It's quiet and peaceful, and balances the loudness of the chaos swarming through my brain.

"Hey," Kace's voice comes from behind me. I didn't even hear him open the sliding door. *Dang.* He showers fast. I've only been out here for like ten minutes.

"Hey," I return the greeting as he joins me. His forearms fall to the metal bar of the balcony, mirroring my position. I glance over to check his proximity to me even though my heart rate gives away how close he is. He's wearing gray and navy plaid pajama pants and a navy Henley with the sleeves pushed up enough to see an entire layer of his forest tattoo. *My Lanta,* Kace in pajamas is hot. How the heck am I supposed to get any sleep tonight with him next to me?

"I called the front desk. They apologized and refunded your room to your card."

I glance at him. "Oh. I would have talked to them in the morning."

"I wanted to make sure it was taken care of." His gaze remains forward.

"Well, thank you. I appreciate it."

He nods, but doesn't say anything else. He doesn't even look at me looking at him, so I draw my attention back to the sky. "The moon looks so big," I finally say. It's not that the silence is awkward. I just don't know what to do with it. "It's like Bruce Almighty got a hold of it."

Kace chuckles next to me, and a surge of pride bursts inside me. I've realized one of my favorite things is being responsible for any sign of happiness in this man. "I can't stop thinking about how we walked in on those people." He shakes his head.

He's thinking about sex? Standing this close to me? Do the two things overlap in his brain? Is there any way? A buzz races across my skin at the thought of him touching me. His arm is so close to mine, I swear I can feel the heat radiating from it.

Taking a breath, I turn toward him. I know he doesn't want me, but I don't know... What if...

"Me either." I lock my gaze with his and run my tongue over my lips, wetting them. His eyes follow the movement, and his breath heats my face. Or is it doing that on its own? *I want him to kiss me.* But what if he runs away again? Fear wins this round, and I clear my throat. "I'm hungry," I say, hoping to break the tension, but it has the completely opposite effect.

"Are you?" There's a gleam in his eye, and I swear on my love for Matthew McConaughey and Kate Hudson acting together that he moves a few centimeters closer.

I nod.

"What would you like, Mya?" His voice is low and seductive, and my body heat overpowers the cool mountain air to the point that a bead of sweat forms at my temple.

"Umm." There's no innuendo here right? I'm imagining it. Yes. I have to be. "A burger sounds good. I think I saw them on the menu."

"A burger?" He searches my eyes for confirmation.

I nod. "Mhmm."

He hesitates. "A burger it is, then." He holds his hand out for me to lead the way.

I walk past him, feeling more confused than ever.

"Wait for me by the door," he says, and I turn back. "So I can put some jeans on."

"Oh, all right." I'm still in the same clothes I've been wearing all day–leggings, an oversized Roxy crewneck and my Uggs. I don't care what anyone says. These boots will always be *in*, and you'll have to pry them from my cold dead feet. I stand awkwardly by the door, willing myself not to look as I hear Kace shuffle through his bag. Part of me is convinced he'll change in the bathroom, but even I know better as I shift my eyes to the side.

I catch him with his flannel pajamas in a pile on the floor, and his jeans at his shins, the moment before he pulls them up. His quad muscles flex with the movement, disappearing into the black boxer briefs tight against his thighs. His jeans slide over his ass as his eyes flick to me. Flashing me a smirk as he adjusts the pants around his waist, he tugs on the zipper and fastens the button. "Alright, I'm ready." He swipes his wallet from the chair and steps into his brown Oxford boots, lacing them quickly.

Meanwhile, I've completely forgotten my craving for a burger in favor of watching Kace tie his shoes. What has gotten into me? I blame the candy cane scene I read in my book earlier. Do I have the urge to mix candy and sex? Not particularly. But everything about the way the guy took care of his girl has left me turned on for the past four hours.

That's it. That has to be. It's not just Kace. It's my book. *But I didn't feel that way about the guy who kissed me earlier.*

"Ready?" Kace's furrowing brows come into focus. How long was I zoning out?

"Uh huh." I open the door, and he follows me out.

We walk down the hallway and the three flights of stairs to the door leading outside. It's a short walk to the lodge bar, but now that the sun has set, it's freezing.

"Brr! It's cold out here." I wrap my arms around my waist.

"Should I keep my eye out for Toros?" Kace asks next to me, completely deadpan.

I stop in my tracks and laugh. "What?"

He shrugs. "You said referencing movies is the way to your heart."

Way to my heart. He could have said 'the way to make things up to you,' or I don't know. Anything else. I'm so confused right now. "I guess you have me all figured out."

"Not yet." The tone in his voice makes me think he wants to know more. What are these mixed signals he's sending me?

He opens the door to the bar for me, and I survey the room. Every booth is full. The couches too. There's two seats in the middle of the bar though, so I lead us there. We each take a seat on a barstool in front of the beer taps. The busy bartender slides a menu onto the bar and lets us know she'll be right back. I glance at the menu to make sure the burger I want is still there, then wait patiently with my hands trapped between my thighs as Kace looks over the options. When he leans back, I'm about to ask him what he's having, but the waitress returns.

"What can I get for you two?"

Kace nods toward me.

"I'll have the house burger," I say. "No tomatoes. And a side salad with vinaigrette please."

She looks at Kace. "And for you?"

"Same. I'll keep the tomatoes though. Thank you."

"Olive theory," I mumble before I registered what I'm saying.

Kace's gaze snaps to mine. "Huh?" he asks, but as soon as the word slips from his mouth, recognition hits, and my face heats in embarrassment. His brow quirks for only a moment before he smirks and gives a sly shake of his head as the waitress takes the menus from us.

"And to drink?" she asks, completely oblivious to the fact that I insinuated that Kace could complete me.

He scans the row of beer taps in front of us. "I'll have the Elk Frost please."

Both of their gazes turn to me. "What would you like?"

I take a breath, willing this stupid crush to go away. I've never been much into beer, but if Kace likes it so much, maybe I should try it. I face him. "Can you pick one for me?"

"A beer?" he clarifies, and I nod. "Are there any you've liked?"

"I haven't tried many."

He scans the line of taps again. "She'll try the pilsner."

The waitress nods and moves to pour both of our beers.

"Beer words are a foreign language to me."

"You'd learn if you liked it. I'm sure all your craft words wouldn't make sense to me."

"Good point. So what's a pilsner?" I ask, forcing myself to focus on his response and not the way his tattoos start at his wrists and disappear under where his Henley is pushed up his forearms.

"Do you want the science of it or…"

I grin, appreciating that he knows I don't care about that at all. "Just the basics."

"Well, then all you need to know is a pilsner is a lager. There's two main types of beers. Ales and lagers–the biggest difference is the type of yeast and the temperature they're brewed at."

I scrunch my brows. This is already a lot of information.

He chuckles. "A pilsner is a type of lager. Think light. Baseball game beers. The Pacific Northwest is known for its IPAs–Indian Pale Ales, but a higher percentage of people drink lagers." He pauses. "You don't care about any of this do you?"

I shake my head, my grin widening. "No, but I like how much you care about it."

His tongue runs across his lip, and then he smirks. I steal an extra second of staring as he reaches for the beers the waitress holds out. He hands the lighter colored one to me.

"Without anything to go on, I'm taking a guess here. This is one of the most popular lagers."

I hold the glass in front of my face, peering through the liquid to see a distorted Kace on the other side. Pulling it to my lips, I take a sip, feeling Kace's eyes on me. The cold beer hits my tastebuds, and I immediately swallow, not wanting it to sit in my mouth. I shake my head, setting the cup on the bar. "Nope. This tastes like college."

He chuckles. "Did you go to college?"

I shake my head. "No, but I imagine this is what it tastes like."

His smile is amused. "It's okay. I'll drink it."

"But you already have a drink."

"A strong one too," he says. "Usually it only takes two of these to get people drunk."

My eyes widen.

"The locals call it 'getting frosted.'"

"I love that. It's like *How to Lose a Guy in 10 Days*."

His brows scrunch.

"Never mind. I can drink that. I don't want you to have to drink two."

"I'll be okay. Get something you like." He nods to the bartender when she looks our way.

Appearing in front of us, she folds a cleaning towel and sets it on the bartop. "What's up?"

"Could we get a different drink over here?"

"Of course." She reaches for my glass.

"No, it's okay," Kace tells her. "I'll pay for this one." He turns to me. "What would you like?"

I glance from Kace to the bartender. "Something fruity please."

"Coming right up." She winks.

I twist in my seat to face Kace. "Thank you."

"No problem." He leans against the back of his seat and pulls his beer to his lips. I track the movement, caught when he eyes me over the rim of his glass. But he doesn't say anything. He just takes a long sip of the amber liquid, keeping his eyes on me.

"Here you go." The bartender's voice pulls my attention to the orange drink with a purple crazy straw.

My eyes light up. "Thank you." I take the glass from her hand, and she walks away, leaving Kace and I alone. Well, alone with the hundred other people in here. But all I see is him. And this pretty drink.

I take a sip, letting the sweet liquid sit on my tongue before swallowing. Mmmm. This is more like it.

"Are you more happy about the drink or the straw?" Kace asks, amused.

I take one more sip before setting the glass on the bar. "Both."

"You're easy to please."

"Rule number thirty-two."

He grins, and knowing he gets the reference is a little thing I definitely enjoy.

Chapter Twenty-Five

Sucking through the straw, I watch the last of my second drink travel through the loops. After eating, we've mostly been people-watching. I don't trust myself with many con-versation topics for fear that they will turn sexual like the one in the car. And now that there's alcohol running through me, I trust myself even less. *Sober* I'm liable to tell Kace he's the sexiest man I've ever seen, with his just tight enough Henley, sitting comfortably on his bar stool, his Oxford boots resting on the foot bar. *Tipsy?* The chance is even greater.

Glancing over at him for the hundredth time, I see he's still half a glass away from finishing the beer he got after he finished mine. "How much do you get paid?"

"For what?" His brows pull together.

I grin. "To babysit that beer."

He laughs, his thumb brushing across the condensation on his glass resting on the bar. "Are you trying to get me drunk?" I love the way he's relaxed in the past hour.

I chew the corner of my lip, fighting the alcohol confidence. "I want to know what drunk Kace is like." *And naked Kace.*

"What was that look?" He raises a brow. Is he not feeling the alcohol at all? Didn't he say his beer was strong?

I shift on my stool. "I have no idea what you're talking about."

He tips his beer back, finishing the second half in a gulp and setting the glass down. Leaning closer, he rests his forearm on the bar. "Tell me, Mya..."

I mirror his position but rest my chin on my palm, and the nearness to him turns up the volume of my pulse. "What?" I think I whisper, but there's a good chance I'm talking louder than I think.

He leans closer, not touching me, but only a few inches from my face. His crisp, woodsy scent overpowers the dozen other smells of the bar in the best way. "Would you rather answer any one question I ask you or drink a beer?"

Fear and thrill rush through me, twisting around the alcohol in my brain like strands of Twizzlers. What could he possibly ask me that would be worse than that beer? "Truth," I answer because that's what this really feels like.

He closes the distance between us, bringing his lips to my ear, his breath warm against my skin. "Was it me you were picturing fucking in your childhood bed?"

I freeze, but the blood rushing to my face doesn't get the memo. Am I embarrassed? I feel a little caught, but I think I'm just turned on. Kace pulls back enough to gauge my expression. I swear I can feel my pupils dilate. There's a pinch in my lip where my teeth are sinking into it. *Kace is making a move.*

What does this mean? Does it matter? What little is left of my clear logic says to pry, but majority rules, and more of me wants to know what it would be like for Kace to touch me the way I've been dreaming about. I lean forward, thankful I'm drunk enough to be brave but not so trashed that I'll fall off my chair. My hand falls to his chest, and I can feel his warmth through the fabric.

Looking him dead in the eye, I whisper, "I pictured it in the bed upstairs too."

"Fuck, Mya." He reaches to tuck a curl behind my ear and leaves his fingers there, tightly intertwined in the strands with his palm resting on my cheek.

"Would you rather," I whisper, "stay here..." I slide my hand down his chest until I reach the hem of his shirt. Slipping my fingers under the fabric, I run them over his abs, feeling them contract at the contact. "Or give me a better look at what's under these clothes."

With one hand still holding my face, the other slips to my waist and he tugs me off the stool until I'm standing between his legs. "I've been wanting to tear these leggings off you since 5 a.m." Despite the flicker of hesitancy in his admission, the eye contact melts me right there on the spot as his hand smooths across my hip to pull me closer by my ass. "Please tell me that's what you want."

I nod.

"Tell me," he insists, not satisfied by my gesture, his expression shifting to a plea for me to want him too.

I slip my fingers through the front loop of his jeans. "The thought of you undressing me has distracted me from *everything* today, Kace."

He groans, and all I can think about is hearing it again in the bed that's waiting for us upstairs. He slides from the stool, dropping his hold on me but keeping us close as he reaches into his back pocket for his wallet. He catches the bartender's attention.

She makes her way to us. "Hey. Ready to cash out?" She flicks her non-judgmental eyes over us.

"Yes, please," Kace says, patiently handing over his card and giving her just enough attention to be polite.

She runs the card on a hand held machine, but Kace's eyes are back on me. He doesn't say anything–just lets his eyes roam my face. My heart thumps in my chest. I want this so badly. What all *this* entails, I couldn't tell you at this exact moment. But that's a conversation for tomorrow. The bartender sets the card and receipt in front of us, not at all bothered by the public display. "Thank you! Have a good night you two." I catch her smile in my periphery and watch Kace pull a twenty from his wallet. He traps it under the clip holding the receipt in place and signs the paper quickly.

"Let's go," he says, lacing his fingers through mine and pulling me toward the front door.

Kace is holding my hand.

Part of me wants to pinch myself to prove I'm not replaying fantasies in my mind. When we push outside, I'm hit by a cold that bites more than a pinch. The snowy air against my heated skin convinces me this is real life.

We walk on the snow dusted brick path that takes us from the bar to the hotel part of the resort, the nip in the air becoming less noticeable the more I focus on the feel of Kace's hand in mine.

He opens the door to the building for us, and with the rush of warm air comes a hit of alcohol registering in my brain as confidence and horniness. He reaches back for my hand before starting the steps, and I latch onto it, following him to the next floor.

We round the corner of the stairwell, and I can't take not being closer to him. I squeeze his hand enough to catch his attention. He freezes on a step halfway up the staircase, and I invade his space until he backs into the wall.

His hands fall to my waist so quickly, it's as if he was waiting for this. I run my hands up his chest, smoothing them across his pecs until I hit bare skin above his Henley. Slipping my fingers around his neck, I intertwine them with the short strands of his hair.

A groan slips from his parted lips as he looks at me, his grip around my waist tightening. His eyes flash from my lips back to my eyes, and I want to kiss him so badly.

All it would take is a tug on his neck and pressing up on my toes, and our lips would meet. God, I want that.

But the little memory Mya in the back of my head pushes play on the clip of Kace running away the last time we kissed.

He hesitates for a second, but then he starts to lean in. Panic sets in. "Race you to the room," I blurt, dropping my hold on him, spinning out of his grip, and booking it around the corner and up the final flight, my boots stomping on each step.

I feel him behind me, and I just know he's taking the steps two at a time. I'm out of breath by the time I run down the hallway. He catches me as I reach the door, grabbing me by the hips and spinning me until my back is pressed against the door. His fingers slide under my sweater, smoothing along my skin, as he leans in, until he reaches my bra.

His gaze meets mine, and my breath hitches. Bringing his lips to my ear, I feel him reach the key card to the sensor next to us. "Once we enter this room, you're not getting away from me."

My god, this man is hot. But my head is buzzing too hard to translate the meaning of his words. Does he mean tonight? Or past that? It doesn't matter. One thing at a time. I reach behind me, feeling for the door handle and pushing down on it when the lock clicks.

Kace pushes both me and the door forward, taking us into the room. My hands fall to his hips for stability. Neither of us bother with the light, but the moonlight casts a dim glow through partially drawn curtains.

He backs me up until my legs hit the bed, trapping both of us in the small space between the bed and the wall. Reaching between us, I grip the hem of his shirt and tug. He lifts his arms, helping me pull it over his head. Taking a moment to appreciate the way his dark forest sleeves bleed into a grayscale mountain on his shoulder, I hesitate with the shirt in my hands before tossing it on the ground next to me. Instead of following the movement, he keeps his gaze locked on me, and the second my hands are free, he takes his turn. He feels along the bottom of the sweater, until he's got both that and my tank top in his grip, and pulls them up and over my head before tossing them into the growing clothes pile.

He leans back against the wall to take me in–now just in my leggings and a light pink lace bra. It gives me the perfect opportunity to see him shirtless in the moonlight, jeans hanging from his hips. But only for a second, because in the next one he's dropped to his knees in front of me.

"Sit," he commands, and I obey, settling my ass on the edge of the bed. Kneeling, he slides his hand around one of my calves, gripping the heel of my boot with the other and pulling it from my foot. He repeats the motion on the other side.

Once my boots are in the space beside us, he loops his fingers under the band of my leggings and tugs. I lean back on my hands and lift my hips, allowing the fabric to slide between me and the comforter. He takes his time, stripping the spandex down my legs and tugging them off, leaving me in nothing but my bra and matching lace underwear.

He runs his thumbs across where the lace lies at the apex of my thighs, and the sensation of pressure over the fabric sends a rush of heat to my core. "Fuck, Mya. I've been thinking about this for so long."

His eyes roam my body, darkening when they snag on my belly button ring in the process of getting off his knees and kicking off his boots. He urges me back on the bed until he's hovering over me. Focusing my gaze on the way his abs are contracted over me, I reach for the button on his jeans. I flick it open and pinch the metal pull, slowly tugging it down the track. With each tooth it unlinks, my body heats in anticipation.

Pushing his jeans down the best I can from where I'm trapped under him, he helps me kick them the rest of the way off. He readjusts himself and settles over me, then dips his head until an inch from kissing me.

An inch from a second chance.

Chapter Twenty-Six

Kace

"Fuck." I pull away from Mya, feeling the distance with every inch our skin gets further apart. Sitting back on my heels, my dick strains against my briefs, and I allow myself a long glance at the goddess splayed beneath me. Jesus fuck, she's hot.

Her skin is soft, covered by nothing but the glow of the starlight and pink lace. The cut of her bra makes me want to rip it off as much as I want to admire how incredible she looks with it on. Her blonde curls are wild against the comforter, and I have a strong urge to run my fingers through them again. I have the desire to touch every inch of her body. But fuck. I internally curse, running my fingers through my hair in frustration, and taking a deep inhale with my eyes closed.

Refocusing on Mya, I'm met with wide eyes. Oh shit. "I don't think I have a condom," I admit, and a visible exhale leaves her. Does she think I don't want this?

Fuck, do I want this. I want *her*.

"You *think*?" she whispers.

I dig through my memory, trying to picture where I could possibly be hiding one. I'm always prepared–overprepared even. There has to be one somewhere. Maybe in my truck.

Note to self: stash condoms in every bag I own when we get home. I glance over at my bag sitting in the chair in the corner of the room. "There *might* be one in my bag." I rub my hands up her thighs.

"Are you sure you want to do this?" she whispers, doubt betraying her.

"I've spent the majority of today trying to convince myself I don't." Her brows furrow, and she moves the slightest bit, like she might try to escape. I slide my hands further up her thighs, slipping my fingers under the lace of her panties. "You're not getting away from me, Mya." I love the sound of her name rolling off my tongue as much as I want my tongue on her. "I want this." She doesn't look like she believes me, so I reach for her hand, placing it over the bulge in my briefs, and relish in the way her eyes widen. She squeezes lightly, taking control of her hand. I groan at her touch, even through fabric. "Trust me. I want *you*."

She smiles, biting into the corner of her lip, and I want to kiss her. But if I don't have a condom, I can't risk getting that riled up. There's no way I'd be able to sleep in the same bed as her. She chuckles. "Are you going to look for one, or…"

"Yes. Yup." I don't want to move from where she's palming me, but the thought of being inside her is motivation. I hop off the bed, heading straight for my bag. Squatting in front of the chair, I glance over my shoulder to find Mya rolling over, laying on her stomach, her chin propped up by her fists and her breasts pushed together, observing my every move.

Opening my duffel, I push my clothes to one side and unzip a small pocket in the bottom corner. Without the bedroom light on, it's hard to see, but my dick twitches as my fingers land on a foil packet like I'm Pavlov's fucking dog.

I hold the wrapper up for Mya to see, and she collapses her head onto her arms folded beneath her, a smile stretching across her face. God, she's beautiful. I spin on my heels, bringing me to eye level with her in this tiny ass room.

I brush a thumb across her cheek, and she leans into it. "Thank the condom gods for blessing us tonight," she says. I chuckle, and she outstretches her arms, taking the foil from me. She tears it open with her teeth, and it's enough to have me fully straining against my briefs again. With the edge of the condom pinched between her fingers, she uses her other hand to reach for my underwear.

Standing, I give her the access she needs to tug them off, and help her toss them aside, leaving me fully erect in front of her. I can't help but wonder if the instant comfort and confidence is the alcohol or *us*. She keeps her eyes on the mission, rolling the condom over my dick slowly, like she's enjoying it, and just when I think I can't get any harder, she caresses my balls in her hand and squeezes.

Fuck me. I'm anxious at the thought of my dick being inside her mouth at some point, but right now, I need it inside *her*.

She glances up at me, and if her hand wasn't massaging my balls, she'd look innocent. "I think it's time for you to fuck me, Kace."

I never expected to hear those words fly from her lips, but it's sexy as hell–a new side of Mya I'm just as enamored by. "Way past time." I join her on the bed, attempting to roll her to her back, but she resists, remaining on her stomach. I slip her bra strap down, kissing her bare shoulder. "What is it?" I whisper against her ear.

"I want..." she starts, but stops herself, burying her face in her arms.

I smooth my hand across her back, loving the way it sends chills racing across her skin. I kiss her shoulder again, then pepper kisses down her arm until I reach the hand folded under her face. She twists her head to look at me. "Tell me what you want, Mya."

Even in the low light, I can see her eyes searching mine–although I don't know for what. I hate not knowing her the way that only comes with time. Not knowing her mind, or her body in a way that would give me all the answers she doesn't say aloud. She takes a breath. "I want you to fuck me from behind."

I chuckle, planting another kiss on her shoulder. "If you're asking for things like that, you can have whatever the hell you want."

She gives me a nervous half-smile, but I refuse to let her get in her head. I move behind her, standing at the end of the bed. Tugging on her ankles, I bring her closer, until her knees are at the edge of the mattress. Reaching up, I loop my fingers on the edge of the lace, sliding her underwear down her legs and revealing the most perfect ass. Apparently all those jump squats she's been doing that rattle the floor from the living room are paying off.

I slap her cheek, not able to resist. The smack echoes through the small room, mixing with the sound of her sweet moan. I think I hear her mutter my name, but I can't be sure, until she says it again. She twists her head enough to say, "Kace, don't make me wait any longer."

With that, I hike her up by her hips, bringing me level with her entrance. She adjusts her knees on the mattress, waiting. I have no fucking clue how we got here, but I'm sure as shit thankful for it. Brushing my thumbs over her opening to test for wetness, she shudders at the touch before melting into it. She backs her ass into me the slightest bit, and I pull her apart with a thumb on each side before using one to rub a circle against her. Another moan leaves her, and my dick twitches at how wet and ready she is.

I press the tip against her, moving my fingers out of the way and using them to spread her as I push in further. Barely being inside her sends a jolt of pleasure radiating through my body. I groan at her tightness and warmth as I push in another inch, feeling her stretch around me.

It takes every ounce of willpower to not bottom out, to not slam into her perfectly tight pussy and see how well she can take me. She whimpers like the anticipation is killing her too, and my resolve shatters. With a thrust of my hips, I fill her completely.

"Oh my god," she cries, her fingers gripping the comforter for resistance as I pull out slowly. With a firm hold on her hips, I rail her again. This time, I slide in easier, with zero friction, her arousal welcoming me inside. *Fuck, she feels good.*

I pull out an inch, pushing back in, then repeating the same movement. My dry spell has me more than ready to explode, and Mya just existing, with the perfect view of her ass and my dick repeatedly disappearing into her pussy, is the pin being pulled from the grenade. There's no going back now.

My grip on her hips tightens as I attempt to control my thrusts with pleasure building in my spine. "Play with yourself for me, Mya," I command. I need her to come with me, and at this angle, I know she can do far better than I can.

She moans with my next thrust, her head still lying on her folded arms as she grips the covers.

"Mya."

Her name on its own seems to get her following directions more than anything. Leaning on one forearm, she reaches between her legs and fuck, do I wish I could see her playing with herself. I picture it the best I can. Her pink-painted fingernails moving back and forth as she presses the pads of her fingers to her clit, slowly at first. But as her orgasm gets within sight, her motion becomes quicker and more erratic. "That's it," I praise her, enamored by every fucking sound leaving her perfect lips, and the way she chases my dick by pushing back every time I pull out.

"Kace," she whimpers, and my name feels like a cross between a prayer and a plea. "I'm so close."

I pick up speed, driving into her at a steady pace. My tightening balls hitting against her turns out to be the final stimulation we both need to tip over the edge. She contracts around me, feeling even tighter than when I entered her for the first time, and pulling the most intense orgasm from me.

My body shudders, my tight muscles going slack. I do my best to continue steady thrusts even though they've slowed. My dick twitches inside her, and I'm rewarded by another wave of pleasure rolling through Mya.

If I didn't just come harder than I have in a long fucking time, I'm convinced I'd already be hard again. When I'm sure she's leveled out, I pull out of her slowly. Slipping the condom off, I knot it quickly and toss it into the trash bin that's only a few feet from me. I'm back to the bed before Mya even has a chance to flip, and I watch her, in what feels like slow motion, turn to her back.

I stand there taking her in. Her cheeks are flushed. Her forearms are crossed over her forehead, and she's looking up at me with a sweet, sedated smile that goes straight to my ego. Knowing I could stare at her all night, but also wanting to climb under the sheets with her, I reach for her hands.

"Up." I wait for her to link her hands with mine so I can pull her to sit. "Get ready for bed."

She gives me a sleepy smile even though I know it can't be later than ten. A glance to the nightstand behind her confirms it's a quarter til. "You can take a turn first if you want. You'll probably be quicker than me," she whispers.

"Alright. I'll be right out." I swipe a clean pair of boxers from my bag and make quick work cleaning up and brushing my teeth.

I open the door to find Mya patiently waiting as she holds her pajamas in front of her. She tries to walk past me without a word, but I snag her by the waist and pull her back flush to my chest, reveling in the feel of her ass against my still semi-hard dick. "Come back soon."

She twists her neck enough to glance up at me, a spark in her eyes telling me she wants that too.

I'm under the covers when Mya comes out of the bathroom in pajama shorts and a sports bra. The little pink diamond heart dangles from her belly button. I have the urge to pull her in by her hips and press my lips to her stomach, but even in the dim starlight, I can see her hesitancy. I fold back the covers on her side of the bed, encouraging her to join me.

She crawls onto the mattress. I toss the blankets over her, and she freezes like she doesn't know what to do next. Wrapping my arm around her waist, I pull her into me. I have no fucking clue what this means. I don't know how either of us will feel tomorrow because I can't even wrap my head around how I feel right now.

Past satiated.

Relaxed.

In control.

Even if it's just for this moment.

As Mya intertwines her fingers with mine, I replay the past hour over and over, like counting sheep, until we're both asleep.

Chapter Twenty-Seven

With my eyes still closed, I feel my mind slowly waking up as daylight seeps into my awareness. This bed is so comfortable, like a freaking cloud. Feeling a slight chill on my chest, I tug on the comforter to curl into it, but I'm met with resistance.

Kace.

Oh my god. My eyes spring open.

Kace.

We had sex.

All of a sudden I'm aware of the weight of his arm draped over my stomach. I twist as slowly as possible, turning to face him and feeling his hand drag across my skin as I do. We never closed the blackout curtains last night so early morning light illuminates the room just enough to make me feel more vulnerable than I have in a long time.

I recall the chain of events. We were drunk, but not *that* drunk. I wanted him. He wanted me too. And the sex. It was so good I can still feel him inside of me as I let the memory play out.

Staring at a sleeping Kace, I wonder what he thinks about it. He looks calm and relaxed. His hair is matted to the side a bit–with an Alfalfa hair–but he's as handsome as ever. The urge to press my lips against his and wake him up with a kiss has me itching to touch him, but I keep my hands folded in front of myself as I lie on the mattress.

I don't know where we stand. My heart thumps so loudly in my chest that I worry it'll wake him. I'm not ready for that. I don't know what to say because I don't know what *he* is going to say. God, I hate conversations like this.

"Stop staring at me," he whispers, and my eyes widen.

Oh my god. Oh my god. Oh my god. I'm not ready. I need coffee or to contemplate my options during an entire listen of One Direction's *Midnight Memories* album before I'm prepared to face the day.

When I don't respond, he opens his eyes, staring back at me. He holds my gaze for a moment, then pulls his hand from my waist. My heart sinks at the same time his hand hits the mattress.

I think I like him–a lot. And not like Brittany Snow thinking she's in love with John Tucker even though she hardly knows him.

"Good morning." His rough morning voice hits my soul just right.

"Hi," I manage.

"What are you thinking?" His eyes search my face, and it feels like the most loaded question I've ever been asked.

A dozen thoughts flash through my mind. Most of them are about Kace and sex, but I can't bring myself to share them. "I saw an owl when I was driving home from Chloe's the other night."

His brows furrow. "What?"

"Yeah. I think it was a baby owl. Just sitting there on the side of the road."

"An owl was *sitting* on the side of the road? Like in the grass?"

I nod. "Yeah, my headlights shone on him and his yellow eyes stared right back at me."

"Him?"

"Yeah. I have no idea how to tell the sex of a bird." The word sex coming from my mouth heats my cheeks and flusters my heart. "But in my head it was a he. He was just hanging out on the side of the road. It felt concerning. Have you ever seen an owl on the side of the road?" *My Lanta*, Mya. How many times can you say *owl on the side of the road*? *How many licks does it take to get to the center of a Tootsie Pop? The answer is way too many to both.*

"Can't say that I have..." he answers with a tone of confusion. "Is this owl a metaphor for something?"

"Umm. No? It's a real owl. I was thinking maybe he was waiting for his girlfriend to go worm picking or something." I'm painfully aware I'm rambling, but maybe I can throw him off enough to completely forget we had sex. Clearly he wants to if the first thing he did when he woke up was pull away from me.

"Maybe he was waiting with your Hogwarts letter," he suggests, surprising me.

I fight a smile and lose, loving that it's the reference he went with. "That's definitely it. Finally, my blue robes are getting dusty."

He adjusts, folding his arm under his head. "Blue?"

"Yeah. Obviously I'd be a Ravenclaw. Have you seen my creativity level?"

"I have."

"And Luna Lovegood is my spirit person, so. Yeah. You'd be a Slytherin, don't you think?"

His brows furrow, and—oh god, why is that so attractive? I need his hands back on me. I *want* to kiss him. My thought train continues to veer to another track and–*kiss.*

We didn't kiss last night. Obviously we didn't because I expertly avoided it since I was scared he'd run away. But now he's here, looking all gorgeous, except... he just deliberately stopped touching me. *Argh.* I don't know.

"Why do you say that?"

"I don't know. You're smart and successful but also grumpy. Seems right. That sucks though." I pinch my lips together, regretting the last thought escaping.

"Why?"

"Nothing. Never mind. So... What's our plan for the day?"

He reaches out, nudging my hand with the back of his knuckles. "Tell me."

"Umm. Just glad we didn't meet at Hogwarts, you know?"

"I'm not following."

I sit, the comforter falling to my waist and making me feel even more vulnerable. To Kace's credit, he doesn't let his eyes wander over my bare stomach or linger on my boobs only covered by a thin sports bra. Although maybe that's not a good thing. I fidget with my fingers in front of me. "We'd be enemies if we met there. That's all. You know unless we pulled some Dramione situation. Which wouldn't make sense if I was a Ravenclaw, I guess. I don't know."

"What's a Dramione situation?" He shakes his head. "Never mind." Sitting, he faces me. "Mya?"

I try to avoid staring at his perfectly toned, bare chest. "Yeah?"

"I think we should just talk about the fact that we had sex."

My eyes shift away from him before coming back, my heart ping-ponging erratically like the bouncing Windows screen-saver on crack. Meanwhile, he's *stoned under the bleachers* cool about this. "Yeah. Ok. What about it?"

"I don't want you to think I was taking advantage of you."

I shake my head, unsure where he's going with this. "I don't think that."

"Still. I'm sorry. We should have talked about it first. Neither of us are in a place to be dating, and sex with your roommate is complicated."

"Uh huh."

"That's what you said, right? That you weren't ready to date. And you didn't want to date me."

I vaguely recall saying that. Weeks ago. How much could have really changed since then? Am I ready for another relationship after three back-to-back? There's no way. Tears spring to my eyes at the thought of losing Kace before I've even had him, and I know my thoughts are the evil version of me trying to gaslight myself because I'm scared.

His eyes shift over my face. "I'm getting the feeling we aren't on the same page."

I shake my head, willing the tear sitting on my waterline not to fall. I've turned the page, but he hasn't. Maybe I've been terrible about voicing my thoughts and feelings in the past, but I'm tired of being that way. I don't have the *time* to continue being that way. *I don't want to be that way with Kace.* "I don't think so."

He's silent. I don't know if he's trying to decide what to say or just doesn't want to say it.

I drop my gaze to my fingers picking at the comforter around my waist. "It's just a crush," I fib, fear raking through me.

He takes a breath. "Last night was... amazing." He sounds genuine, but I sense a "but" coming.

"Just not enough to do it again." I glance up, needing visual confirmation.

"That's not it." He sighs, running his fingers through his hair. Why does this feel like a breakup and we weren't even together? "I just... I can't be in a relationship. I don't trust you not to leave."

He didn't say he doesn't trust *anyone*. He specifically said *me*. I take a breath, pulling myself together because that's my only option right now. "That's fine. I totally get it. It'll be like *Fight Club*. We won't talk about it."

"We don't have to pretend it didn't happen."

I wave my hand to shoo away the comment. "Oh. I won't forget about it. Just don't want to talk about it. You're great at not talking about things, so it shouldn't be a problem." I cringe at my words. I didn't mean it like *that*. Okay, maybe I did, but... "Don't worry. We're totally in sync now. Maybe not JT and the boys level in sync but let's be real, no one is."

Letting my rambling slide, he takes a deep breath and releases it in a sigh. "I want you to stay at the apartment. For the record."

I let out a sigh of relief. "Thank god because I don't have anywhere else to go yet."

"You can stay as long as you'd like." He tilts his face down to look at me better. "Are you sure you're okay?"

"Absolutely." I force a smile. "We still hardly know each other," I say, even though it feels like a lie. "Plus, it's not like we did oral or anything, and that's way more intimate than sex. So... not a big deal. Promise."

He eyes me like he's not sure if he should believe me, and my stupid little brain convinces myself it's because he *does* know me well enough. "I'm sorry about this." He waves his hand between us like it was a simple mix up at the grocery store.

"Don't be. Really. Sex was bound to happen eventually. Two single, attractive people can only be around each other so much before they act on it. My feelings are just misguided by the morning after an orgasm haze." I ignore the gut-wrenching feeling.

He chuckles. "Is that a thing?"

I shrug. "Feels like it." I throw the covers off me, thinking it might be nice to have Lucy Whitmore's short-term memory problem right about now. I slap my hand against his knee. "And it just means it's time for morning after breakfast. Where are you taking me?"

His eyes close for a moment as he shakes his head, amused. "I know just the place."

Chapter Twenty-Eight

I rap my fingers on Kace's bedroom door, then press my ear against the wood, trying to get a clue to what he's doing. I managed to avoid more awkwardness after being rejected this morning, focusing all my effort on acting completely unbothered. When we got back from the mountain this afternoon, he went to the gym, and I'm pretty sure he went on a run after that. I was working on my weekly craft project when he got home. He said hi, but I haven't seen him since. He didn't even come out of his room for dinner.

"Come in," his muffled voice seeps through the barrier.

I creak the door open and stick my head in. "Hi. Whatcha doing?"

"Working." His eyes remained trained on the right of his three computer screens.

"But it's Saturday."

With his hand still on the mouse, he leans back in his ergonomic chair and glances at me. "Weren't you working earlier?"

"Yes. But it's dark out now. Work is over. Let's do something fun." I'm tempted to leave on my own, but I'm desperate for things to not be awkward or distant between us.

"My work *is* fun."

"Yeah. So is reading a phone book. Stop being annoying," I sass, pushing the door open more so I can stand inside his room. My eyes flick to the perfectly made bed, and my thoughts go rogue and dirty, wanting to mess it up. I focus back on Kace, taking a step backward. It's already hard enough being in the room next door when he doesn't want me back, so until further notice, his bedroom is a hot lava pit I refuse to step on for fear of losing the game.

His hands fall to his lap. "What do you want to do?"

"We could go to a bar?" I know exactly which one I want to go to, so I hope he says yes.

"Not really a bar kind of guy anymore." I was afraid he'd say that.

"Okay, but hear me out. There's this new bar–they modeled it off the concept of one in New York City. It's *made* for millennials. It opens at five and closes at ten. There won't even be babies at the bar begging them to play sucky music." I make my eyes look as hopeful as possible, praying I can guilt him into going with me. "Come on, Kace! Evolve with the times," I tack on as a last-ditch effort.

"I'm not a Pokémon."

"If you were, you'd be Charmander. Sometimes you're sad and lonely, and I'm worried about your flame going out."

He smirks. "You don't want to go with Chloe instead?" I already asked Chloe, and she's not available tonight. It's times like these that I wish my sister lived closer and we could do baby-raising things together, but that's not reality. And if I'm being honest with myself, the person I want to go with most is sitting in front of me. I've just been working up the courage to ask him after already being rejected once today.

"No. It's okay though. I can go alone. It's within walking distance."

"Fine. I'll go," he says, and I can't for the life of me tell if I've genuinely convinced him or if he feels obligated.

"Really?!" My grin widens, and he chuckles. "Yay!" I throw my hands up in victory. "First round is on me." I leave his room to get ready but get the distinct feeling that he's shaking his head behind me.

Twenty minutes later, Kace and I walk into the bar, and I'm already in love. In the entryway is a giant circular mirror, made to look like the back of a CD with thin lines in repeating circles and a surface reflective enough to see my light, distressed jeans, white, thin-strapped crop top and sneakers. I love the subtleness of my dangling pink heart belly button ring, but I bet the Playboy bunny one I had when I first got the piercing would be a hit here. "Kace!" I exclaim, not even caring that I'm already an embarrassing level of hype for the nostalgia that I know is coming our way.

"Hmm?" He pulls his attention from where he's already looking into the room.

"Take a picture with me please?" I give him puppy dog eyes, hoping we'll skip the whole part where we bicker before he gives in.

"Sure."

I want to scream, jump up and down and dance like Jenna Rink, but I don't give Kace a single second to change his mind. Pulling my hot pink digital camera from my fanny pack, I hold the silver on button until our reflection in the CD appears on the screen. Kace smirks for only a second before he hides it away. He shoves his hands into the pockets of his bomber jacket, and between that and his jeans, he looks so hot. I smile wide, throwing up a peace sign before I snap the picture. I don't bother checking the photo before sliding my camera back into my bag. I don't plan on posting it anywhere–it's just for me and the delusional version of myself that wants to pretend Kace is mine.

"Thanks." I beam up at him. He gives me a small nod and holds his hand out for me to lead the way into the dark bar. It's pure chaos and magic.

"Fucking hell, I already have a headache," Kace complains as the server walks by with a plate of food that looks like something Shaggy and Scooby would eat.

I spin slowly on my heel, taking it all in. Instead of overhead lights, the high-top tables are bordered with rope lights, giving the room a neon-blue glow.

I clamp onto Kace's arm, his hands shoved in his pockets, and drag him toward the bar. Slipping into an empty space, I examine the bartop. It's hundreds of VHS tapes lined up and set in epoxy. When I look up, the bartender slides a floppy disk coaster in front of each of us. "What can I get you two?" he asks, looking casual in his jeans and tan T-shirt that says, "I'm tired of this, grandpa."

I peek at Kace to see if he's finding amusement in this the way that I am. Instead of paying attention to the bartender, he's scanning the VHS spines. I rest my chin on my palm. "Anything fun?"

He nods to the space behind him where the specials project onto the wall. I look toward its source to see an overhead projector with the cocktail menu written on a transparent sheet. "The *Cool Runnings* Cocktail is peach schnapps, white rum, blue curacao and pineapple juice, and the *Cheaper by the Dozen* is basically an Adios, Motherfucker."

"Oooh." I link my arm through Kace's, not respecting his personal space. "Kace, what do you want?"

He looks over at me, letting me stay close to him, then directs his attention to the bartender. "We'll take one of each, please."

"Coming right up," the guy says. "Are you hungry at all? They made a Bruce Bogtrotter chocolate cake that's pretty fucking good."

Cake with alcohol doesn't sound good, but like...

"She'll have a slice. Thank you," Kace says.

I snap my gaze to him as the bartender walks away. Without permission, I snuggle against his arm. "You're the best roommate. Has anyone ever told you that?"

"No," he responds in all seriousness, and I remember that his ex has been his only roommate. I'm suddenly so sad for him if she never gave him that impression. He is the easiest person to live with.

"Well, you are." I pull away from him, immediately missing his warmth. "Do you want to sit at the bar? Or find a table?"

"Here is fine." He gestures in front of us, and we slide onto the barstools.

I swivel my head to take in the rest of the room. At the end of the bar is another employee dressed in the *13 Going on 30 dress*. The woman next to her is in tight blue jeans and a USA-branded cropped shirt, and I immediately know what she's going for when she climbs onto the bar and sprays something straight from the soda gun and into the Solo cups of a few customers.

In the far right corner, there's a fenced area that looks like a boxing ring, except there are three people dressed in fake sumo wrestler outfits crashing into each other and falling over into giggle fits. "Ever seen *Blank Check*?" our bartender asks, setting our drinks on the floppy disk coasters in front of us.

"Yes," Kace and I say simultaneously, which tickles me so much for some reason.

"That's the idea over there. Games you thought would be epic as a kid but couldn't afford." He's giving us the scoop like it's obvious we've never been here. "And over there–" he points to the end of the room on our left, "is more handheld games." Kace and I follow his gaze to the pull-down screen with *1080° Snowboarding* projected on it. There are a couple of guys on the floor sitting on bean bags really into their game. "Video games. Bop it. Legos. Operation. Hungry Hungry Hippos."

"Basically that scene from *The Santa Clause 2* where he makes all their childhood dream toys appear?" I respond in half-statement, half-question.

"Exactly. Let me know if you need anything," he says.

As soon as he walks away, another guy in a "Vote for Pedro" shirt appears behind us with a metal platter covered in a giant slice of chocolate cake.

I meet his gaze. "Oh my gosh. Thank you." He sets it on the bar top in front of us. When he disappears, I reach for the two forks and hand one to Kace. He takes it from me, but he doesn't make a move to try it.

I, on the other hand, don't mind if I do. I stab through the creamy chocolate frosting and into the fluffy cake for a bite. *"Oh my Lantaaaa,"* I practically moan as I chew. "Kace. This is so good." I glance over at him, noticing he hasn't moved. He's just watching me. "Don't you want some?"

His eyes snap to mine like he's shaken from his trance. Without a word, and still leaning back in his bar seat, he reaches his fork to break off a piece of cake. I watch him bring it to his mouth, chew and swallow. Even in the faint lighting, I can see the way his throat works when he swallows, and his tongue peeks out to lick some rogue frosting off his lip, and right then and there, I realize that he's the person I want to do everything or absolutely nothing with. I could sit here in this bar, partaking in nothing except enjoying his company, and I'd be the happiest girl in the room.

"What?" he asks, even though he's watching me watch him, and I'm pretty confident it's apparent I want him.

The song changes, and I tip my head as if it'll help me listen to the music coming from the speakers. "Holy nostalgia." I grin. "Here (In Your Arms)" by Hellogoodbye. "This song smells like Hollister."

Kace chuckles, and we reach our forks for another bite so in sync that the tines clink. Two of my prongs get stuck around one of his, and the split second it takes to pull them apart sends tension racing through me. We're so close, yet so far all at once, and being around him is the easiest and hardest thing I've ever done. Without a word, we maneuver our bites.

I chew and swallow, glancing around the room. "I forgot about our drinks!" I reach for both of them, one in each hand. I bop them up and down as I sing, "I got two drinks. I got two drinks. I got two drinks. Hey Hey!"

"Would you like me to get you a pickle?" He tries to hide his smirk behind another bite of cake, but my smile widens, so satisfied he caught my reference. "Which one do you want?"

He sets his fork down. "Whichever one you don't."

I ping-pong my gaze between the two, deciding I'll try both. They're both blue from Curacao, so I'm not sure which is which, but I try the one in my left hand first. My eyes widen, and I choke a bit. This must be the AMF because it's straight liquor. "That'll make you give back something you didn't steal," I say, blinking away the moisture in my eyes. Kace smirks as I taste the other one. "Oooohhh." The pineapple and peach flavors flood my taste buds. "Yum." I hold out both drinks for him. "Could this place get any better?"

He reaches for the glasses, and our fingers brush during the exchange. The touch sends butterflies fluttering across my skin. As if on cue, a multi-colored disco ball lights from above, the colored beams streaming from the ball like Carrigan from Casper crossing over.

"Change my address." I throw my hands up. "I live here now."

"Finally I get my space back," Kace teases, setting the drinks on the bar top.

"Hey, rude." I lean in to poke his arm, but the second I move closer, I immediately regret it because all I want to do is kiss him. "Umm. I have to pee. I'll be right back." I barely catch his furrowed brows before I slide off the barstool and find my way to the bathroom.

Since I'm already there, I might as well pee, so I slip into one of the stalls. After I finish, I reach for the lock but freeze.

"Did you see that guy at the bar?" A high-pitched squeal comes from in front of the sink.

"He's so hot. Do you think he's single? God, finding good men at thirty is harder than finding Waldo," another woman adds.

I lean forward slowly, just enough to spy. Through the crack, I can barely make out the giant pink neon light sign on the wall that says, "You're Beauty and You're Grace." My stomach flips. Normally I'd be all over the decor and filing it away in my mental Pinterest board, but only being able to think about Kace is preventing compartmentalization. Plus, I'm pretty sure these three women are talking about the guy I'm sick over.

"I don't know. There was some girl with him a few minutes ago. But it didn't necessarily look like they were in a relationship."

"Maybe they aren't into PDA, but did you see the way he was looking at her? They're definitely together." Oh. I guess they aren't talking about Kace. I'm losing my mind making assumptions over here.

"We should find out. DIBS!" One of the girls screams. "I saw him first."

"No way! You know men in bomber jackets are my weakness. And did you see his hair? It's flawless. His perfectly trimmed facial hair too? God, what I'd do to feel that between my thighs."

The three girls giggle, and I feel like I might be sick. Pressing my forehead against the back of the stall door, I close my eyes and take a breath.

"Fine, but if you strike out and it turns out blonde is his type, I get him."

"Deal."

I peek through the crack again, watching them simultaneously turn to the mirror to reapply their lip gloss. They leave the bathroom with a walk that says they think they're cooler than Paris Hilton in a Juicy tracksuit, and it's not until the door clicks behind them that I come out of the stall.

Chapter Twenty-Nine

I examine the VHS spines again while I wait for Mya. It's mostly chick flicks, but a few classics catch my eye. *Mrs. Doubtfire. Pirates of the Caribbean. The Prestige.* Hugh Jackman is the Jennifer Aniston of men. *The Truman Show. Edward Scissorhands. The Matrix.* I love that series. I wonder if Mya has seen it or if she'd watch it with me. I don't deserve to plan a *not date* after dismissing her when I damn well know I have a "crush" on her too.

Resting my forearms on the bartop, I fiddle with the Rubik's Cube in front of me. I can't believe we didn't kiss last night. I didn't think about it until the car ride home this morning when I replayed the entire experience on repeat, but I can't recall for the life of me if that was my doing, hers or a total fluke. I'm spinning the colors randomly at this point, not even bothering to try and solve it. All I know is I regret not finding out what it's like to *actually* kiss her. I was a fucking idiot for bailing the first time, and it's too late now. Because the overwhelming feeling of doubt outweighs my curiosity, and I hate myself for it. Or maybe I hate Ruby for it.

I lock in an entire row of white squares by accident and decide to put in a little more effort–if only to distract myself from thinking about the way Mya's smile widens at every nostalgic reminder in this place. I didn't want to go out tonight, but that smile alone makes me want to drop to my knees and beg for a chance–amongst other tempting things. Thankfully, we've stuck to our *Fight Club* agreement and haven't mentioned our hookup all day. I'm capable of a lot of things. Hell, I can hack better than Walter White can sell meth. But if Mya brings up last night, knowing I can't be with her, I might lose her altogether.

Where is she anyway? Setting the Rubik's Cube down, I scan toward the bathroom. This place is actually cool, and it occurs to me that maybe Mya holding on so tightly to nostalgia isn't much different from simply choosing to focus on the good in life. That being said, this place feels impossible to navigate between all the colors, games and people, so I don't even notice when someone is standing next to me.

Finally she's back.

I swivel in my bar stool, coming face-to-face with... *not Mya.* I stare at the brunette in front of me. She's pretty if you're into the *Jersey Shore* vibes, but she's not my type.

Contradictory to everything I've believed in the past about the women I've been interested in, my type is Mya.

"Hi," the woman says, her hand falling to my bicep. I follow the motion, staring at where we connect. I don't want anyone touching me except for Mya.

"Uh. Hi." I twist my chair enough that her hand falls away, immediate relief shooting through me.

"So my friends and I made a bet."

I stare back, refusing to encourage whatever the hell this is.

"They think that girl you were with earlier is your girlfriend. Is she?"

"Yes," I lie, although it feels like a trap.

"Well, you fooled me. You don't seem that into her. It looks like you'd rather be anywhere else, to be honest." My gut twists at the thought of Mya thinking I feel indifferent toward her. The random girl clasps her hand around my arm again. "I can fake an emergency if you need an escape plan."

I narrow my eyes, tugging my arm and hoping she takes the hint. "The only escape plan I'm interested in is one with Sylvester Stallone."

She trails her fingers up my arm, touching me without any indication that I want her. Leaning in close, I can smell the alcohol on her breath when she whispers, "You can tie me up if being trapped is your thing, then."

She's close enough to kiss me, and unease settles in my gut. It's not that I'm opposed to tying up a woman and worshiping her body. But not *this* woman, and I'm even more irritated because she butchered my reference.

Intuition makes me glance up. Looking over the woman's shoulder, I spot Mya, who is frozen in place about ten feet away. She's devastatingly beautiful. Simple Mya is my favorite. Even without colorful clothing, she stands out. She looks comfortable in the way that couch rotting with a *Harry Potter* marathon and a pumpkin beer makes you feel.

But right now, she also looks really fucking upset. I stand, completely ignoring the girl failing to get my attention. I should feel bad about being rude, but I don't. I brush past her, taking a few steps that bring me to Mya. I want to pull her into me, make whatever she's feeling disappear. Instead, I shove my hands into the pockets of my jacket. "What's wrong?" I turn to follow her gaze, which is tracking something behind me–the girl going back to her friends in the corner. "What's wrong?" I repeat.

"She was flirting with you," Mya whispers, her eyes glossy.

My brows furrow. "What? I mean, I know, but..." I'm not sure what's happening. I'm clearly not into her.

"I know you don't want to date me or kiss me or whatever, but..."

Panic floods my body. Without thinking, I reach for Mya's face, framing it with my hands on her neck, my thumbs holding her jaw. I bend my knees enough to level with her. "But what?"

"What did I do to make you not trust me?" Her voice is soft and fragile simultaneously, and it breaks me.

Fuck. I can't remember the last time I felt like this. Maybe when I lived in Virginia and Ruby got denied for her dream job. There's an urge inside me to help her, make this better, but my instincts beg me to shut this down and push her away like I have been. The last time I completely let someone in, *she let someone else inside of her.*

If I give an inch, how can I be sure this situation with Mya won't spiral out of control too? I want so badly to get on this ride, but I can't help but stress about the safety rating on the damn track.

Not wanting Ruby's infidelity to bleed into my relationship with Mya anymore, I realize I have to give her *something*–something I can manage for now until I figure out what the next steps are. I need to at least get in the damn seat and click my harness into place.

I sigh, scaling my hands down her arms until my fingers link with hers. She's tense in my grasp, but she doesn't pull away. I tentatively stroke the back of her hands. While it's not grade-A flirting, I'm not running out the door. "Mya," I start, but instead of holding my gaze, her eyes drop to the ground.

"I just want to go home," she mumbles.

"Hey," I say. She doesn't respond. "Mya," I try again, invading her space by moving half a step closer–close enough to get a whiff of her sweet vanilla perfume. I squeeze her hands, and she finally glances up. "We're going to talk about this when we get home."

She hesitates. "You don't talk about feelings, Kace."

"We're going to talk about it." I'm firm, releasing her to pull my wallet from my pocket, moving away from her to hand a fifty to the bartender.

We walk home, the ten minutes dragging on in silence and tension. I itch to grab her hand again to comfort her, but I opt to just move to the car side of the sidewalk instead.

Mya makes a beeline for the couch as soon as we enter the apartment. She pulls the blanket she made for me from where it's folded on the back of the leather and wraps it around her bare shoulders in a way that feels like she's closing herself off.

I toss my keys on the counter, then rub my hands against the front of my jeans, realizing they're sweaty. I squeeze between the couch and the coffee table–past where she's leaning against the armrest, her knees pulled to her chest–and sit on the far cushion. *Fuck.* I lean forward, my forearms resting on my knees, unable to face her.

"Ruby was cheating on me for the last year of our relationship," I admit for the first time aloud. I shake my head. "An entire *year*, and I had no clue," I say more to myself than Mya.

"I'm sorry," she whispers, sounding genuinely upset for me. "But I've never cheated on anyone, Kace." She takes a breath. "I would never cheat on you."

Her confession slams into my chest so hard I swear it knocks the air from my lungs. Not the cheating part, but the way she's openly admitting she wants to be with me. "What Ruby did fucked me up. Partially because of the action itself. Partially because I feel like a goddamn idiot for not seeing it."

"You're not an idiot," Mya whispers, and I glance over to see her staring at the blanket where her fingers hold it together at her chest.

I sigh. "Mostly it's that she should have made it clear that things weren't working between us anymore. She wasted time I can't afford to waste."

Mya looks up. "What do you mean?"

"I want to get married and have a family. I'm thirty-one, and I don't trust anyone. It will take time for me to find someone, and I have to give myself a leg up by trying with someone who doesn't have a track record of staying with men for the hell of it–because they can't break up with someone."

I watch in what feels like a slow-motion assault as my words process in her mind. Her eyes widen. Her body freezes.

Like the asshole I am, I continue, trying to backtrack. "I know that my issues from Ruby are my problem. There's nothing you can do because I'm not in a place to trust you. Your past tells me you can't handle a relationship, and I don't trust that in three months, or a year, or however long from now, you won't hurt me too." *So much for backtracking the attack on her.* Choosing not to dig a deeper hole, I shut my mouth.

She's silent, like she's considering her response, and I give her the space to do so. I have a hundred other things pounding against the cell walls of my chest to get out, but they're more jumbled than a tangled phone cord. "It's not that you don't want someone to be the exception." Her shoulders slump. "You just don't think that person can be me." The sadness in her voice is almost enough to make me take it back.

I take a breath, running my fingers through my hair. *Fuck.* This is why I didn't want to have this conversation. There's no winning. For either of us. I'm not in a place to trust her, regardless of if she deserves a chance. And there's nothing she can do to change that because nothing can make me forget her track record. It's a catch-22. It's something that won't work until I figure out how to get the fuck over it. *Maybe that therapist can get me in on short notice again.* I do want her to be the exception, but that's not enough. "I'm sorry," I say instead of the dozen things that would make her feel better.

Her gaze falls to the hardwood floor, wrapping her arms tighter around herself. "I want to be alone right now."

I nod. "Okay." Standing, I hesitate in hopes of something changing. Of her saying something that will prove I can trust her even though I'm convinced I can't. It's fucked up. The moment I accept that, I walk away, leaving her curled up and alone on the couch as I retreat to my room.

I don't even bother removing my jeans as I flop myself onto my bed, feeling guilty about sleeping here while Mya sleeps on the couch. Or is it that I wish she were in this bed with me and know it's sure as shit my fault she isn't?

Chapter Thirty

"Stupid, stupid glass," I mutter as I throw the glass shaped like a beer can into the trash under the kitchen sink. It shatters into the garbage bag. My next craft is something I've never done. I'm etching designs into the side of the beer can glasses I've got lined up on the counter. I've never used etching cream before. It didn't look hard when I watched the video, but my first try was a complete failure. I made a stencil with my vinyl cutter, but I don't think I pressed it to the glass well enough, and all the lines blurred.

Weeding a new stencil from the black vinyl, I take my time picking out each little letter and piece of my design with my pick. Once I'm finished, I carefully peel the backing off and press the sticker sheet on the cup. Rubbing my fingers over the vinyl, I ensure every part of the stencil is firmly in place on the glass.

I take a deep, calming breath. I've been needing a lot of breaths since last night. I'm more upset by how Kace rejected me than I was over any real breakup. My brain begs me to take the out he's given and leave before I run into the same problem I always do–but my gut tells me to stay.

In the past, my gut has always told me to run, but my brain has always rationalized. *His quirks aren't that big of a deal. Maybe he'll grow out of them. It's not settling–no one is perfect. Don't let a good one slip away.*

This time, my brain tells me to run to avoid getting more hurt than I already am. But my gut... it's telling me Kace could be *the one*. The conflict has me reeling. Distracted. Messing up basic crafts I should have perfected on the first try. I'm tempted to move back to Eugene, but I don't want to be away from Kace. I don't want to feel the way I do about him while simultaneously begging the universe to change his mind. I feel out of alignment. Like when you try to straighten the lines on your phone camera but they never match up.

Reaching for the paintbrush, I dip it into the etching cream a second time. Holding my breath because this stuff smells more toxic than Ross and Rachel's relationship, I dab the white cream over the cutouts in the stencil. I take my time, confident I can do this. When the cream is in place, I set the glass aside to let it do its thing and move on to the next one. I have three designs I'm making. One has cute trees of different heights in an oval frame. In the middle, it says, "Less people. More trees." The second one says, "Live like the mountain is out," inside an outline of a snow-capped mountain. The last one is a chair lift, and it says, "Adjust your altitude." I got the idea when Kace and I were at the mountain two days ago.

I sigh, pressing my palms down on the edge of the counter. What a roller coaster it's been. I thought maybe we would have a shot, but no. Right after I thought he was giving me a chance, he ripped it away. It's not that I don't understand. I get it. I just... I hate it. I hate it so much. I clench my fist, my teeth grinding as I glare toward the front door Kace disappeared through a couple of hours ago. He let me know he was leaving but didn't say more than that.

Abandoning my project temporarily, I walk to the living room and aggressively unfold the flaps of one of my craft boxes next to the couch. Tearing out a sheet of light pink paper and a pen, I slap it down on the coffee table. I already did my Insanity workout this morning. I had a thirty-minute shower concert with Hilary. I ate three bowls of cereal. None of it helped ease my frustration. My feelings are trapped inside me, and I feel so stabby right now that I need to get them out before I lose my freaking mind.

I pick up my pen, angry that it's a pink gel one because that doesn't fit the vibe. But I can never find a black pen when I need it, so I don't even bother. The words feel jumbled in my head, but as soon as the pen touches the paper, they flow out like they've been waiting to see the light of day.

Kace,

For my fifth birthday, my parents gave me a Cabbage Patch doll. At my party, I got a lot of other toys, but I can't tell you what they were because I don't remember. My interests have always been ever-changing. In elementary school, I played a different sport every year to try them all and not get bored. In middle school, I ate lunch with someone different every day because I was worried I'd miss out on knowing someone cool. At my first high school dance, I convinced my mom to get me two outfits so I could change halfway through. I didn't go to college because every month, I wanted a different job that would require a different major.

But it's not me hating decisions or sucking at making them—it's me wanting to experience all life has to offer.

The world has always allowed me to explore everything that interests me. While I exploited that freedom, I never let it translate to my dating life because I'm not a shitty person who cycles through men like toys of the week. Maybe I haven't had a long relationship like you have, but maybe that's because I hadn't found my Cabbage Patch yet.

Growing up, I might have played with a different toy each day, but when I crawled under the covers at night, that doll was always with me. What I'm trying to say is that despite my lack of direction, I always have a home base. I want a home base. I want it to be you.

Wanted.

It turns out that when you finally find the right person, there's no guarantee that you're theirs. And that sucks because with every piece of your puzzle that clicks into place, the more my heart tells me that we could be so good together.

Do you remember that scene in Dennis the Menace where Mr. Wilson grows a flower that only blooms after forty years? Some might say he missed that moment because a robber was in his house. But you know what I think the reason was? It was him focusing on all the negatives in his life. It was him being annoyed by inconveniences that could have been joys.

That's you.

You're the guy who is so busy looking behind you that you're missing what's right in front of you.

You being afraid I'm going to leave is manifesting it.

I hope it's worth it.

Mya

I set my pen down, rereading what I wrote. It took a turn in the end, but I feel better getting it out. I had to write the words he doesn't want to hear because I'll never get to say them. He doesn't want to be with me, and I have to respect that. I get why he has trust issues–to be honest, I would too. I can't fault him for thinking a new relationship right now would feel like a Band-Aid over a gaping wound. He needs to heal more with the proper tools first. That doesn't make it hurt any less, but now that everything is off my chest, it'll be fine. I'll be fine.

Taking a breath, I put the letter and pen both back in the box and return to my craft. This time, when I pull the vinyl stencil from the glass, it reveals a perfectly etched mountain scene.

At least something is going right.

☆ Chapter Thirty-One

☆ ☆

"This is illegal, you know," I tell Mya as I grab my sweatshirt off the hook in the entryway.

"Says the hacker," she sasses over her shoulder from where she's making a cup of coffee in the kitchen.

I roll my eyes even though she's not looking at me. "The good kind."

She turns with two cups of to-go coffee in her hands, reaching one toward me in the entryway. "So you're telling me you've never done anything you 'shouldn't do?' Like ever?" She smiles, and it's so fucking pretty. "You never made a mixed CD using Limewire?"

It's a surprisingly beautiful day in the Pacific Northwest, so she's wearing a tight jean skirt with an oversized sweater. I don't think I've seen anyone wear a jean skirt in years, but fuck can she pull it off. I've had to constantly remind myself all damn morning to stop staring at where her lean legs disappear under the denim–to lock up the vision of my dick disappearing inside her in an unreachable purgatory. Reliving that memory won't do either of us any good.

"I'll take your silence as admittance."

I shoot her a look as I take the coffee. "No."

She hums, bringing the cup to her pink lips, and for the hundredth time since I fucked up the first kiss, all I can think about is wanting to do it again. Every time she's sitting at the breakfast counter eating cereal. Every time she pops her head into my room to let me know she made us dinner or asks a random question because she wants to talk to me. Whenever she's so focused on a project that she chews on her cheek. When she rubs her lips together nervously during a movie she's already seen like she doesn't know the problem will be resolved. This is why I've temporarily sent my feelings toward Mya to a purgatory that only the Winchesters could break into. I was able to snag a therapy session for the day after tomorrow, and I hope it magically changes my need for that.

I draw my focus from where her lips press against the opening of the coffee cup to her eyes, full of amusement. "What?"

She takes another small sip before pulling the drink away. "I was watching you ride a thought train. What were you thinking about?"

"Oh." I clear my throat. Think, Kace. "*Supernatural.*"

Her brows scrunch. "Like the show?"

"Yup," I confirm, wondering if she thinks I'm full of shit.

She brushes it off like it wasn't weird at all. "You know what is so annoying to me?" Apparently it was rhetorical because she doesn't let me answer. "The producers of that show *knew* that Sam's name was Dean on *Gilmore Girls*. They could have given *Supernatural* Dean any other name, but they had to make it confusing for no reason. Like why?"

I chuckle. "I couldn't tell you."

"You know, Kirk would take this job for us."

"I have zero idea who you're talking about." Not like it matters. She could talk about dirt, and I'd still listen to her all day. She's interesting solely based on how excited she gets.

"Kirk. From *Gilmore Girls*. That man has a killer work ethic. He can do any job in the world. If I ever have to write a resume, I'm adding that. Work ethic of Kirk Gleason. Anyone who knows anything would automatically hire me."

"Good thing you seem to have no problem being an entrepreneur." I chuckle. I highly doubt that would fly on any resume. "Are you ready to do this or..."

"Yes!" She reaches for her daisy fanny pack on the counter. Once it's secured across her chest, she pauses, staring at me.

"If you're waiting to bump our fists and let our twin powers activate, you will be waiting a long time."

A bright smile graces her face, her straight blonde strands framing it perfectly. But then it falls a little, and she chews on the corner of her lip. "Kace?"

"Yeah?" My heart thumps against my chest like it has no respect for the fact that I'm supposed to be a thirty-one-year-old man with his feelings under control.

"Never mind." She shakes her head, taking away what's left of her smile. "Let's go. We don't want to be late."

I want to argue with her, to pry, but we have a small window for our job today. "Lead the way." I nod toward the door, grabbing my keys from the leather bowl on the counter. Temporarily ignoring the tension, I follow her out and focus on our task–this time, I'm actually part of the plan.

"Excuse me, Ma'am." The brunette woman stands on the other side of the now open door in a navy blue pantsuit. "Do you have a moment to speak with me?"

"What is this about?" Her brows furrow. I don't know why I agreed to this. Maybe because I feel guilty about sleeping with Mya when I knew we wouldn't be in a relationship and rejecting her *again* after that. She said this job would be better coming from me so it didn't seem like a mistress situation. *The things I'll apparently do for Mya... besides be with her.*

"May I come in?" I glance behind her toward the office. It was easy enough to find her. She works at a local bank as a loan officer, and I didn't want her to feel unsafe by showing up at her house.

"Yes. Do you have an appointment?" She opens the door for me to step inside.

"No. I'm here to make a delivery."

"I wasn't expecting anything." Her face lights. "Is it from my boyfriend?"

Her boyfriend. According to him, they aren't together. He's been trying to break up with her for six months, and she won't take no for an answer. No matter how often he turns her away at his door or how many calls he declines, she persists. She's hitting stalker level, but when I asked him why he didn't file a restraining order, he said he doesn't want to ruin her life like that.

I'm not convinced this solution is any better, but here we are. "Yes, it is." My stomach flips as if I'm the one who should feel guilty about this.

She doesn't take note of my lack of enthusiasm as she reaches for the envelope in my hand. I didn't want to read the letter, but Mya wanted to make sure there wasn't anything criminal in it–you know, more than the action itself.

The woman tears open the envelope, pulling out the typed letter on forged government letterhead. I want to leave, but I promised Mya I'd stay to ensure she reads it and under-stands. I watch her eyes read line by line, flicking from side to side as she follows the words.

"What?" she mumbles to herself. "Witnessed a murder?" Her eyes go wide at that. "In witness protection?" Her mouth falls open. "You cannot contact me." She shakes her head as the words leave her lips, and I watch a tear fall straight from her eye to the paper in her hands. She glances up at me. "Is this real?"

I nod, not wanting to taste the lie on my tongue.

"Oh my god," she whispers. "I hope he's okay." Silent tears run down her cheeks. I'm uncomfortable as fuck but also alarmingly angry. This girl seems so normal. Nice. Hurt. Does she deserve for the guy she loves to take off like this?

He got offered a job out of state, so it's not like she can show up at his house anymore. He also changed his number. But he said he wanted her to move on and not waste more of her life chasing after someone who doesn't want to be caught. It's almost reassuring, but it's still fucked up.

"I can't even say goodbye?" she asks with glassy eyes. If someone was actually in witness protection, they could contact their loved ones through secure channels, but it doesn't matter if she figures that out because there won't be a way to reach him.

"I'm sorry." I reach for the letter. "I'll also need to dispose of this properly." This part was my idea–partially to help the entire scenario feel realistic but mostly to save our asses if she tried to get a hold of anyone in WITSEC.

She hands it over without arguing and falls back on her desk, braced by the palms of her hands. "Thank you for letting me know," she whispers with one final glance up.

I nod and leave her office, closing the door behind me.

Once I'm outside, I slide into the driver's seat of my truck. Mya has it running with Nickelback playing. I'm surprised she knows them.

She reaches for the dial and turns down "Far Away." "How did it go?" she asks, focusing her bright green eyes on me. We're close enough that I can see a lemon-lime shade marbled with the emerald.

"Do you like Nickelback?" I blurt.

"What? Uh. Yeah," she responds with a tilt of her head.

"It's not what you usually listen to."

She cracks a smile. "I know. But everyone's gotta have their favorite emo band." She shrugs. "I love Chad's voice, and I especially love their new song. It's so nostalgic. My favorite part about memories is that no matter what is happening in the present–regardless of whether the people or places still exist–no one can take away the snapshots of your life that make you happy. Songs that remind me of glimmers are my favorite."

Her mind is the most fascinating place, and sometimes when she speaks, I want to jump inside it and live there. For as different as we are, she's able to put feelings I suck at showing into words that make sense. I must stay silent a beat too long because she asks, "Do you hate Nickelback or?"

"I saw them live for my fourteenth birthday." I hesitate before saying the next thought aloud. "It was the best birthday I can remember. My parents were so excited I asked for something they could relate to, we made an entire weekend trip out of it."

The brightness of her smile makes me want to reveal a million more insights into my life. "That sounds like the perfect birthday. I love live music."

"So do I," I admit, realizing I haven't been to a concert in years. Ruby didn't like the music I did, and she'd never sacrifice for a night.

"Okay, so how did the job go?"

Right. "Fine." I stare out the dash, watching the sunlight struggling to break through dark gray clouds. "It's finished."

"Just fine?"

I arch a brow. "As opposed to saying it's great that we broke some woman's heart?"

Her eyes shift to the dash. "Well, when you put it like that."

All the lightness in the car a moment ago is overshadowed. "It wasn't fun. I can tell you that."

"What happened?"

"What do you mean, 'What happened?'" My hands tighten around the steering wheel. "We ruined someone's life with a letter. A fucking letter."

Mya's eyes widen like my words physically slapped her. "It was a nice letter," she whispers.

My stomach churns as I stare straight ahead.

"You knew what the job was, Kace…"

I glance sideways long enough to see her hands in her lap, playing with the hem of her jean skirt. "Yeah. I know. But there's a difference between some Hollywood movie plot in theory and watching it play out in real life. That one piece of paper crushed her, Mya."

"But he wrote it because he cared about her. It was the nicest way out," she defends the guy we met *once*.

My fists clench. "If he cared about her, he wouldn't have dismissed her like that."

"I don't think it was a dismissal." Her brows pinch. "Maybe the premise was a lie, but it's clear that he cared about her."

"Then why didn't he tell her in person?" My teeth grind.

"You heard what he said. It was his last option. He could have filed a restraining order."

"Or maybe we don't know the whole story," I shoot back even though we talked to the guy for over an hour and his details felt true. But there's always *more*, and who knows? Maybe he just realized he could take an easy way out by pawning off the job after seeing Mya work her "magic" at the wedding. *This town feels too fucking small sometimes.*

"Or maybe finding the best words is easier when someone isn't in front of you clouding your thoughts," she snaps.

If only she realized how much she clouds my thoughts. *Fuck, it's frustrating.* Why the hell is she so worked up about this? It's like I've personally offended her. "Well, no one will ever know the whole story when it's all cut off and summed up in a letter."

"Okay. Okay." She holds her hands up in defense. "I'm sorry. I didn't realize this upset you so much. I promise I won't make you help me again, okay?" Reaching into her fanny pack, she pulls out a Blow Pop. She takes off the white and green wrapper and plops the candy into her mouth. My gaze catches on the way her cheeks suck as she leans back in her seat. She pulls the Blow Pop from her lips with a *pop*, and it sets me more on edge. "What?" She gives me a look before twisting the sucker on her tongue.

Jesus fuck, she's hot. With everything else I love about her, it's the milk on top of the cereal. But it's like I'm too damn scared to take a bite knowing there could be a moldy Froot Loop in the bowl. Is that even a thing? I doubt it. Too many dyes and preservatives for them to ever go bad. But that's not the point. The point is that Mya has a bad track record, and even if I could ignore that, she slips in little pieces of her mindset that worry me. Like this job. She genuinely thinks it's fine that he just wrote a letter.

Maybe it's my fucking fault for agreeing to help her in the first place. With this job, and the way the guy sold this girl being a crazy stalker, I thought it would be easier. But watching that girl feel like her world was falling apart, realizing she'll never get to be with the person she loves–fuck, that was rough.

Looking over my shoulder, I shift into reverse and back out of the bank's parking lot. "Are you okay?" she asks, reaching across the console and touching my forearm as I shift into drive.

"Fine," I mutter but feel her staring at me like she wants more of an answer. I'm hoping the therapist can help me find one the day after tomorrow. "I want to get home before the rain starts," I add, feeling like a douche for literally weather-convoing her.

She transfers her hand from me to the dash, leaning forward to look out the windshield as I pull up to a stop light. Gray clouds are scattered in every direction. "I'm sorry," she says, her eyes still focused on the sky.

"For what?"

"I don't like when we argue." She sighs, sitting back in her seat. "I know we're just roommates and all, but whether you hate it or *really* hate it, I like spending time with you. The last thing I want is for you to be mad at me."

The last thing I want is for us to be just roommates. "I don't hate it."

She glances over, holding my stare for a second before she sticks her Blow Pop back in her mouth and turns her focus to the passenger window.

Chapter Thirty-Two

Tapping the birthday card lightly against the newspaper I have spread across the coffee table, gold glitter falls away from the places without adhesive. It leaves a perfect sparkling border around the "Happy Birthday, Chloe!" I've written in bubble letters. I started it yesterday when we got back from our job and Kace went back to work, and I can't help but smile at how cute it looks.

"Do you have plans today?" I jolt at the sound of Kace's voice from behind me, turning from where I'm sitting on the floor.

I set my homemade card off to the side. "Not really. Why?"

He shifts on his feet, slipping his hands into the pockets of his jeans. "I, uh." He clears his throat. "I thought we could do something."

"Okay..." My brows scrunch. "Like what?"

"There's a Lisa Frank expo in Portland..."

My eyes widen. "For real?!"

He nods.

I hop to my feet, already running through outfit ideas in my mind. "I can't believe I didn't know!" I freeze. "Wait. How do *you* know?"

He shrugs. "Overheard some girls talking about it at Little Conejo."

"This is incredible!" I pause, my mind reeling as it absorbs the idea. "You *want* to go with me?" My shoulders deflate when he hesitates. "It's okay if you don't want to. I know it's not your kind of thing."

"No. But seeing you so excited will make it tolerable."

I bite my lip, my grin widening as I try to ignore the flutters in my stomach. "Okay, just give me five minutes."

He nods and disappears into his room.

An hour later, we've somehow managed to find parking downtown and are walking toward the expo, easily spotted since the walls of the building have been temporarily painted with vibrant rainbow stripes.

The moment we're through the front door, we're blinded by neon colors in every direction and my mind races to take it all in.

A hallway to the right leads toward what looks like a room full of paintings.

To the left is a larger-than-life classic Lisa Frank tiger that has been turned into a kid's jungle gym.

There's a square mat on the floor in front of us that must be at least ten feet in both directions. It's a partially colored-in underwater mural, scattered with markers, kids and adults coloring in different parts of the seal, fish and coral.

I glance over my shoulder to gauge where Kace is at–physically and mentally. His eyes are wide, and I can't help but chuckle. "You're regretting this already, aren't you?" He looks so out of place in his black jeans and bomber jacket surrounded by more color than I've ever seen in my life.

I expect him to say *yes*. Or at the very least groan in protest of being here. Maybe even ask to wait in the car. Instead, he surprises me with an outstretched arm. "Lead the way."

I'm tempted to grab and drag him around the place, but I keep my hands to myself. We veer right, heading down a makeshift hallway that I have a feeling wraps around the outer edge of the expo. To our left, black curtains trap us in, and the right wall is lined with paintings in glass frames.

I take in each one, noting they are the original airbrushed art from the 70s and 80s. A pegasus. Hamburgers in space, flying around with Blow Pops, gumdrops and ice cream cones. A frog decked out in princess jewelry. A candy railway. Each one is unique and far more vibrant than you'd expect for art that's nearly half a century old.

When I glance at Kace, I find him taking in the art as much as I am. I stare until he catches me. His brows furrow. "What?"

I shake my head, once again surprised by this man. "Nothing." I grin, turning away from him and walking toward the next exhibit. The hallway of paintings leads to a dark room–three black walls with the fourth being some sort of screen split horizontally. The top features a sky view, and the bottom is an underwater one. Chaotic and colorful animals fly across the top, while others swim in the bottom.

A table sits in the middle of the room, low enough that you have to sit on the floor to use it. Scattered across it are coloring sheets, with outlines of different Lisa Frank creatures. Scanning the room, I plop down, sitting criss-cross, to figure out what it's all about. It appears that you can color an animal, place it in a scanner, and then it's imported into the scene.

They bring your art to life. *How cool.*

I jump when Kace takes a seat next to me, my brows arching when he reaches for a piece of paper with a dolphin and a blue crayon. I pick one with a hummingbird and line up a pink, purple, blue and yellow crayon in front of me. We color for a few minutes with only the excited chatter of other people around us. A kid sits next to Kace with zero respect for his personal bubble, and without hesitation, Kace scoots closer to me. He's sitting cross-legged too, and by the time he stops moving, his thigh overlaps mine. The heat of his body seeps through the tie-dye leggings I've paired with a pink cropped hoodie.

I freeze, my yellow crayon tip pressed into the paper, afraid to move–or breathe. His touch is like Pringles. Once I have a taste, I can't help but want more. Ignoring the heat rushing through me, I drag the crayon across the paper, the yellow wax clumping a bit and making the shading of my bird uneven.

A few minutes later, we're both finished with our art. Mine is a colorful explosion that I know Lisa would be proud of. Kace's coloring matches what I'd expect from him–a typical blue dolphin, perfectly colored. I am surprised by the darker blue line he's drawn around the edge. My sister used to draw that way.

We place our pictures in the scanner, and step aside, directing our gaze toward the screen. At the same moment, my hummingbird flies into the scene and Kace's dolphin appears to leap from the water. My mouth falls open. It's magic.

When I turn toward Kace, he's staring at me. I swear his gaze flashes to my lips, but I must be mistaken. It's dark in here, and he's made it abundantly clear that he doesn't want me like that.

The crease in his brow deepens. "What's wrong?" he asks, and my focus zones in on him, with the moving colors to my left barely invading my periphery.

I survey my body language, realizing my shoulders have slumped, and my earlier excitement has popped like Bubble Yum. *I'm sad Kace doesn't want to be with me.* It sucks that I want this to be so much more because I want to do all these things as his girlfriend–not as his friend.

Then it occurs to me that if I do things like this with him, it'll take away from the valuable time I have to find someone to settle down with–someone who actually wants to be with me before it's too late.

"Mya?" He reaches his hands toward my arms but drops them at the last minute.

I let my gaze search his before shaking my head to clear my thoughts. "Hmm?"

"Are you okay?"

I take a breath, then brush off his concern with a wave of my hand. "Oh yeah. I'm great. This place is hella cool." I look back to where my animated bird is flapping its rainbow wings. "Thank you for bringing me here."

"Yeah." He shoves his hands into his pockets. "No problem."

"Should we get going to see the rest?"

He nods toward the door, letting me lead the way.

Chapter Thirty-Three

Mya and I didn't speak most of the drive home from the expo last night, and shortly after, she went out with Chloe. It's like she couldn't get away from me quick enough–and I only know because there was a note on the counter when I got out of the shower saying she was having a sleepover. Despite never sleeping in the same room at home, I felt her absence. I thought taking her out would be a good thing for our friendship, but we feel even more distant than before.

But fuck, if that didn't make me realize how much closer I want to be. I can't stop thinking about the Olive Theory. Mya thinks it's about opposites making sense together–I could eat her tomatoes and all would be right in the world. That's not what it *really* means though. It's about being willing to make sacrifices for someone because you love them. It's about wanting to support them and being willing to put your small preferences or discomfort aside for their happiness.

Seeing Mya light up over every detail in the expo was worth the chaos of kids and the blinding colors. I couldn't take my eyes off her, entranced by her energy and the way she moved from room to room like she was exploring heaven. She felt a little off toward the end, but it wasn't anything that felt too worrisome.

But this morning, she still wasn't home by the time I hit my lunch break.

Gripping the metal door handle to Little Conejo, I turn at the sound of "I'm Too Sexy," belting from Dave as he comes to a slow stop on his bike.

A chuckle escapes me as I release my hold on the door. "Hey, Dave."

"Kace!" He steps off his bike and leans it against the patio picnic table, the Charlie Brown tree leaning from its place in the milk crate strapped to the back. "Are you feeling sexy today?!"

"Not as much as you are," I tease, thankful he's able to ease the tightness in my chest from my impending therapy session.

"Well, that's a shame. What's got your confidence in a chokehold, dude?"

I shake my head, hoping it comes off as nonchalant, and glance at my watch. "Would you like lunch?"

His nearly toothless grin widens. "I'd be honored to have lunch with you."

I nod toward the table. "Be right back." I make my way inside and order eight tacos before rejoining Dave. I straddle the picnic table bench, twisting enough to face him on the opposite side, the breeze brisk against my cheek. "How's life treating you?"

"Oh, no, you don't." He shrugs off his jacket, worn and hardly recognizable as green. "Tell me about the girl."

Kicking my feet onto the picnic bench, I lean against the connecting wall of the building. "What girl?"

"The pretty little thing who picks up dinner for the two of you sometimes."

"My roommate," I clarify. It's technically true.

"Uh huh. She always buys me a torta, you know?"

My eyes widen. "She does?" I'm not surprised at her kindness, I just didn't expect my two small worlds to collide.

"A true angel, that one. One time, she even humored me with a duet. 'Build Me Up Buttercup.' Do you know that one?"

I crack a smile. "Yeah." I shift my glance to the waitress long enough to take our food tray from her and say thank you.

"Thought ya might. I saw the video." He wiggles his eyebrows as he reaches for a taco. I slide the metal tray closer.

"What video?"

"The buttercup one," he says, his punctuation feeling more like a *duh*.

I raise a brow.

"Little Miss made a music video on her fancy phone. Dancing around and singing."

I nod, pieces of the memory fusing.

"Have you seen it?"

"I was there, but I haven't watched the video." I can feel Mya on my lap, cuddling into me like she didn't realize it was too intimate for how little we knew each other at the time.

"Ah. So you didn't see your cameo?" He continues when I don't respond. "At the end, she's dancing toward you. The way you're watching her... I don't think she notices, but I can see it."

I raise a brow. "See what?"

"That you love her."

My pulse ticks up a notch. That was the beginning. I sure as shit didn't love her then. *But now?* There are two one-syllable words on the tip of my tongue, battling between truth and denial.

"It's pretty clear she feels the same." Dave pushes back the stray piece of hair that's fallen from his ponytail.

I reach for a birria taco and take a bite instead of responding. He shoves the second half of his taco into his mouth and reaches for a napkin before sitting back and waiting. There's no way. It's absurd enough to think someone else can see *I* love her, when I haven't even accepted that myself. But *if* someone else can see it in me, surely I'd be able to see it in her. "I don't think she loves me." The thought steals my appetite.

He narrows his eyes. "Does she have someplace else she could go? Besides your apartment?"

"Yeah..." I'm not catching his drift.

He reaches for another taco. "But she stays."

"Her life is here. It's convenient."

"Convenient to live with a grump and recluse?"

I roll my eyes. "I come here to be around people every day."

"Your best friend is a forty-eight-year-old homeless man," he counters.

"What's your point?" I finish my taco and reach for a second even though my stomach is churning at the conversation.

"My point is that people don't stick around when someone is at their lowest if they don't think said person is worth it."

"Yeah." I end this particular conversation, not convinced that's why she hasn't left.

The rest of lunch is full of bullshit. He distracts me with gossip from the RV camp, acting like he's annoyed even though I know he loves the community that's formed there. He digresses into a few rogue stories about his days over-seas. I try to hang onto every word and stay present, but my mind continuously drifts to the *pretty little thing* I want to be so much more than my roommate.

Thirty minutes later, I walk through the therapist's door, not much more confident than I was the first time.

"Kace. It's great to see you again." Angela welcomes me into the room and sits in the armchair opposite the couch where I take a seat.

"Thanks for making time for me again." I lean forward, forearms on my knees.

She crosses a leg over the opposite one. "What brings you in today?"

I take a breath. "Mya." My stomach flips at the thought of her. "What we're doing isn't working."

"I'm sorry to hear that. Did you start spending more time together?"

"Yes." A confession is waiting to escape, but it's terrifying as fuck. She must know it because she waits. "I want to be with her and stop pulling away." I exhale, running my fingers through my hair.

"When did you come to this decision?"

I sigh. "I think I've known for a while. But I guess it really hit me yesterday."

"What happened yesterday?"

"I took her to an art expo I knew she'd like. It's something I would have dreaded going to with anyone else."

She leans forward, her arm resting on the leg crossed over the other. "And why is that?"

"Anything with her is just *different*. More fun. I don't know."

"You enjoy being around her."

"Yeah, but it's more than that. I'm tempted to kiss her whenever she's close. Hold her hand. Stare at her like she's fucking magic." I scoff at myself when I realize that this probably sounds insane to someone who was led to believe that Mya and I are already in a relationship.

If she catches on, she doesn't show it. "Why do you think you keep pulling away?"

"I know why. My ex cheated." It occurs to me that I'm not as disgusted by the fact as I usually am. If Ruby didn't cheat, I wouldn't have Mya.

"Do you want to share what else you just realized?" Angela observes.

"I know Mya isn't Ruby. She's a better person and a better fit for me by far."

"But..." she prompts.

"I can't let go of the fact that she's a runner by nature. She can't seem to stay in a relationship. I don't want to be a name in the middle of her list."

"You want to be the last one."

I freeze, my eyes bouncing around the room as I consider my answer. "I think so." The realization hits me square in the chest. This isn't a short-term vision for me.

She holds her stare for a moment. "Can I ask you something?" I nod. "What was the first job you ever wanted?"

"Uhh." I scan my memory and chuckle. "When I was a kid, I wanted to get paid to play video games."

"And after that?"

"I was set on designing a new game console for a while. Then I wanted to code websites."

"Now what do you do?"

"Cybersecurity."

"How long have you been doing that?"

"Almost a decade."

"Do you love it? Or wish you had stuck with one of the other avenues?"

"I can't see myself doing anything else."

She hums. "Interesting, don't you think?"

I raise a brow.

"That you had many short-lived dreams before you landed on *the one*."

Her point feels like the colors of a Rubik's cube clicking into place.

A grin slips out as she continues her explanation. "Kace, life is made up of trial and error. The likelihood of finding the best option on the first try is small. There's too much variety in life. Not to mention, with each decision we make, the path being right or wrong is dependent on age, knowledge and situation. The knowledge especially–of what we love, hate, *need*–that doesn't come without experience... without trial and error." She pauses to gauge my reaction.

I press my fingertips together over my knees. "I'm following."

"What if you are to Mya, what cybersecurity is to you? The end of a long road of trying, discovering, searching."

"What if I'm not?" My stomach flips at the thought, my lunch threatening to come back up.

"Is it worth sticking around and putting in the effort to see if you are?"

"Yes." I shock both of us with the speed of my response, feeling my eyes widen. I told Mya I don't have time to waste with her, but I don't think I'd get over her at this point. I watch a smirk grace Angela's face before she neutralizes it again.

"When you went to college, you chose a major that would lock you into certain jobs. You committed. It was the only way to know for sure if it was what you wanted."

"Yeah." Hearing it in different terms unlocks something. My mindset seems to be rearranging its matrix. "Yes. Okay," I resolve. Mya is what I want, who I want to be with, and I can't continue to let anything within my control keep me from her.

By the time I return from therapy, I need sustenance before I can come up with a plan to show Mya I'm ready to make this work. I already scheduled another session for next week because I know that one was a start but not enough. I need help with creating lasting trust, and I'm hoping after a few more on my own, Mya might be willing to go with me again.

Making my way to the kitchen, I scan the main living space. No Mya. Weird. I assumed she'd be here working on an art project.

Opening the cabinet, I reach for a glass. What is that? I pull down a cup that doesn't match my set. It looks like a glass beer can, but there's a design etched on the side. I twist the cup in my hand. It's a mountain, and it says, "Live like the mountain is out" in bold lettering. It's my favorite expression people in the Pacific Northwest use. It's the idea that even on cloudy days, you should live your life with the energy you feel with a clear and stunning view of the mountain.

Mya must have bought these. Or maybe she made them. I glance back in the cabinet to see two others, all with a mountain theme. I examine the frosted fine lines. I'm pretty sure she made these. Not because there's a flaw–they're perfect. They could easily be sold in stores. I just have a feeling she made them. *For me.*

I'm such a dick for snapping at her in the car the other day. It's overwhelming as fuck how attracted I am to her–how much I want to try to be with her. But my mind has finally tipped over the edge that leads me to act on it. Filling the glass with water, I chug almost all of it in a few gulps. I set it on the counter, pressing my palms to the marble. Where is Mya? I scan the room again, noticing her phone on the coffee table.

I make my way to it, pulling a mini sticky note from the screen.

Needed to touch grass. Be back later.

Panic slams into my chest like a child jumping on it. What the fuck does she mean "touch grass?" And why did she leave her phone at home? She could have at least taken it with her. How the hell will I know if something bad happens? How long am I supposed to wait? How long has she been gone? Where would I even look for her?

Walking toward the floor-to-ceiling windows, I tug on the blackout shade. It shoots up, curling in on itself all the way to the top, and revealing a view of downtown Vancouver with a *Twilight* filter.

Everything is a dull blue. The sky. The fog over the Columbia River. The mirrored sides of apartments and business buildings. The air even looks cold.

The sidewalk–*Is that Mya?* I press my face a few inches closer to the glass like it'll help me see seven stories down to where a woman is lying on her back on the cement. She bends her knees, her arms crossing over her stomach. That's definitely Mya. Her blonde hair splays across the concrete in a fan around her head. She's wearing a sweatshirt I've seen her in before with leggings. At least she's not trying to get hypothermia, but what the fuck is she doing out there?

Without bothering to pull down the blind, I head toward the door, swiping my Virginia Tech hoodie from the hook in the entryway. Tugging it over my head, I opt for the stairs instead of waiting for the elevator. I take them two at a time, pausing to catch my breath only when I reach the front door to our complex.

Pushing through it, I take an immediate right, only a few steps away from Mya. She doesn't flinch as I approach, and that's concerning in itself. The storm clouds have opened just enough to turn the air into mist, and the coolness wets my face as I squat beside her, my forearms resting on my knees.

"Hey, what are you–are you crying?" I'm unsure if the water streaming from her eyes and into her hair is rain or tears.

Still looking toward the sky, she doesn't even glance my way. "I needed to feel the rain on my skin," she says, her voice thick with emotion.

"Mya, what's wrong?" I try again.

She finally glances over, giving me confirmation that she's crying. Her voice cracks. "Liam is dead."

Panic surges through me as I drop to my knees next to her, my jeans dampening against the wet cement. "Who is Liam?"

"Liam!" she cries like I'm supposed to know who the fuck she's talking about. I thought I'd been paying attention. I feel like I know a decent amount about her. "From One Direction," she exclaims with aggravation, but it all fades away, and she starts sobbing. Her palms dig into her eyes, her cries racking through her shaking body. I'm so fucking confused, but all I want to do is comfort her.

"Hey. Mya." She continues to cry. "Talk to me. Did this happen today?"

She shakes her head, her hands still covering her eyes. "No. It happened a while ago. But I just... I forget sometimes.

But a post popped up and reminded me that he's dead," she manages before she chokes on a cry. "He was so young and–" She sucks in a breath. "It's not fair." She sniffles so hard I'm concerned she hurt her brain. "And why is life so confusing? How am I old enough to experience tragedy?" Another sob cracks in perfect unison with pronounced rain-drops. *I don't think this is all about Liam.* "My Tamagotchi died again." She lets out a sigh that feels devastating. "Britney's conservatorship destroyed her. Don't even get me started on the Nickelodeon documentary. Everything is falling apart."

She's spiraling.

I readjust myself, lying down next to her. The cement is cold, even through my hoodie, but I move close enough to feel her faint body heat.

She removes her hands from her eyes to look at me. "What are you doing?"

"Feeling the rain on my skin."

She releases a sad laugh, then sighs as she brushes some of the rain from her face. "Seriously, Kace?"

"I'm not leaving you out here alone, and I have a feeling you're not ready to go inside yet."

She tilts her face back toward the sky and closes her eyes. "I feel like Brittany Murphy spinning around and around in that teacup with Dakota Fanning." She goes silent. "I'm spinning round and round, and nothing feels okay, but I don't know how to get off," she adds like she knows I was confused at the reference. "I'm thirty, and I have nothing to show for it. I live in an apartment with a guy I'm not in a relationship with. I have an unstable job. I wing every second of my life like nothing matters except the present. But what fucking good is that, Kace?" She cries for another second, attempting to take breaths but choking on her sobs. I want to take her inside, to hold her, calm her down, but I think she needs to get this out, and if she doesn't, I won't know how to help her in the first place.

Batting at her eyes, she continues. "I know it's my fault for not leaving guys until they leave me. I'm not trying to be a bad person or lead them on or waste their time. I settle because I'm afraid. I'm terrified it's so late in the game that if I leave the wrong person, it doesn't guarantee I'll find the right one. What if I'm alone forever?"

The angel on my shoulder tells me I could be the right person for her, but despite wanting that, the devil makes another appearance and throws a punch when she reminds me that settling is her bad habit. "You're not going to be alone forever," I reassure her.

"How do you know that?"

"Because anyone would be lucky to be with you. You're always coming up with projects to brighten people's day–thank you for our new glasses, by the way."

"You're welcome," she whispers, refusing to look my way.

"You're smart enough to figure out any project you're inspired by." I shift to face her a bit, the cement cold and wet under my side. "You're fun. Outgoing. Adventurous. Beautiful. You're everything so many people wish they could be, and instead of acting like you know it, you help everyone else live brighter too. Who wouldn't want to be with you?"

"You," she whispers, and like the fucking idiot I am, I let it hang in the silence between us. My heart thumps in my chest, my mind reeling with all the words I could say. I don't know which ones are right, and I don't have the tools to knock down my walls and figure it out. "Gwen Stefani was right," she mutters but doesn't follow up on the thought. I'm pretty sure she's talking to herself. "At least I know how to spell bananas," she continues, and a part of me wishes I had first-class tickets for her thought train. It's as wild as Phoebe Buffay's. "I'm just having a midlife crisis. Or a midnight crisis. One or the other." She sighs.

It's only six in the evening, but I get her point. "How about we go upstairs? I'll make you the best comfort food, and we can watch TV. You don't have to fix everything tonight."

She glances at me, eyes full of vulnerability as she takes a deep breath. "Alright."

I stand and reach for her hands. She slips them into mine and squeezes them tight as I pull her to her feet. I refuse to let go of her hand as I lead her back to our place.

Chapter Thirty-Four

Mya

"Here you go," Kace says, holding out a bowl of pasta when he joins me in the living room. I press send on my text to my sister, asking if I can come home, then take the food from him.

"Thank you." I settle the dish on my blanket-covered lap and pick up the fork. It looks like fancy mac and cheese with miniature tube noodles in an orange creamy sauce–although there are tiny red specks that make me think it'll be spicy. It's garnished with parsley, and my mouth waters. I haven't eaten since breakfast. "This looks good."

He sits beside me on the couch. "Comfort ditalini is what my mom calls it."

I grin. "I love that. My mom makes us popcorn salad."

He scoops pasta onto his fork. "What's that?"

"We'd go to Blockbuster on Friday nights when I was a kid. And then mom would make it as our movie treat. Popcorn with our favorite mix-ins. M&Ms. Mini marshmallows. Pretzels. Nerds. Milk duds. Red Hots.

"So... trail mix?"

"No!" I laugh.

"A stomach ache then?"

"Definitely that but somehow in a way that makes me crave them."

He gives me a half-smile. "I get it. Some of my favorite beers aren't my *favorite*, but I consider them so because I drank them with my dad."

"Just like that," I say, hating and loving when he understands me. This week has been emotional, to say the least. I feel torn enough breaking up a relationship, even when logic tells me it is the right decision. Kace and I argued. Then he took me on the perfect date that absolutely was not a date and twisted my insides all over again. Then I went down a celebrity social media rabbit hole, and it was like the trigger to the meltdown about my life that has been on a countdown timer for months. Now I'm spiraling like a penny in a wishing well. "Do you see your parents often?"

"Not since I moved here."

"Were they upset that you came out here?"

He shrugs. "At first they thought I was moving to Canada."

"I swear most of the country confuses Vancouver, Washington with Canada even though this one was founded first." I chuckle. "They don't want to come visit?"

"Maybe when..."

Stirring my pasta with my fork, a burst of steam releases. "When what?"

"Nothing." He takes a bite of his dinner.

I set my bowl on the coffee table without trying it first and turn toward him. "Maybe when what? When I move out?"

He shakes his head. "It's not like that."

"I know I've been here longer than you planned. Do you want me to leave?"

"No. Mya, stop. I want you here. Just eat your dinner, okay? I found us a show to watch."

"You did?" My brows pinch as I reach for my pasta and settle back into the couch.

"Yeah. I know how much you love Hilary Duff."

A grin splits my face for the first time tonight. "What can I say? That girl can do no wrong."

He gives me a side glance that looks more like an eye roll as he reaches for the remote. "Anyway. They came out with a *How I Met Your Father*. And Hilary plays the girl version of Ted."

"Sounds great." It's not as great as him saying, "The perfect thing for us to do tonight is consummate a relationship," but here we are... having a roommate date night that I'll forever wish is *more*. I wonder how long I'll last before I can't handle it any longer.

I take a bite of my pasta, flavor exploding on my taste buds. It's the perfect blend of creamy and spicy. "Wow. This is 'I hope there are leftovers' good."

He chuckles. "I'm glad you like it."

"Thank you." I allow myself only a quick glance in his direction before focusing back on the show's opening credits.

"It's the least I can do."

What does that even mean? I assume he feels guilty for not wanting to be with me, so he's trying to make up for it in other ways.

The next ten minutes pass with only a few chuckles between us. I already love this show, and maybe Kace is right. I don't have to fix everything tonight. I don't have to determine the path for my future. I don't have to accept Kace doesn't want to be with me. I definitely don't have to figure out my business taxes. I can do all of that tomorrow.

"You good?" Kace's voice overlaps Francia Raisa's. That woman is a saint, donating a kidney to Selena Gomez. I've loved her ever since *The Secret Life of the American Teenager.*

"Yeah, why?"

"You won't stop fidgeting."

"Oh." I retrace the last few minutes in my mind, realizing I've been shifting and adjusting my legs trying to get comfortable. "Yeah. I'm just usually a legs-on-the-couch person. Sorry."

He hesitates and then says, "It's fine. You can stretch out." I open my mouth to speak but immediately close it. The man leans back and offers me his lap, and I'm more shocked than when Duke realized Viola was a girl. Because... His lap. For my legs to sprawl across. What in the fresh hell temptation is this?

"I'm not going to bite you," he adds, looking at me like I'm the crazy one.

"Alright." Leaning against the arm of the couch, I swing my bare legs over Kace's lap. When we came inside from the rain, we both changed–me into my pajama shorts and an oversized T-shirt and Kace into black sweatpants that hang perfectly on his hips, swapping his Virginia Tech hoodie for a plain gray tee. I wiggle around until I'm comfortable. The couch isn't *that* long, so when I scoot down to lean against the armrest, my knees bend over Kace's lap.

Feeling exposed, I pull the blanket I made for Kace from the back of the couch and settle it over my legs. I cuddle my arms under the chunky knitting, my fingers fidgeting with the string of my pajama shorts as he helps me adjust the blanket over my feet. Once I'm settled, he rests one forearm across my shins and his other hand over the blanket on my thigh. "You good?"

No, I'm not good. The man I'm in very strong like with has his hand on my thigh, and all I can think about is the last time he sent pleasure surging through my body. My heart is beating a billion times a second, and I might pass out from my nearness to the man I've been daydreaming about for far longer than just that mountain trip. But yeah. "I'm good," I whisper, forcing my focus on the TV.

With the blackout shades, it's so dark in here that the only light coming from the TV is hardly enough to see anything in the room. It's making me even more tuned in to every little movement from Kace's side of the couch. I don't even know what's happening in the show anymore. Did we finish the first episode? Are we onto the next one?

Kace adjusts himself, slouching as he leans back against the cushion. In the next moment, he slips his hands under the blanket and repositions them to exactly where they were topside.

One arm is draped over my shins, but now his hand grips my calf. The other hand rests mid-thigh. I subtly swipe my tongue over my lips to counteract how dry they've become.

His thumb brushes across my calf as one scene on the TV transitions into another, and my stomach flips.

His hand smooths across my thigh as characters have indiscernible conversation, and I fight the urge to squeeze my legs together.

I chew the inside of my lip, giving a silent pep talk to the butterflies in my stomach about getting excited over nothing.

But then his hand slides the smallest bit closer to my core. Each centimeter of movement turns me on more. His hand freezes, and so does my breath. His hold on my thigh tightens, and I feel the pad of each finger where it presses into my skin.

His hand slides further until his pinky swipes under the hem of my shorts.

God, I want him. His fingers inside me. And exploring every inch of my skin.

But then they pull away. His hand slides toward my knee where he grips like it'll hold him in place. No. I internally groan. *Come back.*

I scoot down, my head falling to the armrest and my ass scooting closer to him. His hand grips my skin, but when I let my leg fall away from him, it naturally slides down my inner thigh. Even in the dark, I can see Kace's gaze snap to me.

He holds his stare, then wets his lips. "Mya," he whispers, and the way he says my name feels like another rejection.

I run my tongue along the roof of my mouth, wetting it enough that I'll be able to speak. "Yeah?"

Groaning, he lets his head fall back against the couch. Giving me a sideways glance, his lips barely part like he's going to speak, but then he seals them shut again.

I hold his gaze, waiting.

"You're turning me on," he says begrudgingly.

My hands tense where my fingers play with the hem of my sleep shorts, my heart rate skyrocketing at the admittance. "And you don't want a repeat of the night at the mountain," I assume.

"Of course I want that," he confesses like it's a secret he's been holding onto. "I want to make you fall apart on my couch."

"So, what's the problem?" I ask in a tone that's split between snapping and frustration.

He sighs. "I think we need to talk first."

I don't want to talk about *us* again. I know how the story goes. Right now, I want to feel better, not worse, so I stuff the negative thoughts into a box with all the ones from earlier. "You said I don't have to fix anything tonight. I don't want to talk. I want to feel good."

The TV characters continue on with their lives in front of us while we're stuck in a long moment, frozen like a website trying so hard to load behind the scenes. Attempting to speed the connection, I link my pinky with his and give the slightest tug.

"Mya," he repeats, this time in a warning tone and with a battle simmering in his eyes.

"Kace," I echo. I want to be inside his mind, know every thought running around even though I'm scared of the enemy in his head. "We've already slept together."

His eyes flick over mine, the resolve in them finally dissipating as his middle finger brushes along my panty line, the pad pressing against my skin and transferring the energy of his internal war. How he looks at me feels like a cross between desire and sincerity. I don't dare believe he needs me the way it feels like I need him right now, but I feel more wanted than I have in a long time. He wets his lips. "Are you sure?"

I relax against the couch, letting my legs fall open wider as I zone in on his hand on my inner thigh. "Yes," I tell him, feeling more powerful thanks to his question and letting my eyelids close.

He shifts ever so slightly in my direction, and the feel of the glow from the TV in my periphery fades until the only thing in my focus is where Kace touches me. Still under the blanket, the hand furthest from me runs up my shin, feathering across the skin on the inside of my knee before sliding onto my thigh.

My god. My heart flutters, my pussy tightening at the anticipation. The hand that's been inching up my leg makes its move. He slips it to the apex of my thighs, running his thumb over my entrance through my shorts. A sigh escapes me at the contact, the lace of my panties rubbing against where I'm already beyond turned on and ready. "I do want you to feel good, Mya," he says as he hooks two of his fingers onto the inside of my shorts and pulls them out of the way. "You deserve to relax and to not worry about anything but letting go."

I melt further into the couch at his words and touch.

He sighs. "Promise we can talk later."

"I promise," I mindlessly agree.

With the commitment, his other hand joins in, and he brushes his thumb down my slit. I let out a gasp at the same time he groans. "Fuck, Mya. You're so wet." He rubs a finger in small circles against my opening. Without warning, he slips it inside of me, pressing until he bottoms out. He angles himself more toward me, and I twist to give him better access. He pulls out of me slowly, letting me feel every place he touches inside me. With the next thrust, he pushes a second finger in. He doesn't retract them until he's as deep as possible. His thick fingers slide in and out slowly and steadily without any friction, heat already building in my core.

My heel nearly slips from the couch cushion, and I relax my leg, draping it over his knee to give him better access. On the next thrust, he hooks his fingers, curling them upward as he pulses inside me. "Oh my god, Kace." I bite into my lip.

My pussy tightens around his fingers the second his thumb rubs against my clit. "Fuck," the rare curse leaves my lips as my hand flies to my hair to tug on the strands. My other hand falls to his bicep, fingernails digging into his skin.

Knowing I'm close, he doesn't deviate from the motion. His hooked fingers hit my G-spot with every pulse, the pressure of his thumb against my clit steadily sparking my every nerve to life. *All of this without even looking. Imagine what he can do with the lights on.* The thought of him scanning my naked body with a look that says he's deciding how he wants to worship it sends me spiraling over the edge.

"Oh my god," I choke out as my orgasm floods my body. My pussy tightens around his fingers. Sparks of pleasure jolt through me from where he touches my clit. A wave of white-hot heat ignites every cell.

My fingers clench in my hair and on Kace's bicep as I ride the wave. It seems to last forever, and he doesn't stop until every bit of tension leaves my body, and I melt into the couch. Oh. My. God.

A blow as devastating as my orgasm was powerful hits me with the realization that I won't get that every day for the rest of my life. That I can't have Kace. I fling my arms over my eyes, choosing to focus on the experience I just had instead.

My breathing is labored as he slowly pulls his fingers from me. He tugs my underwear and shorts back in place before running his hands down my thighs. He stops when they're at my knees. "You're so fucking beautiful when you come," he whispers, and it just now occurs to me that my eyes might have been closed, but he was watching me come undone at his touch. Heat rushes to my cheeks even though they are already flushed. "Look at me, Mya."

I shake my head, and he brushes his thumb against the inside of my knee, sending both warmth and a chill through me. "Tomorrow?" I force myself to pull my arms from across my face. "I'm not fixing any problems tonight."

"Okay." He squeezes my knee and reaches for the remote. "Tomorrow."

He clicks to restart the episode but doesn't let go of his hold on me. Right before the episode ends, I whisper, "I wouldn't be settling with you, Kace."

When I look up, he's drifting off to sleep with his eyes closed and his head leaning against the back of the couch. I pretend he heard me and tonight is a night like any other where we fall asleep on the couch.

Chapter Thirty-Five

Kace

Groaning, I reach to tug on my neck before opening my eyes. Fuck, I've got kinks everywhere. Appraising the situation, my hazy vision scans the room.

I'm on the couch, leaning at the most awkward angle known to humanity, but the warmth of Mya's legs is replaced with the blanket she was using last night.

Mya.

I jolt upright, searching the space. Her side of the couch is empty. The room is dark as fuck. The only reason I can see shit is from the natural light coming from the crack in my bedroom door. I glance toward the entryway. The bathroom door is open, and the light is off. *Where the fuck is she?*

The panic surging through me propels me to the kitchen. The clock on the oven glows *8:32* in neon white. I haven't slept this late in a long time, and it no doubt has to do with resolving to be with Mya. Despite my "don't sleep on a couch when you're over thirty" aches, I feel rested.

Rested but panicked. Because what the fuck. Where is she? She's always here in the mornings. Hell, she's usually not even awake at this time.

I check the leather key bowl on the breakfast bar. Her Tamagotchi keychain, Jeep fob, and the pink apartment key I made for her are missing. If she took her apartment key, she's planning to come home, right? I breathe a sigh of relief at the thought. I heard her whisper she wouldn't be settling with me last night as I drifted off. So why would she leave?

Wanting to be sure she's not here, I check my bedroom. The bed is still perfectly made from yesterday. There's something on the corner of my desk though. It's a stack of papers.

Fuck. It's her taxes. She asked me to look these over before we went to the mountains, but I haven't had a chance, given that I've spent every second working to avoid thinking about Mya. I flip through the sheets, pulling one closer to my face when it catches my attention. She made estimated quarterly tax payments? My brain tries to make it make sense. Mya is the girl who rarely has anything planned further out than a week, but she's been on top of her taxes which is the worst part of owning a business. I hate that I'm surprised by this, but I am. Surprised and attracted? Business intelligence is sexy as fuck. I've always been impressed by Mya's ability to run her business, but this is another level. And seeing that she's capable of planning and being organized like this... I've underestimated her.

This isn't the tipping point though. I was already there. Last night... fuck. Last night. Getting to watch her come undone at my touch... She's so fucking beautiful. But it's more than that. The second her legs hit my lap and she snuggled into the couch, I knew there was no going back. This is what I want. Mya next to me every damn night.

She's it. And whether it works out or not, I'll kick myself forever if I don't give her a chance–give *us* a chance.

My heart pounds against my chest, reminding me Mya needs to want that for us to have a chance. She needs to be here. And she's not. *Where the fuck is she?*

Dropping the papers to my desk, I return to the living room. The coffee table is clear. Our dinner plates and her cell phone are no longer there. I glance to the far end of the couch, to where she keeps her things stacked between the sofa and window. Relief floods me when I see two boxes neatly pushed into the back corner of the living room.

But... her suitcase isn't here. Or the duffel bag she brought to the mountain. Which means all of her clothes are gone. Frantic, I make my way to the bathroom. The white granite is clear–all her skincare and makeup products missing.

Mya is gone.

This wasn't supposed to happen. She's not supposed to leave. Today we were supposed to figure it out. My head is spinning. Her boxes are still here. I know they fit in her car. So she's just gone temporarily. She'll be back. Unless she thought moving them would wake me. Why don't I call her? Jesus fuck. Of course. I can just call her.

I swipe my phone off the kitchen counter and find Mya's contact. I press *call* and pull the phone to my ear. It goes straight to voicemail.

I try again. Same thing. *Shit.*

Setting my phone on the counter, I go back to her boxes. I tug on the blackout curtain beside it to give me enough light. I know I shouldn't go through her things, but I'm losing my mind here trying to figure out if I've lost her.

I unfold the perfectly pinwheeled top of the box, looking for any clue as to what's going on. A few leftover window clings from her project a couple of weeks ago are on top of a stack of light pink paper. I don't know what I'm thinking. Her craft box isn't holding some secre–

I'm either delusional or my name is written on the underside of that paper. It's backward, so I could be wrong. I shouldn't snoop, but I'm pretty confident it says my name.

Without any more thought, I slip the paper from the box and flip it over. My heart drops to my stomach like a falling elevator at the confirmation.

Kace,

For my fifth birthday...

I scan the letter, then reread it a second time more slowly. *Fuck.*

You being afraid I'm going to leave is manifesting it.

I hope it's worth it.

My eyes shift over the final two lines so many times I'm sure they'll change.

But they don't.

Dropping the letter to the floor, I lean against the couch and run my fingers through my hair.

A rustle comes from outside the apartment door, and my eyes snap to the entryway. I wait for what feels like forever, but there's no follow-up sound. No keys jingling in the hallway. No key sliding into the lock and twisting. No door opening. No Mya popping into the space with a perfect smile, ready to tease me for my misunderstanding.

Just me, alone in my apartment because I was too afraid of ending up alone.

Chapter Thirty-Six

"Aunt Mya!" my nephew, Hendrix, yells as he squirms from my sister's arms and runs toward me. The crochet "Little Foot" I made him is tucked under one arm as he catapults himself into me on the couch.

"Hey, buddy. Who do you have there?"

He squiggles on my leg, leaning back to show me. "Olaf!" He shoves the dinosaur in my face like I'm not the one who made it.

I chuckle. "Olaf... like the snowman from *Frozen*?"

"Uh huh." He grins wide. "I love him. Thank you."

"You're welcome." He snuggles into my chest, and I'm so happy that even though I haven't been home in months, our Facetime dates have been enough for him to remember me.

"He won't put it down," Ella says, sitting on the couch beside me. "I love your hair, by the way." She reaches to touch the tips. Anyone could look at us and know we're related. My hair nearly matches hers now, except she has lavender streaks running through her blonde waves.

"Thank you. I do too." I grin.

"Here you go, Mya." I glance up to see my brother-in-law handing me a cup of coffee. He's wearing plaid pajama pants and a three-quarter-sleeve baseball shirt. His perfect rock-star hair is pushed to the side, and his eyes are tired. He's definitely transitioned from lead singer and guitarist in a band to full-on dad mode, and every day I'm thankful my sister has someone so wonderful to do life with.

I bet Kace would make a good dad. A good husband. A good everything if he'd let his guard down. I sigh, pushing the thoughts aside as I reach for the mug. It says "Rock Star Dad" in AC/DC font. "Thank you... Wait. Did you make this?" I cringe as I wait for an answer. Mack hates coffee.

He chuckles. "Hey, give it a chance. Ella has forced me to perfect my coffee-making skills.

"Okay, good." I grin, bringing the steaming beverage to my lips. I take the smallest sip at first, but the moment the caramel goodness hits my tastebuds, I go back for a full gulp. "Thank you." I reach to put the mug on the coffee table because I don't trust the way Hendrix is flying his dinosaur around.

"So, what's new?" Mack asks.

"Nothing much, really." I know my shifty eyes give away the lie.

"You're not living with 'a total hunk' that you're crazy about?"

I shoot him a look, one brow raised, semi-aware of my sister giggling next to us.

He holds his hands in surrender. "Ella's words, not mine."

A sad laugh escapes me. "I don't know."

"Mommy, Olaf pancakes, please," Hendrix interrupts, clearly bored by our conversation.

"Okay, sweetie," my sister says. "Should we go make every-one breakfast?"

"Yes!" He reaches his hands out, and Ella pulls him from me and into her arms. They wander to the kitchen, leaving me to wonder if I will be eating snowmen or dinosaurs.

"What don't you know?" Mack says, snapping my attention back to him.

I sigh. "It feels like I don't know anything."

"None of us do," he says confidently, leaning back into the couch.

"You guys seem to."

He chuckles. "Come on, Mya. I love your sister more than life, but you know she did not always have it figured out."

"Yeah," I admit. "I know. But she had you to help her. I have no one."

"What about this Kace guy?"

"I feel like we'd be so good together. We balance each other. He's calm, organized and safe. I'm chaotic and spontaneous. He grounds me in a way I know I need, and I'd like to think I help him live in the moment. But we're similar in ways that work too. We like the same foods and shows. He understands my love of nostalgia and how my brain works, even if it frustrates him sometimes. But he's got a mental block. He doesn't trust me not to hurt him because I haven't been in a long-term relationship."

"You just hadn't found the right one yet," he says like it's obvious.

"Exactly! I don't get why Kace can't see that."

He mulls over a thought. "Can I tell you a story?"

I nod.

"Before Ella, I was with someone else."

I mean, obviously he was–he's twenty-nine. But it's still weird to think about. He and my sister are so perfect together that it's easy to forget they haven't been married forever. "I remember. You were still hung up on her when you and Ella met, right?"

He nods. "I was convinced I'd never find someone again. I brushed Ella off without a second thought and ghosted her for a while. Coming from someone who has had their heart ripped apart by someone they thought was *the one*, I can tell you it's not easy to move forward–even when someone is as incredible as your sister. It's terrifying to put yourself in the position to possibly get hurt again."

"How did you know when it was time to let go of your ex and give Ella a chance?"

He leans forward, his forearms on his knees. "I knew I gave my all to Maci. At the end of the day, it wasn't enough. I realized that if it were meant to be, it would have worked out *because* I gave it my best shot. My best wasn't enough for her because it wasn't *right* being with her."

"So you're saying if Kace doesn't want to be with me, I should just accept it?"

"I don't know if Kace is your Ella or the one who comes before. Only you can determine that. What I can tell you is that all you can control is whether or not you give it your best shot. Once you do that, moving on or staying stuck is your choice."

I groan. "Being an adult is harder than staying alive in the Oregon Trail game."

Mack chuckles. "You're going to figure it out, Mya. You're always welcome to stay with us."

"Thanks, Mack." I lean into him for a side hug, and I can't help but think about how well Mack and Kace would get along. I can picture them playing an after-dinner game of Guitar Hero together or making hot cocoa for everyone on Christmas Eve.

"Anytime." He stands to help his family in the kitchen. As I sip my coffee and watch the three of them from a distance, colliding waves of emotions hit me. I feel so behind not already having what they have. It feels like my ovaries are shriveling up and all the fish in the sea are being caught. Time isn't just ticking–it's sprinting past us all in Nike Air Maxes while some of us are still tying our shoelaces. The tiny rational part of my brain tells me I need to get back out there as soon as possible to up my chances of reaching the finish line.

I don't want it with just anyone. I want it with Kace. But I've exhausted time and energy trying to convince him we should be together, and he's hardly given an inch. It would be worth the wait if I knew we'd end up together. I'd rather be even more behind on the timeline I've set for myself than be on track but unhappy. But his mixed signals don't give me enough indication of hope.

Setting my goal to devise a new life plan this week, I join everyone in the kitchen as Ella is placing pancakes–a combination of snowmen and dinosaurs–onto a serving plate. We gather around the table, and I force myself to sit in this moment and enjoy it. I don't want to be jealous of what my sister has. That won't get me any closer to getting what I want. Aside from that, I *am* happy for her. She deserves this life and so much more.

Mack hands me a plate covered in sizzling bacon on a paper towel. I use the tongs to layer two slices over my stack of pancakes right as the doorbell rings. Our heads all turn toward the noise.

"Are we expecting anyone?" Ella asks Mack.

"Don't think so," he answers, setting the plate on the table. "I'll get it."

Focusing back on the food, I reach for the syrup and drizzle it across my breakfast.

"Hi," I hear Mack say from behind me.

Whoever is at the door clears their throat. "Hey, uh." I freeze mid-cut of my pancake. "Is Mya here?" My heart rate skyrockets, and I look across the table to my sister with matching wide eyes. "I'm Kace."

"Hey, man!" Mack's voice warms like he's known Kace forever. "Yeah, she is. Hold on. I'll grab her for you. I'm Mack, by the way. Mya's brother-in-law." How the hell did Kace get here? And why isn't Mack concerned that someone he's never met showed up completely uninvited and unannounced? Whoa. That was uncharacteristically safety-conscious of me. *What is he doing here?*

"Nice to meet you. I've heard good things," Kace says, and I get the feeling they're shaking hands.

"Feel free to come in," Mack says.

"That's okay. I don't want to intrude."

"You're not at all. I'll let Mya know you're here."

"Thank you."

A moment later, Mack appears in the kitchen. My eyes flick from my sister to her husband and back again. "Are you going to make him wait, or should I bring him some bacon?" Mack asks.

Chapter Thirty-Seven

Mya

"What is he doing here?" I whisper.

"Go find out, stupid." My sister waves me off with her hands.

"Okay, okay." I push back from the table, the chair legs scraping against the tile. Looking into my reflection on the microwave door, I run my fingers through my hair, tucking a strand behind my ear.

With each step I take toward the entryway, my heart thumps inside my chest. When he comes into view, I freeze. He's devastatingly handsome in his jeans, T-shirt and bomber jacket. His hair doesn't seem up to his standards of put-to-getherness, but it might be a stress thing. Why is he here? He's tugging on the back of his neck, nervous in a way I've never seen him.

"Kace... What are you doing here?" I manage. From some-where behind me, the record player kicks on, and the crisp sound of Daughtry on vinyl fills the air.

"You weren't home when I woke up."

"Umm. Yeah... I came to visit my sister." I scrunch my brows, glancing around me.

"Visit?" His eyes pin on me, full of hope.

"As opposed to?"

His body deflates. "Moving here."

"Movin–what? I left you a note."

"Yeah, I read it." His head tips back, and his fingers run through his hair like he's upset.

"What's going on? Are you okay?"

"No, Mya. I'm not okay. I woke up to find that you packed all your shit and left."

"My suitcase, you mean? I brought the whole thing. I didn't want to wake you by sorting through it."

His face scrunches in confusion. "I tried calling you."

I cringe. "Sorry about that. My car charger broke, and since we fell asleep before I could plug my phone in, it died on the way here. Thank god I no longer need printed MapQuest directions to get me places."

His fists clench. "And the note?"

"What about it? Did it fall off the milk container? I was wondering if tape loses its effectiveness in the fridge. I should have left it on the counter. Sorry. You know my brain doesn't function well in the morning."

"What are you talking about?" His fist flexes before running through his hair again.

"What are *you* talking about?"

"I'm talking about the note you wrote me. About how you don't want to be with me."

Oh. *That note.* The blood drains from my face, and I divert my gaze to the carpet. *Shit. Shit. Shit.* "You weren't supposed to see that," I mumble to myself, shaking my head.

He's frozen in my periphery, speechless.

What do I say? Is it a good thing he found it? I didn't plan on him reading it. It was a pretty harsh letter. And yet... I glance up. "Kace..."

His gaze meets mine, and I swear both our hearts are beating in sync at full volume. "Yeah?"

"What are you doing here?" I bite my lip.

He takes a breath, stepping into my space. He opens his mouth to speak but closes it, and my eyes lock onto his lips as he wets them. I'm suddenly acutely aware that we haven't kissed since the first time. While it was a total disaster, I want nothing more than to be reminded of how it felt to have his lips on mine.

He slips his fingers into my hair, cradling my face and searching my eyes. My breath hitches. My brain short circuits. I will myself to be more *light as a feather* and not *stiff as a board*, but what the heck is happening right now?

His worried eyes shift back and forth across my face. "You don't want to be with me anymore. Is that true?"

I shake my head, his skin brushing against mine with his gentle hold. "That's all I want," I admit, my fingers fidgeting between us. "Being with you is all I think about."

"Fuck, Mya," he mutters. His grip on my hair tightens as he closes the space between us, and his thumbs brush across my cheek. "I thought I lost you."

"Lost me? I thought you didn't even want me." The way he's touching me seems contradictory, but emotion wells in my chest at the thought that it could still be true.

He shakes his head in amusement. "I'm losing my god-damn mind over you. We're past *want* at this point. I *need* you."

"Really?" I ask like an idiot because... excuse me, what?

"I know I'm a moron. I'm sorry it took me so long." He takes a deep breath like the oxygen will provide him courage. When he exhales, his breath is warm against my skin, and I want to steal it in a kiss. "I was scared."

My hands softly grip his waist. "I'm not going to hurt you, Kace."

He shakes his head. "I don't want you to promise that. It's not something anyone can guarantee because shit happens."

"Okay. Well, what *do* you want then?" I beg. I'll give him anything if it means we have a chance.

"I just want you." He's looking at me like I'm the eighth wonder of the world. "Exactly how you are. Except completely moved into my apartment. My bed. My life."

This time, I'm speechless.

"Say something," he says over the loud beating of my heart.

I grin. "I knew you did illegal things with your hacking."

I catch a sliver of an amused shake of his head, and then his mouth is on mine. His lips press against me, soft but commanding. He doesn't waste a single second, swiping his tongue, asking for access I happily give him.

My hands slip under the hem of his T-shirt so I can feel his skin against mine as our kiss deepens. It's already everything I've ever wanted since the first time and worth the painfully long wait for this moment.

Our tongues tangle, and with each kiss, we're brought closer together. His fingers slip further into my hair, cradling the back of my head, and my stomach flutters. My grip on his waist pulls him flush to me. Kace groans, and I can't help but smile at it.

Knowing I can kiss him anytime I want now, I break the connection. He chases my lips, closing the small distance again to give me a single kiss. He pulls back just enough to press his forehead to mine, his grip falling to my ribs. He brushes his thumbs right below my bra line, and I curse the long-sleeved tee that separates us.

I can't help but smile. "I didn't peg you as a stalker."

"I couldn't wait another second," he says breathlessly. "And now that I know it's even better than I imagined, I'd break a hell of a lot more laws."

"We have so much time to make up for. Do you know how many times I've wanted to kiss you in the past two months?"

He grins quickly before kissing me again. "Not as many times as I've wanted to kiss you." His eyes shift over my face.

I chew on my lip, fighting back my smile. "What are you thinking?"

"About how we should go have breakfast with your family."

I deflate a bit. It's not that I don't want him to spend time with my family. I just want him to myself first, now that he's *mine*. "Really?"

He leans until I can feel his breath against my ear. "And the whole time, I'll be thinking about how I can't wait to be inside you. With you being *mine* this time." My cheeks flush, and I chew the corner of my lip. He pulls back to take in my reaction and chuckles. "You're so fucking cute."

Pressing my face to his chest, he wraps his arms around me in a hug, and everything about this feels perfect. "I don't want to wait to be alone with you," I say into his jacket.

"We've got time." He pulls back, slipping his hand into mine. "But we drove separately, and going home means we have to be apart for two hours, and I'm not ready for that."

My grin widens. "Okay, fine. Pancakes it is then." I tug him toward the kitchen. "But you have to promise you'll still want me in your home no matter what embarrassing stories my sister tells."

He stops, and it jolts me a little. Pulling me back into his arms, he says, "Our home," and kisses me senseless again.

Chapter Thirty-Eight

"Finally." I exhale, shutting the door to the guest bedroom behind Kace. We ate breakfast and then spent the entire day together. Kace seemed comfortable, chatting with both Mack and Ella effortlessly. He even disappeared with Hendrix for a while.

It was the perfect family day. We went to the park, got ramen at my favorite Japanese spot in Eugene, and somehow convinced Hendrix to discover the magic of *Ice Age* instead of *Frozen*. He asked if Scrat was friends with Olaf, and Kace told him a whole story about what they do when they hang out. When Kace told me he was ready for a family, it's clear now he truly meant it. I know in my heart that he's it for me. I can picture us in the same way I see Ella and her family, and he's the only one I can imagine in it.

I opted to skip inviting my parents to lunch because I worried it would never end. But once Hendrix went to bed, Ella canceled it out by acting as if it were urgent to play Twenty Questions with Kace... like eight times over. While I appreciate that I learned a few new things about him, I've never wanted my sister to shut up more in my entire life.

"What?" he teases. "You didn't want to hear about the chameleon I had when I was eight?"

"I would love to hear more stories about Godzilla another time." I grab his shirt at his stomach and tug him closer to both me and the bed. "But you told me you were eager to do something else this morning, and I want that more."

He threads his fingers through my hair, gathering it in one fist and holding it out of the way as he leans to kiss my collarbone. "What did I promise you earlier?" His breath against my skin sends a chill over my body like a tidal wave. Tugging my neck to the side with his hold on my hair, he kisses his way up my neck. A moan escapes as I slip my fingers under the hem of his jeans. He whispers in my ear, "The things I want to do to you..."

My fingers find the button on his jeans and pop it free. "Do them." I tug his zipper down one tooth at a time.

He groans. My name sounds like a plea when it leaves his lips.

"Hmm?" I grip the hem of his shirt and tug upward. He reluctantly lets me pull it over his head.

"We're at your sister's house. They're right up the hall."

"I'll be quiet. I promise." I grip his hips and lean back enough to take in the way his V disappears into his black briefs. Biting my lip, I look up at him with pleading eyes. Just for good measure, I slip my hand inside his jeans, palming him and squeezing his balls.

"Fuck, Mya." He groans, and his head and eyes roll back a bit. I grin, pleased with myself. I know I've got him. He kicks his jeans off as gracefully as possible without breaking our contact, then walks me backward to the bed. When the back of my legs hit the mattress, he reaches for the hem of my shirt and pulls it over my head in one smooth motion.

His thumb brushes across my cheek before he trails his finger down my neck, following the strap of my bra and over my breast. His hand continues across the bare skin on my stomach until he reaches my belly button. He leans back to take me in, his thumb brushing over the skin next to my piercing. "You're everything I want," he murmurs, and I can't wait to spend my life being the object of his affection. His fingers reach my jean shorts, and he makes quick work of the button and zipper, falling to his knees as he tugs the denim and my underwear to the floor.

Smoothing his hands up my legs, he plants kisses along my inner thigh–slow and controlled. He pauses when he reaches the apex of my thighs. Using his thumbs to spread me, he drags his tongue up my slit. "Oh my god," I try to say, but I'm pretty sure it comes out incoherently. He sucks my clit into his mouth, releasing it with a pop.

He buries his face between my legs, dipping his tongue inside me before trailing it up my slit again. I gasp as arousal floods my body and brace my hands on his shoulders.

He squeezes my thighs with his hands, pulling me closer, and the view of him on his knees is enough to make me come already. But I want to be more comfortable. I want this to last, so I pull away from his grasp and scoot across the bed.

Without hesitation, he slips out of his briefs and follows me. Before he has a chance to hover over me, I nudge him to the mattress, pressing him onto his back with my hands on his chest. He stares up at me with questioning but feral eyes, and if I weren't so excited for the pleasure, I'd soak up watching him want me.

Instead, I crawl down his body until I reach where he's already semi-hard. Leaning on one forearm, I squeeze his balls with one hand, using my thumb to guide his cock into place. I drag my tongue up his length, hearing him groan as I suck his tip into my mouth. "Fuuuck." He groans, his hands falling to my head. Right as I'm about to take him to the back of my throat, he tugs on my hair.

I peer up at him, and he tugs again. Panic rushes through me as I return face-to-face with him, hovering over his body. "What's wrong?"

"What's wrong is you're not sitting on my face. I've only had one taste, and it's not enough."

I grin, feeling more comfortable with Kace than I ever have with another man. "All you have to do is ask nicely," I tease.

"Mya, get your pretty little pussy in my face. Now," he commands, and I'm turned all the way on. I begin to do as he says, but he nudges me to turn around. I oblige without a second thought, positioning myself over his face and aligning his cock with my mouth. At the same moment I swirl my tongue around his tip, he flattens his tongue, licking the length of me. A mutual moan escapes both of us, and I feel the vibration of it to my core as he dips his tongue inside me.

I descend on his fully erect length, sucking him into my mouth until he hits the back of my throat. The way he squeezes the back of my thighs, traveling them toward my ass, encourages me to keep going. I squeeze his balls as I retract my mouth, sucking hard the entire way.

As I slide back down, he flutters his tongue inside me so quickly I nearly come on the spot. I freeze my motion, the pleasure raking through me nearly paralyzing. He sucks my clit into his mouth again, and I cry out as much as I can with his cock filling my mouth.

I return my focus to him, sucking as I bob up and down, massaging his balls and loving the way his thighs tense. I pull back too far, and he pops from my mouth. He uses the opportunity to pull away from me, sliding out from underneath and pushing me onto my back.

Before I can get a word in, he levels his face with mine, pressing his lips to my neck. Straddling me, he slips his hands under my back, fumbling until my bra is unhooked. In one smooth motion, he tugs it off me with a grip on the front and sits back on his heels to appraise me.

I wait patiently as his eyes roam my body before landing on my face, his hands gripping my sides and his thumbs rubbing across my skin. "I'm sorry it took me so long," he admits. "I regretted it even in the midst of pushing you away." He palms my breast, his thumb brushing over my nipple.

I groan at the contact, and when he grinds his hips against mine, my back arches at the feel of his cock against my pussy. "I'm just happy we're on the same page now," I manage.

"Me fucking too." He hesitates a moment, his tongue licking over his lip and his eyes locking on mine like he's baffled that we're here–together. I run my hands up his thighs, and it snaps him back to action. He descends on my breast, massaging one with his hand and sucking the nipple of the other into his mouth, swirling his tongue around the peak.

He moves to kiss my lips, and as he does, his fingers find their way to my entrance. With small teasing circles, he toys with me. "Mya," he whispers, and it occurs to me that my eyes have fluttered closed.

I open them, our gazes locking. "Hmm?" I manage before letting out a moan when he plunges two fingers inside me. My back arches at the touch.

"How do you feel about us not using a condom?"

I try to focus, but it's hard with his fingers working inside me. "You don't have one?" I ask between labored breaths. I've never not used a condom.

"I do… But I want to feel you so fucking badly."

My eyes flutter closed again at the shots of pleasure jolting through me every time his fingertips land just right.

"Baby?" He pauses the motion, his fingers frozen inside me.

I force myself to focus and look at him. "I got tested last week. After the first time."

"Are you on birth control?"

I nod. "An IUD." I hate birth control, but at least it's a hormone-free one.

He continues to withhold movement. "Tell me what you want."

"I want to feel you too, Kace. Please," I beg.

He groans, pulling his fingers from me. I whine at the loss, feeling my opening close. But in the next moment, his cock is in place and slowly pushing inside me.

He inches in, my arousal erasing any friction in the way. When he's as deep as possible, the pressure inside me heats my core. He pulls out just as slowly, and without the condom, I'm aware of every place our most sensitive skin touches, and it's almost too much. He thrusts down, his lips crashing onto mine simultaneously to him bottoming out again. *My god.*

I kiss him back hard and let my hands wander up his sides. They slip around his back, my fingers digging into his shoulder blades when he thrusts into me again. He breaks our kiss just long enough to say, "Fuck, Mya. You feel so fucking good." Then his mouth is back on mine, and my mind whirls with the memory of our first time and how much closer I feel to him now–how confident I am in our connection now that he's let me in.

He reaches between us, rubbing his thumb against my clit. It strikes perfectly with his thrust inside me, and I cry out. His hand from the arm he's balancing on is over my mouth in the next second. "Shhh," he says, slowing his pumps. I nip at the inside of his fingers, and he smirks. "Oh yeah?" I swirl my tongue over his skin, dragging it between his fingers and trying to hold back my giggle. "You little brat." He removes his hand only to replace it with his lips.

After one quick kiss, he pulls back. "Are you going to be quiet?"

I nod, smiling.

"Good girl. Now what do you say we come together?"

Instead of words, I lift my head off the mattress enough to kiss him. His return is so forceful it presses me back to the bed. His tongue tangles with mine, and my fingers dig into his skin as he resumes his thrusting.

Rubbing my clit, he picks up his pace, applying more pressure and hitting deeper inside me with each plunge. I gasp for a breath in our kiss, the pleasure building inside making my lungs forget how to function.

Right before I can hardly take the tension anymore, I fall over the edge. It feels like both a feather floating to the ground and a wave crashing down on me. I can't breathe, and yet, every cell of my body has never felt more alive. I break our kiss to focus on my orgasm, and Kace's lips move to my neck. His nips and pecks across my skin intensify every sensation.

His thrusts quicken, and he groans against my neck. I feel him swell inside me as my pussy clenches around him in waves. *Holy shit.*

He pumps a few more times, each one reminding me how full I feel and extending my orgasm. He comes to a stop, collapsing onto me but holding his weight up just enough. With sweat along his hairline, he brings his lips to mine for a kiss.

He searches my face like he needs confirmation that was as amazing for me as it was for him. "How was that?"

"Pretty solid." I grin. "I'd put you on my Mount Rushmore."

"Hey!" He pinches my side. I try to squirm away, but he has me pinned.

"I'm kidding. I'm kidding. It was better than watching *The Vampire Diaries* for the first time."

"Even though we didn't do it under your Damon Salvatore poster?" He rolls his eyes, and I giggle.

"All I need from now on is you."

He brushes his thumb across my lips. "Thank you for waiting for me," he whispers.

"No chance I wasn't going to."

Chapter Thirty-Nine

"So, I was thinking maybe we should leave the apartment this weekend," Mya says from where she's sitting on the floor making crafts on the coffee table. This week's project is a mashup between a coloring book and a deck of cards. She ordered blank cards and is drawing outlines of different mandalas on the faces based on the number, and then her customer will color them in. Her creativity is insane, so I have my laptop set up out here for that reason alone. They say it's best to surround yourself with people who are on your level or higher, so clearly it's in my best interest to be around her.

That, and I feel like I spent so much time trying to stay out of her orbit that I want to make up for it now. The past week since we've returned from her sister's has flown by. We went out once for groceries, to the craft store, and I went to therapy. Besides that and work, our time has been spent deep in the honeymoon phase. Sex. Tacos. Cereal. Comfort ditalini. Movies. Cuddling. Teasing. Touches every time we're close enough. All the things I love about a relationship–the things that make this feel right.

I haven't questioned Mya or my decision to be with her. Once everything clicked for me, I was all in. She's a little crazy and lives life more freely than I do, but I need someone to help ensure I enjoy life in all the right ways.

I glance up from my keyboard. "Yeah, I'm down. I want to take you on a real date."

"Actually…" She stands, making her way to where I'm at in the kitchen. I twist my barstool and make room for her to stand between my legs. I grip her waist, and her hands fall to my chest. "I want to take you out."

I chuckle. "Is that so?"

She nods. "Mhmm."

"Where does Mya Holloway take her boyfriends on dates?" I ask, masking the panic coursing through me. I hate surprises and not having a plan. Unfortunately for me, that sounds like Mya's April 25th kind of date, and I know I'll likely have to pay that cost to be with her.

She grins. "Well, you see… It just so happens that BOYS LIKE GIRLS are going to be in Forest Grove this weekend."

My thumbs freeze where they're rubbing across her back. "Really?"

She nods. "I know how much you love them, so I got us tickets."

I'm torn between pure excitement and off-the-wall anxiety. I hate driving anywhere near Portland. It's stressful as fuck. Plus, I've never been to that venue.

Before I react, she slides her fingers to the nape of my neck and plays with my hair. The gesture immediately relaxes me as she continues. "The show starts at seven. It takes about an hour to get there, so I thought we could leave at four. That way we won't be rushed. There's a highly rated brewery near the McMenamins venue that we could try. And it's all within walking distance of a free parking area with security."

I stare. "Did you plan all that?"

"Yes... Does it not sound fun?" I can hear the panic in her voice. "We don't have to go if you don't want to. I just thought–"

"Mya," I cut her off. "I meant..." I pause, trying to find the right words. "I mean this in the nicest way. I assumed you'd be the type of girl who buys last-minute tickets and figures the rest out when she shows up."

"I am." She nods, still unsure if I'm on board or not. "But you like it when things are planned. I didn't want you to have to worry about anything so you could have fun."

I tug her closer, and I have no doubt she can feel me hard between her thighs. She melts into me. "Thank you. It sounds perfect."

Her smile returns. "I'm so glad. I can't wait."

"I think you should buy me a T-shirt," Mya announces once we're through security at the outdoor venue. She's walking backward to face me, holding her hands out for me to grab.

"Is that so?" I take one of her hands in mine. She looks so fucking cute in her ripped jean shorts, black combat boots and my black and white flannel tied around her waist. Her black crop top reveals a sliver of her stomach that distracts me whenever I look at her. She crimped her hair and tied half of it back in a black and white checkered bow. It's a far cry from her typical color vibes, but she barely got me out of the apartment when she showed me.

She nods, her smile bright. "Duh. I want to remember our first date forever."

"So what you're saying is we can burn the JCPenny pictures then?" I had no idea how the photographer captured any-thing worth keeping, but lo and behold, three different shots were emailed to Mya. I was shocked to see they truly made it look like we were a couple then.

"No way. I'm keeping those forever. We're making them centerpieces at our wedding." Her eyes widen and she freezes when she realizes what she said. "I mean…" She chews on her lip.

I pull her into me and kiss her perfectly pink lips, hoping to reassure her that she doesn't scare me anymore. "Let's get you a T-shirt. Also, you taste like Dr. Pepper."

She releases me to dig into the front pocket of her shorts, pulling out a maroon Lip Smackers and wiggling it in front of me. "Discontinued flavor." She uncaps it and swipes it over her lips. "But tonight is going to be the best night ever, so I thought it was worthy of an appearance."

Thirty minutes later, Mya is wearing an oversized tee repping my favorite band, and standing next to me in the front of the general admission section, bouncing on her toes. This venue is sick. The sun is setting behind the stage and trees surround the grass field we're in. There's a VIP section in front of us, but we scored standing room right behind the rope that divides the two sections.

A red glow highlights the drum set, and John Keefe comes into view. Fuck, this is cool. A spotlight focuses on Martin Johnson, still looking straight out of the 80s with his rock star mullet, black leather jacket and black leather skinny jeans. With a few strums of his guitar, the intro to "Two Is Better Than One" starts.

A chill runs through me when the chorus hits–from the slight breeze or Martin's voice, I'm not sure. I glance at Mya. She's singing the lyrics, swaying back and forth in her own little world. Everything about her screams *life*. I can't believe I fought this for so long, and I can't believe she's mine.

My eyes remain on her for the rest of the song. When it ends, she turns toward me with a smile that's harder to see now that it's dark outside. "What?" she asks.

"Remember when you told me you wish I could experience my own energy because I'd hate it?"

"Uh... yeah." Her face crumples into worry, and I can't help but smile.

"I wish you could walk into a space and experience your own energy so you can see how magical it is."

Her face softens. "Thank you for that."

I nod toward the stage. "I didn't know you listened to them."

She shrugs. "I didn't before. But I've had them on repeat all week just for tonight. And now I love them."

"I love you." The words tumble out without permission, but I've never meant the sentiment more than I do with Mya now.

Her grin widens, and she turns toward me, looping her arms around my waist. "Really?"

"Really," I confirm, my heart thudding in my chest to the drum beat of the next song.

"I love you too." She stands on her toes to press her lips to mine. "I love you so much."

I pull her closer, and she squeezes into my side. My attention is pulled to where Martin stops strumming his guitar to speak into the microphone. "Alright everyone, get your phones out," he says. "Right now. This is your chance." Everyone around us switches their phone to video mode, pointing the camera toward the stage. "We're playing 'The Great Escape' chorus for you. Then you're putting them away so we can go back in time for three minutes to enjoy music like we used to!"

The crowd roars, most of them jumping up and down at the start of the chorus. I glance down at Mya in my arms. "Don't you want to record this for our first date memory?"

She tilts her head to look up at me. "I'll never forget this."

Chapter Forty

"You've really never been to Ikea?" Mya asks for the seventh time today as we stand outside the absurdly large bright blue and yellow warehouse.

I quirk a brow and wait until she turns to look at me. "I do not consider myself a materialistic man, but I refuse to work hard and still pay for furniture I have to put together myself."

"It's about the experience." She smiles, and I know I'd follow her into any maze–even one with a port key to a cemetery at the end. Thank fuck this one will only end with, hopefully, a few minimal purchases.

My lease was up for renewal last week, so I looked into moving us to a two-bedroom so Mya could have her own workspace to create whatever crafts and chaos she wants–especially since we both decided it would be best for my sanity and All That and a Bag of Crafts if we stopped the Unhitched business. I want her to have everything she needs to make her work the priority she wants it to be, but she also deserves more than to have a workspace that takes more time and effort to put together than her actual crafts. Contrary to her belief, this is all for show–or as she would say, 'the experience.' I ordered her the DreamBox storage closet that she's constantly going on about, and it comes later this week. It will serve as every piece of furniture she'll need wrapped in one.

"Whatever you say, babe." I let her lead me through the front doors, surprised when she passes the yellow carts and bags and heads directly to the escalator.

Stepping off the moving stairs, she takes my hand, tugging me toward the chaos. I can see signs, which might give the appearance of organization, but I'm not sold. Combine that with the fact that I'm a plain and simple decorator, my hell would literally be to be trapped here for eternity. But what's the phrase? *Happy wife, happy life.*

Mya isn't my wife yet. She's only been my girlfriend for a couple of months, but not only will she be my wife someday, I already have a ring. I don't know if it says more about me, considering I didn't so much as shop for a ring in the eight years I was with Ruby. Or if it says more about Mya, that she's got me so locked in by just being herself. I haven't planned a proposal yet, but only for the sake of *trying* to do things in order.

"Oh my gosh. This is so cute!" She holds up a stuffed owl at the entrance to the maze. "It's Hedwig!"

I chuckle. "I have a feeling Ikea is too cheap to acquire the rights to Hedwig."

She rolls her eyes. "You're one of those guys who points out all the plot holes in Hallmark movies, aren't you?"

"Absolutely," I tease without hesitation.

She smiles, but then it fades as she runs her fingers over the wings of the owl.

I watch her for a moment, feeling a shift. "What's wrong?"

When she glances up at me, her eyes are glossy.

"Hey." I slip my hands along either side of her neck. "Talk to me."

She shakes her head. "It's not a big deal."

"If you're upset, it is a big deal," I say the words as if I've known her my whole life and been there for every crushing moment, and it's weird as fuck to me that I haven't.

"I'm so happy with you, Kace," she whispers, and my stomach drops.

Blood rushes through my ears. I thought what we've been doing *works* for us. I've happily gone on every weekend adventure she's planned for us, and she's seemed more than content spending the weekdays creating routines and traditions together at home. We've been completely transparent about anything that bothers us. At least I have... "Why do I feel like there's a 'but?'"

She focuses her gaze on where she's picking at the fuzz on the stuffed animal between us. "I still can't shake this feeling that I'm so far behind."

My heart palpitates as I flashback to the day on the sidewalk. I did not handle that breakdown in the way she deserves, and I refuse to make that mistake again. I pull her into the first section of the maze, which is apparently living room themed. I'm pretty sure we're not supposed to sit on the staged furniture, so I guide her to a modern dark gray and sage living room mockup that has a divider wall blocking off part of it so we aren't completely out in the open.

"Hey." I brush my thumb across her jaw to draw her attention to me.

"Hi." Sadness laces the whisper, and she's still fidgeting with the owl.

I don't want to invalidate any feelings she has around this because I've had some of them myself. It fucking sucks thinking your dreams have an expiration date. "What do you feel behind on, and what is your timeline for when you want to achieve them?"

She glances up at me like she's surprised by my question. Or maybe thrown off. Her eyes flick to the entertainment center next to us as if she needs to recall a memory. Looking back at me, she takes a breath. "I just..." She chuckles, and it makes me smile despite knowing she's sad. "I grew up thinking I'd be thirty, flirty and thriving."

"You are all of those things." I brush a tear from her cheek.

"I know. I feel selfish. I have a job I love. A guy I love. One who's giving me my own crafting room." She gives me an appreciative half-smile. "But I can't get it out of my head that once you're thirty, you're supposed to be married and have kids. You're supposed to be a grown-up."

"For starters, the divorce rate for first marriages is around forty percent. So a lot of those people who made choices *just* to stay 'on track' are setting themselves up for failure."

She gives me a sad chuckle. "Is that supposed to make me feel better?"

I smirk, but then level with her so she knows I'm serious. "Mya, I'm all in. Timeline matters far less when I'm not going anywhere. We have the rest of our lives."

"You're not worried about me wanting out in another month?"

"I know you're not going anywhere. Partially because I trust you, and partially because you and I are endgame. Except I won't die on you like Tony Stark."

The corner of her lip turns up at the reference. "Even if I can get past the marriage thing–" She cuts herself off. "I'm not telling you to propose or anything."

"I know," I assure her, silently happy to hear we're on the same page.

"Even if I can get past that, I'm worried I'll be too old to have kids once we're ready."

"There's no rule saying we have to go in order. If you want to start a family right now, I'll knock you up this month. I'm *all in*, Mya. So if you want that now, it's yours. If you want to wait a year or two, I'll be here for that too."

"Yeah?" She looks at me with hopeful eyes that I pray she doesn't pass down to our future child or I'll never be able to say no to anything again in my life.

"I would put a baby in you right here on this couch if you asked me."

"Shut up." She laughs and slaps my chest, still clutching the owl with her other hand. "You would not participate in exhibitionism."

"Try me." I'm dead serious. "I would do anything for you, Mya Holloway."

She holds the owl in front of her, and even though it's blocking her beautiful face, I can feel her smile.

"Yes. I will get you Hedwig."

She lowers the bird. "Really?!" Her eyes light in a way that far exceeds my hope.

"Absolutely. It reminds me of the first time we had sex. You were on some rant about an owl on the side of the road and then rambled about how if we were at Hogwarts we could never be together."

She sighs happily. "I love it when you listen to me."

"Is that so?" I glance around the mock living room, wishing we were at home. I pull her close and whisper in her ear, "I love listening to every little sound you make. Especially when I wake you up in the middle of the night."

"Kace!" She tries to slap my chest, but I'm holding her too close. Her cheeks are flushed, but she still says, "Don't make me horny in Ikea."

I chuckle. "Sentences you never thought you'd hear for $200, Alex."

"I love you," she says like it's both intentional and habitual, and I love it. "Come on." She slips her hand into mine and tugs me through the maze. We pass at least ten other mock living rooms. This place is surprisingly easy to navigate.

We walk through the workspace area, and Mya's eyes catch on a few things. The next section is kitchen models. My eyes scan the few setups around us. Tugging Mya backward a little by her grip on my hand, I peek into one of them.

"Oooh!" She squeezes my hand. "Do you actually want to look at something?"

"Uh huh. But not this one." I lead her to the next model. It's not right either. They're all a little too open-concept for me.

I stop in front of the third one and scan the area around us. It's a Tuesday morning that I took off work specifically so we didn't have to brave the crowds of Portland. There's no one except a couple of older ladies past us and into the dining section.

"This one," I tell Mya, and her brows pinch.

"This one? It doesn't seem like you."

I glance at the blaring white kitchen. Yeah, definitely not me. But an entryway on the other side leads to a pantry area.

Mya follows me, peeping her head around the corner like she's Sully looking for a monster under the bed. *Fuck, I love her.*

When I'm in the nook, I pull her in with me. Her hands fly to my chest for balance, and her eyes go wide. "Kace. What are you doing?"

I kiss her in response, just once, but I keep our lips pressed together as I lift her by the waist and set her on the pantry counter. She spreads her legs enough to give me space between them as she deepens our kiss.

I tug her ass to the edge of the counter, noting the drawer handles behind her legs. Plus, if she leans back, she'll hit her head on the white shelves lined with clear plastic storage containers filled with fake food.

Running my hands up her thighs, my fingers slip under her short floral skirt. I fucking love this outfit she wears–the skirt paired with a thin white tee knotted at her stomach to reveal a sliver of skin and the pink heart perfectly framed in her belly button. *Note to self: buy her more crop tops.* I grind against her, already hard in my jeans, and kiss her again.

She drops the owl on the counter beside her, weaving her hands into my hair at my nape as she kisses me back for a second before breaking it. "So much for not making me horny in Ikea," she whispers breathlessly.

"I didn't make any promises." I slide my hands further up her legs, brushing a thumb across the silk. "Fuck," I mutter under my breath. "You're already wet."

She leans forward, bringing her face closer to mine. "I'm so turned on right now, Kace. Please don't tease me."

"Me? Tease you?" I smirk. "Never." God I feel like a new person since letting myself love Mya. I feel comfortable saying whatever comes to mind. I feel safe to let out the side of me that wants to have more fun. I feel confident that I can live on the edge because even if she can't catch me, she'll never let me fall alone.

I press my thumb against the apex of her thigh, sliding it under her panties and over her slit. She lets out the sweetest moan as her head falls to my shoulder. "Kace, I want you so badly."

"You know all you have to do is ask."

Her gaze snaps to me even though I can tell focusing is hard as I rub circles against her opening, trying to get her as wet as possible. "Stop. You are not going to have sex with me in Ikea."

"Is that a dare?" I challenge.

"You don't care that we could get caught?"

"I mean, I'm not trying to go to jail, but..." I trail off. I have no idea what else I was going to say because all logic is out the window now. "I'll keep an eye on that mirror." I nod toward a mirror on the other side of the doorless entry to the pantry that gives me a solid view of anyone within ten feet.

She bites into her lip and eye fucks me so hard, it's all the approval I need. She reaches for the buttons on my jeans, only fiddling for a moment before they're unsnapped and the zipper is down.

"Try to be quiet," I remind her, and she mimes zipping her lips and throwing away the key. The promise is immediately forgotten the second I plunge my thumb inside her. She lets out another moan but catches herself, biting into my shoulder to keep herself quiet, and fuck is it hot. After I massage her until she's soaking wet, I tug her back to the edge of the counter as close as she can get.

Pulling out of her, I free my throbbing dick from its constraint and move her skirt out of the way as I push into her. Her teeth dig into my shoulder as I thrust with little resistance, my dick twitching inside her, begging for more.

I glance at the mirror to my right and hold the stare for a moment, making sure there's still no one around us. Then I pull out of her slowly. It's so slow it's pure torture. But it's also pure pleasure as I feel my length sliding out of her pussy. I plunge back inside while keeping a firm grip on her ass for leverage. Holy fuck, I already feel like I could come.

"Mya," I whisper against her hair, freezing my thrusts. Her pussy clenches a bit as she looks up at me–as if me saying her name pulled her closer to the edge. She gives me a hazy grin.

"Hmm?"

"You're so goddamn hot. There's no way I'm going to last long."

Her smile widens like she's proud of herself for that.

"Tell me what you need to get you there with me."

She chews on her lip before answering. "Play with my clit," she whispers. "Kiss my neck." She tilts her head to give me access, her hair falling behind her shoulder. Holding eye contact, she adds, "And bottom out. Every. Single. Time."

Fuck me. I could come just listening to her talk. Instead, I pray to whatever sex gods will listen that I can last long enough to fulfill her three wishes.

With one hand still gripping her ass, I bring my other to her clit, giving her just enough pressure to melt into my touch. I glance up at the mirror one more time for good measure because more than hating jail, I would hate anyone else seeing my girl fall apart like she's about to. With a clear coast, I kiss up her neck, nipping and sucking lightly as I thrust into her. The containers lining the shelves above her rattle every time I fill her, but there's no stopping now.

Her fingers tighten their grip on my hair at the same moment her pussy clenches around my cock. Waves of her orgasm tightening around me send me flying over the edge, coming inside her. I continue to thrust, slowing the movement as we both level out.

Between heavy breaths, Mya holds my gaze, her lips parting. "You give me everything I've ever wanted."

Still inside her, I pull her close, not ready to separate even though I know we need to. "Not yet. But I will."

Chapter Forty-One

"Ready?" my sister asks with her camera in hand as the gondola reaches the top of the mountain. She's wearing her silky, light pink bridesmaid dress. It's short like mine.

Except mine is white.

My skirt is silk and twirls to perfection. The thin straps lead to a flowery lace bodice that makes my boobs look fantastic–although there are a few other things helping my cleavage today. My favorite part of my outfit though, although no one has seen yet, is a garter I made from the Betsey Johnson dress Kace bought me on our first *not date*. He's going to get such a kick out of it.

"I'm so ready." I grin at my sister, and she snaps a picture of me with the luscious green mountain on the other side of the clear ski lift bubble. We opted for a spring wedding mainly so I could wear the dress I wanted and so our guests didn't freeze. Kace did plenty of snowboarding over the winter anyway.

When the gondola door slides open, Ella steps onto the platform from the moving pod first so she can photograph the first look. I step out next, careful not to trip in my pink heels, and stop only a few feet from Kace's back. With the lift peaking at the ridge, the view of the mountain's valleys behind him is insane.

His hands are in his pockets casually, and I wish I could see his face to know if he's nervous or not.

I'm not nervous at all. I'm thirty-three, and time has been ticking away faster than ever. I read a study once that explained the phenomenon of time seeming quicker as you age. It's all perspective. When you're a kid, one day takes up less of your life. The older you get, the less significant each day seems in comparison to the thousands of other days you've lived before it.

Maybe that's why I cling so hard to moments of nostalgia–they're like hitting *pause*, letting me savor every frame. But standing here, about to marry Kace, I don't need to live in the past anymore. Because while most days speed by in a blur of adult responsibilities and planned routines, this moment feels exactly like those endless childhood summer days–pure magic, stretching out before me with infinite possibility. No matter how fast time moves after this, this day will always be one of my favorites, preserved perfectly like a polaroid in my heart.

I take a breath and glance at my sister. She gives me a nod, and I tap Kace's shoulder. When he turns, there's not a single shred of nervousness in the way he takes me in. He scans my hair, in loose waves with baby's breath woven into the strands. His gaze lingers on the soft sparkles on my chest. Then he roams the rest of my body, and I'll never forget the way this feels.

He steps toward me, carefully slipping his fingers into my hair and pulling me into a kiss. I smile against his lips, still obsessed with the way they feel against mine three years later. "You're so damn beautiful, Mya Levitt."

"Thanks." I grin, pulling back to appraise him and so giddy about hearing him say my new name. His black suit is crisp, and he's as handsome as ever with his perfectly manicured scruff and deep brown eyes that I never get tired of staring into. I smooth my hands over his chest. "You look so handsome."

"Thank you," he says, but then just smiles at me, brushing his thumb across my cheek.

My eyes search his in hopes they reveal what he's thinking. "What is it?"

"I love being in your orbit. I can't wait to be your husband."

I grin. "I can't wait either. But first, I have a gift for you."

"Oh yeah? What is it?"

I glance over his shoulder to where Mack stands next to Ella. I reach my hand out, and he delivers the can he's been holding.

Kace's brows furrow as I hand him the beer. "Beer? Now?"

"It's your favorite." He twists the can in his hand to get confirmation that it's the Best Day Ever IPA from Brothers Cascadia. "I was thinking we could use it to celebrate."

"You hate beer…"

I grin. "I like this one." My heart flutters in anticipation. I feel like I tried rushing life with everyone before Kace, but when I realized I felt so secure in him being *the one*, I didn't want to rush anything. That's why it took us three years to get married, and I'm more than okay with it. But now it's the part of the timeline I've drawn hearts and stars around in my mind.

"Why do I feel like I'm missing information here?"

"I had this can specially made." I try not to laugh as he examines the can, not spotting the difference yet. "Check the label."

He holds it closer to his face, immediately seeing the corner that's peeled up. Pulling the label back, I watch his eyes flick back and forth as they read each line.

The best day ever
wouldn't be complete
without the best news ever.
Don't you think so,
Daddy?

Kace glances at me, then back at the can. Back at me. Back at the can. "Is this what I think it is?" he asks, his voice full of emotion.

I nod, willing the tears on my waterline not to mess up my makeup.

"We're having a baby?"

"We're having a baby," I confirm.

"I'm going to be a dad?" His eyes are still wide, and it makes me laugh.

"Yes."

With all the clarity he needs, he wraps his arms around my waist, spinning me around. I laugh through the first rotation, but the second and third get me. "Kace," I say through a nauseous laugh. "You're making me sick."

He stops spinning immediately, settling me softly on the ground. "Fuck. I'm sorry. But also it's a little bit of our baby making you sick." He glances at my stomach even though I'm not showing yet. I'm only nine weeks along, but we've been trying for the past year. "*Our baby*," he says again, amazed. "I love you so much."

"I love you more," I whisper back, worried if I use my full voice, it might break.

"There's no fucking way." He shakes his head. "Well, I guess this makes our honeymoon a babymoon, huh?"

"I guess so. Are you going to tell me where we're going yet?"

He smirks. "Covington, Georgia."

I frown. "We're going to Georgia for our honeymoon? Babymoon? Whatever."

"Unless there's a Mystic Falls somewhere else."

A laugh bursts out of me, a few tears finally escaping. "For real?"

He nods. "Are you good with that?"

"I've been wanting to go forever."

"Since you were twelve. I know." He chuckles, and it's the sweetest sound. My stomach flutters, and I know it's not from our baby, but I smile at the thought of it being him or her soon.

I glance outside our bubble to find my sister crying, leaning her head on Mack's shoulder with his arm around her. Dave, Kace's best man, is off to the side flipping the ring box in his hand, and I swear he's singing "Build Me Up Buttercup" as he and Chloe watch us. I spot my parents next to Kace's within earshot of us. His mom and dad moved to Washington last summer to be closer, and our cabin will be completed in a few months. It's up the road from his parents' place.

I refocus on my soon-to-be husband. "What did I do to deserve you?"

Squeezing his arms tighter around my waist, he says, "Right place, right time, babe," with that smirk that still makes my heart flutter.

I think back to the Valentine's Day that changed everything. "You never did tell me why you chose *my* table that night."

"I've thought about that a lot." He reaches to brush his thumb across my cheek. I can't help but smile and lean into the touch. "I think the universe knew what I needed in my life and jumped at the opportunity to turn my misstep into the Yellow Brick Road."

"Who would have thought that you of all people would be the one to save me from a lifetime of boring dates?" I tease.

"Just your basic white knight." He kisses my nose before pressing his forehead to mine.

I grin. "My Seth Cohen in a bomber jacket."

He presses a kiss to my lips before pulling back and taking my hand in his to lead us to the altar, my heart on the verge of exploding.

Out of all the places I've been and all the time that's passed, I'm thankful for every second of it leading to the breakup that gave me my life. This life.

I can't help but think about how if it were 2007, my Facebook status would read: **Mya Levitt is feeling** *happier than she's ever been.*

More by Tisa Matthews

If you loved this story, check out the **Finding Home** series on Kindle Unlimited.

Book 1: ***And Then There's You***

Book 2: ***I Love You, So What?***

Book 3: ***Can We Just Be Happy Now?***

Book 4: ***Tied Up In Riches***

While books three and four can be read as standalones, books one and two of the series should be read in order for the best experience.

Book 4.5: ***Home*** is an extended epilogue featuring a POV chapter from each main character in the series! It's meant to be read after you've finished the series!

Acknowledgements

I've always been a lover of nostalgia. There's something so beautiful about the simplicity of a time before smartphones and GPS–even though I thought my life was over multiple times with each boy who broke my heart, college roommate who was nutso or got lost in the middle of a suburb with only cows in every direction and no signs pointing the way out.

But I've never wanted to go back to the 2000s as much as I do now–back to a time when my mom was alive. I'd say this book saved my life, but I won't because it wasn't my life that needed saving.

Grief is the most incomprehensible pain. There's nothing anyone can say or do that truly makes it better because the one thing you want is something you can never have again. Losing my mom has been the most devastating experience that has changed me to my core. I haven't slept in months, and the fact that I somehow managed to write a story I love with words that make sense is something I'm so proud of. In that sense, this book did save me. It was the only thing that truly pulled my mind from reality, that kept me focused on something long enough to temporarily forget that I'll never be able to call my mom again.

During a time when I could hardly get through a conversation without crying, I couldn't function well enough to go to work, Mya and Kace were there for me.

There were a few other people there for me in ways I'll never be able to repay them for because they not only helped this story become what it is but for helping me push forward in a time I wanted to do nothing.

Arianna: I would still be spiraling like a ham if I didn't have you. There are no words to describe how thankful I am for you pulling me off the ledge the hundred times I bolted toward it. Grief has made my insecurities come out from hiding, and you were there every single time to help me move past them. You read every chapter as I wrote it to hype me up when I deserved it and help me make it better when it was needed. You shared your friends when I thought having more beta readers would fix all my doubts. You came up with the cutest cover idea and let me ask your opinion a million times on repeat. You loved Mya and Kace so fiercely when I wasn't giving them the love they deserved. You answered my phone call and sat with me when I couldn't get out the words that my mom died, and every moment since then you've let me work through the process you know all too well. Thank you for being my pool noodle. I'd be drowning without you.

Kristen: If I had to choose someone to fight for me, it would be you every time. I'm so thankful for the way you side with me, not because I'm always right, but because you put in the effort to see my vision so clearly. You help keep my characters in line with my vision for them when suggestions from others muddle my thinking. And you reminded me to drink water when I could hardly take care of myself, so you're basically responsible for my brain function. Thank you.

Jillian: My strong suit has never been developmental edits. Without hesitation, you hopped on board to help me organize this story and find its missing pieces. You're always there to hype me up and help me when I need it even when you have a million things of your own going on. Thank you.

Isabella: My first editor. You popped into my life at the end stages of editing this book, when everything was overwhelming and helped me make so many final touches to elevate this story into one I'm so confident about. Thank you for always answering my questions, brainstorming with me and being the coolest gen-z-er I know.

Sarah: Your energy and vibe always brighten my day. Your love for Kace and willingness to throw down for him against any slander is my favorite. Thank you for rereading scenes and playing devil's advocate when I was waffling between two suggestions. I appreciate your help with this story so much.

Shelby: The number one hype girl. Hands down the best beta commenter. You made the editing process so much more fun for me than it's ever been before. Thank you for being you and for sharing all the stories *Unhitched* references reminded you of.

Dawn: Thank you for spending so much time correcting all my toxic writing traits and listening to me cry about my frustrations way too damn much. I'm so glad I have you in my corner.

Sophie: Thank you for rereading chapters and helping me brainstorm a million things. I appreciate you making time for me last-minute more than you know.

My author friends, Heather, Sam, Tiffany, Patricia, Kortney, Kim, Cassandra, Jessi: Thank you for taking time away from your own writing schedules to help me edit this story. I'm so grateful to be part of an author community with people willing to share their knowledge and perspective so we can all learn and grow together.

Rose, Meesha, Ashley, Leah, Stephanie, Mandy-Kay, Kayla, Jason, Lauren, MK: Thank you for taking the time to read this story, offer feedback and suggestions and talk through my questions. Each detail and edit is important, and so many of the ones I've made in this book are because of you.

My boss and coworkers: You covered my shifts. You fed me. You hugged me. You let me cry in the cooler. You gave me ridiculous and unusable book ideas when I needed to brainstorm, and I love you all for every bit of it. You gave me the capacity to work on this project, which was everything I needed to get through the last few months, and I'll forever be grateful for that.

To both my parents: Thank you for giving me a childhood I loved enough to center an entire book around the nostalgia of it. There were ups and downs, of course. There were times we didn't have a lot of money. Neither of those things are what I recall when I think about the past. I'm so lucky to have the childhood I had, full of love, and experiences, and I'll never take that for granted.

Drew: Growing up has always felt a little scary for me. I get trapped in my head, wishing I could go back to a simpler time, but you're always here to ground me. You show me how much I can love the present and help create a version of it that I'll look back on years from now and miss just as much as I miss the past now. I'll never be settling with you.

About the Author

Tisa Matthews is a millennial and elder emo at heart—some of her favorite music being emo covers of 2000s pop songs. She still has a ceiling covered in glow-in-the-dark stars at her parents' house and regrets getting rid of her Razor Scooter, but she'll never toss her enV flip phone even though it hardly works. She's always been a Zac Efron girl but has recently questioned why we've been ignoring his brother this whole time. Her AIM screenname was SwimFreak340.